STONE MIRROR

STONE MIRROR

A NOVEL OF THE NEOLITHIC

Rob Swigart

Left Coast Press, Inc.

Walnut Creek, California

**Left
Coast
Press**
Inc.

Left Coast Press, Inc.
1630 North Main Street, #400
Walnut Creek, California 94596
http://www.LCoastPress.com

ISBN 978-1-59874-016-5 hardcover

ISBN 978-1-59874-017-2 paperback

Library of Congress Cataloging-In-Publication Data

Swigart, Rob.
  Stone mirror : a novel of the neolithic / Rob Swigart.
      p. cm.
  Includes bibliographical references.
  ISBN-13: 978-1-59874-016-5 (hardback : alk. paper)
  ISBN-10: 1-59874-016-4 (hardback : alk. paper)
  ISBN-13: 978-1-59874-017-2 (pbk. : alk. paper)
  ISBN-10: 1-59874-017-2 (pbk. : alk. paper)
  1. Neolithic period--Fiction. 2. Turkey--Fiction. 3.
Archaeology--Turkey. I. Title.
  PS3569.W52S76 2007
  813'.54--dc22

                          2007004820

Printed in the United States of America

The paper used in this publication meets the minimum requirements of
American National Standard for Information Sciences—Permanence of
Paper for Printed Library Materials, ANSI/NISO Z39.48—1992.

07 08 09 5 4 3 2 1

Cover design by Andrew Brozyna
Text design by Lisa Devenish

Contents

Preface / 9

1 NOW

Time / 11 • The Excavator / 12 • Jones, Listening / 13 •
First Contact / 15 • Object Lesson / 17 • On the Road / 19 •
Hill of Mirrors / 21 • Plans / 21

2 THEN

Shelsan / 25 • Mala / 27 • No Name / 28 • Pretender / 30 •
First Grand / 32 • Sun Demon / 34

3 NOW

Why It's Important to Dig / 41 • The Project / 44 • Mellaart / 46 •
Dig House / 48 • DANTE / 50 • Özgür / 53 • Negotiations / 55 •
Underworld / 57 • On the Mound / 59 • Could Be Anything / 61

4 THEN

Boy Going Under / 63 • Stone Mirror / 66 • Pinnak on the Roof / 67 •
Walk of the World / 68 • First Egg / 72 • Empty Place / 74

5 NOW

Speculation / 79 • A Hunch / 81 • Home Plate Don't Move / 82 •
Satchi at Night / 83 • Bringing It Up / 84 • Saturday Morning / 85 •
Preliminaries / 89 • The Word / 90

6 THEN

The Stranger / 93 • Invitation / 97 • Gathering / 99 •
Blood Lust / 100 • Spirit Flight / 103

7 NOW

Fast Forward / 107 • Scholar / 108 • Rolf / 111 • Débitage / 112 •
Congeries / 114 • Lurkers / 116 • Men in Black / 117 •
Introduction / 118 • Reflections / 119 • An Interruption / 120 •
In the House / 122 • Eye of the Storm / 123

8 THEN

The Great Bull / 125 • The Mountain of Frozen Tears / 128 •
Tsurinye / 130 • Possession / 133 • The Snare / 134

9 NOW

The Media Get the Message / 137 • Go Ask Alice / 139 •
What the Dead Bones Said / 140 • Precautions / 141 •
Calamity / 143 • The Leisure of the Theory Class / 145 •
Speed Dial / 148 • Not the Territory / 148 •
What's Bred in the Bone / 150

10 THEN

Full Circle / 151 • Harvest / 153 • Pinnak and Temkash / 155 •
Long Road / 158 • Homecoming / 159 • Counting the Dead / 162

11 NOW

Evil Eye / 165 • Dead Reckoning / 166 • Air Play / 169 •
Mother Love / 171 • No Crocodiles / 173 • Line of Sight / 175 •
The Problem of Authenticity / 176 • The Dealer / 177 •
Network / 179

12 THEN

Shelsan's Return / 181 • Night / 182 • In Dreams / 183 •
The Leopard / 184 • Widow / 186 • Painting the Dead / 187 •
Clans / 189 • Pinnak / 191 • Fire in the Air / 192

13 NOW

Locking Up / 195 • New Friends / 197 • Afet / 198 •
Survey Marker / 199 • Good Company / 200 • Glimmers / 201 •
Call / 203 • Aftermath / 203 • Dawn / 205 • Iskembe / 206

14 THEN

Year, Turning / 209 • Passing / 210 • Building the Sky / 212 •
Light / 213 • Wet-Time / 214 • Final Combat / 215 •
Bucranium / 218 • Unborn Moon / 219 • Night Spirit / 221

15 NOW

Questions / 223 • Alice on the Road / 224 • First Steps / 225 •
In the World / 227 • Feed Your Head / 228 • Plan B / 230 •
Ripple / 232 • Schedule Change / 232

16 THEN

Under the Tamarisk / 235 • A Turn / 237 • Last Rights / 238 •
The Offer / 239 • Moving In / 240 • Invocation / 242 •
Getting Ahead / 244

17 NOW

Plan B Executed / 247 • Package / 248 • Homecoming / 248 •
Double Vision / 249 • At Sea / 251 • Reasonable Doubt / 252 •
But / 254 • The Island Princess /256 • Goddesses /256 •
Alice's Revenge / 257 • Season's End / 258

18 THEN

Harvest and Plant / 261 • Setting the Stage / 263 •
Pinnak Descends / 264 • Endings / 266 • Shelsan's Shelter / 267 •
Light / 268 • To the Sunset / 270

EPILOG • NOW

Wonderland / 273

Glossary / 275

Selected Bibliography / 285

About the Author / 287

Preface

Archaeology and archaeologists have provided material for novelists for a long time—Agatha Christie (*Murder in Mesopotamia*, 1936), D. H. Lawrence (*The Plumed Serpent, Quetzalcoatl, 1972, c. 1951*), Doris Lessing (*Briefing for a Descent into Hell,* 1971), Tony Hillerman (*A Thief of Time*, 1988), James Michener (*The Source*, 1965), and Jean Auel (*Clan of the Cave Bear*, 1980) are just a few. Their works are fiction above all, and they vary greatly in their adherence to archaeological accuracy.

Archaeologists also sometimes try their hand at telling their stories in fiction. Adrien Arcelin, one of the first archaeologists to work at the Paleolithic site of Solutré, wrote a novel called *Solutré ou les chasseurs de rennes de la France centrale* (*Solutré or the Deer Hunters of Central France,* 1872). Adolph Bandolier, who has a park named after him near Santa Fe, New Mexico, wrote *The Delight Makers* (c. 1918), a novel about the Hopi. Others, such as Sir Mortimer Wheeler (as Steven Mithen, *After the Ice*, 2004) and David Webster (*The Fall of the Ancient Maya*, 2002), have interlaced short dramatic passages in factual books.

But it is a special challenge for a novelist to write fiction about archaeology that is scientifically accurate and contemporary enough for use as a textbook. *Stone Mirror* is my second, the first being *Xibalbá Gate: A Novel of the Ancient Maya* (2005).

I spent many years writing fictional stories and scenarios for the Institute for the Future (a small think tank in California) as a way of dramatizing forecasts. Describing the future and recounting the deep past are similar: there is scant direct evidence and much context to consider; results are tentative, speculative, and subject to constant revision; and intuition plays a large role.

I'm not an archaeologist, but I've tramped around ancient sites in North, Central, and South America; Southeast Asia; the Mediterranean; France; and Anatolia, and I have had a lifelong interest in the stories people left on the surface of the earth, stories written in the material they left behind, their architecture and their garbage. What people throw away is often more telling than what they carve in stone, which after all is what they wanted the future to know and not necessarily what they were really like. Accident and contingent events are the archaeologist's friend; the burning of a palace in Mesopotamia has often fired temporary writing on clay and preserved it for us in the future. This in itself is a drama worthy of telling.

Stone Mirror is fiction. It is as accurate a portrayal of the often hot, dirty, and tedious work of archaeology as I could make, and as careful a speculation about the inhabitants of central Anatolia 9,000 years ago as I could invent. It has been a lot of fun. I've been fascinated by this distant culture since my first visit to Çatalhöyük in 1999. Those people chose to live in the middle of a swamp in very close quarters. Why is a mystery, but as archaeologists uncover more of their daily lives, we get an increasingly clear picture of the choices they made; however, any description of their daily lives remains speculative.

Good speculation, whether about the future or the past, is based on good information, available physical data, multiple points of view, and luck. I've been fortunate to encounter a number of professional archaeologists who generously shared their knowledge and time.

It's always a danger to begin listing acknowledgments. In spite of this, I must give special thanks to Dr. Ian Hodder, director of the Çatalhöyük project, who generously allowed me to spend time on the site, granted me the status of visiting scholar at the Archaeology Center at Stanford, and has at all times been supportive. He read the manuscript in draft and made many suggestions, all of which I took. I got many valuable comments from Dr. Cornelius Holtorf as well. The book is better archaeology, and better fiction, for their attention. *Stone Mirror* could not exist without them, but of course they are in no way responsible for any lapses or errors, which rest as always with the author.

Dr. Mihriban Özbaşaran was also especially helpful through a number of email exchanges. Others include but are not limited to project artist John Swogger, Shahina Farid, Mirjana Stevanović, Louise Martin, Tristan Carter, and Ali Ümut Türkcan. Conversations with Michael Balter, author of *The Goddess and the Bull: Catalhoyuk: An Archaeological Journey to the Dawn of Civilization*, were extremely helpful. To the countless others I have inadvertently overlooked or otherwise slighted, I plead innocent of premeditation. I thank you all.

1 Now

Time

The object was fixed in darkness. Around it swirled shouts, wails of lamentation and rage, the hard sounds of things breaking apart, dust, and chaos. There were passions: hatred and terror. And there was death.

In time, all faded. Then there were footsteps, the muted clatter of brick placed on brick, the cutting of wood, the cries of children; and, less often, the scrapes of digging, burial, and more grief.

Gradually the living receded, growing ever more faint as the years came and went and dirt piled upon dirt. The voices died.

If the object could be said to do anything during all the noise and confusion, it would be that it dreamed, and in dreaming did its work. Dreams are inward, reflections of things neither seen nor heard, but their effects are real, and timeless, and always ready to return.

Millennia passed in a silence modulated only by the clicks and whispers of insects, worms, small burrowing animals, the languid reaching of roots, the infinitesimally slow sifting down of soil particles, salts, and moisture. After a time even these ceased, and only the occasional deep, sub-base rumble of distant tremors in the earth disturbed the stasis of the object and its home.

Above in the middle world the seasons came and went; the harshness of cold-time; the terrific heat of warm-time; snow and rain. The world grew warm and dry, but below in the dirt the temperature stabilized.

The ruined town and all the lives it had held were gone from sight.

Then the object could no longer be said to dream, even after what it had done, after all it had meant. It simply was, a made thing, drained by time of its human significance.

Until Satchi Bennett brought it up again into the light.

The Excavator

Satchi leaned over the railing of the roof terrace and contemplated the street six floors below.

It was a broad avenue with trolley tracks running down the center. He could see cars, taxis, and a small bus called a dolmus. It was evening, and the street was brightly lit, the noise of traffic pleasantly distant and abstract, unlike the staccato bray and sputter of conversation behind him.

Satchi had turned his back on small talk. Jones, seated at the bar with the man from the Ministry might think him antisocial, but he didn't really care. What the hell, he *was* antisocial!

Jones was a great man, of course. Things happened around Jones because he was a celebrated archaeologist, host of dozens of television specials and movie documentaries, appearing against backdrops of jungle, desert, pyramids, or other picturesque ruins. His magnificent mane of gray-blond hair would ripple in a gentle breeze, adding motion to his famous smile. His sonorous voice soothed and excited by turns. Things happened to Bryson Jones because . . . well, he made them happen.

Despite all this, Satchi thought this junket was a time-killer. He hated to kill time, but for the moment he had nothing else to do. Susan had politely but firmly asked him to leave three years before, so he had no family. He was between projects, along for the ride. He had few friends; he didn't care much about people, after all.

What he really cared about was dirt.

As a boy in Toledo his favorite toy was a large yellow dump truck. He could sit on top of the cab and fill up the back. He still had the little plastic shovel. He would push with his feet and drive across the broad expanse of his mother's back yard. It was enormously satisfying to build the mound of dirt, load after load. Usually his mother would come out and order him to put the dirt back where it came from, thank you. Unmaking the hole was almost as satisfying as making it. Later he would learn that this was called backfilling.

He loved dirt. He loved the way it looked, its colors and textures, its sense of density. He loved the feel of it, dry or wet, trickling through his fingers. He loved its smell. But most of all he loved the things it hid. When he uncovered them little by little, it was a tantalizing striptease of the buried past. That, he told himself, was why he had become an archaeologist.

Of course, a Freudian might have had other ideas.

The traffic below was distant, the way objects buried in the soil were distant. The distance was like time. From up here it was like looking down into the past.

Such thoughts were drifting through his mind like large, placid fish when a man leaned against the railing next to him. Something about the intent way he held his cigarette between the third and fourth fingers and puffed at it in short, sharp intakes while staring intently at Bryson Jones attracted Satchi's attention. The shapeless gray sports jacket he wore over an open-necked shirt, through which a tangle of black chest hair grew up to join his three-day stubble, sagged to one side. Without taking his eyes off Jones he dropped his cigarette, crushed it underfoot, and immediately lit another. After a moment he patted the side pocket of his jacket.

Satchi felt a stirring of disquiet.

There was a story everyone knew. God knows, Jones himself never tired of recounting it. A few years before, Jones had been making a documentary on the multicultural prehistory of Indonesia. Apparently the subject matter offended a certain young man's nationalist agenda. He'd apparently brooded for days, tracked Jones back to Kuala Lumpur, burst into the lobby of the hotel where the archaeologist was giving a press conference, and fired four shots from a small-caliber revolver. Three of the bullets put neat holes in the concierge's teak desk; the fourth shattered an expensive chandelier. The police apologized politely. The would-be assassin was well known. He had, they said, a history of mental troubles. They whisked him away, leaving Jones shaken but unhurt.

It was ridiculous to think that the object in the man's pocket was a gun, but it was heavy, and the man seemed nervous. Best not take chances. Satchi edged closer.

Jones, Listening

Bryson Jones, perched precariously on a metal bar stool, was listening attentively to the man from the Ministry of Culture and Tourism. It was an ordinary night, warm and comfortable, a night for small talk and dinner.

The man from the Ministry repeatedly mopped his receding hairline with a large white handkerchief as he explained some of the more important features of the region. For instance, did Dr. Jones know Konya, this lovely city, was once the capital of the Seljuk Turks?

Of course he did.

Anatolia, the whole of Asian Turkey, in fact, was one of the oldest continually inhabited landmasses in the world, filled with archaeological sites from the Palaeolithic to the Republic. No doubt Jones knew all this as well.

He sounded like a travelogue.

Jones, ever mindful of the potentials of image, glanced down into his glass of *rakı*. The ice was slowly melting, releasing thin white streamers from the small cubes, like the slow release of stories from the ancient past. It would make a nice picture if he ever did a documentary here. Rakı was a kind of national drink.

He looked up with his most ingratiating smile. "Anatolia is rich in heritage, Mr. Nevra, perhaps the richest in the world. Turkey is a fortunate country, indeed."

The sun was sinking below one horizon and a full moon was lifting above the other, a satisfying symmetry, the hands of the universe so evenly balanced, rising and falling.

Jones gave an encouraging smile. Mr. Nevra said Konya was home of the Mevlani Sufi order, better known as the whirling dervishes, founded by the poet known to the world as Rumi.

Jones was diplomatic, amiable, and quick-witted. He had the gift of conveying an impression of sympathetic attention, as if each word were a revelation. He didn't produce this effect for any special purpose, but if for some reason it turned out there was a purpose he was prepared. Bryson Jones believed, above all else, in being prepared.

Mr. Nevra went on talking and mopping his forehead. Jones went on listening.

To the west, the sky was still striped with pale rose, lavender, and green; everywhere else it had turned velvety and dark. To the east, the full moon was drifting up between the metal arms of two cranes hovering over a round, half-built office tower. A trolley rattled past six floors below. The first stars were just visible.

Jones smiled, and sipped, and nodded, drinking in every word. Every encounter was a possibility, every meeting freighted with potential, with hope. There was no such thing as coincidence.

First Contact

The stranger shook himself like a dog emerging from water and reached once more for his jacket pocket. Satchi leaned forward, but the man merely patted the pocket and flipped his cigarette over the railing. Satchi let out a sigh, torn by the absurdity of the situation. He, Satchi Bennett, prepared to protect Bryson Jones! It was doubly absurd, since there clearly was no danger.

Why should Satchi Bennett, who didn't care much for his fellow man, want to protect Bryson Jones, who cared very much for people, especially if they could do something for him? Why, indeed? This was why Jones had detractors, people who called him a media whore, a prima donna, an egotist.

But Satchi didn't dislike Jones, either. It was simply that they lived in different worlds: he liked dirt, and Jones liked celebrity. And, Satchi added without irony, it was true Jones had a gift for raising money and sponsoring big projects, and big projects were what paid Satchi's wages. True, his wages weren't much, as his exwife had been fond of repeating, but it was what he did.

Without someone to do the actual digging, people like Jones would have theory without data, empty. Yet without people like Jones, there might not be any digging to do. So Satchi waited expectantly.

The big man approached Jones and Nevra. The Ministry man stopped his monologue and said, "Well, Dr. Jones, I hope you will allow me to introduce you to my cousin, Özgür." He listed his cousin's qualifications (some archaeological training), interests (Anatolian civilizations), and pedigree (third cousin on his mother's side). The pedigree also involved a surname with too many unpronounceable vowels for easy assimilation. Jones did not try to repeat it.

Satchi pursed his lips: this guy had simply been waiting to meet Jones. Why had he, Satchi Bennett, been alarmed? He was just another fan.

Jones shook hands and was immediately drawn into a new round of small talk – it was hot this year, wouldn't he agree? But it was not as hot as two years ago. Jones agreed that it was hot, but expected that it would be hotter in August.

Özgür spoke idiomatic, if somewhat stilted, American English. Jones was a professor, was he not?

Yes, he was.

Even Satchi, who did not count social skills high on his list of necessities, recognized that this apparently aimless exchange was going somewhere, and that it had something to do with the object in the jacket pocket.

Dinner appeared. Conversation everywhere faltered, there was much scraping of chairs, people sat at the tables scattered around the roof terrace; muted talk started up again. Satchi looked around, hoping to eat alone, but it was too late. Jones was inviting him to join them.

Conversation dragged on at length about absolutely nothing. For instance, apparently the Konya Plain was experiencing something of an economic boon, with heavy investments in agriculture. Wheat seemed to be the staple crop – wheat and sugar beets. Both officials seemed particularly proud of the sugar beets.

The starters came and went. Many of them contained eggplant. The main courses arrived. They too contained eggplant.

Özgür turned to Satchi. "And what is it you do, Mr. Satchi?"

"Satchi's my first name. My surname is Bennett."

"Really? And where would such a first name come from, then? Perhaps it is Indian?"

"A baseball player. Satchel Paige. Before I was born he played for the Cleveland Indians."

"Ah, I see."

"My father was a Cleveland fan. I'm an excavator."

"Satchi digs," Jones said. "Diggers always leave theory to people like me. Theory, and explaining it," Jones added with a smile.

Özgür murmured something about the importance of theory and fell silent. Sticky concoctions of honey and nuts arrived, followed by small cups of thick Turkish coffee.

With an ingratiating nod Mr. Nevra found pressing business elsewhere.

Satchi watched the coat pocket, but Özgür gazed pensively at the full moon and appeared to have forgotten about it. Then he shook himself and poured Jones a glass of rakı. "You know of Çatalhöyük, of course."

"Of course, a large Neolithic settlement that flourished between around 7600 and 6200 BCE. There's a model long-term archaeological project under way there."

"Yes, of course, it's a very famous place." Özgür nodded vigorously. "And are you visiting other sites, Dr. Jones, like Çatalhöyük?"

Jones studied the surface of his drink. "Besides Çatal we're going to Pinarbaşi, and to Aşıklı Höyük, but I believe they are not quite contemporary with it. Why do you ask?"

Silver-yellow moonlight caught Özgür on his right cheek, and the harsher light from the interior of the restaurant lit the front of his face. In this odd cross-illumination his eyes appeared unusually large and menacing.

Abruptly he coughed lightly and reached into the pocket. Satchi tensed.

Özgür pulled out a package wrapped in a handkerchief. "Tell me, please, what you make of this." He placed the handkerchief on the table with a slight thump.

Object Lesson

Bryson Jones's life had been a series of such seemingly random, chance encounters that had turned into golden opportunities. When the object hit the table his perfect teeth gleamed. "What might this be?"

Özgür carefully folded out one corner of the handkerchief after another until a black lump sat alone in the middle of a white square. It was vaguely hemispherical, roughly twelve centimeters in diameter, a mottled white on the rounded part, polished black on the flat surface. Jones tapped it with a fingernail and produced a small clink. "Obsidian," he said. "Where's it from?"

"Most likely from Göllü Dağ." It sounded like Gillew Dah.

"I meant, where was this object found? This is a mirror, wouldn't you say, Satchi?"

Satchi was examining it intently. "Yes," he replied after a moment. "Very fine work."

Özgür leaned back and laced his fingers over his stomach. "A farmer."

Jones murmured encouragement.

Özgür continued. "He had it in his house. A tax inspector saw it. He realized it might be of archaeological value and brought it to my office."

"And you brought it here, to show me?"

"Your reputation is great, Dr. Jones. I had thought you might be interested."

"That," Jones waved his long, elegant hand, "depends."

The recorded muezzin from a mosque to his left drowned him out and he stopped. Almost immediately an even louder recording started up from the other side of the hotel, the sound over-modulated. When they fell silent he started to speak, but was once again interrupted.

Özgür made a little wave. This would take time.

Jones picked up the lump of obsidian and after a moment's examination gave it to Satchi.

The excavator lightly touched one of the white flecks. "Plaster," he murmured. In the smooth surface he could see the right side of his face, clearly illuminated by the lights from the restaurant. It peered back, small and dark, yet sharp. The polish was high, the result of many hours of patient grinding. Someone had put a lot of effort and skill into this object.

He turned it slightly and the full moon appeared, hovering over the table just a few centimeters away. Satchi could see the seas and the craters in exquisite detail.

The call to prayer ended.

Özgür went on as if nothing had happened, "Depends on what?"

"Depends." Jones repeated, putting the mirror face down on the handkerchief. "On where it was found. This mirror has no provenance. We've already lost most of the information its context could have given us. So it depends on where it was found."

"Yes," Özgür agreed. "I understand." He looked around. Three people were talking at the bar. Otherwise the terrace was now deserted. "You have heard of a town called Çalikükköy?"

Jones looked at Satchi, who shook his head. Neither of them would even be able to pronounce it without practice.

"Of course not," Özgür continued. "Few have. Very small village about fifty kilometers. . . ." He waved his hand vaguely.

Satchi, following the gesture, could see Altair burning halfway to the zenith of the night sky.

Jones nodded.

Özgür continued. "There is a hill on the farm, fairly large. It has a local name. Aynalı Tepe – Hill of Mirrors." The final undotted "ı" of Aynalı sounded like the "u" in cup.

"Ah."

Özgür leaned back in obvious pleasure. "I think it might be an archaeological place, a site, yes?"

"The name's suggestive," Jones murmured. "They've found other mirrors there?"

"Perhaps, yes. Of course, although I am not a practicing archaeologist, merely an official of the local government, I thought if you were interested we might discuss the future? After all, it takes two hands to make a sound, as we say."

Bryson Jones did not believe in chance. Bryson Jones was the right man to have this piece of information, and so it came to him.

Satchi could see Jones was already making lists of funding sources, specialists they could approach. He would need surveyors, faunal and human remains experts (there would certainly be burials), an obsidian specialist, . . . and an excavator.

With a sigh Jones folded the corners of the handkerchief over the mirror and handed it back to Özgür. "Before we discuss the future," he said thoughtfully, "perhaps we should take a look?"

On the Road

Three days later Özgür and his driver collected Satchi and Jones. They sat in the back, and while they drove he rested his arm on the back of his seat, half-turned so he could talk to them.

While Satchi pored over several sheets of topographic and geological maps, the Turk asked Jones what he thought.

"I've done a little checking," the archaeologist said, dropping into his lecturing mode. "You know the so-called Neolithic Revolution began after the last ice age, around 10,000 BCE – Before the Common Era – but Çatalhöyük proved it had extended westward by 7500 BCE."

"Yes, yes," Özgür interrupted. "But the mirror suggests Aynalı Tepe is Neolithic, doesn't it?"

Jones shrugged. "Suggests, but we won't know until we see it."

"But it could be contemporary with Çatalhöyük, couldn't it?" Özgür's hope was palpable.

Jones replied, "Carbon fourteen, or obsidian hydration on the mirror, perhaps, might give us approximate dates, and the artifacts we find might fill in some of the blanks. It all depends on what we find there. For instance, what characterizes Çatal, as opposed to the earlier but overlapping settlement at Aşıklıhöyük, is the highly decorated nature of some of the dwellings, with wall paintings and mounted animal heads or plaster moldings: Mellaart's 'shrines.' If Aynalı Tepe is a contemporary, and if it has similar art, that makes it more important." He leaned forward and tapped the Turk on the shoulder. "There was a brief survey of Aynalı Tepe in the 1950s, but there are many such mounds in Anatolia, most of them looted, ploughed under, or turned into local parks, and most of them Bronze Age, or much earlier than Çatal. So we don't know yet: it could be Chalcolithic or even Byzantine." The archaeologist leaned back with a smile. "But you're right, the mirror does suggest Neolithic."

The van rolled through flat farm country criss-crossed by cement aqueducts and narrow canals. Some of the fields glowed pale green with early crops, but most were a uniform dusty brown. A couple of times they passed man-high piles of cattle dung drying in the sun – fuel for cooking fires, as it had been for thousands of years. The smell was pungent.

Mountains dimly outlined in the haze ahead of them seemed no closer when they abandoned the paved main road for a dirt track. An enormous plume of tan dust rose behind them and slowly settled in the still air. After a quarter of an hour they passed through a small village. Özgür said, "Çalikükköy." A small mosque on the central square went by in a blur. On the far side three men sat on white plastic chairs in front of a two-room tavern. They lifted glasses of tea as the van swept by. Satchi turned to look back, but the dust had swallowed them.

A few minutes later they pulled up in front of a house of whitewashed mud brick and a tile roof. To one side were several mounds of the now-ubiquitous dung, an ancient tractor, and a few chickens.

The farmer came out, and there was much pressing of hands and exchanges of rapid Turkish. Satchi detected the words efendim and tamam. The latter he understood to mean "OK." The farmer kept glancing at Jones, looking into the palm of his hand, taking off his cap to scratch his scalp and stare at the sky, putting the hat back on, scratching his cheek with a dirty fingernail (and a slight rasping sound), then glancing around and clearing his throat. He had probably never received such attention before. Özgür presented Bryson Bey and Satchi Bey. The farmer's grip was firm, his hands work-roughened. He gave off the same powerful odor as the stacks. A few hundred meters behind the house they could see the mound. "Aynalı Tepe!" the farmer said with a broad, melodramatic gesture, as though he had built it himself.

Hill of Mirrors

Aside from the house and a few drooping poplars along a short section of the road, there was little to see. The mountains were still distant purple blotches against the pale, empty blue of the sky. The fields cracked in the heat. A flock of sheep went by in the distance, bells clanking. Insects made occasional whirring sounds in the dry, spiky weeds, a bird called. The sun was bright, and Jones put on a San Francisco 49ers cap. The east side of the mound was brightly lit, the west in shade.

"What do you think, Satchi? Rough guess?" Jones was squinting up at the artificial hill.

"We should pace it off," Satchi said thoughtfully, "but a couple of hundred meters on a side; maybe ten high." He kicked at the ground, sending up dust. "According to the geology report this is alluvial soil, lakebed or shoreline sediment, similar to Çatalhöyük. Like the area around Çatal, this was probably marsh 10.000 years ago, here on the other side of the alluvian fan. River came north from the Taurus Mountains, water was trapped in the bowl of the Konya Plain."

"We'll do some coring, but I agree it was probably the same environment in the Neolithic. We just have to confirm that this site was Neolithic," Jones added. He turned to Özgür. "Where did the farmer find the mirror?"

The farmer led them to the west end and pointed at the ground about halfway up the slope. "*Burada*," he said, *here*.

They gathered around the spot and gazed thoughtfully at the weeds.

Plans

They found no mirrors, so they continued to the top. Jones and Satchi watched the ground carefully, pausing frequently to show each other something before moving on. Satchi remarked on the absence of decorated pottery fragments, even on the surface. "We'd have to test," he said, "but so far we're not seeing anything later than Neolithic. And it appears the surface has eroded toward the south. Here, for instance." He squatted down and scraped with a fingernail, exposing a slightly different color. He tapped it. "Mud brick, I think, just under the surface." He was talking more to himself than to Jones.

"If Neolithic," Jones said, "this is a major find."

"Too early to say for sure," Satchi cautioned, picking up a fragment of gray-black cooked clay. He scratched the surface and sniffed, jiggled it in his hand to test its weight. He wet his thumb and rubbed it, turning it over and over. "Hmph," he grunted, carefully replacing it where he found it. "We'll do a surface survey, get good statistics, but there's quite a bit on the surface, which means we *could* be standing on top of the walls of an ancient settlement. The survey will tell. If true, we wouldn't have to excavate through thousands of years of later material overburden to get to the Neolithic. It would be right under our feet." He spoke as if they were already doing the project.

They reached the top. On three sides they could make out the dim outlines of mountains marking the edge of the plain. The sun, now overhead, was a blinding orange disk; nothing stirred.

"Hello," Jones said at the edge of a funnel-shaped hole about three meters across. "What have we here?"

Satchi crouched and picked at the gray soil visible on the sides. It was mottled with small objects – potsherds, bits of bone. "Treasure hunters' pit," he grunted.

"How long ago?" Jones asked.

Satchi shrugged. "Not so long – a winter, perhaps two. The sides are slumping, but the cut is still relatively fresh, not many erosion channels." He glanced at the farmer, who was busy talking to Özgür.

"How deep?" Jones asked.

Satchi spread his hands. "From the diameter they could have made it all the way down to original soil. And they left their ladder."

Jones contemplated the pit, and then the surrounding plain. Though Satchi had never worked with Bryson Jones before, they had known each other for many years and he could guess what was going through his mind. "This place is under threat," Jones said thoughtfully.

Abruptly he stood up, made a fork of his first and middle fingers and looked sight lines across the mound. He stamped on the ground, scuffed a few areas, picked up and discarded fragments of stone, baked clay, and dirt. He brushed his hands on his pants and walked purposefully the length of the mound and back. He tugged at his lower lip. "Survey, yes," he said. "And a guard for the place."

"Right," Satchi agreed. "A season, six weeks perhaps, for a surface. Second season for subsurface, bring in some remote sensing equipment, see what's underneath."

"Then trench excavation," Jones said.

"Right," Satchi agreed. "Depending on the survey, but certainly we'd want to trench from the west of the crown, to get the occupation sequence and join up to the looters' hole to provide context for whatever they destroyed. Then we decide, depending on what we see with remote sensing."

"Özgür," Jones said, making an effort to control his excitement. "What about permits?"

"You want permits?" Özgür's surprise was feigned.

"Of course," Jones said curtly. "This is a new site, probably contemporary with Çatalhöyük. You'll get the credit for the discovery."

"No, no, *efendim*, I'm not interested in credit. . . ."

"Permits?"

"Yes, *efendim*, permits. I can help . . ."

"I'm sure you can. Satchi, listen!" He squatted again and slapped the ground with the palm of his hand. "You hear that."

Satchi gave a crooked smile. He'd seen Jones do this act before, on television. Was it in Israel?

"That," Jones continued without waiting for an answer, "is the sound of the past. Under our feet people lived their lives, generation after generation, hundreds of years of occupation, a settlement growing, expanding, then contracting and disappearing under the earth. Why? Perhaps the lake dried up, perhaps there was no more wood. Disease? Invasion? Peoples' lives, Satchi: birth, reproduction, and death. Tending their crops, their flocks. The first farmers, Satchi, the first to get a real sense they could conquer nature, control their own destinies."

"They didn't grow anything much around here," Satchi said.

"No, too wet, unsuitable for agriculture – this was all swamp 9,000 years ago. But nearby, Satchi, in the foothills over there, was good land for dry farming. I bet we find domesticated grain here, carried here on someone's back, as at Çatal. We'll find houses, the places they lived, the stuff they lived with, the tools, the food, the toys, and the dead. Perhaps even art. They were so different from us. They saw the world differently, their spirit-haunted, animal world, tied as they were to the cycles of the sun and the moon, the seasons of growing, the reproduction of animals, all so different from our cars and airplanes and Internet. Think about it, Satchi: the deep past, here under our feet, always under our feet. Human beings lived and died here. We'll bring them back, Satchi, we'll bring back their lives, the things they loved and died for, how they saw the world, the pain and disease, the daily labor. The animals they hunted, fought, killed, ate, or the animals that killed them. And the jealousy, envy, hatred, and fear." He stood and looked for a moment at a horizon no one else could see.

This, too, was familiar from a dozen television specials. Was it, Satchi wondered, a wish or a warning?

Softly Jones added, "We'll dig them out, Satchi. We'll give them life again, the people who lived here 9,000 years ago."

2 Then

Shelsan

Shelsan sat up in thick darkness.

The sound overhead had been brief, yet it lingered like an echo. Not a footstep, not yet. It was too early. Not the sound of wood breaking, or an animal bone. Was he hungry?

He listened to Mala breathing. She was beside him still, slack in sleep. On her other side the boy's breath rasped faintly, one time.

It was not quite absolute, the dark. There were glimmers here and there, racing spots of light, a faint glow. He sniffed and smelled her. He listened more closely, but the boy made no further sound. He had been hot these three days and had scarcely eaten.

There was a noise from the sunset-side sleeping chamber – a scrape of cloth, bare feet on the plaster floor: Little Boren. "Babi?" he whispered.

"What is it?" Shelsan's voice was muffled, almost drowned in the close dark.

"It was something up."

So the lad had heard it too. "Yes," he whispered. "Spirit Father or Water Bird, perhaps. Go back to sleep. I will go up."

Mala stirred, awakened by their voices. "Hush. What's this of Water Bird? What?"

A new light, another glimmer in the darkness, and then a sudden cold stone knife sliced the dark, cut the dark, divided the dark. The storage bag of hackberries near the hearth became a shape in the liquid light: full moon again.

"Even if it isn't Water Bird, it says Come out," Shelsan told her.

"It says no such thing!" If Mala had been standing she would have had her fists bunched onto her wide hips. The boy on her far side stirred and whimpered. "No such thing," she repeated more softly, and turned back to comfort the child.

Shelsan stood. It was still cold; his skin puckered into plucked bird flesh. He grabbed his bear fur cloak from the hook, threw it over his naked back, and pulled it tight around him. Mala's warmth had long faded.

"Why?" Little Boren wanted to know. "Why does it say Come out?"

"It wants something," Shelsan muttered, and didn't long consider whether it was something Water Bird wanted really, or something Shelsan himself might want.

He climbed outside. Colorless light turned the plain of rooftops into irregular patches of pale white surface and yawning pits. Things stirred in those wells of darkness, breathing and stamping. Some were animals, of course, sheep in pens or tied to roof structures, dogs near the Edge, hunting in the night.

Something flitted briefly on Pinnak's roof, a shadow. When Shelsan turned to look, it was gone.

Pinnak's two sheep bleated once in the triangular pit between their houses, formed because Pinnak's Second Grand had not built his house true to theirs, and his wall slanted away on the sunrise-side. Pinnak was Mala's cousin, son of her mother's brother; a leopard had killed him by nine dry-times ago.

Other sounds, more distant, came from the swamp, from the thick wood, from the river. Some were animal. Other things, too, came at night and cried at the stars, at the moon, things that were not animal, nor were they human. They made sounds that belonged to nothing known in the Place, to that world outside, to the swamp and the forest, and they did not like people.

He looked around. Everything was motionless as far as he could see. The Place was deep in sleep.

What had wakened him on this windless night? It could not have been that shadow on Pinnak's roof, for the shadow made no sound.

Overhead, stars spilled across the sky, a flood of cold light half drowned by the moon, round and mottled with the Wasting to come. It hung like a grain sack halfway to the top of the warm-side sky, slightly orange, as if it reflected distant fire. Tomorrow it would begin to shrink. Shelsan, dazzled, looked away from it toward the cold-side sky, where a trail of stars hooked toward the Pivot, the unmoving one.

The flap over their roof entrance had fallen ajar. It was this that had let in the stone cold knife to cut the dark. He pulled it closed and heard the stick handle clatter against the wall above the ladder. They would have dark again down below.

He made a circuit, starting with Pinnak's roof. There was nothing to be seen there but the usual pile of debris of Pinnak's incessant stone working and his baskets of night soil still full and stinking. Pinnak always left them until people complained and told him to take it away from the Place, or at least dump it into one of the pits. Even then he waited, just to irritate them. Now he would be snoring down below, wedged like a dung beetle between his two women, surrounded by his swarm of brats. How many were there now? Four? Five?

On the roof of the House on the cold-side Shelsan could see the two sleeping forms. That was normal. The old man, Mala's slant-uncle tied by copulation to the Snow Clan, coughed when he was inside and complained often of the dark and the smoke. Up here in full moonlight he slept soundly. He was once a great hunter, so they said. They said he had more than fifty cold-times, fifty dry-times. There were few in the Place who could claim so many. His woman was not much younger, a silent wraith who seldom spoke, like many from the Snow Clan. They had children in the house beyond, and two who lived inside and they all kept to themselves.

No one was out on the sunset-side where Mala's Sorrow Clan cousins lived with their men and children except a goat tied on the roof, but it was asleep and did not stir.

"I'm here," he called, but there was only silence. Water Bird had called him to come out for some reason known only to Water Bird herself.

Unless that shadow had been Pinnak climbing down into his house. He was always smiling and acting friendly, but you never knew what he was really thinking, and he had a malicious side that would bear watching.

Shelsan gazed down into the pit between their houses, deep in thought. After a moment he shrugged and relieved himself into the black opening. Pinnak's sheep bleated and backed away.

Mala

When Shelsan had gone Mala lay awake, staring into the glimmers of light. They moved eldritch around the room, lighting here and there: on the skull of First Grand, Spirit Father of the House, the hackberry sack, the oval top curve of the dark opening to the back storage on the cold-side.

The boy was so hot to the touch, so frail. Only two cold-times! It wasn't fair. If it really was the Sun Demon, there was little to be done.

The eldritch lights moved over the dome of Spirit Father's skull. He seemed to be looking down on her.

What did they want of him, of her? What had she done?

Could it be because she had gone with Shelsan, after all? Spirits, Waterbird or Spirit Father, they were punishing her by sending Sun Demon for the boy? Because the small boy was Shelsan's son? Could that be it?

But Big Boren had been gone so long! She needed someone, and Shelsan had been kind, even though he came from the far sunrise-side, and was from the Locust Clan. He was a good hunter, and lucky too. The Animal Spirits had favored him, and she had accepted him into her home.

Yet now they were punishing him as well.

Little Boren was sleeping again. She could hear his smooth breathing, sense the rise and fall of his chest. He was becoming a man, Little Boren was, and so fast. Shelsan would have to take him soon on his Walk of the World, introduce him to all the plants and animals. And this, even though he was not Shelsan's!

Yes, Shelsan was a good man.

The stick handle clattered briefly against the wall, and the glimmering lights went out. First Grand's skull vanished into the darkness. The child whimpered beside her; she pulled him to her breast and soon fell asleep to the sound of his feeble sucking.

No Name

"What was it?" Mala asked when Shelsan descended again. Her voice woke the boy, and he pushed away from her with a small cry.

"Nothing. It was nothing."

"So Nothing woke you? Nothing pretended to be Water Bird or Spirit Father? Nothing called you outside?"

He grunted and lay down beside her.

"The boy is sick," she hissed. "I hoped they were coming to help us, Spirit Father or Water Bird. I was hoping."

"Leave it, Mala."

But she could not leave it, and later she said, "The little one's worse, Shelsan. You're his father. If he dies, he will never have a name. You must go to Temkash again. You must bring him again."

"You want me to go to Temkash?" This was surprising. Temkash was Mala's half-brother, prime mate of Denn'ik of the Wind Clan, distaff nephew of Shelsan's maternal slant cousin, but he lived at the Edge beyond which there were no other Houses, and he would have nothing to do with his Clan. His was Last Egg. There were periodic rumors another would come to his edge, begin to build, and then Temkash would no longer be at the Edge, he would be pulled farther and farther into the Place.

Shelsan knew Temkash would not stand for this; he had built as close to the water as possible so it could not happen. He clung to the Edge, said he needed to be there, see what lay beyond, stay close to the wild world outside the Nest. After all, he was a Pretender, the most feared in the Place, and what he wanted, he got.

They knew, all the many thousands who lived in the Place, that Temkash could easily slip away from them. He would go to the Other Side, dancing and jabbering at them in a silent gesture language, hands weaving incomprehensible words in the air, and the People would stir uneasily and look at one another. When he did that he was no longer human.

Sometimes, when he went to the Other Side, he brought things back – a new word, a description of a plant no one had seen before, a cure for toothache, and the People would be glad. But once at least, so they said, he had slipped away and a few days later the woman from his sunrise-side had died.

Shelsan had told Mala he was not sure about this since no one saw the Pretender leave his house, but it was true the woman had died screaming, and when they asked him, Temkash only showed his worn brown teeth. There had been bad blood between them.

But when the little one grew hot, she had sent Shelsan to ask Temkash to come. And he did come then, and looked at the boy, and told her it was probably Sun Demon in the boy. Mala asked what the boy had done, and Temkash answered curtly that he didn't know. What had she done, she or the others, what had *they* done? She swept her hand around the Place to take in the Grands, neighbors, cousins, all the houses and their Clans.

Again, Temkash said he didn't know. The spirits had their own reasons. Who could guess them?

So Mala, her eyes darting to the boy and back, had asked more anxious questions, and Temkash had turned his lips down into his beard. He gave her a sour look and climbed the ladder to the outside. Sun flew in, flew out again as the smoke flap opened and closed.

"Go to him," she urged Shelsan, and he could hear the fear. "Bring him back."

Pretender

Of course Mala had hesitated to send for Temkash again. No one ever wanted him, not really. Sometimes he refused; sometimes, it was said, he killed instead of cured. But Mala, her eyes veiled with pity, with concern, with love even for her man-child, could see Sun Demon eating the boy from the inside, the way his cheeks, so fat and full, caved in; the way his eyes sank back into his skull. So she sent Shelsan again. "He's family; he can't refuse." So Mala said.

But when Shelsan asked, down in the dim hollow of the Pretender's solitary house there at the Edge beside the water, fourteen roofs away from Mala's house, Temkash answered in his gruff, unpleasant voice, "Why should I?" and turned away to pull a strip of dried meat hanging from a roof beam and begin chewing on it.

Shelsan said, "The child does not move. He barely eats."

Temkash barked, "Sun Demon! Of course he doesn't move."

"You're the only one," Shelsan tried. "The only one who can help." He looked at the walls, plain, dirty white above a peeling red panel. Indefinite shapes leaned against them, long sticks, broad masks, tall shapes of reeds bundled into human or animal forms.

"Not a reason," Temkash answered, tearing off another bite. He kept his back to Shelsan. "Try Tzam."

"Mala wants *you*," Shelsan insisted. "Tzam is a slant uncle of the Spider Clan. Wrong house."

"Not interested," Temkash muttered, frowning darkly at the molded shape of his ancestor bear high on the sunrise wall.

Shelsan lifted his shoulders and dropped them. He could not command a Pretender. No one could. He could have added, "Family," but he did not, for he knew it would do no good. Temkash would come if it suited him.

So he made his way toward the ladder through a haze of ancient smoke and nameless smells. He had to step over the great disorder of Temkash's floor, the heaps of skins, round platters of grain, the piles of bark scrapings, dried mushrooms, tubers, and twisted roots. Shelsan knew some of the objects – bits of notched wood or circles stretched with skin – contained strange sounds: drums or rattles.

Other things made, or twisted, light; he'd seen them before when Temkash worked, when he brought spirits down from the upper world, when he rode his animal, how the light seemed to flicker or fade around him. Temkash was strong.

Near the hearth was a pile of animal heads and legs. Some were dried, with clinging patches of hair or fur. Others were naked bone, defleshed and cleaned. Some were painted in garish reds, blacks, and whites, in zigzag or chevrons, loops and nested circles.

At the bottom of the ladder he almost bumped against a small woven cage hanging from a rafter. It was full of living spiders, beady eyes peering out through the mesh.

He started up the ladder, thinking he could not go back to Mala if Temkash would not come to help the boy. He would have to take Little Boren and leave the Place. He'd been thinking of this for some time. Perhaps he should go now, today. It was a good time for Little Boren to take the Walk of the World anyway.

"Wait," Temkash called. His mouth was full.

Shelsan paused on the ladder. He could hear the other man swallow in the silence. Finally he backed down the ladder. "What?" he asked mildly.

"Ah!" Temkash chopped sideways with the edge of his hand.

Shelsan waited.

"I require something."

Again Shelsan waited.

"Frozen tears." He held his hands apart. He spoke of the sharp, transparent stone from the black mountains.

"That is large."

"It is what I require just to try. With a Sun Demon I can promise nothing. Sun Demon is strong, and determined. You have seen what it has done? That woman six roofs down toward the warm-side? One day she comes back from her fields, she and her man last Unborn Moon. Next day the Sun Demon has her, and the day after that she is dead.

And then there were the two children next to her, three days after, gone, one, then the other." He sighed. "It is difficult. Very difficult."

"I'll have to go to the Mountain. There's nothing that large here, not in our house, not in the Nest, not in all the Place."

"By cold-time, then." The Pretender stooped down to gather things from the floor, then paused and looked up at Shelsan. "Have as many of the Sorrow Clan as possible come tomorrow at first sun. They must be there, do you understand? I will call upon the Lineage Head."

Shelsan's heart sank. First the frozen tears – the obsidian – and now this.

"If the boy lives or not, we must eat." Temkash pulled a long branch from a heap on the floor and stood, glaring.

"All right," Shelsan whispered. He left the Pretender crushing dried leaves into a wooden bowl.

First Grand

When he came up from Temkash's dwelling it was nearly midday. It had grown quite hot, and the air was thick with moisture steaming off the broad, shallow water below the Place. Whenever someone dumped their slops into the pits of abandoned houses, dark clouds of flies were disturbed and spiraled upward, buzzing angrily. Fire smoke filled the air, and already the smells of roasting meat lay in flat layers over the uneven roofs.

People greeted him as he made his way toward First Egg. He barely acknowledged them with a bob of his head. There was too much to do to get ready, and little enough time.

Shelsan took his best hunting spear, the one with the precious flint blade, from the rack on his roof and set off toward the warm-side swamp. He climbed down the outside ladder and made his way along the river. It was the middle of the day, not the best time for hunting. The river moved slowly between low banks, carrying its burden of the leavings of butchered carcasses, fragments of discarded wood, human and animal waste. From time to time a small fish rose to the surface, mouth gaping as it tried to eat something too large for its mouth. Frogs complained on all sides.

He knew Mala would ask why he didn't just butcher a kid or a lamb. Anyone else would have done that. No, he had to go hunting, try to get something from the outside, something wild.

Yes, he would say, as he always did, the old ways were best, the ways of Waterbird Mother, of Spirit Father.

He found the tracks as the sun was in its last run for the western darkness, a family of swine. He followed and soon heard them grunting in a stand of rushes by the river.

There was little wind, but what there was helped him. He stayed downwind from the group and watched patiently. Finally a yearling boar emerged from the thicket and drifted along the waterside under the shelter of a line of tamarisks, rooting at the soil and turning it over with his tusks. Still Shelsan waited. It made its way closer, until Shelsan could see its tiny eyes, focused intently on its meal.

Shelsan didn't have to move at all. His spear caught the boar under the shoulder and must have hit the heart because the beast collapsed onto its side, kicking at the ground, and gradually fell still. It hadn't made a sound.

He had to keep his eye out for the big boars, for they could be dangerous, but he was still downwind, and butchered rapidly. He cut and lashed some poles together and dragged the meat back.

There was much cheering and bawdy laughter as he hauled his kill up the ladder to the Place. "Mala will fuck him good tonight, for sure," someone shouted.

"Oh, be quiet, Itzal," a woman answered. "His boy is sick. He's called for Temkash."

"Oh. Sorry, Shelsan, I didn't know."

It was late in the afternoon but the sun was far from darkness when Shelsan stopped at the Widow Klayn's. "May I come?" he called down, and she called back, "Come."

She was a member of Wasting Moon Clan, a pretty woman with her hair coiled tightly to the back of her head and three vertical lines of tattooed dots on her cheeks. Shelsan gave her a joint of the pig and basked in her smile of gratitude. It offered more, but there was no time, and he made his way back to Mala's with the remainder of his kill.

She was waiting on the roof, holding First Grand's skull. "It was lit by the Moon Spirit last night," she said, holding it out.

Shelsan nodded. "Temkash will speak with him." He took the skull and sat cross-legged against the flimsy side of his roof shelter. Mala brought him a water skin.

He held the skull up and looked into its empty eyes. "Well, old First Grand, we will need you now so I'm going to give you a new face."

The skull was naked, had been for many generations (Shelsan knew twenty names going back). It said nothing, and he did not sense, as he sometimes did, that the ancestor was smiling.

No, today its expression was blank and indifferent.

But the baby was his, his and Mala's, and he had to try to appease, to cajole, to tempt.

He took a handful of the baked lime he had brought from the distant hills to the sunset-side. This he mixed with water, adding crushed sand and limestone powder. Once he had kneaded it into a smooth white paste he carefully molded it around the skull in layers, filling in the eye sockets and nose and wrapping a band around the back. The dome of bone that remained on top had been polished over countless years of wear and attention.

Mala brought food, and he ate, waiting for the plaster to dry.

As the sun was going under, he took a brick of hematite and scraped off a small heap of powder, mixed it with oil, and carefully he painted red bands around the plaster. He circled in the eyes, too. The skull of the oldest Grand now had a fresh, new face with polished bone and red, inward-looking eyes. Only the few remaining crooked upper teeth showed signs of the old man's age.

When the night's darkness was complete, Shelsan carried First Grand down into the house and put him back into his niche.

Sun Demon

Shelsan, one among the many, leaned against the sundown pillar, his arms crossed. He was scowling at the tangled ceiling. Ropy roots dangled, some rats scurried. Lamps along the edge of the walls, from the niches, from beside the hearth.

Temkash was preparing himself, above, out in the sky, out in the feeble light of first sun. From time to time his heavy footsteps dislodged dust, which drifted down. Some fell in the child's impassive face. The boy was staring up into that same tangle, but his eyes saw nothing.

One of Mala's distaff Sorrow Clan cousins near Shelsan backed against the wall and dislodged the Head of First Grand, which toppled forward. Shelsan caught it before it hit the floor.

The cousin, squinting nervously, gave him a grateful look and tapped his own forehead for luck.

Now Temkash began to moan, and the quiet murmuring ceased. *Ooah*, he moaned, *Ooh-aah*. His feet began to beat on the roof, a hesitant rhythm at first, and more dust fell.

Mala kneeled before the hearth and blew on the dung ash. Spirals of dry gray flakes rose and spun. There was a burst of flame. She fed the flame with chunks of dried fuel, and it grew large in the hearth. Shelsan saw sweat start in the furrows of her forehead. Her hair, once so dark and sleek, was loosely coiled, tangled, and streaked with the color of ash. She was no longer young, more than thirty cold-times and heavy with her years. Shelsan didn't know how many more.

"Eeeah," Temkash moaned up above. The pounding of his feet grew more rhythmic and gained speed. He was at the opening above the ladder, above the hearth. Streamers of dust, dirt, and insects fell from the thatch. The sounds were without words, the thumping, and the cry of pain, the cry of fear. It went on a long time, and the four hands' of people down below stared at the opening above the hearth where the ladder came down from the upper world.

It was a deer cry he made, a deer in pain as the leopard seized it. The boy suddenly gave an answering cry, and Mala turned.

The boy's face was still again, his body rigid on the platform. Temkash's anguish was the same as the boy's. Sun Demon was taking them down together.

The flap flew back and Sun Demon fought with smoke, a vicious spiral clawing into the outer air, harsh light striking down into the house, cracking it open it to the outside, to the danger.

Then a figure appeared in the opening and began to back down the ladder.

Shelsan could not say for certain it was a man, just that it was a figure wrapped in skirts of skin, layers of woven reeds, chains of hollow bird bone that clattered, and Shelsan knew they came from water birds. A stab of real fear ran through him, top to bottom: Water Bird was the founder of the Place. Water Bird had built the Nest and laid the First Egg, this crowded chamber.

He pushed the fear aside.

Halfway down the figure stopped and turned, arms stretched up to hold the flap open. Bright light filled the opening. His head crest was the cranium of a huge bear. Fierce yellow incisors raked down in front of his brow. The bear's narrow eyes were plastered and painted red. A spray of vulture wing feathers seemed to glow with an inner darkness behind the skull where bear became bird, carnivore and carrion eater. All Shelsan could see was the morning sunlight become Sun Demon dancing on the crimson skull-top, the feather crest in shadow against the shadowed wall. The human face, the little bit that was visible, was painted blood red between the skull and the tangled beard.

The man-beast waited on the middle step, head near the ceiling, motionless. Only the human eyes under the brim of the bear's upper jaw darted feverishly, never pausing, never still. The skull and its semicircle of feathers hovered, as if detached from the man, gone flying by itself.

With a strange, inarticulate cry, this time a bird of prey, Temkash dropped his arms like folded wings, the flap fell to block the sun and gloom returned.

The chamber was filling with smoke probing for an opening. Already the ceiling was shrouded in haze, and the liquid layer of it hid the thatch, the beams.

Temkash, or what had been Temkash, stood, rising to its full height, and it was enormous, a great beast still moaning, a stain, a blot, against the wall. The lamplight flickered.

Suddenly it pulled something from the folds and hollows of its clothing and put it to his lips. It blew and a shrill scream filled the small space, stopping all breath. The bear's head turned, looked around the small room at the people pressed so closely together. It repeated the shrill scream, trilling fast, and the beast jumped from the ladder, legs tucked under, arms crooked, claws extended, into the crowd, crashing into Pinnak. Pinnak was a big man, a heavy man with a shining scalp, a red face, and enormous forearms, but he shrank back before the beast-man.

Others tried to leap out of the way, but the beast-man that had been Temkash knocked against them, slashing with his claws. There was nowhere to go; bodies swayed, rebounded from the walls like ripples.

The beast crouched, panting, and the people pressed back. It turned toward the hearth and sniffed. Something flashed in his hand: with a hiss the smoke changed color and billowed out. Shelsan could see blood run in sheets down the walls.

The beast turned to the crowd and multicolored lights flickered from his hand, swirled up in all directions; sharp rays shot through the smoke. Some of the people crowded in this hot, close room went blind and cried out in terror. Fat Pinnak cowered near the sunrise-side, but his eyes, glittering with malice, were sharp and observant.

The light stopped swirling and seemed to settle gradually around the niche containing Eldest Grand's Head, the red-painted, plastered skull of the lineage founder. *The Head seemed to open its eyes, to look around the room.* Shelsan shivered, though it was hot. *The skull was looking directly into him.*

As suddenly as they started, the lights winked out. In the dim, flickering light that remained, the bear-man was crawling on his hands and knees toward the boy. The Head vanished into the gloom near the ceiling.

Shelsan did not move from the sunset pillar, though the others jostled against him. His fingertips touched the curved horns of a Great Bull, its skull set into the pillar beside him. Third Grand had killed that bull in a great battle, and had given a feast still remembered in the songs of the Sorrow Clan. Shelsan gripped the horn and resisted the press of bodies.

Only the boy, lying face up on the sleeping pallet, had a clear space around him. He was small, the boy, still an infant, and didn't seem to be breathing. But who could breathe in all that smoke and crowd?

Shelsan shook his head. This was his boy, yet it seemed he was not. Shelsan felt more attached to the boy's older half brother standing in the back near the grain storage, the one still known as Little Boren even though his father Big Boren was gone to the mountains and never returned these past four cold-times.

Ooooah, Temkash moaned his beast-moan. He blew his little bird-bone flute, and it screamed impossibly high and loud in the confined space. Only the vague outlines of people, their heads and hair, were visible through sweet dung smoke the color of a days-old bruise. Their eyes sometimes glinted.

Oooah. The bear-man shuffled close to the ground toward the boy, and the people made space as best they could. His sandals dragged dirt and ash from the hearth onto the clean white floor. Shelsan had plastered it only a few moons ago, before the Sun Demon climbed into the boy to devour him.

Now Temkash was touching the boy with the tip of his bone flute. There was no reaction except the nearly invisible rise and fall of his tiny chest.

The Pretender began to grunt, crouching beside the sleeping platform, *Uf-uf-uf.* The grunting started low, it started slow, but it grew quickly louder and faster, this *uf-uf-uf.*

Suddenly Temkash threw out a sparkling cloud that hung in the smoke above the boy's face, little lights twinkling in the gloom. All time stopped. No one moved. The small tallow lamps flickered.

Something stirred in the rafters; a wing came down and swept over the heads of the people in the room, the soft whoosh of a vulture, the breeze of its passage.

"You do not, you are not, you cannot, be not, don't!" the bear-man shouted. There was silence. *The small motes glistened in the smoke. They began to fall onto the boy's impassive face.*

The Pretender blew a rising note on his flute. It continued impossibly long. No one had breath so long. Someone screamed near the sunset wall, and the scream joined the sound of the flute. They both stopped abruptly, leaving stunned silence. A lamp went out, and Shelsan heard Mala sobbing.

The Temkash beast stood. He held his palm up and inhaled deeply. His back arched, and he began to tremble. Blood flowed from his nose. He fell to the floor, screaming in pain. His bear-skull crest fell off, exposing tangled hair shiny with grease. He writhed on the ground, clawing at the plaster. Even from where he stood, Shelsan could see the long curving marks the Pretender's thick fingernail claws had gouged in the soft floor. "*Aaah. Aaah,*" Temkash screamed. "Get it off. Pull it. Out. Not dark. No!" He stopped and began to mumble, as if talking to himself or to something unseen. "I've been there," he mumbled. "Was it? Will be, then, now, what? It's too long, too long. Do we remember? I do. First Grand was dead. No, he will be dead. He is there, I saw him, he is there, was there."

He mumbled to himself for a long time after that. Try as he might, Shelsan could understand no more. The sound became a low, rhythmic chanting, and the room was so thick with smoke he couldn't see the other side where Pinnak crouched. His own breath began to catch in his throat.

Temkash sat up suddenly. "No, it won't be. I can't, don't." He put his hands up, as if pushing something away, something that was trying to sit on his chest. Something did sit on his chest and he fell back. His breathing caught and he stared wildly around, his hair spread on the plaster. Finally he took one long shuddering indrawn breath. Blood seeped from the corners of his eyes and trickled down his cheeks, blending with the red paint.

They all stared. He was breathing heavily, his hands hooked, lying on his back. *Above him something turned in the smoke just under the ceiling. It might have been the head of a great aurochs, one of the gigantic cattle of the region. Light seemed to glide along one shining horn to a shattered tip that bristled with wicked spikes.*

"He's here!" Temkash shouted suddenly. "Look!" He pointed in the direction of the roof entrance. The smoke was too thick, the room too dark. Shelsan could see little but the layers of smoke. *True, the smoke writhed against the ceiling as if alive, and the vague shapes of hanging storage bags, water skins, dried herbs seemed to be moving as well. The entire room was alive, the walls expanding and contracting as though breathing.*

Shelsan leaned toward Mala. She was crouched over the boy, her hand on his forehead. The others in the room, so many of them, began to mumble, nonsense words, noises, growls, animal sounds. They began to tremble as well, the whole packed mass of them shaking. Someone collapsed but couldn't fall, held up by all the others. *Lights flickered, the walls pulsed, zigzag lines writhed along the edge where the wall met the ceiling, lines of many colors that shimmered against the darkness and wriggled like snakes around the room, faster and faster.*

Temkash's heels drummed at the floor. One of his sandals fell off. His foot left blood on the plaster.

Suddenly the boy sat upright, his eyes staring, white showing all around the iris. There was fear in those eyes, yet he was only two cold-times, two warm-times, hardly a Person at all so what could he fear? Shelsan started toward him.

It was in that frozen moment, when all motion had stopped, that the Grand's Head toppled once more from its niche. This time Shelsan was not fast enough to catch it, and it fell to the sleeping platform beside the child. The red plaster cracked and a large section fell off, exposing the gaping hole where its eye had been.

The boy vomited weakly and fell back, suddenly slack, small, and empty.

Mala started, and soon all the women joined a harsh, piercing ululation that filled the small room like the smoke. Shelsan's eyes watered and his throat rasped. *He saw something dark rise up from the boy and drift aimlessly near the ceiling, as though looking for an exit, and he wanted nothing more than to climb the ladder into the sky and run to the swamp. There at least he would be able to breathe.*

The wailing went on for a long time, gradually tapering off. In the silence that followed, Shelsan heard only an occasional sniff. No one spoke. Another lamp went out.

"There was nothing I could do," Temkash said in an ordinary voice, sitting up. "Sun Demon was too strong. You saw it. Nothing. Nothing."

3 Now

Why It's Important to Dig

"Global warming!" Jones said. Though the man on the other end of the line couldn't see, he swept an elegant hand in the air. "Like today, the Neolithic was a period of climate change, though then the causes were not human. Around 15,000 years ago the ice started to relax its grip. The steppes and mountain slopes of the Near East grew warm and moist and fat with plants and animals. You might think of all that abundance as the tree of knowledge, because human beings began to dimly understand they didn't need to wander in search of food: it was all around them."

The man on the other end of the conversation murmured attentively.

Jones continued. Around 12,300 years Before the Common Era, during a period called the late-glacial interstadial, oak woodlands spread, along with trees like pear, pistachio, and almond, edible roots like wild turnips, and, above all, wild grasses. "The temptation was too great," Jones emphasized. "Some wanderers stopped going after their food; there was no need. Everything was close to hand, so they settled down and let the food come to them. And of course warming was happening all over the world, so the so-called Neolithic revolution happened to greater or lesser degrees elsewhere, though usually later."

The Natufians, he continued, dug circular pit houses with dry-stone walls and thatch roofs gathered into permanent settlements. These, he noted, were not yet farmers, but hunters and gatherers. They collected acorns, fruit, and other plants from the steppes and slopes of the Mediterranean hills at places like 'Ain Mallaha north of Lake Tiberius. They cut grain stalks with wooden sickles embedded with flakes of flint, ground acorns into flour, stored food in plaster-lined pits, and hunted. When they died, their bodies, adorned with shell or bone necklaces, bracelets or bonnets, were buried in unmarked graves inside abandoned houses, sometimes with their pet dogs.

It was a first attempt at settlement, and did not last. The climate changed again, and a cold, dry period called the Younger Dryas began around 10,800 BCE and lasted 1,200 years. The garden fell barren. The Natufians abandoned their homes and went back to following the food.

Finally warm weather returned and stayed.

Settlements appeared all over the Middle East, from the source waters of the Euphrates River in a broad curve down through the Levant – the Fertile Crescent. They have names such as 'Ain Ghazal and Jericho near the Dead Sea; Çayönü, Göbleki Tepe, Nevali Çori, Mureybet, Abu Hureyra, and Bouqras along the Euphrates; and further west Aşıklı Tepe and Çatalhöyük in Anatolia. "We are beginning to read a narrative in the development of cultures in this region," Jones said. "For example, ten thousand years ago people at Jericho, which Kathleen Kenyon excavated in the 1950s, plastered human skulls, probably to remember the dead or honor a lineage founder. Plastered skulls reappear to the west around nine thousand years ago at Çatalhöyük. And the architecture at Aşıklı Höyük, which was occupied around 7600 BCE, continues at Çatal."

Because just the right combinations of plants and herd animals flourished in the region and the abundance endured, settlements gradually, tentatively, unevenly, succumbed to the temptation of growing crops and domesticating animals.

It was never intentional. Wild plants dropped seeds before they were brought home from the surrounding areas. The seeds that clung to the stalks made it back to the settlement. When some accidentally fell on fertile ground nearby, they sprouted, people noticed, and soon they were deliberately saving and planting the seeds. Naturally enough they began selecting for the biggest, juiciest seeds. Weeding and watering and fertilizing seemed to help the plants grow.

Then they began to evolve. The grains that grew under human supervision were those that "waited for the harvester." Over generations they turned into domesticated wheat and barley and could no longer survive in the wild. Humans had tamed nature. At the same time, though, nature had begun to domesticate humans, who were now condemned to a life of toil, tending their crops.

"You might say," Jones murmured, "Eve offered Adam a loaf of bread rather than an apple. He took it, and human society changed forever."

Over the next five millennia the Near East underwent what Gordon Childe called the Neolithic Revolution. Its "Neolithic package" included architecture, pottery, and ground stone tools.

This picture proved to be a bit too simple, though: many sites contained stone vessels and no pottery. Some had burials under the floors of living houses; some had art, painting, sculpture; others did not. So our understanding of the Neolithic gradually changed, and today it is viewed as a much more complex progression than people thought even as late as the mid-twentieth century. For example, there was no pottery at Jericho. Kathleen Kenyon called this phase the Pre-Pottery Neolithic A, to be followed, naturally, by the Pre-Pottery Neolithic B. Soon periods, locations, and cultural assemblages were proliferating.

Settlements grew ever more crowded. Food surpluses led to population increases. This led to conflict between settlements. Leaders emerged. Conflict became war. Labor became specialized, with some farming and others investing in defense. Methods of social control, such as organized religion and centralized political power, emerged. In many places we find art that clearly has ritual significance. There is evidence also of human and animal sacrifice, even cannibalism, for instance in the so-called Death Pit at Domuztepe, a sixth-millennium Halaf period site in southeastern Turkey.

Meanwhile animals had also fallen under human control. Herd animals, such as sheep and goats, were the first. Humans simply replaced the leader, and the animals followed. Of course, they now had to live in crowded, unnatural conditions. The inevitable result was that they passed diseases back and forth much more easily than they had in the wild. Soon those same diseases, such as influenza, were jumping to the humans with whom they lived. Over generations these animals, too, evolved, becoming smaller, meatier, and incapable of surviving on their own. Now they, like the plants, needed humans to care for them.

Diet changed. People ate less diverse foods, since it was so easy to grow a small number of crops. They ate more starch and less animal protein. The jaw and teeth, no longer needed for grinding tough natural grains and uncooked meat, gradually diminished in size. "In fact," Jones said, "bioarchaeologist Clark Larsen claims the reduction in tooth size after the development of agriculture was nearly universal. In China, for instance, people have much smaller teeth than

Europeans do. This is a reflection of the longer period of time they have had agriculture."

In many areas stature also decreased, health suffered, tooth decay became rampant and obesity commonplace. Infant mortality went up and lifespan decreased. "Perhaps it was a Faustian bargain," Jones continued. "We may have art and music and satellites, but we also are living with the consequences of decisions made during this period. This is why Aynalı Tepe is so important: it's another tile in the mosaic picture we are developing of the origins of what we call civilization. Actions taken 9,000 years ago have consequences today. The Neolithic condemned us to lifetimes of labor."

"Do you think you'll find something . . . significant?" the lightly accented voice on the other end of the line asked softly.

Jones barely hesitated. "Of course."

"Then what level of funding will you need?"

Jones let out a silent sigh. Now it was only a matter of reeling in the fish; or, better, harvesting the grain.

The Project

Satchi had to admit that when Jones undertook a project, it proceeded at a dizzying pace. His reputation and contacts opened doors and wallets.

Within days Jones had written up a research proposal. "We believe this to be an important Neolithic site," it said. "Our purpose is to confirm this, determine how large it was, and its relationship with Çatalhöyük and the regional culture of the Konya Plain, including trade patterns for goods like obsidian, shells, and animals. Most important, it is imperative this site be protected from further destruction by erosion and looters."

By the end of September he had already acquired several hundred thousand dollars in preliminary funding from what he called "a private donor," the excavation permits were approved, and an architect was at work on drawings for a Dig House.

By late the following spring a group of graduate students marked the beginning of Season One by creating an overall site grid with a zero point at the southwest corner. Once this was done, the survey showed the mound was an ellipse, with its long axis oriented more or less north-south, 227 meters long and 172 meters wide. The students and faculty drew relief maps. The highest point was 9.33 meters above the plain and 1,032 meters above sea level. A surface collection program followed. Bits of late Byzantine pottery to fragments of bone, obsidian, and charred remains were collected from 2 by 2 meter squares at 10-meter intervals over all of Aynalı Tepe. The numbers and locations of all artifacts were logged, and from this they extrapolated the average density across the entire site.

A month later they had added a general regional survey and done the data entry for preliminary Geographical Information Systems and geological databases. These, as well as satellite and aerial photographs, confirmed Aynalı Tepe had occupied a slight rise in marshy terrain beside a now-vanished river.

Özgür was appointed state representative, which gave him both a salary and significant administrative power over the site. Jones worked hard to keep him happy. Since Satchi's initial misgivings about the man had not diminished, he was grateful for Jones's continuing intervention.

Late in Season Two a British documentary crew interviewed Bryson Jones outside the farmer's house. On the tour he pointed to the protective fence. "First thing we built," he said. "To stop further looting and preserve Aynalı Tepe for the future."

He let them past the half-built Dig House and up the mound, describing what the Aynalı Tepe Project expected to find: households like those at Çatalhöyük – they hoped with bull crania and figurines, burials and stone tools; perhaps even art. At the summit he pointed to the collapsing treasure-hunters' hole: "People who do things like this are thieves, common criminals. We must put a stop to it. We don't want to see what happened in Iraq after the American invasion, when the museum was looted and hundreds of ancient sites plundered. As long as ancient artifacts have value, there will be unscrupulous people who will steal them for profit."

He paused to let this sink in while the camera lingered on the hole. "We'll never know what they found – they left us only their ladder. No doubt some private collector purchased whatever they looted from Turkey's national heritage and has them locked away for private viewing, permanently disconnected from the past, swallowed up by a greedy and evanescent present."

The documentary went over well. Aynalı Tepe was becoming known. "But, Satchi," Jones said later, "the Aynalı Tepe Project is far bigger than just a few cable TV shows. We'll get an award-winning documentary out of this. You find me something new and surprising, and we'll turn the world upside-down."

Satchi said. "I'll do my best, but we have to go carefully, and I can't dig up something that isn't there."

"Not asking you to do that, Satchi, certainly not. But there's something there. Something special. I feel it. Call it a hunch."

Mellaart

At the beginning of Season Three Satchi gave a seminar to the new members of the team. The Seminar Room was dark. The screen glowed behind him. On it was the image of a plump man in glasses lounging with a cigarette, a bemused smile on his square face.

"James Mellaart!" Satchi said. "This was the British archaeologist who discovered Çatalhöyük in the late 1950s and excavated there for four years in the early1960s. He was a colorful, flamboyant figure, who unfortunately was later caught up in controversy, even scandal of the so-called Dorak Affair. Ultimately he was banned from excavating in Turkey."

Mellaart was excited when, in 1958, at age 33, he visited the mound near the town of Çumra southeast of Konya. No one expected large settlements in Anatolia, not ones so old, anyway. All the action was supposed to be further east, at Jericho, and Jarmo in Iraq. Anatolia, according to Mellaart's boss at the British Institute of Archaeology at Ankara, showed "no sign whatever of habitation during the Neolithic period." Mellaart had recently been digging at Hacilar, a copper-age site, but when he saw Çatal he knew it was earlier, and much larger than Jericho. Mellaart believed Anatolia was a pivotal location in European prehistory and planned to prove it. To this ambitious young archaeologist Çatalhöyük was a godsend.

"What about the Dorak Affair?" Francy, the redheaded graduate student from California, asked. There was a murmur from some of the other volunteers in the Seminar Room. It was shortly after sunset, and many of them were tired. One, a sophomore from the University of Cincinnati, was asleep.

Satchi shrugged. "Briefly, Mellaart claimed he had been shown a collection of priceless artifacts. It was a stunning announcement but was backed only by drawings he had made himself. The Turkish government was interested in where these artifacts might have come from, and when he could produce neither the woman who he said showed them to him nor any proof that they existed, their suspicions grew. If they existed, they had to have been looted. So they threw him out of the country. You can read up on it in Michael Balter's book *The Goddess and the Bull.*"

Mellaart uncovered 150 buildings in a densely settled agglomeration of house structures in up to twelve layers of occupation over at least a thousand years. And this was a tiny percentage of the site, which meant this was the largest "city" of the time.

There was an impressive consistency in the organization of the houses, with a hearth and roof entrance to the south, platforms, side and rear storage chambers, and sometimes wall decoration – paintings, bull crania, sometimes plaster or plaster moldings in the shape of a woman giving birth, or perhaps a lizard or a bear. He was convinced the more highly decorated houses had religious significance and dubbed them "shrines." No one knew before this that that there were any Neolithic sites in Anatolia. And he found the now famous "goddess figurine," the fat seated woman with her hands resting on the backs of two leopards.

After Mellaart was forced to leave Turkey the site was more or less abandoned until the early 1990s, when Ian Hodder decided to undertake a reexcavation. He designed a twenty-five-year project, using the latest excavation and analytic techniques. Our project is similar to his, both in its goals and its methodology.

Hodder worked much more slowly and carefully than Mellaart did, beginning with a surface survey and then slow, methodical digging, sorting, and analysis. One conclusion they reached was that the shrines were, in fact, houses that were simply more highly decorated than others. There was no evidence of streets or public places, no evidence of divisions of labor. Each household seemed to be a self-contained unit. It was a surprising discovery. This was not a town in the sense we would think of it.

"Over the years a series of reports have come out of the Çatalhöyük project," Satchi concluded. "They are models for the rest of us. We have them in the library. Read them carefully."

The lights came on, and there was a general rush toward the door. Francy stayed behind. "I still want to know about the Dorak Affair," she insisted. "What do you think? Did the treasure exist? Did Mellaart really see it? Was he smuggling artifacts out of Turkey the way the government suspected?"

Satchi shrugged. "I'm an excavator," he said. "I dig. Mellaart was an interesting archaeologist but perhaps a little too interested in fame for my taste."

"There are really archaeologists like that?" she asked innocently.

"No comment."

Dig House

It was a June morning early in Season Three. Satchi was waiting impatiently in the center of the open courtyard of the completed Dig House for a truck to arrive. He was staring absently over the roof at the summit of the mound where a polymer mesh awning suspended on a network of tubular supports shaded the excavation.

They had confirmed that the site dated to the Neolithic, around 9,000 years ago. Despite the heavily eroded architectural remains of what was probably a seventh-century Byzantine farmstead on the north end, dated by a bronze cross and some pottery in a small midden, the Neolithic settlement was largely undisturbed. A surface scraping of the crest of the mound had uncovered the tops of the mud-brick walls of an agglomeration of buildings constructed side by side, as at Çatalhöyük. They didn't have carbon dating confirmation yet, but everything he had seen convinced Jones that Aynalı Tepe was at least partly contemporary with Çatalhöyük.

The subsurface sampling had also uncovered a garbage pit surrounded by abandoned houses. Satchi felt there must be a house beneath it: a midden here would be like a landfill in Central Park. It was odd enough for Satchi to plan a remote sensing pass over the area, and the equipment was due any minute. It would save them a lot of work and might give some clues to why Aynalı Tepe was abandoned, but the road outside the gate remained stubbornly empty.

Still, it was satisfying, seeing the open square of the nearly completed Dig House. The east side contained dormitories and bathrooms (sunrise through the dorm windows, Jones had said, would help the team wake up). The northern corners housed kitchen and dining, meeting rooms, offices. To the west were laboratories and meeting rooms, whereas the south, facing the mound, held the Secure Room, with barred windows on both sides. It was here that all particularly valuable finds would be kept. Next to it was the Situation Room, the heart of all the remote-sensing operations to come – soon, Satchi hoped. If Ben's damn machine didn't arrive today, he'd have to extend the trench toward the looters' hole tomorrow, which meant taking people off other tasks.

Everything was running smoothly. Satchi stepped over a flowerbed and walked slowly along the veranda.

Jones had decreed that the project would have the best equipment money could buy, powered as much as possible by solar. "Sure it costs a little more to get off the grid, but it's worth it," Jones said. "We make a statement. We're environmentally friendly. We're good for the country. And what's more, it's true." Some solar panels on the south-facing roof were already providing hot water. Others generated electricity for the computers and other electronics, such as high-speed satellite Internet.

Satchi had asked him how a private donor could afford all this.

Jones waved his hand negligently. "It's a company called Shenzhen Holding Trust."

"What's that?"

"A philanthropic organization."

"You're kidding."

"Let's just say it comes indirectly from an anonymous billionaire with an interest in antiquities and a keen eye for tax policy."

Satchi grunted dubiously but didn't probe further. His concern was the dirt, not the money. He was grateful for the amenities, though he thought ruefully it wasn't like the romantic old days when they'd had to live in tents in the desert.

Archaeology had gone high-tech, complex, and collaborative, with dozens of scholars in different disciplines coming and going. A work crew from the village was hammering together the final sets of shelves and workbenches for the labs. Within days they would be crowded with people such as Lodewyk Barhydt, a Dutch medical doctor who specialized in human skeletons, and the Finnish archaeological art conservator Hellä Rautanen, due to arrive early next week for a preliminary look at the site. By later in the summer they hoped to have some art for her to conserve.

There would be people to examine animal bones, chaff from ancient grains, mud brick, the remains of charcoal and fire ash, clay figurines, and stone tools. They expected chemists, geophysicists, ethnographers, experts in worked stone, botanists, and ecologists.

Satchi would have to coordinate them all, make sure they had beds, keep track of how many were staying for meals, arrange transportation. It all distracted him from the dirt, but it was part of his job.

Beside the gate Mehmet, the permanent guard, was painting his new house. He and his young family would move in within the week. He saw Satchi, pointed down the road, and waved. It must be the truck, at last. Satchi glanced over at Özgür, seated comfortably on one of the ubiquitous white plastic chairs, sipping a glass of tea. Yes, he thought, looking at his watch, things were going well.

It was time to worry.

DANTE

A woman emerged from the kitchen with a tray and proffered small glasses of hot tea. Satchi, watching Mehmet and the gate with some impatience, declined with a smile.

Özgür took a cup, replacing it on the tray with his empty. With a deep sigh he sipped noisily and exhaled a long plume of smoke. "It is good, this Dig House," he said affably.

Satchi nodded.

The representative's smoke turned brilliant white when it floated from the shadow of the overhang into full sunlight. "Your Doctor Jones is someone who can do things."

"Yes, Mr. Tasköprülüzâde, the Dig House is good." Satchi could finally pronounce the man's last name without stumbling, and he always made it a point to address him formally. "But I wouldn't say he's *my* Doctor Jones."

"OK, sure, not your Doctor Jones," Özgür replied. "But he made you Field Director, so perhaps you are *his* Mr. Bennett, no?"

Satchi didn't bother to answer. Özgür was charming, irritating, sly, and useful by turns. He knew Satchi didn't have a Ph.D. and always referred to him as "Mr. Bennett." Satchi found it helped if he maintained his distance and didn't react to the representative's petty snipes. The important thing, he reminded himself, was the dig, always the dig. Personal conflicts were irrelevant.

He took a deep breath and was letting it out slowly when a horn sounded from the gate. Mehmet pulled it open, and a panel truck rolled into the courtyard and stopped alongside the veranda.

"At last," Satchi said.

The project driver climbed out and stretched before volunteering that he had had made it from Istanbul in nine hours because Bennett *efendim* had made it clear his cargo was very important. But, he insisted, he had never gone faster than the speed limit.

"Yes, I'm sure," Satchi agreed, nodding vigorously. "*Çok önemli*, very important. *Çok iyi*, very good." He opened the back of the truck and looked at the large blue case with the word DANTE stenciled on it in red.

Özgür joined him. "I'll get workmen to help unload," he said.

A young man in baggy cargo pants and a T-shirt sporting the image of an upright trowel with a glinting highlight off the tip of the blade came around the back. "There she is," he said proudly.

"Ben?" Satchi said. "I thought you were coming on the bus tomorrow morning."

"No way I was going to let this thing come down here without me," Ben said. "She's my baby. Francy here yet?"

Satchi nodded. "She got in yesterday. Don't tell me . . ."

Ben laughed. "Wishful thinking, perhaps, but hope springs eternal. We went to Cabo San Lucas together for Christmas, but it's been a long time, what with her being in England for the semester and me in California."

"Ah. But it does sound as if the romance is progressing. Congratulations." Ben and Francy had been a notoriously on-and-off couple for some years.

Ben squinted, twisting his mouth up to one side. "She's an old-fashioned girl, you know."

"These days I'm not sure what that means," Satchi observed.

"It means she wants parental approval to get married. I think it's quaint. Our problem is my Portuguese mother and her Irish one. It's complicated."

"Tell me all about it later," Satchi said. Özgür returned with three workmen. "Özgür, this is Ben Veira, one of Doctor Jones's prize graduate students. He's a talented excavator and a wizard with electronics. We're glad to have him."

"Grew up playing Doom, that's all," Ben grinned. "Not a wizard, just a child of the times."

The workmen lifted the case onto the veranda. "This Dante is what, actually?" Özgür asked with a frown.

"DANTE – Digital Anisotropic Noninvasive Terrestrial Explorer." Ben beamed. "Dr. Jones pretty much gave me carte blanche, if you know what I mean. Spare no expense, he said. She's a beauty, I promise."

Özgür lit another cigarette. "You can tell me perhaps what it does?"

In response to Ben's inquiring look Satchi said, "Mr. Tasköprül-üzâde's an archaeologist, Ben. He's also the government representative on site, which means he's ultimately responsible for everything, including not just permits and visas, but everything we find. Think of him as an important member of the team."

"Got it." Ben popped open the case. "Well, see, DANTE's a complex of remote-sensing instruments – fluxgate magnetometer, electrical resistance, side-scan radar, and so on, all built into one box, and because of the software I've written it's way more sensitive than anything built so far. It'll allow us to get a peek at what's underground without having to dig, hence the 'noninvasive' part. I've fixed it with telemetry, with software to interpret in real time, you see, on the computer. And anisotropic, well, that's because it's directionally dependent, so the proximal regions remove larger soil particles . . ." Ben explained how software helped increase resolution of the distal regions. "Gives us greater flow-through, see?"

Özgür did not see. He was frowning, visibly annoyed, and interrupted. "It looks like a bomb."

Ben laughed. "No, not a bomb, I assure you."

"Explosives are not allowed," Özgür said.

It was Ben's turn to frown. "No explosives. Archaeologists don't use them."

"Özgür is an archaeologist," Satchi repeated.

Özgür nodded. "So you look underground?"

"Right." Ben relaxed. "I thought of calling it Beatrice, but I couldn't think of a way to make that work as an acronym – too many letters – and I liked the idea of Dante, you know, being given a guided tour of the underworld, so even though this baby is the tour guide and not the tourist I thought, what the hell . . ."

"Yes," Satchi interrupted, "thanks, Ben. We have to call it something, and DANTE's just fine."

Ben gazed lovingly at the barrel-shaped instrument, the laptop and various cables, a small platform with runners, a folding antenna. He lifted out a thick binder. "The user manual," he said.

"Must be 500 pages," Satchi observed dryly.

"Six fifty." Ben hefted it.

"Is that enough?"

"I hope it's enough for a Ph.D. Let's get it to the Situation Room."

Özgür lit another cigarette. "One minute."

Ben turned. "Yes?"

"This . . . instrument, it sends radio?"

"Telemetry, sure. Why?"

"Radio is not permitted."

Ben's voice went up a register. "What do you mean, not permitted?"

"What I say." Özgür looked up as the woman reappeared with more tea. He took a glass. "It is not permitted to send radio."

Ben leaned toward him. "Why not? It's a research instrument, and a damned expensive one, too."

Özgür shrugged. "You cannot use it."

Before Ben could respond to this, Satchi took his elbow. "Ben, a word." They walked away.

Özgür

Özgür sat comfortably and watched Satchi and Ben walk toward the Situation Room. He took a sip of his tea. Let them have their little private word. He, Özgür Tasköprülüzâde, did not mind.

But he did mind. At the beginning everything had fallen into place just the way he planned. He'd contacted Jones and now Aynalı Tepe was on the map. He was the government representative.

He should be happy.

But it was no longer going well. He had to admit, and Özgür was not one to admit things easily, not even to himself, that he had a sour taste in his mouth, and it wasn't from the tea, or the cigarette, which he abruptly flicked away.

First there was Jones. Jones was always polite. He shook Özgür's hand warmly and consulted him on decisions. Yet Özgür always felt he wasn't sincere. Jones wasn't *really* paying attention, as though his mind was somewhere else and Özgür was an afterthought.

He wanted the famous archaeologist's full attention. After all, it was he, Özgür Tasköprülüzâde, who had showed him the stone mirror. Aynalı Tepe was his discovery. Yet in spite of all Jones's solicitousness and thoughtful nods, Özgür never quite felt appreciated. In fact, he felt Jones was suspicious, as if he thought Özgür had stolen the mirror or something.

Well, he thought, one who handles honey licks his fingers. It can't be helped. He was in charge, and that was something.

It was different with Bennett. Özgür's resentment of him had bloomed like a bottle of ink dumped into the still, clear water of his soul. He understood what rankled him. For one thing, the excavator was curt to the point of rudeness. But beyond that was the patronizing way Satchi lectured him about basic archaeology. He, a trained archaeologist!

Deep inside Özgür knew the truth: his undergraduate degree was from a mediocre provincial university. He also dimly knew he had done little with the limited knowledge he had acquired and had just coasted through a series of low-level government jobs thanks to his cousin.

When the mirror came his way, though, everything became clear. Allah had blessed him, and he knew what he must do. So why did they treat him this way?

It was because these Americans and Europeans had more money, better resources, access to the media. People paid attention when they spoke. They dismissed Özgür; people were nice to him because he was the representative, not because he was smart and competent, not because he was a peer.

One particular day really stuck like a nettle on his skin. Özgür had asked Satchi about dirt. The man seemed so interested in it, as if it were a substance of great power and magic. He hovered over the trench. Sometimes he dropped to his knees and sniffed it.

It was dirt. What was so special? Özgür wanted to know

Dirt, Satchi said, was infinitely mysterious. You got a feel for it – the way it moves: it flies, settles, dissolves, flows, fills; and the way people dig it, trample it, drag it around, move it, sift it, leave things in it, buried deliberately or by time.

It could drift through the air, flow in sheets down slight slopes, or cascade down steeper ones. It changed all the time through the action of living things such as rodents and bacteria and plant roots and fungus, through the chemistry of salts and contaminants such as human and animal waste, fire and fire residue, through the physics of freezing and melting. It came in all sizes, from dust to boulders. Over time it moved the things it contained, both vertically and horizontally. Everything that disturbed dirt left traces, and archaeologists could decipher them and tease out the story they told. People lived on it, in it, among it. In the end they returned to it.

"To you," Satchi said, "to most people, in fact, dirt is just brown stuff that gets in the way. But it is a living thing."

As if Özgür needed to know all this! What Özgür did know was that dirt covered up things that could change his life if he could just get them out of the ground. As Satchi had said, dirt was in the way.

He lit another cigarette and sat back in his chair. He could be patient.

Negotiations

"What's with this guy?" Ben demanded above the din of hammering in the Human Remains Lab behind them.

"Keep your voice down," Satchi replied. "He's the rep; we have to keep him happy."

"Stopping us from doing archaeology will keep him happy?"

"Of course not. He's the one who showed Jones the mirror. In a way he thinks of this as his project."

"So why didn't he just get his own damn permits and do his own damn project?" Ben's voice went up.

Satchi smiled without humor. "Money, perhaps, among other things."

"Yeah, right. So what do we do?"

"I'll have a talk with him. He wants something. We just have to find out what it is."

"You think it's really not permitted to use telemetry?"

"Possibly, but it's the first I've heard of it. Fear of terrorism or something, perhaps, but I'll make him understand it's harmless. He can watch everything we do, he's the boss, the man in charge, blah blah, you see? We need the underground survey – we think Aynalı's like Çatal, but we won't know for sure without this survey. We won't know where to look, and there will be things down there. He doesn't like me, but . . ."

"Treasure," Ben interrupted, snapping his fingers. "This guy's a treasure hunter."

"Not necessarily," Satchi began, then saw the workman carrying the case away. "Wait a minute!" he shouted. "*Dur! Yapma!* Stop." He ran after them.

They put the case down. "What's going on?" he asked Özgür.

"They take it to Secure Room."

"You're going to lock it up?"

"Of course, yes. You must have permit to use radio. It is a military thing."

"We don't use military frequencies, just short-range telemetry, enough to cover the mound, that's all."

"I can't know that," Özgür said reasonably. "I couldn't take responsibility."

Satchi looked into the distance for a moment. "All right, Özgür, whom do we ask?"

Satchi glanced at Ben, who listened intently with a strange bemused smile, as if he found the situation interesting but not personally relevant. Satchi suppressed an angry comment. He was no longer sure whom to blame. Perhaps if DANTE had arrived when Özgür was away they could have simply begun using it and it would have been a *fait accompli*. Too late for that, though. "Özgür?"

"Ah, yes." Özgür looked around. "Whom to ask? That is difficult. Besides the Ministry of Culture and Tourism, I suppose the armed services, and the Directorate of Electronic and Technical Intelligence might have to know. Perhaps Turk Telekom? Even the Health Ministry – possible bad radiation effects."

"But we have permits!"

"Yes, *efendim*, you have permits to dig, but you do not have the necessary permits for radio. Cell phones, for example, can be used by bad people to set off bombs."

"We have cell phones already! And we are not terrorists."

"No." Özgür smoked in great tranquility. The workmen sat down along the edge of the veranda and chatted quietly.

Satchi thought it over. "What would it take?" he asked.

"Pardon, *efendim*?"

"Let me rephrase." Satchi did not trust his Turkish and spoke carefully in English. "How can we acquire the necessary permits to work with DANTE?"

"Ah, yes. I would have to spend some time on this problem."

"Would you spend some time on the problem? Please, Özgür!"

Özgür turned down the corners of his mouth and raised his eyebrows. He looked at the top of the mound over the roof. He examined the flowers along the border of the veranda. "All right," he said at last. "It will take time, but I will try."

"Thank you," Satchi said, his voice tight. "Everyone will appreciate it. I will appreciate it. You're the best, Özgür."

Özgür nodded and signaled to the workmen. He seemed satisfied.

When DANTE was on the floor of the Situation Room and the representative had taken the workmen away, Ben patted the bright crimson letters: DANTE. "Yes!"

"Yes, what?" Satchi frowned.

"Yes, that Özgür's something. I think he just wanted somebody to recognize how important he is."

Underworld

It had taken Özgür six weeks to get the permits for DANTE, but now Satchi, Ben, and another graduate student sat in the darkened Situation Room and stared at a computer screen. Satchi tapped it. "Down," he said quietly for perhaps the twentieth time that morning.

The only light came from the monitor and several rows of LED readouts. The only sound, aside from the breathing of the room's three occupants, came from the air-conditioning.

All morning they had worked the instrument hard, doing rapid, low-resolution scans of the top of the midden area, which Satchi had decided to study first. If house floors lay underneath, his hunch would be confirmed.

Özgür had retreated to the veranda, where he was no doubt sipping tea and watching with dark suspicion, but at least he was out of their hair for the time being.

They were now rescanning the area at finer resolution, slowly building up a three-dimensional map of a 10-meter square at grid coordinates 127,76. They already had mapped the walls and floors of the neighboring houses, but here the midden went down at least another layer.

So far they had seen mostly visual white noise, though in fact the sensor image of millions of soil particles packed into a random density pattern was mostly green. "Should be called 'Green Noise,'" Ben snorted. "GN."

The screen displayed 1.3 by 1 meter horizontal slice of the earth just over 2 meters below the surface. This had taken all morning.

Ben muttered, "More GN" and tapped a key. The screen fragmented into a chaotic, multicolored mass and began to redraw itself from top to bottom as the machine outside began a new scan.

A narrow shaft of intense August sunlight found its way through the imperfect window shade and illuminated a white oval on the worktable to his left, though it missed the stone dagger one of the students had uncovered in the trench the day before. He shrugged; it couldn't be a sign from the local deities.

One of the student volunteers adjusted the blinds, and the light blinked out.

"Thanks," Satchi said. Not that he would have taken it as a sign if the light had hit the dagger. Not really. Satchi's belief in science kept his feet firmly on the ground into which he was now peering. He leaned back in his chair and glared at the image, daring it to reveal something surprising, something that wasn't dirt or rock or fragments of fallen roof or just plain garbage. Another dagger would be nice.

Ben grunted something indistinct. The screen wavered, swirled into a pattern of false colors (still mostly green), and stabilized. "What's that?" He turned to Satchi. "Field Director?"

Satchi sighed and shook his head. Embedded in the noisy matrix of dirt was a blob of dark green running off to the right. "Probably a false reading." Although he loved the science-fiction quality of Ben's high-tech view of the past, he had too much experience to trust the machine completely. The images often turned out to be chunks of rock or irregular distributions of slightly denser soil. Remote sensing was still more art than science, and in Satchi's view only looking closely at the soil, and touching it, would confirm reality. "Keep going."

"It's interesting," Ben said. "If this was a house, it was deliberately destroyed and never rebuilt. People living all around it dumped their garbage there."

"Not unusual," Satchi said. "Maybe the family died out. No heirs to rebuild." He had the habit of tugging at his lip when he had to make up his mind about something. The digging season was always too short, and time was precious, especially with an expensive machine like DANTE; he didn't want to waste it in futile examinations of natural anomalies. But this one was curious enough to give it more study.

"OK, Ben, center it." He glanced at the digital clock on the screen. "Jones'll be all over me if we don't make sure, especially if it turns out to be something important. He's pushing for a big find. Helps with the funding. Benefactors want publicity, and publicity comes from exciting finds that attract *National Geographic* or *ArchaeologyNowOnline*. It makes for lousy archaeology and is a distraction from real science, but we have to do it to pay our way."

Ben spoke into a microphone, "Hey, Francy."

A voice came back a little tinny from the tiny computer speaker. "Yes, Ben?" The voice was politely neutral. Ben and Satchi exchanged glances.

"All business," Satchi mouthed.

Ben's mouth turned down a little.

"Move half a meter west, please," Ben said.

The image fragmented and restabilized.

"Hmph." Ben put his forefinger on a dark band running diagonally across the upper left of the screen. "*That's* part of the wall to the east."

Satchi leaned forward. "The neighboring house." He scribbled a note with the coordinates and asked Ben to start recording. The blob was now centered, a dark circle with a lighter halo.

"Shouldn't be there, should it?" Ben asked. "I mean, it's in the exact center of the midden."

"At the level where the midden turns to fill," Satch said. "Above is garbage, below is much cleaner. And it looks like a sphere."

"Or a sort of a football shape. You can see how the sides slope away. Maybe just a big stone, something natural someone brought here because it looked nice."

"Paper weight?"

"They didn't have paper! Oh, you're not serious." Ben tried, without much success, to conceal his irritation. "Anyway, the top's embedded in a matrix of irregular material. Below really is cleaner."

"The object, by the way," Satchi made an impatient gesture at the screen, "is not stone."

"I guess it wouldn't *be* a stone, would it?" Ben said. "I mean, it seems they were careful about sifting the soil when they buried a house, weren't they? Like at Çatal? So the fill wouldn't sag and collapse under the new building. Besides, there's not much rock around here. Stone would be exotic and expensive. Be weird to leave it in the middle of a buried house, no?"

"Mm." Satchi was distracted, pulling at his lip again. "Go down until you find something, like a floor. Then build us a 3-D, 5-millimeter scale, of that object. I'm going out to take a look."

On the Mound

A hundred meters away the team was working under the awning. Satchi kept his eyes down and walked quickly through the sunlight. Once under the shelter he raised his eyes.

In August the fields were a parched pale tan. Wheat. For millennia people had been growing it here, not to mention barley, peas, and flax. With irrigation they were getting two crops a year in some places. That was today. Eight or nine thousand years ago, though, this was swamp.

Traces of the river were barely visible as a subtle variation in the endless yellow. Only by allowing his eyes to fall out of focus and then letting them drift along the slight alteration in the elevation of the land could he make out its course, and even then it was vague, just a hint. But 8,000 years ago there was a river there, or a sluggish stream, more lake than river, but moving water, source of drink and life for the town. No doubt it was had been filled with filth and death as well, at least downstream. This had been a big settlement, perhaps four or five thousand people dumping trash into the river. The survey team had found stone tools and animal bones for miles along that old course.

"This had better be something," he muttered, moving over to the technology team.

Francy was watching over DANTE. A series of lights flashed along one side of the bulbous machine with each pass. When she saw Satchi, she pushed her cap back on her head, "Ben's doing a 3-D."

"We saw something."

She gave him the benefit of a lopsided grin. "Just over 2 meters?"

Satchi marveled at her affinity with the machines. She seemed to know what they were doing just by looking at them. "You can tell by the lights," he suggested.

She shook her head. "Lights tell you only that DANTE's doing a scan, nothing about depth. It's a guess based on elapsed time and number of scans since this morning, and now how fast they repeat."

"They also tell you he's doing a 3-D?"

"Sure. Always the same – scan, scan, scan, pause to change depth, repeat. By the rate I guess 5-millimeter scale. There've been six passes so far, – seven – so the object is not so small." She kept count without looking.

"No wonder Ben likes you," Satchi muttered.

She looked sharp. "He likes me?"

Satchi pretended he hadn't heard. "Something different, looks like 25 centimeters or so across, can't tell how deep."

She showed more of her teeth. "Going to dig it up?" Her bright red hair was escaping from under her cap.

"I doubt it, though as far as we can tell everything above it is midden."

"Then you're going to dig it up," she said firmly.

Satchi grimaced. "Let's wait and see, OK?"

Francy shook her head. "Nope, you're going to bring it up. Bryson Jones is coming back tomorrow. You'd like to have something to show."

"Besides that flint knife Kevin found last week?"

"A fine knife," she agreed. "But not unusual. This sounds unusual."

"And you deduce all this because I'm having Ben make an image?"

"Because I know you, Satchi Bennett. When you make an image it means you think it might be important, and when you think something might be important you can't help yourself, you want to see what it is. And Dr. Jones will want to see it for sure, especially if it's unusual. So what do you think, statue? Figurine? Tool? Time capsule?"

He grinned back at her. "Manifold from a 1992 Ford Taurus."

She snorted. "What if you're wrong? What if it's not important?"

"I'll wait until I see the full image."

While he waited, he watched one of the undergraduate volunteers carefully brush dirt off something. Satchi could see it was a pebble of no particular interest, but he said nothing. Experience was important. The boy looked up at him expectantly and showed the pebble. Satchi nodded and smiled. "Keep going," he said. "This place is full of interesting stuff."

DANTE had fallen silent. "Scan's finished," Francy called.

"OK," Satchi said. "I'll go see what we have."

"You're going to dig," Francy muttered.

Could Be Anything

Ben was leaning back in his chair, hands clasped behind his head. His eyes were closed.

"What is it?" Satchi asked.

"Damned if I know," Ben answered without opening his eyes. "Could be the signature of a football made out of oleomargarine, for all I know."

"Does margarine have a signature?"

"Everything has a signature."

"OK." Satchi leaned toward the slowly rotating object. "Could be a skull."

"Yes," Ben agreed. "I thought of that, but it's a bit too big for human. Animal?"

Satchi manipulated the mouse and turned the image over. "Look at the bottom, the way it seems flat."

"So it's a tchotchke for the mantel." Ben half-opened an eye under a lifted brow.

"Good, except for one thing."

"No fireplace?"

"Mph. What do you think it is?" Satchi asked.

Ben shook his head. "You won't get me that way. Could be anything – bone, clay, stone, shell. I said everything has a signature. I didn't say all signatures are easily distinguishable. It's hard to define even the edges of that thing, the way it smears into the soil around it. Quartz scattering, probably. Here's what I will say: it's a roughly spherical or ovoid object, complex in structure and probably man-made, approximately 1,500 cubic centimeters. It's located 2.06 meters below ground level on an eroded mound; which would probably make second level down out of eight or nine, that is, toward the end of occupation. Best guess at the moment. Carbon dating we'll tell us more, but say 9,000 years old. It's in a household context, so it was put it there deliberately. . . . And before you say anything, there's no sensor evidence of disturbance, so it wasn't planted after the fact. Probably. It was buried when they destroyed the house, and it was a house because 1.5 meters below this object, more or less, is a floor. Probably. So this was a house before it was a garbage dump. Probably. But that thing's in the wrong place, you see, out in the middle of the room, up in the air. It should be at the side, or on the floor. So it's weird."

"Very well, Mr. Veira." Satchi sighed. "I'm glad Özgür isn't here today. He'd have to call Ankara to get permission just for us to make a printout of that thing."

Ben grunted.

"He did get us a permit to use DANTE," Satchi reminded him.

"Yeah, that's true," he grudgingly admitted.

Satchi went back to the dig. Francy smiled sweetly, but Satchi saw her question. "All right," he muttered tersely. "It seems to be an artifact."

4 Then

Boy Going Under

Shelsan swallowed his disgust at the tiny body, at the Sun Demon, at all of Mala's kin who had come to witness the child's death and Shelsan's shame, at all the spirits that maligned him, at Temkash and his failure. Disgust fueled an impotent rage that generated only blinding smoke, like a fire from dung that had not been properly dried.

The body, crooked into its fetal shape, was cooling.

The boy must be warm, Mala told him last night after the feast when everyone had gone. He must be near fire, she said, because he could not go under the earth. He must go to the sky, not just because the Sun Demon had taken him, but because he had not yet become a Person and so could not be placed on the cold-side where he could descend to join the ancestors. For these reasons he must be buried near the hearth. His spirit was too light and would float up, out through the entrance hole and into the empty sky. He would be forever gone.

Where does she learn these things? Shelsan asked himself. Hunters left their dead for the world to reclaim, for the birds and jackals. That was their return. What was all this about going down or going up?

Of course he knew the answers to these questions. He could name every one of Mala's Grands and say where they were buried in which ancestral Egg, back to First Grand. It was his duty as her man to learn these things. But he was a Locust Clan hunter, and her Sorrow Clan ways still seemed strange.

All morning she had been lying with her face to the wall on the sunrise platform. She had pulled her goatskin cloak over her head, so she certainly wasn't looking at the black, stylized carrion-eater wings he had painted on its lower half to remind them of death, and of Water Bird, the first founder.

Shelsan had waited for her to clear the debris from the funeral feast. It was he who had provided the meat, he who had brought Temkash, he who had sired the dead boy at his feet; it was she who cooked the food and cleared the debris and cleaned the hearth.

Now, the morning after, food and fragments of bone were heaped near the oven, along with torn woven mats with bits of pork and flat bread still lying on them. Someone had dropped a skin and now it slumped in a pool of drying lentil stew. The heat had grown intense, as it always did in the warm-time, and the food was beginning to stink.

No matter how long he waited, Mala did not move, and finally he gave up and set to work.

He drove his precious flint mattock into the filthy plaster next to the oven, breaking it apart and digging deeper into the soft soil beneath. Temkash had failed, leaving him with this mess, this angry woman who wouldn't move, and a stiff, bent carcass that only yesterday had been a boy; his boy. The girl didn't count; she had been born dead. Now Shelsan was the last of his line.

There was little place left for a death that had come too soon. There, on the other side of the hearth, he had buried his obsidian, all his precious frozen tears and worn blades. It was there in case of need, and there was often need. Beyond the cache he had buried his infant daughter, born dead this past cold-time, but she had been so much smaller than this one and took little room.

Little Boren watched him work. Little Boren had almost fourteen rounds of the sun and had grown up inquisitive, always asking questions. "Why do you put him here?" he asked now.

Shelsan told him that the boy must rise with the hearth smoke. The house, he said, was an egg; it had held the family since Second Grand had died and since Big Boren's father had rebuilt the house. There were only two ways out of the egg: one was into the sky through the roof entrance. The other was into the ground. That was reserved for the dead who had become people. And now . . .

"Second Grand is underground by the sunset wall, isn't he?" Little Boren mused. "Now Little Brother is by the hearth. Why is the hearth always on the warm-side?"

"Why do you think?"

"Because the hearth is warm, and the sun stays in that part of the sky, especially when it goes far down in the cold-time."

"Very good. Inside is as outside. Down is as up."

"OK. But there must be others under the floor, Babi."

"There are," Shelsan said, pushing aside the mound of dirt and broken plaster. He glanced from the small body to the hole, and then set to work once more. "First Egg itself is old. Some day soon we'll have to build again."

"Do we tear the house down, the way they did to the sunrise-side three roofs?"

"That will be the way, yes." The hole was now large enough for the curled body. Shelsan took strips of leather and angrily tied the legs tightly flexed. He wrapped a strip around the head and bound the child's jaw closed. Then he dropped the body into the hole, covered it with a small woven mat, and stood back. "Mala!" he called.

She stirred at last.

"He's going under. If you want to do something."

She rose unsteadily to her feet, took a step, and cried out.

"What is it?" Shelsan asked, but she sat down on the edge of the sleeping platform and rubbed her foot. "Come on," he said impatiently.

She took something from the floor and made her way to the tiny grave. This was the second of her three children to go under. She smiled wanly when Little Boren took her hand.

A thin blade of sunlight found its way through the entrance flap and set fire to the base of the sunset pillar. Shelsan moved to block the light.

Mala regarded the body, her face twisted with remembered pain. "So small," she mumbled absently, turning in circles as though looking for something. Finally she took a small shell from a niche near the hearth. The shell had been the little one's favorite plaything, at once cup and bed and digging tool. She dropped it on the body.

Shelsan's disgust returned. He rejected this dead one. It was not his boy, this pathetic lump onto which he scraped dirt. Soon there was only a dark oval on the plaster floor to show where it was.

"He's sleeping, but he won't wake up, will he?" Little Boren asked.

"He's gone," Shelsan said shortly. He waved his hand vaguely. "Somewhere else."

"Where?" The boy would not stop asking.

"You're too young. I'll tell you when we go on the Walk," Shelsan replied.

"When will that be?"

"Soon enough! Now stop." He scuffed the dirt with his sandal, pressing it down. "I'll plaster it later," he said. "When we get back."

Stone Mirror

Mala held up a lump of black stone. "What's this? I stepped on it."

"Frozen tears, but not from our cache." Shelsan took it and turned it over. "Look."

She stood beside him. They saw faces side by side, dimly reflected in the smooth black surface, a couple, his wide cheekbones and deep-set eyes, her straight nose and lined cheeks. "Where did it come from?" she asked.

"I don't know." He turned it again and their faces slid away.

He looked around the room at the sleeping platforms, draped in skins and woven mats, at the sunrise and sunset pillars, one decorated with the bull's skull and curving horns. There were crawl holes in the back wall between the platforms, two of them, leading into the storage chambers. One held a three-moon supply of lentils, their staple food; they had an excess of lentils, he thought, but not enough of anything else. The other contained nothing but rat droppings, a pig skull, and some scraps of leather.

Little Boren hopped up and down. "Let me see, let me see."

Shelsan gave it to him and shrugged. "Someone dropped it yesterday," he said, scooping the remaining dirt into a basket.

Mala would not give up. "Who would bring such an evil thing in here? This is cursed. You see? Faces? Ghosts in the stone. Frozen tears, grief. And when? Who has been trying to harm us? Who killed the boy?"

He drew back and rolled his eyes. "There were nearly four hands of people in here yesterday," he said. "Little one was dying, remember? Anyone . . . no, wait. There was a moment when Temkash was in the other world, when he was Bear, and lights flickered in his hand. Did you see?"

"I'm not sure," she admitted, here eyes lowered. "The day, everything that happened . . . I saw blood on the walls."

"I remember," Little Boren announced firmly. "He was crouching near the hearth, and the lights were flashing. He was holding something. Is this it?"

"Yes," Mala said with an effort. "I think it might be."

Shelsan said, "He was bringing in the healing spirits, no? Those were the spirits flying around the room, Water Bird and the others. But he was just tricking us. There were no spirits, just lights." There was something sour in his mouth and he pursed his lips.

"Why are they called frozen tears?" the boy asked.

"Because the stone is like the water that hangs from trees in cold-time, boy." He turned to Mala. "We will go now," he said. "I will take Little Boren and we will go for his Walk of the World. We will come back with Frozen Tears for Temkash." The sour taste in his mouth would not go away.

Mala stared without comprehension. Then, wordlessly, she closed her eyes and groped her way back to bed, lay down once more facing the wall, and covered her head.

After a moment Shelsan picked up the basket of dirt and carried it up the ladder. Little Boren followed.

Pinnak on the Roof

The sky above was wide, a pale lavender, interrupted only by a great orange sun climbing the sunrise sky. In the distance irregular ridges were etched against the empty dome, but there were so many other houses Shelsan and Little Boren could not see bare ground. It was as if the Place went on forever, roof after roof, house after house, egg after egg. Little Boren shrank against a sunward wall as if cold.

Shelsan looked across a plain of rectangles, each at a slightly different level, so the plain lifted and fell as his eyes moved over it. Everywhere ladders connected the roofs, or, if there was a small gap between the houses, plank bridges. From the entrance holes, protected by lean-tos or tents of leather or brush, smoke drew straight vertical lines into the air. Here and there on the roofs people gathered around hearth fires. The roofs were crowded with huts of brush or wattle amid tall heaps of dried dung for fuel, racks for weapons or drying fruit, sheaves of grain for fodder, spaces for weaving or cleaning grain. There was movement and sound – talk, and here and there from the pits formed by houses not squared with each other, the bleating of goats. Crows flew overhead, landing to feed on scraps. It was familiar, the buzz and patter, the endless movement, the work and talk, yet Shelsan's disgust would not leave him.

He walked along the wall-top path to the corner. The neighboring house angled away, leaving a triangular gap between the two buildings.

Pinnak was seated cross-legged against a brush-and-mud fence on his roof, carefully knapping a long obsidian blade. "Sorry about the boy," he said, looking up with a cheerful smile.

Shelsan grunted and dumped the basket of grave spoils into the gap. This man, Pinnak, had eaten their food; he had breathed their air. Now, as usual, he was sitting in the shade of his wattle fence, working a lovely blade of frozen tears. Yet he had never been known to hunt.

"That blade will break first time you use it," Shelsan observed.

Pinnak showed teeth with neither humor nor lightness. He held the blade to the sun and looked along the scalloped edge, a hand's length leaf shape tapering to a fine point. He put it down on a piece of leather draped over his thigh and pressed a bone tip against an edge, flaking off a tiny morsel. He examined it again and grunted in satisfaction. "Don't intend to," he said at last.

"Then why make it?"

"Luck."

He may have been one of the best stone knappers in the Place, or, if not the best, certainly one of the fastest, but he was a fool. Worse, an envious and angry fool.

Shelsan made a sign, asking permission, and Pinnak pretended not to notice, engrossed in his work. Shelsan waited patiently, eyes on the other man's face.

Finally the fat man shifted uneasily. "What is it?"

"We'd like to cross."

"Ah," Pinnak said, waving his hand. "Go ahead." He continued working on his blade, though it was clearly finished.

"Come, Little Boren." Shelsan took a sack of woven grasses, a bow, a bundle of arrows, and his best flint-tipped spear from the rack of hunting gear near the entrance. He had reached a decision. "We're going." He started across Pinnak's roof with long, determined strides.

"But we don't have any food with us," the boy protested, running to catch up. "We don't have anything for travel."

"We'll manage," Shelsan replied shortly, climbing to the next sunrise roof.

"Are we going far, Babi?"

"Yes." Shelsan said, moving faster and faster. "Far."

Walk of the World

Shelsan's anger was a hard ball of poison in his belly; or it was one of the newly dead dragging at his heels, wheedling and complaining.

And so he ran. But the ball stayed hard and knotted, and the dead one followed, its voice sometimes high, sometimes low; man or woman he could not tell. Perhaps it was his son, the boy-child he had just buried.

All he could have said was that his anger pursued him. He didn't try to hide it from Little Boren, and the boy stuck close to him in silence. Shelsan paused briefly by a place called Sand Hook, a ridge in the marsh thick with tamarisk, and looked back. The Place loomed, filling half the horizon with a blank tan wall. He shrugged and led Little Boren toward the warm-side and across a broad plain dotted with low shrubs and broad meadows of soggy ground broken here and there by open sheets of shallow water. In the distance the mountains rose up against the sky. They kept the river with its line of rushes to their right and stayed on the driest ground.

When they next turned back to look, the Place was already a low patch of unnatural color that sprouted a thicket of vertical lines: smoke of countless hearths.

Shelsan took a deep breath. Ahead were weary days of walking, but behind was the din of talk, shouts of rage or complaint, bleating goats, and barking dogs and screaming children. Here the only sounds were the cries of high flyers and thrumming of frogs, occasionally interrupted by a thunderclap of wings when they disturbed a flock on the open water. The birds would clatter into the air in a rush, circle, calling to one another, then slowly settle again, splashing to the surface to float gently amid ripples circling away and falling still. Between times there were endless clouds of insects, and the smells of wild cattle dung and decaying vegetation.

He was angry he had to go to the mountain, angry that he had to pay Temkash, angry that the child had died, angry that Mala had taken it so hard. It seemed the damp and rot and stench also spoke his anger.

But gradually, now that he and the boy were outside, away from the Place, he began to outrun his anger. The ball of poison in his belly came to be an empty hollow after all. He began to relax and slow his pace. Irritating memories – Pinnak with his toy blades and superior smile, the burial, and the failed healing – faded, and the voice of the shambling dead one faded too. Now the sun was almost to its highest point.

He led the way into the trees along the river. "Time to eat," he said, not unkindly, the first words since striding across Pinnak's roof.

"Good," Little Boren answered. "I'm hungry."

"I know."

They worked their way around a hummock of tamarisk and began to gather food along the riverbank. Little Boren pulled up plants to show Shelsan from time to time and ask if they could eat them. Once or twice Shelsan said yes, and soon his sack was full of mallow, mint, and other plants, plus snails and a squirming heap of fat, angry frogs.

Shelsan asked Little Boren to name the ones he knew and taught him the names of the ones he didn't. He described their nature and their qualities, their habits and their homes. "Snails have small spirits," he said. "But they are many, and together they are large. The water could not live without them. Frogs, on the other hand," he added, holding one up in the air, "make much noise, and so call us to them."

Near a place called Bear Kill they stopped to strip the leathery skin off six of the frogs and wrap their rubbery flesh in leaves. Frogs were always better cooked, but the few scraps of wood here were water-soaked. Shelsan told Little Boren when they got to Dak's Cave at the mountains there would be dry wood and he could make fire. Tonight they could cook the rest of the frogs.

Before they ate their noon meal, Shelsan held some of the food on his open palms and said, "May the hunt be good."

The boy answered as he had been taught, "May the hunt be good."

Shelsan raised his hands to the four directions, to the sky, to the earth.

"May the bull come to you," Shelsan said.

"May the bull come," the boy answered.

They ate slowly, smacking their lips and tossing the frog bones behind them into the river, as required by its spirits.

When they had finished and were resting before the next stage of their hike to Dak's Cave, Little Boren pointed. "Babi, why do we call that mountain to the sunset-side Angry Bear?"

"It's always been called Angry Bear."

"But why? I understand why we call the sunrise mountain Water Bird Landing, because we are Her people, but I don't understand Angry Bear."

Shelsan thought this over. "A Grand from First Egg, perhaps, met a bear."

"And the bear was angry," Little Boren concluded, satisfied.

By evening the Place was out of sight in the deep marsh. Even the tall sticks of fire smoke were gone. The sky was an empty mortar turned over their heads. The sun had been the pestle that ground them with its heat. Even the evening wasn't cool, but at last they reached the sharp, white hills and came to a rock shelter where the sand was dry.

"Here is called Dak's Cave," Shelsan said. "Here Third Grand Distaff passed a cold-time. He was a great hunter, Dak, in his time."

He led the boy to the fringe of ragged trees and showed which dry cedar sticks they could bind together with sinew for a hearthboard. He bent a willow stick from the stream bank into a fire bow, looped a stick into the bow cord. They took turns drilling into the hearthboard, and slowly the shreds of cedar gathered, heated, burst into flame. Shelsan spitted the frogs and held them over the fire while the boy ran up and down the sandy spit gathering stones. When he had a double handful of the rare items – all stones in the Place had come from far away, and Dak's Cave was far away – he sat down cross-legged near the fire.

"I smelled the frogs cooking," he said, as if to explain why he had stopped collecting. He began to arrange his treasures on the sand before him.

"Here," Shelsan said, handing him a frog, its flesh charred and crisp.

They ate and threw the bones into the fire, as the fire spirit demanded.

When they had finished the boy started his questions again. "Is the Place the only Nest in the world? The Place is full of people much of the time, but we haven't seen anyone else since we left."

"There are other Places, so it is said, not so far away, a day or two of walking. It is said that one other is larger than the Place, perhaps much larger. We exchange with it some; you know this, Little Boren, you have seen them, they come from the sunrise, cold side. We give them seeds, or we give them meat, sometimes we give them worked stone. And they give us things, too, baked clay statues, arrow shafts. The other place is not a Nest, not an Egg. It is said they are cattle people, from the Great Bull, but I don't know about this. We avoid their place. They do not like strangers there, so I have heard, and so we stay away."

"Are they enemies?"

Shelsan looked at him sharply. "Why do you say that? We have no enemies. They stay in their Place and we stay in ours. The world is large, as you will see. The Place, our Place, is the only Nest, made by Water Bird Mother long ago."

"How long ago?" Questions again.

"Long," Shelsan answered. "I know twenty Grands." The stone chips in front of the boy glittered; he took one in his hand. "You see this?"

"Yes."

"This is frozen tears from the mountain, where we are going."

"Pinnak has a lot of that. So do you. How did it get here?"

Shelsan handed it back to the boy. "Someone brought it. See the edge. It is a tool, no good now, of course, but once . . ."

Little Boren nodded and dropped the chip. "You like it here, don't you, Babi?"

"Here, Little Boren?"

"Away from the Place. You're different here."

"Am I?" Shelsan said thoughtfully; he knew it was true.

Little Boren nodded and changed the subject. "What about the Grands? You said twenty? That's all the hands and feet, fingers and toes! And when Water Bird Mother laid the first Egg, that was a house?"

"You ask too many questions, Little Boren. I will sleep. When I wake I will tell you of these things." Shelsan settled back against the wall of stone and soon was snoring loudly. Little Boren shrugged and watched the stars move up the sky.

First Egg

The next evening Shelsan leaned back against the cliff. The sun, at the horizon, shone into his dark face, tinting it orange. "It was the beginning," he began, settling into the story. "It was the beginning, and Water Bird was happy in her nest. This happiness went on forever, which is the time that was before, when there was neither day nor night. She raised her young, and they flew off, and again she raised them. She lived beside the people, beside the hunters. She gave herself, and always she was there. That is why we thank her still.

"But I will tell you why we thank her now, why we say she built the Nest. It is because one day the Giant People came. They drove her from her nest, the nest she had used since the Beginning, forever ago.

"She rose into the air with a great cry, but when she spiraled down and tried to settle, her Nest was gone, and in its place were fields of wheat, and sheep and goats. Her nest was gone, so she wandered then, she wandered far and wide, flying, looking for a new place to build her Nest. She flew warm-side and cold-side, but always toward sunset, because behind her the giant People had taken everything. Wherever she goes in this time she finds desert and waste; the world has turned hot. The few small places where she sees abundance, there are others who drove her away again.

"And so it goes for many seasons, and she grows weary, her wings are tired, they are heavy, and she thinks, 'I will find no place for a Nest,' and she despairs. Her wings move slowly, and she too moves slowly. Soon she will be unable to fly and will fall to the earth and die."

"She will?" Little Boren demanded.

"Hush," Shelsan answered. "You ask too many questions. Of course she didn't, because finally she found a place of abundance, where there are no giant People, and so she circles around, and builds a Nest, and she lays the First Egg."

Little Boren fed small sticks to the fire. "Then what happens, Babi?"

Shelsan's voice changed tone, grew rhythmic and strange. "After a time and a time, a space of land rose, and grew dry, and a space of dry earth appeared among the plants and the water.

"This is a place of abundance, and there are no giant People. This is a good place, and so Water Bird circles around, and builds the Nest, and she lays the First Egg; she comes down and puts the First Egg, which is First House, in the center of the water plain, the Nest in the center, surrounded by mountains, and Water Bird guards the Egg. The Egg is First House. First Grand Father, First Grand Mother, they are inside the Egg, are curled inside the Egg, they are waiting inside."

He fell silent, and Little Boren had to ask him to continue, because he knew the next part was important.

"Outside the Nest there is wind, there is rain, there is snow, and the floods come again. Water rises up around the Nest. There are great sounds, terrible sounds, for the Great Bull is running across the sky, and then there are the cries of Water Bird, who fears to lose her Egg. First Grands, too, are afraid, from the roaring, the howling, the cries. Their flesh shrivels and their bones rattle, and they shake with fear, and words stop in their throats; they cling to each other. And so they lie with one another.

"But the First Grands, waiting inside the house that is the Egg put down by the Water Bird, dream of what is outside the Egg.

"Heat comes, and the water falls back, and the Egg begins to crack, to open, to crack open, and there is the sky, out there, above. First Grands, Father and Mother, climb up and look out, and see the land is full of food, of lentils and wheat, of animals. They go out on the top of the Egg, they look this way, they look that way. They see the plants everywhere, they see the water winding among the trees, they see the animals in the open spaces. Above is the sky, and across the sky the boats of the sky, so they climb down outside the house and go walking, First Grand Mother and First Grand Father. They are young and don't know about the earth, having seen only the inside of the Egg. At night they come back to the Egg, but each day they go farther. They see the animals everywhere, the sheep, the goats, the pigs. Water Bird Mother provides. The food is all around them, and all around the seasons, too.

"Then First Grand Mother's belly began to swell . . ."

Shelsan paused and waited, but there was no voice out of the dark. He touched the boy, saw he was asleep, and he too lay down. He awoke once and wondered what had awakened him this time. He listened, but there were no sounds but the ones that belonged here in the wild, and he dropped back into sleep.

Empty Place

The next day they set off along the foothills toward the sunrise, then toward the cold-side. They walked for fourteen days, following water so they could drink, and sometimes Shelsan killed a bird, and sometimes they ate leaves, nuts, fruits, or tubers from the ground. The sun circled through the warm-side place, and the moon too. Now it was almost gone, the Wasting complete, and they had not seen another human being, another child of the Water Bird, only the animals, the deer, the pig, the wolf, the sheep. One time only they saw a Bull standing with his cows and calves, but they were far away, and Shelsan said it was best to leave them alone. The Bull was a danger, even this far; it wouldn't do to anger it without reason.

There was a mountain to their right, toward the sunrise, and marsh-land to the left. They made their way over rough country, and passed the mountain called Water Bird Landing, which they could see from the Place. They came to a cliff and continued along it until a river came through, and they turned toward the sunrise-side again, up the river. Shelsan paused once and sniffed the air.

"Do you smell salt?" he asked the boy.

Little Boren sniffed the air as well, and said no.

Shelsan grunted and led the way along the river's edge. The water ran fast, and then it slowed and the land was flat. Low trees and shrubs lined the river and made a thick green wall to either side.

"Babi?" Little Boren asked later, when the hills were closer and the land had grown dry.

"What is it?"

"Is something following us?"

Shelsan froze. "Why do you ask that?"

"You're quiet, like you're always listening."

"I am always listening, little one. You, too, should be listening. We are far from the Nest." He reassured the boy, but remained uneasy and listened harder.

It grew cool and clear. The heat lifted, taking the worst of the insects. They moved through spaces between hills, and the river ran faster. There were more trees. Ahead they could see new mountains growing larger, outlined against the pale sunrise-side sky. "The Mountain of Frozen Tears," he said, and added under his breath, "I hope."

And of course Little Boren asked, "Why did you say salt?"

"It is said that near the mountain there is a big water and that it is full of salt."

"Why?"

But Shelsan said he didn't know, that he had never seen it. "It is said our salt comes from there. I thought I smelled it, back there at the cliff, but perhaps I was mistaken."

On the fourteenth day they passed among hills and in a valley beyond they came upon something strange.

As long as he had lived, Shelsan had felt the circles of time, the days and nights, the seasons of growth and harvest, the births and deaths in the Place. People said it was always like this and always would be. Water Bird had formed the Nest, the Place, and then the world had always been the same.

Yet he wondered sometimes. The Place had changed. The stories said there had been one Egg, and then there were others alongside, and more, until now the Place was many tens of roofs across. He could stand up there and the land was below; from his roof he couldn't even see it, only the distant mountains, the ones they had left behind many days ago.

The People had been building houses on houses through many Grands. Could that also be a circle? Would the Place begin to shrink and finally disappear, and another Place begin; another Nest, another Egg?

Shelsan knew of only one other place. Some of the People had been there and come back to describe it. It was larger than the Place, they said, but much the same. Roofs across, like the Place. But, as he had told Little Boren, it was not sacred to Water Bird, that other Place. The people there were not People, not children of Water Bird either. They had their own spirits, their own Powers, their own Grands. All other people wandered like Water Bird before she made the Nest, and the giant People were long gone or far away, they were not in time, they were stories.

So what lay before them, what they looked at in astonishment, was so unexpected, so strange yet familiar, that Shelsan could not speak, and for once even Little Boren was without questions.

It was like the Place, but empty. Slowly Shelsan understood that what he saw were houses, like the Place. They were strange, though; empty and desolate and roofless, their living spaces to the sky, cold-time, warm-time, rain, and snow.

And most astonishing of all there were two nests, divided by a straight, empty space! He and Little Boren could see trees ahead of them, their branches tossing in the breeze.

Where were the people? Air whispered through the tall dried grass, some still heavy with clusters of seeds. Crows called out as they flapped from one ruined wall to another, or into the trees up the slope of the mountain toward the warm-side.

Where were the talking, shouts, children? Where were the bleating sheep, the goats, and barking dogs? This cool, well-watered valley was deserted.

Old Kark, six roofs warm-side, had told Shelsan once of going to Mountain of Frozen Tears. He had brought back a tear almost too large for one man. It had made him greatly respected for the rest of his days. But he never spoke of a place like this.

Shelsan stirred himself and started forward.

"Wait!" Little Boren cried. "Where are you going?"

"To see," Shelsan said, looking straight ahead.

"No," Little Boren said. "It's full of . . . ." But he couldn't say what it was full of. No one. Nothing. Spirits.

Shelsan stepped forward and slowly walked between the two lines of buildings. Through strange openings in the walls he could see scattered roof timbers.

A chorus of cicadas suddenly began a loud, continuous shrilling, fell silent, and started up again.

He leaned into one of the buildings. The boy had caught up with him and stayed close, his eyes wide. They could see sleeping plat-forms, as in the Place, and a hearth against the warm-side wall.

But the walls had openings in them, and were strangely empty. He could see no cattle skulls, paintings, or moldings of the bear ancestor, as in Temkash's house. Did they not honor the spirits? Did they not summon them into the Egg, as at the Place? It was unsettling. And dirt had piled up, in places all the way to the strange openings. No Person would allow dirt to accumulate like that. It was against the Powers, disrespectful of the ancestors.

Shelsan sniffed. The air was strange, too; without animal smells, the ripe odor of middens and latrines, the familiar sour smells of life, as in the True Nest, the Place.

What had happened? Where were the brick makers? It was the season; they should already be at the water, shaping and singing. The first bricks at the Place would already be drying in the sun. These houses were made the same way, but beginning to fail. How many seasons had passed without people?

They soon came to the edge. This was a small settlement, much smaller than the Place.

Perhaps the Sun Demon had taken everyone as it had taken the child.

There was a shout. They turned, and something was walking toward them, holding a spear lightly, as though hunting. When he shouted again, it was nonsense, as a newborn might babble.

The man, if it was a man, was half-dressed in outlandish draperies, with a wolf skin looped around his loins. He glared at them out of a beardless face under a mound of dark hair twisted around his skull. He took three or four more steps toward them, stopped, lifted a spear and stood as if to throw.

Shelsan balanced his own spear over his shoulder.

The two men faced each other, each waiting for the other to make the first move.

5 Now

Speculation

Francy was smiling so sweetly that Satchi could think of nothing to say, so he shrugged and walked away.

"You're going to dig it up," she called after him.

He turned. "You're just trying to get my goat, but it won't work; I don't have a goat." He made a broad gesture, taking in the mound. "These people had goats. And we're *not* going to dig it up, we're going to excavate. There's a difference."

He prided himself on doing the least amount of damage – after all, archaeological sites this age were a nonrenewable resource, and archaeology a destructive science.

"Call it what you want, you're going to dig it up," she sang. "You know you are. I know you are. Everybody knows!"

He walked along the trench toward the looters' hole, deep in thought. Over the past weeks they had excavated a small but informative sample and had used DANTE over much of the site. As expected, Aynalı was a densely built, three-dimensional jigsaw of house floors and roof debris, middens, and storage bins. The excavation so far had turned up obsidian, baked clay figurines, a few imported flint tools, decorative beads and shell, animal bones, plant debris, fragments of white and red plaster, and nine burials, four of them flagged for future excavation. They had found no sign of streets or public spaces. The material culture of Aylanı was similar to Çatal. At its most densely populated there were upward of 500 houses.

There could be surprises, perhaps wall paintings, moldings, sculptures. So far, though, they had found nothing to attract *Archaeology NowOnline* or *National Geographic*. But what was important was the dirt, always the dirt.

With a fatalistic shrug he went to supervise placement of the excavation. Soon enough the string outline was in place, and he called lunch.

The staff speculated about the mysterious artifact over eggplant and tomatoes. "Bet it's a bull cranium," Francy suggested. "About the right size. For a little bull, anyway."

"No horns," Ben said. "And it's too small, even for a little bull. Really, Francy!"

"A goddess figurine, then. The goddess worshipers will love that."

"It'd be bigger than any so far, assuming they're not just fat ladies suffering from arsenic poisoning."

"Why arsenic?" Francy asked.

"Increases appetite after a bout of malaria. Apparently it works way too well – the people at Çatal were obese."

"I bet it's a goddess," Francy repeated with a toss of her head.

"Look," Ben said. "The so-called goddess figurines are just fat ladies, probably heads of household. Mrs. Smith of the Leopard Clan."

"Come on, Ben, everyone knows they're goddesses, seated on thrones, with leopards sometimes. Ever since Marija Gimbutas analyzed the European Neolithic figurines back in the seventies everyone agrees they're religious. Even Mellaart said so."

Ben glowered at her. "Gimbutas," he said slowly, "was a great archaeologist. After all, she was at Harvard and UCLA."

"Are you being ironic?" Francy demanded.

He ignored the question. "Everyone agreed she knew an enormous amount about Bronze Age Europe and Lithuanian folk art. And everyone agrees her so-called Kurgan hypothesis, her idea that warrior horsemen from the Pontic steppes spread in successive waves of invasion into Europe and conquered the peaceful indigenous Neolithic goddess worshipers, was an interesting idea."

"Yes, but she never said there was one Mother Goddess, she spoke about various goddesses . . ."

"Yes, yes," he said impatiently. "But she still thought they were matriarchal, and they were probably no more matriarchal than anyone else. Besides, most of the figurines she claimed were goddesses were probably just toys, or women fulfilling normal gender roles for the time. And Colin Renfrew thinks the Indo-European homeland was right here in Anatolia and that it spread into Europe slowly along with agriculture. And linguistic evidence suggests that Indo-European might be a whole lot older, so despite all the support she got from Joseph Campbell and her devoted following of ecofeminists and Mother Goddess worshipers she was constantly leaping to conclusions the data does not warrant. And then there's conflicting DNA evidence . . ."

"What makes you such an expert?" she demanded.

"I'm a nerd and I read a lot," he said smugly.

It drove her crazy when he did that. "Well," she huffed, "if it is a goddess, the goddess people will sure pay attention."

A Hunch

Days passed and the team settled into a routine. After three weeks they had removed an enormous amount of midden material, leaving a pit 10 meters on a side. House walls were exposed on all four sides, though they were plain and unadorned with exciting art. All work now focused on the central house, which had been purposely destroyed and never rebuilt, though the houses on all four sides had been rebuilt before the community itself ceased to exist.

Jones arrived. "Well, well," he beamed. "I hear we have something."

"A potential something," Satchi agreed.

The mound was busy. Wheelbarrows went in a continuous stream to the sifting grates where a crew carefully logged, sifted, and sorted the soil before sending it on to the flotation tank at the foot of the mound to the east, where charcoal and plant remains would accumulate at the surface and could be siphoned off. A team was busy measuring and recording fragments of bone, dung, fragments of plaster, charcoal, and fired clay from the midden material.

The trench from the west side was advancing slowly toward the looters' hole. Lodewyk Barhydt, the Dutch human remains specialist, squatted beside a burial, sketching the bones. "Infant," he told Francy, waving his pencil. "Postoccupation. Probably a local farmer." He glanced up from time to time as if trying to track the progress toward the artifact, though it was well outside his specialty. He was not immune to the general heightened awareness of the potential new find.

Jones bent over the DANTE printout. "Mm, mm," he murmured. He straightened. "Yes, it does look interesting."

"And big," Satchi said. "Roughly 25 centimeters."

"Too big for a skull," Jones murmured. "Think it's made of plaster?"

"According to DANTE," Satchi said, "it's not homogeneous – there are different materials, a couple of dense places – the data's ambiguous. I'm sure the next-generation remote sensing instruments will do far more, but this is what we have so far."

"Context?" Jones asked.

"Midden. Below, clean dirt. There's a floor below, so the house was deliberately terminated. The really strange thing is its location." He tapped the printout. "It's nearly 150 centimeters above the floor level, away from the walls. It wasn't left in a niche or buried in a posthole."

"Very strange," Jones agreed. "How long before we can bring it up?"

"A week."

Jones took Satchi aside. "This place is special; I've got a feeling about it. The placement, the size, the elaborate decoration, they all mean something." He looked around at the students and specialists bent over their work. "I don't think we have a week. Özgür will be back on Saturday, and I'm not sure he'll be pleased. If we wait until he's back, he could stop the dig while he asks his superiors what to do or tells us we need some new kind of permit. Best we have this object in the Finds Room before he gets back, so full speed ahead. Friday's the day off, so you have until eight Friday morning. That's five days. Work all night, blow the budget; I'll get more money. I want the best man to bring it up. That's you." He rubbed a finger along his hairline. "I just have a hunch."

Home Plate Don't Move

Satchi said, "Deliberate haste."

"What does that mean?" Francy asked.

"It means we work as fast as we can, but deliberately. 'Just take the ball and throw it where you want to. Throw strikes. Home plate don't move.'"

"Don't tell me. Satchel Paige? What the hell is he talking about."

"He always gave good advice. It just means do your best, deal with whatever you can actually do something about, leave the rest alone. The artifact isn't going away, it'll still be there Friday morning."

The days and nights passed.

Wednesday evening, just before eight, when the western sky was still pale with the remains of the departed sun, they had to stop. One of the diggers had found the tip of a bone. After a conference around the table they sent for Jones.

"What is it?" he snapped, still out of breath from his run up the mound.

"Burial. I'm putting Lodewyk on it."

"But we can keep going? We'll get the object?"

Satchi shrugged. "Sure. I just don't like this rushing. But, sure."

They worked under lights until ten. The awning overhead hid the stars. "It looks like one of those nighttime traffic accidents," Francy said.

"Be quiet," Ben cautioned her. "This is science."

Satchi at Night

He punched the pillow and turned over. A few moments later he turned the other way. Finally he sat up and examined his watch. He could make out from the faint glow that it was 2:43. He lay back with a sigh.

The darkness overhead, which he knew was the bottom of the upper bunk, was nearly absolute. No lights leaked through the thin curtains.

Had something disturbed him? No, he'd been awake for some time. Bits of the dream came back. He had been talking to Susan. Or, rather, she had been talking to him. Her words weren't clear, but he knew she thought he was incapable of relating to people.

How had they met? He couldn't remember. Someone must have introduced them. His father, the fanatical baseball nutcase, had been bugging him to settle down. He had a business, his father had, making industrial solvents. "You can clean up in this business, Satchell," his father would say. It was his endlessly repeated, and increasingly feeble, joke. Industrial solvents were used for really tough cleaning jobs: grease, tar, nuclear waste.

Satchi gave serious consideration to industrial solvents. They could, he thought, be useful when it came to dirt, a way of separating things, making fine distinctions.

Finally he had proposed to Susan. He must have, because they were married. And then he'd gone to graduate school, where he remained blissfully unaware of her constant outward drift.

"Did you hear it?"

It was Lodewyk from the bed opposite.

"Hear what?" Satchi asked.

"I don't know. Some kind of sound woke me up."

"What kind of sound?"

"A scream? Oh, never mind. I was probably dreaming." The Dutchman soon drifted off to sleep, evidenced by a series of even, gentle snores.

Satchi stared into the darkness. Had he heard a scream?

It was probably just Susan telling him he always had his head buried in the dirt, and soon enough the rest of him would follow, permanently.

Bringing It Up

By ten p.m. Thursday they had reached a small, multicolored patch. According to DANTE there were floors at level one on all sides, but this house definitely belonged to level two.

The workmen climbed out to make room for Satchi. A domed surface protruded from the floor.

He used the tip of his trowel to delicately pry up a patch of soil. From time to time he dislodged a small stone or other debris, tugging it carefully from the matrix and putting it in a bucket with the dirt. When the bucket was full one of the students hauled it away.

Ben had set up a video camera pointed at the object for those who couldn't get close enough to see. Deep black shadows leaped drunkenly as Satchi moved around. As he worked, more and more of the object emerged from the dirt, revealing increasingly strange designs: horizontal chevrons, nested circles, zigzags. Satchi looked at it with enormous satisfaction. It was almost spiritual, this uncovering. Ben shot gigabytes of photographs from every possible angle.

"What is it?" Francy wondered, for the hundredth time.

"Ritual cult object," Ben suggested between shots. It was the archaeologist's perennial response. They had front-row positions. Almost everyone else from the crew was standing silently in a semicircle, watching. "A ball for some kind of weird sport. Want some beef jerky?" A supply of snack foods had been going around the group all night. They stood in a small island of brilliance in the midst of a desert of dark. No other lights were visible. This late even the Dig House was dark.

"No, thanks, I had some." She rubbed her stomach as if it hurt.

Satchi ordered more lights. They drove away the shadows but created hot spots in the computer images.

Hours passed and nothing much seemed to happen. The artifact (and everyone now tacitly agreed it was "the artifact" and not just an object) appeared so slowly that some people wandered away to talk, smoke, or nap. Midnight passed. A couple of journalists were on hand filming as well.

When he had exposed 7 or 8 centimeters Satchi said softly, "What might these be?"

Two small half-moons appeared at the soil line. He dug carefully for another hour until he had exposed two circles around 5 centimeters in diameter in one side of the artifact. He scraped some of the dirt away, and the circles became depressions. He stopped. "It can't do this here. It has to go to the lab."

"Well, Ben, it isn't a ball," Francy said. "It's beginning to look like a . . . a Halloween pumpkin?"

"I heard that," Satchi muttered. "Can't be. First, it's hard. And they didn't have pumpkins." He added thoughtfully, "On the other hand, they probably did have some version of Halloween. And it does look scary."

People began reappearing, and the buzz of conversation grew louder. Word spread, and by two thirty in the morning Jones himself had reappeared, followed by a retinue of journalists, who had been gathering all day.

The night had grown cool, but near the lights it was warm enough. Ben chewed his jerky from time to time. Francy paced nervously, her hands clasped behind her back.

By three thirty Satchi had uncovered it all, and even Ben had to admit that it did look like a bulging carved head, with shallow eyeholes leaking painted red tears and a fan of multicolored rays. Underneath a triangular plaster nose were two rows of what could only be painted teeth.

Saturday Morning

"Not acceptable!" Özgür shouted into Satchi's face, his nose almost touching the younger man's. Despite the relentless spray of spit, Satchi gazed mildly back into the representative's eyes. "This . . . is . . . not . . . acceptable! Do you hear?"

Mid-morning sunlight poured in through the back windows of the Finds Room onto a group of students leaning against the far wall, eyes wide. Francy and Ben, near the window, exchanged looks and rolled their eyes.

Satchi nodded gravely. Of course he could hear. Özgür had been ranting for nearly ten minutes, and no one else had spoken. He, Özgür, state representative, was going to shut down the dig. He was going to bring in the police. He would forbid publication. He was going to make sure none of them would ever work again.

The storm, though anticipated, had been startling in its ferocity.

The room collapsed into silence. Özgür glowered at Satchi before turning to Bryson Jones, leaning comfortably against the floor-to-ceiling shelving, apparently at ease. On a shelf beside him the source of the representative's wrath stared vacantly. It could have been the archaeologist's second head, though the eyeholes, still filled with dirt, gave the impression of blindness.

Lodewyk hovered near the door. Behind him, on the other side of the courtyard, a knot of journalists, including the crew from *ArchaeologyNowOnline,* chatted among themselves. Satchi hoped they couldn't hear the representative, though it was unlikely. He had a loud voice.

Jones's posture seemed to goad Özgür to greater fury; he began to sputter. Finally he pursed his lips and strode past the line of terrified volunteers without a glance in their direction. He made his way around several open boxes containing fragments of cooked clay, soil samples, burned animal bone, and a human forearm from the trench. At the window he glared into the sunlight for a few minutes, his hands clasped behind his back. He rocked forward, almost touching the glass with his forehead. Finally he turned around. "Look, Jones." He dropped all pretense at good manners. His voice was quieter but trembled with suppressed rage. "You were to dig up nothing without I was being there. Nothing! Not this, is for sure!" He pointed at the strange head. "I should have been there before you were bringing it up. Before. I am the representative." His voice started to go up again.

"Certainly, Özgür," Jones said soothingly. "Perhaps we should have waited, but you must understand this is a very important find. Once we had discovered it we had an obligation to rescue it."

Özgür stepped back. "Rescue? From what? What is the meaning, rescue?"

"Ah, well, you see," Jones spread his hands. "Since you left . . ." He put a slight emphasis on *left* that implied the representative had somehow been derelict. "People have been coming round. Strangers, too. We've been . . . concerned."

Özgür frowned, looking down at the open boxes. "People?" he said slowly, his voice now dangerously quiet. "What people?"

"People, yes." Jones moved away from the shelf. "For instance, only yesterday there was a delegation from town. I couldn't follow all they were saying, but I'm pretty sure they were unhappy we didn't hire more of them. One suggested he should be the guard and not Mehmet, who isn't originally from the village, though his wife is. Another was quite angry and went on for quite a long time, I must say, complaining we had hired so many of the women to work in the kitchens. I had the feeling he thought the women were getting too much power, or too much money. You see, it's delicate, and you weren't here to help us negotiate with them. None of us speaks Turkish well enough. We count on you, Özgür."

"It is not important, people from the village," Özgür said after a moment's thought. "You have taken up that thing, it is property of the Turkish government. I am the representative. I found Aynalı Tepe. I should have been here for something so important."

"Of course you should have been here, Özgür, no question about that. But this . . . head is of great scientific value, and we were concerned for its safety. I take full responsibility. It was important to get it off the mound and into the Finds Room. Mehmet's a good guard, but he can't stay awake all night. If someone wanted to go up there with a shovel and take it, it wouldn't have been difficult. I can't keep guards up there watching it twenty-four/seven. Too many people know about it. Really, I was saving it for you, Özgür. I thought you'd want to see it before the reporters, before the rest of the world."

When the representative caught his breath he asked, "What is it?" His voice was considerably quieter.

Jones arched his eyebrows. "Well, although, we can tentatively date it to 8,900 years ago, to be confirmed, of course by radiocarbon dating of the underlying wood residue, and although we know it's made of decorated and painted plaster, there are many things we still don't understand. We don't know what it is, for example. It's not just plaster. There are things, so far unknown, inside it. And we have to ask ourselves the meaning of the designs. We can state they are very unusual. It does resemble roughly contemporary plastered and painted skulls from Çatal or Jericho, though it's larger and much more elaborate, with that strange nose. Other examples were painted red or black, and the eyes were set with shell or bitumen, and they were often modeled to look more lifelike. So perhaps they were meant to bring the dead closer to the living, to remind them of the dead person, or even to be something like a living presence. Or they could be involved in ancestor cults. We just don't know. Similar skulls have been found in Syria and Jordan." Jones spread his hands. "There seems to be a widespread cultural phenomenon here."

While he spoke Özgür started playing nervously with his pack of cigarettes. He slid one out, put it in his mouth, and looked around. He took it out of his mouth and put it back in the box, and put the box back in his shirt pocket. "Dr. Jones. I'm disappointed. This was not our agreement. I am representative here and that thing, as all other things of archaeological significance found here, is my responsibility." But he had lost his momentum and his voice was calm.

"Absolutely, Özgür," Jones said smoothly, moving to the desk near the door. "You are one hundred percent right, and that is precisely why we haven't cleaned it yet – we were waiting for you."

Satchi was impressed by the audacity of this modest distortion of the truth. In fact there hadn't been time to do anything but get it down to the Finds Room before the rep arrived.

Jones tapped a key on the computer. He gestured at the screen just coming to life. "We're taking very good care of it, Özgür; you needn't worry. It'll be safe here; this room, as you know, is always locked unless the lab director is present."

"It should go in the Secure Room," the representative said, recovering some of his authority.

"It would really be better here, where the specialists can examine it."

"The Secure Room," Özgür insisted. "Only I have the key. It will be much safer there."

"All right," Jones conceded, and Satchi could tell this was what he intended all along. "We can move it there to work on it, no problem." Jones tapped the monitor screen and told the Finds Room director to log it out to the Secure Room.

Özgür glanced at the picture of the artifact. "All right," he said. "But don't let this happen again, Jones *efendim*. Something this valuable is property of Turkish government and must be protected. As you said . . ."

He was fiddling nervously with his cigarettes again. Finally he put one in his mouth. "Now, if you will excuse me." He pushed his way past Ludowyk and out into the courtyard.

From where he was standing, Satchi could see how eagerly he brought his lighter up, as if something else was bothering him.

Preliminaries

After Özgür was gone, Satchi asked, "What people?"

Jones looked elaborately innocent. "Pardon?"

"What people. You blew him off with that nonsense about men from the village."

"But they did come here yesterday, men from the village. They did want jobs. And some of them were quite unhappy that their wives are earning more than they are."

"Yes, but that's not what you were talking about."

"Well, Mehmet mentioned there were a couple of other men hanging around." For once Jones shifted uncomfortably. "He thought they were journalists, but they didn't come in. Mehmet said they walked around the perimeter and went away."

"This worries you," Satchi said.

"We'll discuss it later," Jones said, adding. "Come on in, Lodewyk."

The Dutch specialist bobbed his head and entered. He lifted his glasses to the top of his head and leaned close to the head. "Very interesting," he muttered. "Is there a cranium inside?"

Satchi shrugged. "It seems the head was probably set on a post."

"A post?"

"Yes," Jones said. "It was mounted on a post and then buried in situ when the house was terminated. Normally they would have taken everything down and filled the lower walls with clean dirt. But this was left standing. There must be an explanation."

"You found wood?" Lodewyk repeated.

Satchi grinned. "We'll have to wait for the archaeobotanist to be certain, but it looks like it was set on an oak pillar. Kind of like a Neolithic floor lamp. Right, Francy?"

Francy gave a little wave. "I said you'd dig it up."

Lodewyk returned to the artifact. "Looks like a woman, wouldn't you say? Something about the curve of the cheek?"

"A woman?" Satchi shook his head. "I don't know, Lodewyk. It looks more like a bird monster, something to scare the children."

Jones, however, was rubbing his hands together. "No, no, no. It could be a Mother Goddess."

Satchi gaped. "A Mother Goddess? Come on, it's a plaster head with a pointy nose and painted teeth. How could it be a mother goddess?"

"Well," Jones shrugged. "Think about it: a sculpted plaster woman's head placed in the center of a building, facing south toward the hearth. Perhaps this building was a shrine, not a house at all. Mellaart thought there were shrines at Çatal. Call this a cult building devoted to goddess worship. I remember there was a small silver statue of a bull at Ashkelon they called a 'Golden Calf.' Generated lots of publicity."

Satchi interrupted. "At Çatal the houses had bull crania and moldings shaped like figures he thought were women giving birth. Lots of elaborate decoration."

"Yes," Jones smiled. "That's my point. We don't know yet about the walls or the floor. We're going to excavate this house completely. But consider. This could be the first real cult building found in this area."

"OK, we'll find out when we dig," Satchi said. "If it was domestic, we'll know. But all the shrines at Çatal were really houses; people lived in them."

"I know," Jones laughed. "Don't worry, I won't say anything specific. If people want to believe it's the Mother Goddess, well, there are many points of view. The more attention Aylanı Tepe gets, the easier it will be to keep our funding angel interested." He gave a little wave and went out to talk to the flock of journalists who had been gathering in the courtyard.

The Word

Ludowyk was absorbed with the goddess, so Satchi loitered in the doorway to watch Jones hold court. Özgür waited at his side, puffing smoke. While he wasn't exactly shoving to get there, it was clear he wanted to be in front of the camera.

After a few moments Jones called out for anyone interested to assemble at the truck. They had set up a video monitor in the back. When a satisfactory group had gathered around, Jones nodded, and the cameraman started the tape.

The floodlit area was surrounded by darkness. Then the cameraman started to take a series of dramatically lit close-ups of the head, with its blind eyes and tortured face, before Satchi lifted it in the slanting dawn light.

Later, in front of the shelves in the Finds Room, Jones described for the cameras the excitement of uncovering this mysterious object, larger and more impressive than anything found so far. He tripped off one or two first impressions, casually slipping in a reference to the Mother Goddess.

Özgür had wandered away and was speaking on his cell phone, waving his cigarette around. His loud, rapid Turkish began to interfere with Jones's soft-spoken description of the artifact, and Satchi went out to ask him if he could move away from the door, but when the rep saw him, he moved away.

Later, when the journalists had left and a semblance of calm settled on the dig, Satchi told Jones that he thought Özgür was hiding something. "It was strange, Bryson, but when I went out he stopped talking."

"I suppose that's normal. Probably telling people about the find. Be good for the project."

"I'm sure you're right," Satchi said. He was watching the reporters across the courtyard talking excitedly on their phones.

Word was getting out.

6 Then

The Stranger

Shelsan, spear balanced over his shoulder, could hear wind sighing through the pine boughs behind him. He could hear small animals scurry through the tumbled walls of the deserted houses. A hawk cried overhead. Behind him Little Boren breathed quickly but made no other sound.

The stranger had not moved.

The sky was pale but the mountain beyond the hillsides was a dark and suddenly threatening presence. The Powers were like that sometimes – not quite there, but felt. The woods, which had been warm and protective before, now teemed with unknown, unknowable things: darkness, rough trunks, hidden depths, leaves that thrashed restlessly back and forth but never in all that motion revealed what was behind them. Shelsan knew they were the spirits of the departed people who had once lived here.

He lifted lightly on the balls of his feet and inhaled, drawing into himself the scents of pine, his own sweat, burnt stone, dust, and the ancient odors of houses long abandoned. He released the breath slowly.

The other man's eyes glittered, the only motion. His oddly feminine face might have been carved of wood.

"He's a hunter," Shelsan murmured.

The boy, just behind him and to one side, grunted.

"See how he stands?" Shelsan continued calmly. "He's ready for a bull to charge; that's the way to stand, one foot a little forward. Watch him. The bull could go left, or he could go right. So the hunter waits. Only at the last moment does he move. His eyes are soft. He does not stare, Little Boren. Remember that. He does not fix his eyes on the bull, not on the eyes of the bull, not on the sharp horn, nor the wide nostril that smokes like a house entry in cold-time. When the bull charges, the hunter won't know which way the horns will twist, to the right, to the left. When you hunt the bull, and one day soon you will, you wait, like this man, this man who is dressed like a woman."

"Will you charge him?" Little Boren asked. "Will you throw your spear?"

Shelsan almost turned in surprise. "Why would I do that?"

"He threatens, doesn't he? He holds his spear as if he will throw. Wouldn't it be better to attack first?"

"Why would it be better? I don't know him. And I too hold my spear as if I will throw. He has done nothing."

"But he might," Little Boren insisted. "He might do something."

"And he might not," Shelsan said reasonably. "Might is never good enough. Be ready. If he throws his spear, you must feel which way he aims. Know that and you know which way the spear will fly. You must not be there when it arrives. It's easy as long as you don't stare."

"I'm not staring."

Shelsan could hear the resentment. "Good," he answered shortly.

They stood a while longer without moving, and then the stranger made a complicated motion with his head and let the butt of his spear drop to the ground.

Shelsan responded with the same movement.

The stranger spoke again.

"I don't understand," Shelsan called. "Where are you from?"

The other tilted his head as if listening to something far away. Then he broke into a smile. "Yes, then," he said in something that sounded like the speech of the People. "You . . ." He jabbed toward them with his free hand, fingers extended, palm down. "From Khrm?" He was hard to understand. The words were strangely formed, with odd gutturals that sounded as if he were clearing his throat.

"I don't know . . . Khrm." Shelsan did his best to imitate the sound.

"You speak like," the man insisted. "I am Basatzaun." There was a catch in his throat just before the end.

"Shelsan. Not from Khrm. From the Place. And you?"

"And you?" Basatzaun repeated, frowning. "Um, and you." He tipped the point of his spear toward the sunrise-side without lifting it from the ground. "I from," he said, adding an unfamiliar word.

"Far?" The stranger had wild effeminate hair twisted around the back of his head, and his face was painted with red and black streaks much the way Mala painted hers for the Water Bird Festival in the wet-time. The patterns weren't exactly the same, but certainly it gave the impression this was a woman.

"Far, yes," Basatzaun said, holding up his free hand, fingers splayed.

"A hand of days!" Shelsan said. He gestured Little Boren forward. "That is far, though not as far as Little Boren and I have come. And you speak the language of traders."

"Traders, yes. Days, no." Basatzaun bobbed his head. "I come more far. Moons."

"We look for Mountain of Frozen Tears," Shelsan said slowly, wondering if such a thing could be possible, for a man to walk a hand of moons just to find frozen tears, if that was why he was here. Surely there were places closer to his home.

The other pushed his lower lip out and squinted at the sky. "Not know . . . frozen tares." He jutted his hip to one side as though taking the first step of the egret dance reenacting Water Bird Father's courtship.

Shelsan touched the tip of his spear, the clean, black, efficient blade, with his forefinger. He had knapped it himself and tied it to the haft only three days ago, saving his precious flint point in his sack. "Tears," he said. "Frozen tears. My blade is from the Mountain of Frozen Tears," he said.

"Ech," Basatzaun said, bobbing his head again. "Sure. Round Top."

"Round . . .?"

"Top, Top. Mountain." He lifted his own spear. "Also. You go there? Not good to go Mountain of Frozen Tears. Better wait."

"Why?"

"Eh, why?" Basatzaun seemed on the point of saying something when an arrow shot past his face with a whistling sound; he hesitated the barest moment before darting to his left with a cry that sounded like, "Run!"

He vaulted through an opening in the crumbling wall of a house.

Shelsan grabbed Little Boren's arm and pulled him toward the wall. Another arrow whistled and Little Boren screamed. Shelsan vaulted the low, crumbling brick and yanked the boy after him.

The far corner had collapsed. He led the way up the treacherous slope to the next building.

A strange baying sound rose up behind them, accompanied by shouts from across the open space, coming swiftly closer. Shelsan stopped. A long shaft dangled from Little Boren's calf. Shelsan saw at once its feathers were from the vulture. He paused only long enough to pull it out. Blood gushed from the wound. Shelsan scooped a handful of spider web from a corner and pressed it over the wound. "Come on," he said, pulling the boy to his feet.

The stranger had vanished as if he had never been. Shelsan wondered if he were a spirit, a visitation from beyond. The Pretenders said sometimes they could see spirits, the ones especially who meant harm.

But Basatzaun hadn't intended harm; Shelsan was certain of that. Perhaps he had come just to warn them.

Though Little Boren moved painfully, they scrambled through the ruins, away from the shouting.

A tree had fallen across the third house, tilting down. Shelsan walked up it, balancing with his spear. At the top he turned. Little Boren hesitated at the bottom. "What is it?" he hissed.

The boy started to scramble toward him, pale with the effort. Shelsan reached down and the boy lunged for his hand. He pulled him up and the boy whimpered deep in his throat. They made their way along the top of the house wall, stepped across to the next, and were at the end. "We'll have to jump," he said.

Little Boren was looking down, his eyes wide. At home he would never jump to the Outside from a roof. Why was there no ladder?

"Come," Shelsan ordered. "I'll lower you. Try to stay off the leg."

An arrow whistled overhead. The boy took Shelsan's hand and slid backward over the edge. They dropped to the ground and he led the boy, now limping badly, into the woods. They plunged on through the trees and undergrowth until the light faded. The trees had thinned, and they were among hills covered with low shrubs and scrubby grass. The sounds of pursuit had faded, and they stopped to rest. Both were covered with scratches, but they were alive.

"Babi?" Little Boren whispered. "Who were they? Why did they attack us?"

"It wasn't us they attacked, little one. I think they must be enemies of Basatzaun. They thought we were with him."

"What were they saying?"

"Too many questions. I have no answers."

They walked among man-high shrubs. The breeze, which had been light, even pleasant, among the buildings, began to moan in the branches. Inside the moaning was another sound, short, and so sharp it cut. Shelsan held up his hand. Little Boren bumped into him.

"Eeeyah," Shelsan called.

An answering voice came from somewhere ahead and to their left: "Eeeyah."

To Little Boren it was the call of the dead lost in the marsh around the Place. Sometimes in the dry-time when the leaves fell they moved among the trees at night and flickered with a strange light. Little Boren could remember a woman from the warm-side Edge who had gone there and not come back. Many had gone out to look for her. They hunted for days but found no trace, and after that they said she was now one of the lost that cried in the night. Little Boren shivered.

Basatzaun loomed up out of the darkness, grinning. "Good now," he said. "Boy right?"

"He's injured. Arrow. Who were those people?"

"Erh, bad. Bad, bad people, food herders; won't trade, try to kill, always try, afraid we take their tame food! Mud-people! We avoid them, but they follow us. Not get Basatzaun, though, eh? Not this time." He clamped Little Boren's leg with one surprisingly strong hand and scraped off the cobwebs with a dirty fingernail. The wound was red and angry. He clicked with his tongue, poking at the wound. Little Boren went pale and sweat started on his forehead, but he said nothing.

Suddenly the Basatzaun slapped the wound with his open hand. Little Boren screamed. "Good," he exclaimed. "No poison." He let out a long, piercing whistle, and he sat down cross-legged with a grin. "Now we wait."

Invitation

The night grew cold but they agreed there would be no fire in case the "food herders" were still around. Under the sky's great river of light Shelsan rummaged in his sack and found some dried meat to share. They ate in silence, huddled together.

High clouds drifted in, shrouding the stars in a gauzy veil. Wolves called from the south and from the open land to the west, an eerie conversation from two directions.

The conversation between Shelsan and Basatzaun was a lizard with a broken back: it started, paused, rushed, stopped. But slowly they found words to share, the way they shared their meal.

"You're a hunter," Shelsan ventured.

At first Basatzaun did not understand, and Shelsan had to mime drawing an arrow, an animal falling. "You hunt. Hunter."

"Pah!" Basatzaun made a spitting sound. "Hun-ter? Not like mud people, food herders. Those people forget to speak to animals, to bring forth, to forgive, be forgiven. Kill people only."

"Tell us," Little Boren said. His voice was weak.

"I can tell this, I can tell the great herds have grown thin," Basatzaun said, still with many breaks and pauses, and much repetition, but his voice grew strong, and though they missed many of the words, his meaning became clear: "The mothers drop few young, fewer every year. There was a time, I have heard, so it is said, that the herds darkened the open spaces to the horizon, and the thunder of their passing lasted days, days during which men could not speak, could not act together because of the noise. But it did not matter then if they could not act together, because the game was plentiful, and bellies were always full."

Basatzaun collected his thought in silence. The high clouds dissipated, and silvery starlight threw an eerie glow over everything. The needles of the low pines, the leaves on the shrubs, the pointed tops of the grasses around them, all turned liquid and white, and they realized that a predawn dew was falling.

Basatzaun continued. "Yes. Then, in those days, those times, there was a balance, like standing on a round stone in the middle of a great river. The stone could roll, could go sunrise, or could go sunset, but if the hunter stood just right the stone did not move. That was what it was like, in the old days, in my grandfather's time, so it is said, so I have heard, standing just right, just so." His voice trailed off in the darkness again. It seemed he had fallen asleep when he added, "Every animal that dies gives to us. We must give to them. But there are too many now who have stopped giving. This is why the animals grow thin on the land, why we must roam farther each year, why we have had to leave the old lands. It is why we are here, and why we cannot have a fire."

"It is why Water Bird Mother left the ancient lands," Shelsan said.

The sky had turned pale and light. The wolves had fallen silent.

Basatzaun got to his feet. "Good that day comes."

Shapes loomed up out of the bushes around them. A short, stocky man was outlined against the sky. He crossed his arms on his chest, palms on opposite shoulders, and said, "Kaixo!" His head was shaved on one side, and jagged tattoo lines covered his cheeks. He carried an impressive supply of hunting equipment tied to his belt and slung across his back—bow, arrows, a long-bladed knife, loops of cord, sacks. Three rabbit pelts hung over his shoulder. Four other men waited behind him.

"Kaixo!" Basatzaun answered, crossing his own arms.

They spoke together for some time, occasionally examining Shelsan and the boy. Once or twice they spoke the name of Khrm.

Finally one of the men, for they were all men, turned to Shelsan. "You speak language of Khrm?"

"No, I don't know Khrm," Shelsan answered.

The man smiled, showing more gaps than teeth. "You speak like Khrm. That is fine. You come with us, yes? Khrm is friend. Tomorrow big day, big feast."

Basatzaun said, "There has been a hunt for cattle. It is the time of year, the middle of summer. So we will feast."

"Feast?" Little Boren seemed to forget his pain for a moment.

The new man, the stranger, said. "Big. Near empty house-place, they say too dry, they say the people grew sick until no one left. Yesterday you were there. Place of ghosts. Near there. In the morning we will take you in. Basatzaun like you, so we take you in, make you blood."

Gathering

Little Boren, limping alongside Shelsan, asked, "What did he mean, 'make you blood?'" They had not slept, but the boy made no complaint. His curiosity seemed to give him life.

The forest was still drenched in shadow. Shelsan was uneasy, for they had turned back toward the abandoned place, the place of lost spirits. Though they hadn't seen their attackers, they must still be nearby. It was only a small comfort there were now seven of them, and all but Little Boren had weapons. He realized he would have to make some for the boy; after all, he was nearly fourteen summers now. "I don't know," he said. "We'll find out."

It was mid-morning when they stopped, not, as Shelsan expected, at the settlement, but in a flat open space with two buildings larger than any house built on foundations carved into the bare rock. Forest surrounded the clearing on three sides. A broad, shallow river flowed along the fourth, the one they had traveled beside just the day before. So, as Basatzaun promised, they were near the empty Place.

Here, though, it was crowded with people, some dressed as outlandishly as Basatzaun in layers of skin and fiber, others wearing almost nothing but a string around their waists. Still others were dressed quite normally in buckskin skirts and sandals of woven reed. Most faces were painted, tattooed, or scarred in neat parallel lines. Naked children darted underfoot, shrieking and cackling with laughter. There were stacks of spears and bundles of arrows outside the largest building. Despite the heat several family groups were gathered around fires.

Several men were butchering the carcasses of enormous aurochs beside the river. They lined the heads neatly along the riverbank beside stacks of legs. Women scraped the hair or scraps of flesh off the skins and spread them in the sun. Some skins, already finished, were drying or being worked by others seated in circles. "There must be hands and feet of people here," Little Boren said. "Where are they from? Who are they?"

"Hunters," Shelsan said. "People who follow the food, and don't expect the food to follow them."

"Come," Basatzaun said.

Shelsan and the boy followed him to one of the buildings. He threw aside a skin covering over the side entrance.

"Wait here." Basatzaun went in, and the skin dropped into place behind him. A few minutes later he came back and gestured for them to follow.

Blood Lust

The dark smelled strongly of blood. A frame covered with freshly skinned cattle hides separated the entrance from the interior and shut out most of the light. Blood still dripped from the skins. Only a few lamps glimmered in the dim, smoky interior.

A man handed a horn cup to Basatzaun, who passed it to Shelsan. "First you, then boy," he said, making a drinking motion with his hands.

A low chanting began. Shelsan looked into the cup, but the liquid was opaque. He sniffed and the odor caught in the back of his nose. Cautiously he took a sip.

"You must finish," Basatzaun said.

Shelsan took a larger mouthful, looking at him over the rim. The taste, acrid at first, was not unpleasant after a moment. He swallowed and looked into the cup again. It was more full than before, so he drank again. Now it was full to the brim.

Basatzaun took the cup and gave it to the boy, who drank and immediately fell into a coughing fit. The stranger waited impassively until it was over and then pushed the cup at the boy's lips. Finally he took it away and disappeared around the frame of skins.

"I don't understand, Babi," the boy began. "How can people speak, speak and I don't them understand, understand, I don't? What are they chanting, sounds like the Pretender, but I don't know words . . . words?"

"They're strangers, Little Boren. We must wait. Patience." It took an effort to put his own words in order, and so he fell silent.

Dark liquid dripped onto the floor; it was red, almost black, like water on the swamp at night. Light came from somewhere, from everywhere. Were they making blood?

After some moments, or many moments, or none, the frame shook and flew back with a sound like wind, revealing a semicircle of standing figures. A round pool filled with glistening liquid marked the center. A dry, shallow channel carved into the floor passed from the pool beneath the feet of the figure in the middle.

Little Boren couldn't take his eyes from the pool.

One stirred and stepped forward. It had been standing with its animal head lowered, staring at Shelsan and the boy. It stopped and lifted its head, revealing a set of wickedly tipped horns.

Now that their eyes were adjusting they could see that all were dressed in skins that bulged and drifted when they moved.

The figure lifted a staff and flipped it horizontal. Long, pointed blades tipped both ends. They dripped a thick liquid.

Someone seized Little Boren from behind. He cried out, but a hand clamped over his mouth stopped the sound. He was pushed to the ground before the animal creature. The figure seemed to grow taller, to raise the double spear, to plunge it into the boy.

Shelsan started forward, but someone held him as well.

The figure lifted the spear, reversed it, and plunged it once again into the boy's body.

Little Boren lay still. His blood flowed toward the pool, filling it slowly. It reached the channel and began to flow between the figure's legs, and into the darkness beyond.

He pulled the spear from Boren's body and twirled it twice, sending drops of blood in a great arc. Then he stepped back to his place in line.

Two others stepped forward, one with the skull of a wild boar, the other the head of a great bull. They lifted the boy, put him on his feet, and stepped away.

Shelsan expected him to fall; instead he looked around groggily. His glittering eyes passed over Shelsan's without recognition.

"What have you, have you done?" Shelsan's mouth was filled with flax and the words were lost.

One of the men, Basatzaun from his voice, turned toward the boy and began to chant a long list of single words. Shelsan looked down. Red liquid was pulsing in time with his own heartbeat along the channel in the floor.

Basatzaun stopped, and the semicircle opened, revealing a bench against the back wall. The channel of blood disappeared under it.

Whoever restrained Shelsan now pushed him forward. He stumbled, trying to avoid stepping in the liquid. The boy stood to one side, eyes glossy and black. Someone prodded him, and together he and Shelsan came to the bench, were turned and urged to sit.

The figures now spun slowly, facing them. They began chanting in unison, a low and monotonous, endlessly repeated series of open throat sounds. Small lamps flickered into life around the room until a dazzling light filled all the space. The semicircle began a slow sideways shuffling dance that wound in one direction, then another, overlapping itself in an intricate pattern that exposed the entrance. The skin frame and the leather flap over the door were gone. Shelsan distantly realized the building faced the sunset-side, but even as the thought arose it submerged again. He was blinded by sunlight. A great shape filled the doorway, there was much agitation and scuffling, some rasping snorts followed by a pained bellow, and an enormous bull stumbled through the entrance into the room.

It stopped over the central pool, breathing wetly, eyes rolling. Garlands of small white flowers were wound around its neck and horns, brilliantly illuminated by the afternoon sunlight pouring through the entrance.

Three powerful men, naked and glistening with sweat, surrounded the beast. They lifted enormous cudgels and their powerful chests flexed and rippled. The bull stared at them resentfully, as if it knew what was about to happen.

With a great cry they leaped forward. The clubs flashed as one against the animal's head with a terrible wet sound. They lifted the clubs again and swung at the beast's head over and over, first together, then in a rhythmic sequence. The bull struggled, staggered a step or two, and slowly collapsed to its knees. After a long moment it toppled sideways, breathing rapidly, tongue hanging into the pool.

Vague shapes moved around the chamber, extinguishing the lamps. Basatzaun removed his headdress and handed it to someone behind him. He kneeled beside the great head and with one swift stroke cut the bull's throat with a flint dagger. A great spout of blood filled the pool. Soon it was flowing along the channel under the bench where Shelsan and Little Boren were seated. This time it had the thick flinty smell of real blood.

The rest of the figures removed their headdresses and became men. They clapped one another on the back with exultant cries. Basatzaun led Shelsan and Little Boren, still limping, outside where, blinking at the light, they were greeted by a great cry and cheering.

Little Boren, still dazed, looked down in wonder at his body. He was untouched. "Babi," he whispered. "He speared me. I saw him. I felt it. Why am I not dead?"

Shelsan said, "Always, Little Boren, you ask too many questions."

Spirit Flight

The smell of cooking meat attracted them, and they wandered among the roaring campfires. Hands reached whenever they passed, inviting them to share. Someone began to play a drum, and people here and there started singing unfamiliar melodies in strange, halting rhythms. More people had arrived while they were inside the building. They smiled and exchanged halting words. They ate, and soon Shelsan was dancing with others, arms around one another's shoulders, men and women. A sliver of moon slid down the sunset-side and disappeared beyond the river.

Little Boren could not dance. His calf was swollen and red, and he winced in pain when he took a step. But he ate and drank with relish.

The revelry went on until many were asleep. Shelsan found a woman to lie with, and afterward he found himself, unable to sleep, wandering along a river glistening with stars.

Days passed quickly. Shelsan learned that the people who had attacked them had no spirits of their own, or had only bad spirits. So Basatzaun said. Of course, he added, looking away, Basatzaun's people had helped themselves to the food they grew. It was a moon ago. But that was only natural. They were great hunters, Basatzaun's people, who had walked many moons over broad mountains to hunt.

He said sadly that because the animals they hunted had grown scarce these last years, each wet-time they had to go farther. And that made the grain those people grew all the more necessary. It was only natural.

The moon grew fat and lit up the nights. Little Boren could no longer walk, and began to mumble in his sleep. Shelsan feared the Sun Demon was in him, but Basatzaun said no, it was the arrow that left a trail of grief in the boy's leg.

Shelsan made a poultice and put it on the wound. It seemed to bring some relief, but the boy soon fell sick again, and mumbled more, and his words made no sense. Perhaps he was speaking the language of Basatzaun's people? But no, they could not understand him either.

Basatzaun brought a girl to take over the boy's care, a slender young beauty with midnight hair, wide eyes, and skin pale as a lily. "This is Tsurinye," he said. "Her name means White. She will cure. She has a great gift."

Shelsan asked her how old she was, but she just stared at him with wide eyes and didn't answer.

"Thirteen cold-times," Basatzaun replied for her. "She doesn't talk much."

"I see that."

She stood awkwardly beside Little Boren, sucking on her lower lip and shifting from foot to foot. Her eyes darted back and forth as if she were following a rapid conversation. "Buh!" she shouted, squatting suddenly. She touched his temple, his chest, then the wound. Her eyes rolled back so they were entirely white.

She leaped up and ran in a circle, careless of anyone in her way. With each completion the circle grew wider and people had to jump aside. An old woman gently steered her, barely diverting her widening spiral around a fire. A keening sound came from her, neither a human nor an animal sound.

With her arms out like wings she ran, her dark hair flying. Her legs were churning now. A line of people formed along the riverbank and with gentle hands kept her from falling in. She paid them no attention, keening still, until her hand brushed against a tree trunk at the edge of the clearing, and as suddenly as she started she stopped, her fingertips against the bark.

What happened then seemed impossible. Shelsan didn't see her do it, but she was high up the tree, and the top was bending down, swaying wildly back and forth. The girl emitted a series of sharp, piercing cries, like a hawk would make as it plunged toward its prey, a cry that could terrify and paralyze.

The tip of the tree dipped low to the ground, as if to brush against it, then rose swiftly, only to dip on the other side. The gyrations grew more violent, more uncontrolled. The cries came one after the other, then, seemingly, together, as if there were now two hawks circling and plunging.

And then, as suddenly as she had begun, she stepped lightly from the tree on one of its descents, and walked calmly into the woods. A few moments later she returned with armfuls of leaves. She squatted serenely by the river and soaked the leaves for several minutes, then mashed them into pads, which she placed on the boy's forehead, crooning to him under her breath a low, breathy keening song with many gaps and sudden leaps of rhythm.

"It is a healing spell," Basatzaun said.

And so it came to pass Little Boren grew cool again and opened his eyes, and when they fell on the face of the girl whose name meant White, he could not take them away.

And so Shelsan would have to go alone to the Mountain of Frozen Tears.

7 Now

Fast Forward

The global telecommunications networks worked at light speed. Fiber and satellites sent the images of Bryson Jones and his artifact to every part of the world, from Kuala Lumpur to Kodiak, Tierra del Fuego to the Andaman Islands. There was no inhabited place on earth where people could avoid seeing the "Startling Discovery," as one headline shouted from a huge screen in Times Square. Jones's face and the artifact floated side by side in the darkness of the void, like an image of Good and Evil.

Yet, in the end people wondered what made it so startling. The blogosphere, newswires, and cable networks were both intrigued and puzzled by it. Provenance, historical context in the Pre-Pottery Neolithic, and archaeological significance were for specialists; ordinary people were not moved by academic enigmas. They wanted simple mysteries easily solved.

Pundits found it difficult to account for its sudden sensation and the buzz it created. After all, no one could say exactly what it was, and certainly not what it was used for, what it meant. Could it be that people were intrigued by the odd fact that it had been set on a post, as MaeAnn Swanson, the noted anthropologist, mused? Most people would shrug at that, she answered herself. Things on posts were ordinary. Today many things are set on posts – mailboxes, street signs, floor lamps, coat racks, ashtrays. Even back then there was nothing startling about things on posts. Skulls. Warnings. Border markings.

Perhaps it was the elaborate plastering? But, no, that couldn't be it. Lots of cultures made things out of plaster. Plastered skulls, wall moldings, and floors had even turned up at Çatalhöyük. Why, kids played with *papier maché* and Play-doh in kindergarten.

Yet once they had seen it, even in its current state, before cleaning, people could not tear their eyes away. There was something both grotesque and compelling about the dirt-covered dome, the prominent nose or snout, the streaks, grooves, and lines of color, the blood tears from the round hollows that looked so much like eyes.

All who saw it felt a shock of fear. What made the artifact an international sensation was that shiver of something otherworldly, supernatural, outside or beyond the physical world.

One prominent professor of semiotics declared it the work of a gifted artist, a genius, even, someone who still had access to the haunted world of mankind's most primitive nightmares. Based solely on his brief view of the object on television he concluded that this object was telling the world, our world, far in the future of its making, that there was something deeply buried in both our past and in our psyches, something we had to face. That something, he suggested, was the terror that made you want to scream, to run, when you could neither scream nor run. It was the fear that paralyzed, froze the mind. It was the fear that killed.

This thing was the stuff of nightmare.

The public at large would embrace the artifact. After the initial shock it turned up everywhere, on T-shirts and place mats, in advertisements and Halloween masks. The image would have its day.

But that was in the future. For now, there were other parties with more specific interests.

Scholar

Professor Lena Marie Troye crossed against the light, talking into her cell phone.

"You're absolutely sure?" she repeated, jumping back to get out of the way of a Cherokee driven by a fresh young blonde. Two small children in back were watching a video. Then it was gone.

Lena Marie had been at Starbucks ordering a mocha grande when Gayle called to tell her about the discovery in Turkey. Since she didn't have her laptop to check for herself, she had canceled her order and rushed out.

There was a break after the Cherokee. She sprinted across the plantings in the road divider.

"I'm sure," Gayle said.

Lena Marie stepped off the divider into the eastbound traffic. Although this was a quiet college town and stately elms in their lush summer foliage lined the main street, cars still screeched and drivers still shouted. Lena Marie paid no attention. Some things were more important than negotiating with other people in the physical world. If true, what Gayle had told her was the biggest news since Marija Gimbutas first published *The Gods and Goddesses of Old Europe* back in 1974. The Neolithic, Gimbutas had maintained, was a peaceful period in mankind's history, a matriarchy ruled over by a benign Mother Goddess eventually destroyed by patriarchal pre-Indo-European warriors from the Pontic steppes.

"I don't want this to be another fiasco, like that goddess statue they dredged up from the sea near Bodrum, the one that so *obviously* turned out to be a boy. You remember."

"Yes, Lena Marie, I remember. But this time it's Bryson Jones," Gayle answered. "On the Discovery Channel. I just happened to turn it on. No rush, I've got it TiVoed."

Jones and his team had found the head of a real Goddess, larger than life, made of shaped and painted plaster! "I'll be there." Lena Marie flipped the phone closed and dropped it into her purse, neatly sidestepping a BMW.

More cars honked, but she made it safely across and started jogging toward the university, four blocks away. She passed the Baltimore, a retro soda fountain and cheap restaurant, and a series of used-book, CD, video game, and clothing stores. A block from the campus she slowed, aware of the unbecoming sight of a full professor jogging in street clothes, even on a fine summer day when there were no classes and few students to see.

"It's real," Gayle said as soon as Lena Marie burst into the room. "I watched it again to make sure." Before Lena Marie could sit down, Gayle was fast-forwarding through the commercials and program announcements until Jones's face appeared. The Goddess's face hovered by his shoulder like a supernatural presence. Both faces were surrounded by darkness. The cameraman had a gift for melodramatic lighting.

Lena Marie leaned forward and paused Jones in mid-sentence.

The Goddess face was pained. She suffered for humans' behavior. She suffered for the future, when the warlike males would destroy her peaceful realm. Her worshipers did not give her what she deserved, what she demanded. That much was clear from the dark hollows of her eyes, the strangely avian beaklike nose, and the tortured markings on the face.

"She's beautiful," Lena Marie said softly, releasing the pause.

Jones was talking about the shape of the head, which had female characteristics.

Lena Marie paused again. The camera lingered on the lower part of the face, showing the grotesque painted teeth. Possibly, she mused aloud, someone from the Bronze Age warriors had added them to subvert the Goddess's peaceful, egalitarian order.

"Really, Lena Marie, I don't think so," Gayle said hesitantly. "It was buried in the house. They date it to 6900 BCE."

Lena Marie glanced sideways. "There must be an explanation," she said. "That's a woman's face. Look, there are so many of the signs, even those v-shaped marks on the cheeks. She would never have a grimace like that unless she suffered."

"It may be a little too early to draw conclusions." Gayle had grown much more cautious since the goddess-who-turned-out-to-be-a-boy.

Lena Marie began pacing the room. "If we wait," she murmured. "If we wait . . ."

Gayle looked up expectantly. Lena Marie sat down again. "Go ahead," she said. "Let's see the rest."

The footage was still raw, barely edited. Only two days before, Jones had put out the word that they were going to bring up something interesting. If it was a gamble (and Lena Marie thought it certainly must have been, for how could he have known?), then it had paid of handsomely.

They saw the excavations under the awning, the bright lights and harsh shadows. They saw Francy staring thoughtfully as Satchi carefully pried the object from the ground.

And finally they watched as he raised the head into the dawn light.

It was as if the Goddess were being reborn.

"We can't wait," Lena Marie said when the program was over. "No, we certainly cannot. If we do, that bitch Swanson will get there first, she'll get her hands on it, and we'll have a problem being heard over the kind of noise she knows how to make."

"So," Gayle grinned. "When do we leave?"

Rolf

The clouds had been threatening Paris all day without delivering. It was unseasonably cold, too, as if the threat of global warming was some kind of scurrilous Green Party lie. Yet, Rolf thought, only a few years ago thousands of people had died in the worst heat wave in recorded history. Would it rain? Would it not? Nature was unpredictable.

Man, however, was not. He had only to look at the six television screens set into the dark wood bookcases in his office to see the inevitability of human nature. CNN, France One, the BBC, all echoed, in infinitely repeating mirrors, the rounds of human folly.

Since Rolf made his living from the avarice of his fellow humans, their predictability was his friend.

As an example, he had before him on the leather surface of his Louis XIV desk (a very fine reproduction) a handwritten letter from a man in China, a man who stated clearly that he eschewed electronic communication and would not use a computer, a telephone, or a fax machine. He trusted, and here Rolf let an audible bark of amusement escape, the national postal services.

But it was possible the man was right. There were laws, after all, that prevented people from opening the mail, or at least made it more difficult. And email, telephone conversations, faxes, it seemed, could all be traced, tracked, and flushed out by the software wizards of various national or corporate intelligence agencies.

Perhaps a handwritten letter, written on plain thrift store paper, albeit perhaps with an expensive fountain pen, was the safest after all.

It was a polite letter written in a fine, even exquisite, hand in English. "Dear Mr. Butcher," it began. "In my travels about the world more than once I have come across your name as one of a reputable and particularly discrete dealer. I am interested in contacting such a person." The letter went on to discuss, in vague and overly polite terms, his trust in the mails and an extensive private collection of antiquities. He was not, however, interested in selling but in making some modest additions. He proposed a contact. There was no name, just the address of a mail office in Chongming, China.

Rolf had been pondering this single sheet since he had returned from Geneva. Was it a trap? Interpol? FBI? Would even Interpol go to such lengths to lure Rolf Butcher, who was, after all, a respectable dealer in antiques, a man from a robust, if petty bourgeois Alsatian family, with offices in Paris and Rome. He was a man of spotless reputation and a pillar of the Third Arrondissement. They had nothing on him, he was sure of that.

The postmark was three weeks in the past. Rolf had been out of town but readily available by email or cell phone. He hadn't received a letter like this in years, so its unexpected appearance in his Paris office piqued his curiosity.

"All right," he said. He spoke English habitually, even when alone and speaking to himself. Most of his dealings were in that language. The result was that he was losing his northern Alsatian roots, leaving only French and English as serviceable languages. "I'll answer, Mr. Anonymous."

He started to type on his desktop computer but stopped almost immediately. Perhaps he should meet this stranger on his own terms. He took up a pen, but after gnawing on the end for a few minutes, put it down. Handwriting, after all, was individual, like fingerprints. Better, in the end, to use a cheap office printer.

While his reply was printing he leaned back in his chair and glanced idly at CNN. When he saw the strange head with empty, dirt-filled eyesockets he turned up the volume.

Débitage

Afet Orbay leaned over her laboratory table. Its white surface was blackened by close to four hundred tiny fragments of glasslike obsidian, sorted by color and size. She held a magnifying glass in one hand; with the other she pushed her hair back behind her ear. It was a habitual gesture, more utilitarian than vain. Occasionally she considered having her hair cut short but never seemed to have the time.

The stones were from a collection of what archaeologists called débitage, the waste flakes knapped off stone. "There you are, my pretty," she said aloud in faintly accented English, gently prying up a small flake with a pair of tweezers and turning it over. Under the magnifying glass the small triangular piece was gray-green, shiny, and translucent. She moved it across the table, hovered over a small grouping, examined it under the glass, moved a fragment aside to make room, and carefully placed her prize in its place.

She smiled and straightened, once again brushing her hair behind her ear.

"Almost perfect," she said to the American graduate student.

He moved to the table, and she showed him under the glass a long, slightly twisted flake of obsidian with one sharp edge facing a battery of tiny flakes. "You're sure?" he asked. His voice quavered. It seemed to happen every time he was near her.

Her smile exposed a set of perfect white teeth and etched a tiny pattern of crows' feet at the corners of her dark eyes. The American, though some years younger, fell back a little, as if hit by a sudden breeze. "You may be sure I'm sure," she said. "There are a few small chips missing, but this group was found in situ. As you see, they fit together. They make a blank almost the way it came off the outcropping at Göllü Dağ 9,000 years ago." She held the glass over the assemblage. "See?"

He bent over it and examined the complex, three-dimensional jigsaw. "Yes." He glanced quickly sideways at her silhouette against the huge north-facing window. As usual she was intensely focused on the patterns on the table.

He glanced at his watch. It was a little before eleven in the morning, almost lunchtime. "I wonder if you'd . . ."

She nodded and straightened, letting the magnifying glass fall to her side. "Of course, it will never be the way it was. Once a stone has been knapped, it is forever altered. It may leave a useful blade like this one, well used, you can see, but it can never again be what it was, and glue is a poor substitute for the fires of a volcano."

"Of course," he murmured, retreating to his side of the room.

The secretary put her head in the lab door. "Dr. Orbay?"

"Yes, what is it?" Afet put the glass down.

"There's a Mr. Bennett on the phone for you."

"Bennett?"

"That's what he said."

"All right." Afet followed the secretary, wondering who Bennett was. She took the receiver from the woman's desk. "Hello?"

"Dr. Orbay? This is Satchell Bennett, Field Director at Aynalı Tepe."

"Oh, yes, that's where I heard the name. What can I do?" After a moment's silence she realized her mistake and added, "For you?"

"You may have heard about our find last week?"

"I'm afraid not, Dr. Bennett; I've been very busy. I have a report due the end of the week, analysis of some of the débitage at . . ."

"I'm not a doctor," Satchi interrupted. It was a reflex. "Listen, I don't want to bother you, but we have something here, and they say you're the best in the country."

Afet couldn't imagine what he wanted of her. She was a lithics specialist, but hers was laboratory work, the slow, careful sorting, cataloging, reassembling, with long hours of examination, searching out the patterns, feeling her way into the physical processes that went into the creation of tools, the origin of the stone, what kind of tool it was, how it was made and used. She studied typology, function, technology. She was not a field person, and lithic analysis was hardly an emergency science.

"An unusual artifact, a head, plaster," Satchi was saying. "It's attracting a lot of attention, and we don't want to make any mistakes. Besides, I think you'll be interested. There's something inside, probably stone. We have a team – human remains, plaster, conservation. We'd like you there, too, if you're interested. Just in case it is stone. And I'm willing to bet it is."

She glanced across the desk at the secretary, busy filling out forms on the computer. The secretary glanced up briefly and smiled.

Afet looked around the office at the bookcases and filing cabinets, the heaps of journals and old glass-fronted wooden cabinets crammed with fragments, pottery, figurines, plastic baggies of soil and plant debris. It was all familiar and comfortable.

She sighed. "All right. When?"

"Tomorrow, if possible."

Congeries

Just after eight in the morning the Thursday after the artifact was uncovered, Lena Marie stepped from her Konya taxi onto the gravel of the courtyard. She glanced around while Gayle struggled with the suitcases. "A congeries," she said.

The courtyard was alive with disordered but purposeful activity. People of all ages, genders, and sizes rushed in and out of doors, along the veranda, up to the mound, back into the court. Lab and office doors were wide open. A ping-pong table had been pushed to one side and was littered with laptops. Students bent over them or engaged in heated discussion, absently brushing away flies. Two delivery trucks and a film crew took up space near the kitchens.

"A congeries is right," Gayle huffed, dropping the last suitcase on the veranda with a sigh. "Are we in time?"

"I hope so," Lena Marie answered. There was no one to greet them, so she stopped the first person to walk by. By luck it was Satchi.

"I am Lena Marie Troye," she said.

"Yes?" he replied politely.

"Professor of Folklore, Gravidian College, Connecticut."

"Yes?"

"We're here to see the Goddess."

"The God . . . Ah," Satchi grinned. "Yes, sorry. We've had so many people calling lately I had forgotten. Of course. Welcome to Aynalı Tepe. What . . ." The taxi turned around with a deafening crunching of tires on gravel and sped away through the entrance, momentarily interrupting him. ". . . can I do for you?" he finished.

"Where is Doctor Jones?"

"He left yesterday, I'm afraid. A meeting in Geneva. He'll be back in a few days."

"Very well, we'll talk to him when he gets back. Now, I'd like to see Her."

"The find? Of course you want to get right to it. We're doing a preliminary examination this afternoon, as soon as another specialist arrives."

"That's all right," Lena Marie said sweetly. "We're patient, and we have to wait for Jones anyway. For now I'd just like to see Her. I presume MaeAnn Swanson isn't here yet?" It was only a half-question. Lena Marie was pretty sure she had beaten her rival.

"No. I haven't heard about her."

"Surprising, but good news."

"Since you're staying," Satchi continued, "I have to warn you the dorms are full. We have an overflow crowd."

Lena Marie beamed. "That's quite all right, we're equipped for camping and can sleep under the stars on the earth, closer to the Mother Goddess."

"I see." He glanced at Gayle, pursing her lips at the pile of luggage. "Well, I'll have one of the students give you a tour as soon as I can find one who's free. Meanwhile, come this way and I'll show you the find." He carefully avoided mentioning the Goddess.

"Thank you," Lena Marie said. "That would be lovely."

Özgür was chewing on an unlit cigarette in the Secure Room, a baseball cap on his head, and speaking into a cell phone in rapid Turkish.

When he saw Satchi and the women he terminated the call and flipped it closed. "Ah," he said genially, switching to English. "This must be your stone person."

"No, I'm not a stone person, whatever that is." Lena Marie put out her hand. "Lena Marie Troye. Gravidian College. Connecticut. A pleasure. You are?"

The representative responded with a bleak smile and muttered, "Özgür Tasköprülüzâde." His hands were full with phone and cigarette, and he did not shake hers.

"Yes, well, very nice to meet you, Mr. Tezkup." Lena Marie put her hand down. "Where's the Goddess?"

Satchi watched this exchange with a twinkle in his eyes.

"Excuse me?" Özgür said.

"The Goddess. Where is she?" Lena Marie pronounced each syllable carefully.

"The . . . goddess. Would that be she there?" Özgür pointed his cell phone toward the bookcase.

Lena Marie inhaled noisily. "Ah." She took a few steps and peered closely at the head. "Just look, Gayle. Look at her."

"Don't touch," Özgür said tersely.

Lena Marie stared at him over her shoulder. "What do you take me for? It is you who should not touch. Men!" she added, turning. With her forefinger a couple of centimeters away from the plaster she traced the deep furrows in the brows and cheeks, the circular eye openings, the thin, painted upper lip. "It almost looks like some kind of helmet, doesn't it?" she said. "A Neolithic precursor to Athena, perhaps."

Gayle clucked agreement. Soon they were deep into a private conversation about the iconographic history of the divine feminine.

Lurkers

Mehmet approached Satchi. "Those men again."

"What men?"

"You know, they were here before, I told Dr. Jones." Mehmet's English was slow and careful. He took his job seriously, and when there was nothing for him to do he studied English out of a book.

"The ones who seemed to be looking the mound over but didn't come in? I remember. They were back?"

Mehmet nodded. "Yes, those men, same. This time they came to gate, asked many questions, about the television people, but mostly about the object."

"The whole world seems to be interested in our spooky head," Satchi smiled. "Any idea who they were?"

Mehmet shook his head. "They did not say. Just asked questions. Where was it? Was it really Neo . . . Neolithic?"

He, Mehmet, did not trust these men. They pretended they were simply curious, but he was sure they wanted something. They weren't like the others, the scholars arriving almost hourly, or the women who had arrived this morning. These men wore black formal suits. They spoke Turkish well, but with an accent. It was hard to tell where they were from. One thing that was strange: they parked their vehicle half a kilometer away near the stand of poplars and walked to the gate. Why did they do that?

"I don't know," Satchi answered doubtfully. "Maybe they needed exercise."

Men in Black

Ben drove into the compound at 11:46 and rushed around to open the passenger door. The slim woman who stepped out thanked him and walked straight toward the office. "Please, Dr. Orbay," Ben called, running after her. "You should have some lunch first. It's almost over. And as you can see, no one's in the office."

"Very well." She followed him into the dining hall and collected a plate of salad.

As soon as she was seated at his table, Satchi stood and tapped his water glass with a spoon. When the room quieted down he said, "We have a lot of visitors these days. Most are honestly interested in our work, but this is no time to get careless. We can't afford to lose anything, no matter how small, and with all these people around it would be easy for something to go . . . astray. If you see a couple of men in black suits, for example, please report them."

Francy tapped Ben's arm. "Men in black?"

He winked. "Mehmet saw them."

Satchi continued, "Since our artifact is drawing so much attention, it's especially important for all of us to be vigilant."

"Excuse me, please, there is something I don't understand," Afet said.

"What?"

"I'm am specialist of obsidian. I am here for the stone, but I understand this artifact is plaster? You are Dr. Satchell Bennett, and I must know if this is correct."

Satchi smiled widely, perhaps because her hair formed an intricate gossamer web on either side of her face and trapped stray sunlight falling through the dining hall window. "I'm sure there's stone of some kind inside, and because the object was in an unusual context, and is itself unusual, we wanted a lithics specialist on the team. I for one am very glad it's you." Her expression was grave, but when she lifted her hand to tuck her hair behind her ear Satchi looked away and his eyes met those of Lena Marie Troye, standing beside his chair.

"Mr. Bennett?" Lena Marie's voice was husky. "You've truly have found something extraordinary."

"Yes."

"I feel confident it's a depiction – a portrait if you will – of the Avenging Goddess. Something happened here, in this place. Don't you feel it?"

"Is this what you meant?" Afet asked Ben.

Ben nodded. "Dr. Troye is interested in the history of the Goddess." He lifted his eyebrows. "We don't know if it's a goddess. Maybe when Dr. Jones gets back . . ."

Introduction

In the middle of the afternoon break Hellä Rautanen, the conservator, an angular woman from Helsinki University, was ready. The *ArchaeologyNowOnline* camera crew, along with Lodewyk and Afet, were gathered around the table. Lena Marie and Gayle stood near the door. Özgür hovered between them and the conservator, his eyes in constant motion, as if he expected to spot a thief at any moment. Several of the dig crew were present as well.

Satchi took the artifact from a box and placed it on the workbench with a slight thump.

Francy called, "Shouldn't we name it? We can't just keep calling it 'The Head.' I mean, can we? It sounds like the bathroom or something, like on a ship."

Satchi grinned. "What would you suggest?"

"Me? You want me to name it?"

"Who better?"

"I don't . . . I mean, I'm just a . . . All right, how about Elvis?"

Someone stifled a laugh, but Dr. Troye was outraged. "You can't call Her Elvis! She's the Goddess!"

Francy sighed. "You're right. How about Alice, then? Like Alice in Wonderland?"

Satchi asked for objections, but Lena Marie had fallen silent.

Ben whispered, "Alice in Wonderland? Magic mushrooms?"

"I was really thinking of Alice Cooper," she whispered back. "But don't say anything."

Satchi put both hands out. "Very well. Everyone – *ArchaeologyNow Online* – meet Alice."

Reflections

Satchi sent the crews back to work. He promised a special seminar later on what the conservator found.

A few visitors gathered at the entrance to the Secure Room to watch Hellä prepare Alice. The tension was palpable, like nerves pulled tight in the back of the neck.

She put on white cotton gloves, hesitated for a moment, took a deep breath, and lightly stroked Alice's cheek with the delicate bristles. A few fine particles of dust fell to the pristine white surface of the table with each stroke. She was careful not to touch the object.

Lena Marie and Gayle remained to observe. Satchi was torn between going up to the mound and staying. As he dithered in the doorway, pretending to be lost in thought, he wondered if he was right to have called that woman all the way from Istanbul. He glanced at her frequently, and each time nearly lost his concentration. He had looked up her name, Afet. It meant "woman of bewitching beauty" in Turkish.

It also meant "calamity."

The first meaning was certainly true: every time she tucked her hair behind her ear his heart leaped. "Stupid," he muttered.

"Excuse me?" she asked.

He shook his head.

With a fleeting smile she leaned forward to look intently at Alice. Her own face had clean, sharp cheek bones, a sensuous curve to her mouth, and porcelain ears nestled in her long, dark hair. Satchi saw how delicate her fingers were, smoothing her hair back. They were the kind of fingers that could sort débitage without hesitation, strong and competent.

As for the second meaning, calamity, what's in a name?

Hellä looked into the camera. "In the absence of Doctor Jones," she said, "I will describe what I am doing here." She cupped her palm over the dome of the head without touching it. "Alice is built of plaster, and plaster this old, that has been buried so long, is very delicate. I'm going to clean the bottom first. It's flat and covered with residue we believe to be wood, probably oak. Alice had been set on a pillar in the middle of the room.

"Then I'll clean out the eyes. These are Alice's most interesting features, and we're all curious to see what's inside." She offered a severe smile to the camera. "Some plastered skulls have eyes inset – bits of shell or bitumen – and there's something inside here. We don't know what."

She turned Alice around slowly, examining the surface. "As you can see, the designs cover the object from top to bottom and all the way around. Were they supposed to represent hair or some kind of headdress? Are her features animal? Feline, perhaps, or avian? The nose could have been a muzzle, snout, or even, perhaps, a beak."

She spread a piece of white cloth on the table and very gently tipped the head on its side onto the cloth.

With a small dental tool she began picking at the soil on the base, toppling it out onto the smooth surface of the table and brushing small piles of it into a plastic bag every few minutes. These would be analyzed later. The bottom of the head was covered with flat, undecorated white plaster. She put down her pick and stretched.

An Interruption

A loud male voice said, "But I simply must see it!"

Özgür was blocking the doorway. "Who are you, sir?" he asked, though his politeness failed to conceal his suspicion.

The man was in his mid-forties, clean-shaven, short dark hair, a healthy tan, and muscular arms sticking out of a sleek, short-sleeved turtleneck of white silk. His jeans were clean, starched, and pressed. The overall impression was favorable. Perhaps, thought Satchi, a bit too favorable, too studied. At least he wasn't wearing black.

"Rolf Butcher," the stranger introduced himself, extending his hand so vigorously Özgür instinctively shook it. "Doctor Jones, Bryson Jones, suggested I have a look around. I'm here to do that. Look around. I understand you have found something important, so I'm also here to see that. Someone outside told me it was in here. So here I am." He showed an array of very large, white teeth in an affable smile.

Probably capped, Satchi thought.

"Very impressive," Rolf continued. "All done in a couple of years, I understand, the Dig House, the laboratories. Well-funded, I'd say, but projects like this can always use more, no? Well, well, that's why I'm here."

Özgür fell back before this onslaught, and Rolf Butcher pushed his way past him to the table. He made eye contact with everyone in the room, one at a time, and nodded in a friendly way.

Afet smiled back when he took her hand and patted it gently. "A pleasure to meet you," he murmured. Looking around he added, "Yes, very nice facilities. And you, I recognize you, the Field Director, yes, Doctor Bennett?"

"I'm not a doctor."

"No matter, you're very good, your reputation is great, really. I saw you on CNN."

"Did you?"

"Yes, indeed. You're quite famous."

"Where are you from, Mr. Butcher?" Satchi couldn't place the accent.

"Paris, mostly," Butcher said offhandedly. "And this must be the mystery find." He gazed down at the head, lying on its side. With a glance at Satchi he said, "Do you mind?" and without waiting for an answer bent down for a closer look. Several people leaned forward, ready to stop him if he tried to touch it, but his hands remained clasped behind his back. He stared into the empty, dirt-filled eye sockets. His breathing seemed quiet and controlled, as if he wanted to avoid contaminating the object.

He straightened. "Yes, indeed, it is very interesting, this object, quite extraordinary. Similar to ones found at Jericho, or at Çatal. But when I saw it on CNN I said to myself, I said, Rolf, that is a very unusual piece, a work of art, and a very odd one. Most such heads are quite plain and white, or perhaps painted red. Sometimes little black eyes made from bitumen, yes, as at 'Ain Ghazal? Or eyes of cowrie shells, too. Were they trying to bring the ancestors back to life, do you think, give them new faces? Red is the color of life, isn't it? Blood, or ripe strawberries, yes? But this is too large, and far more highly decorated. It is a skull, isn't it, inside?"

"We don't know yet," Satchi answered dryly.

"Of course, not yet. But there's *something* inside, isn't there. One sees this object on television, and one asks oneself what the people who made it were thinking? What did it mean? It's important to find answers to these and other questions. Yes, very important. Thank you so much. I'll let you get back to work."

He stepped back into Lena Marie, who put her hands out. He turned and apologized. Their eyes locked for a moment. "Excuse me," he murmured, taking her hands, as he had with Afet's. "You're the Goddess scholar, aren't you, Doctor Troye?"

"Why, yes."

"Now, this is indeed a pleasure. I have so many questions for you. Could we step outside to talk, just for a moment?"

Lena Marie looked at Satchi, but he was watching Hellä at work. She could see it was going to be a while yet before the eyes were clear. "Of course."

In the House

The excavation had expanded. Ben was grumbling to Francy that he should really be taking notes in the Secure Room and not be stuck up here digging. "Besides, I like to watch the work. That conservator's got amazing hands. And besides, again, I'm not really an excavator, I'm a tech guy."

"He trusts you here." Francy was seated cross-legged next to the discolored area that defined where the hearth had been. "He put you in charge."

"For today," Ben said. "You and I, we're the DANTE team. And you're the excavator, I'm the geek."

"Yeah, Ben, sure."

One of Lodewyk's graduate students walked over. "Find anything?"

Ben gestured at a curve of bone sticking out of the dirt on the northeast side. "Just him, or her, if you want to excavate the burial. It's a little later, a level above, in the house to the east and will have to be removed before we can get to the wall."

Lodewyk's student nodded and started working the soil around the bone. "Adult," she muttered.

Ben squatted and scraped at the dirt over the floor. Though dirty, the plaster was in fairly good shape. To the east a lip marked the beginning of a raised platform.

In the center of the floor was a discolored circle. "Weird, isn't it?" Ben said. "Finding a post in the middle of the house. Support posts should be at the sides."

"Look at this." Francy drew her trowel along discolored plaster near the hearth. "It's a different texture."

"Obsidian cache? No, too big, probably another burial. They liked to bury kids near the hearth." He scraped away some soil too. "Here's another one."

Eye of the Storm

Two more hours had passed, and several people had wandered away. Lena Marie and Rolf came back and waited by the door.

Hellä pushed the dental pick into the soil over the eye with a very soft click, audible in the tense silence of the room. She leaned back. "Something hard."

Infinitely slowly she pecked away the dirt.

A small black spot appeared. She worked without haste until she had exposed a circle of pitch black a little over two centimeters in diameter. It filled the orbital cavity.

"Not shell, not bitumen," she said, turning the head a few degrees so the socket faced the camera. The light caught the darkness and set it afire.

"A mirror?" Afet breathed over Hellä's shoulder. "It's a mirror."

She cleaned the other eye. Expertly set into both sockets were finely ground, perfectly polished circles of deep black obsidian.

8 Then

The Great Bull

Grief grew in Mala as the grain in her patch of ground three hours walk from the Place grew, slowly ripening toward fullness. Though she neglected to go see them as she should, she knew the tops of the stalks would be heavy with seed and that the time to harvest was coming fast, yet she passed silent days with her feet hanging over the roof at the warm-side Edge watching the marsh dry out. The wheat was growing, but her grief was growing, too, so heavy now she could not move.

This year was certainly more dry than last, but her eyes were filled with water and she did not see well. She had seen well enough to know the floods had retreated early and the animals had grown strange, moving to different places, and at different times. There were fewer frogs than she remembered. Even snails were scarce, and the wild cattle came ever closer to the Place. One huge bull especially stared at her from a distance, puffing hot steam from his nostrils. She stared back with neither fear nor desire, though he was clearly a god and wanted something of her. She had grown to hate spirits and gods, the wild ones, the ones of the hearth, all of them.

The bull waited every morning. On the third day he ambled away, disappearing through cluster of rushes that brushed dryly against his flanks with a sound like the whispering she sometimes heard from Pinnak's house. Perhaps the whispering concerned her. She did not care. Perhaps they, Pinnak, and the rushes, were saying her man had left, her son had left, and, like Big Boren, they would never return.

She was indifferent. Let them come or not come. Shelsan and Little Boren were certainly at the Mountain of Frozen Tears by now. If they came back Shelsan would pay Temkash, but the boy had died and she did not care either if the Pretender got his stone or not. She was as dry heat and dust, empty as the marsh in front of her. Only her eyes filled from time to time.

People died, so they said, when Temkash was around. And he was around, every few days, asking about Shelsan. His house was close to this spot at the Edge, only two roofs away toward the sunset-side, so it was easy for him to come to her. "When will Shelsan come back, Mala?" he would ask, standing behind her. "When? Speak, woman."

She did not speak. What was there to say? Shelsan was gone, Little Boren was gone like his father; the baby girl was gone, and the boy who never had a chance to become a Person, he, too, was gone. Temkash had failed her, and her life was black with grief. She could have said this to Temkash, that it was so, that he had failed, that she drank nothing but sadness, but she did not. Her tongue was stiff in her mouth and would not move.

Some evenings she want back to her own house, across all the roofs, making her way slowly toward the center where First Grand had built First Egg in the Nest. Those nights she slept on her own roof, and ate sparingly from her stores, lentils and peas and the remains of last year's wheat. When she did not go back, when she stayed at the Edge, someone would bring her a wooden bowl of meat and lentil stew and she would eat without pleasure, and smile grimly and give thanks.

When she made her way again across all the roofs, she asked permission to cross if someone was about, or walking quietly along the wall tops if not. People spoke to her, but she barely answered. Always she ended up sitting at the Edge again, staring at the empty land toward the warm-side.

At first, Pinnak came several times a day. "I can move into your house with you, Mala. Your lineage is direct from First Grand. We could gain much together."

Once only she looked up at him with haunted eyes. Then she turned once more to the dry land.

"All right, I know I have two women in my Egg. But I will leave them if you let me move in with you, I promise." He went on like this for some time, but she had stopped listening. Finally he stopped coming.

There came a day when a woman spoke behind her, saying, "Come, Mala. We have grief, all of us. You are not alone."

Mala glanced over her shoulder. "Widow Klayn. I did not expect you to come here." Her voice was dry as the marshland. She turned again to the void.

"I lost my man four cold-times past," Widow Klayn said. "Since the Great Bull gored him, I have been alone."

"You are yet young," Mala replied. "And Shelsan gives you his attention."

"He does it out of kindness, because we are kin," Widow Klayn said flatly.

"And you, you come here to me out of kindness, do you?" Mala asked bitterly. Her grief was a lump of charcoal in her throat.

The widow squatted beside her. "No," she said. "Not out of kindness."

"What, then?"

It was the hottest time of the year. They sat side by side and stared at the empty marsh. The sun had moved a little in the sky before the widow spoke again. "We share loss. Your children, my man. Through Shelsan we are kin. Perhaps you cannot have more children, Mala."

Mala was about to speak, was about to ask, "How do you know this?" but just then the same bull appeared at the far end of the empty land where the willows drooped in the heat not far from the rushes and walked toward them. Widow Klayn gasped.

The bull approached, stopped, came closer, stopped again, staring at Mala. He stepped forward delicately through the hummocks and heaps of kitchen waste thrown from the walls until he stood beneath her, looking up.

His great chest heaved and collapsed with each long, shuddering breath. His flanks were streaked with dirt and sweat. He must have been half again as tall at the shoulder as Mala, with horns that spread fully her own height. One horn tip was broken, leaving a ragged set of wicked spars like leopard teeth; the other tip was sharp and polished. His breath rasped in his wide nostrils, and he stank of sweat, and half-digested grass, and something unnamable.

He was old, this bull, but still proud and strong.

"I know those horns," Widow Klayn whispered. "He's the one killed my man."

The bull pawed twice at the dusty ground and snorted. Mala stared and they locked eyes, woman and bull.

It was a shock, that look he gave her, for he saw deep into her, into her loss and rage. His large brown eyes, bright with intelligence and malice, saw to the very base of her, to that place that nourished her grief, like the ground from which the wheat sprouted. The muscle of his neck, his withers, his flanks, bunched and loosened.

His mouth opened, and his tongue twisted this way and that.

"What does he say?" Widow Klayn asked, her voice so hushed she could not say which feeling was greatest, the fear or the awe.

"Death," Mala answered. "Someone will die."

The Mountain of Frozen Tears

Shelsan left the boy with Basatzaun and the hunters and made his way toward sunrise and the Mountain of Frozen Tears. He moved with care, avoiding people. If he saw smoke he made a wide circle. If he heard calls, he crouched in the underbrush until the sounds had moved away. He feared the mud people who grew their food, attacked first, and did not share.

The land sloped gently upward. Twice at dusk he paused to snare food, and to sleep. On the third day he reached a barren place, carrying the small carcasses of birds and rabbits. The mountain rose before him, and he understood why Basatzaun's people called it "Round Top." His father and his uncles, all he knew who had come here before, had described often enough the barren reddish ground, the black outcroppings, the bleak blue sky. Yet seeing it for the first time was a shock. It was clear the mountain itself was a god – there was an active, restless spirit in the place despite the desolation. This was not a place to trifle with; it demanded reverence, especially if one wanted to take frozen tears from it.

They had told him also of the lake, but this water, wrapped around the base of the mountain, reflected only empty sky and the dark dome and blocked him.

He picked his way along the rocky shore, keeping the lake to his left, looking for a way to cross, when heard the sharp, rhythmic tapping of someone working stone.

He walked toward it, passing a series of shallow gullies on his right. In wet-time they would discharge water into the lake. Now they were dry, and it was from one of these that the tapping came.

He approached cautiously. It was the custom, he knew, for people to share the mountain, to come and go in peace, so as not to anger the god that had wept for them. It was said when the mountain was angry it belched fire and choking smoke and killed those who had angered it. There were plenty of frozen tears for all, so they said. But Shelsan was cautious, and approached with care.

He followed the sound around a bend in the gully wall, then around another.

A man and two women sat by a small, smokeless fire. The women were preparing a meal while the man worked a beautiful core of frozen tears against his thigh. Tiny shining chips flew away from each careful tap of his hammer stone, and in due course a long, delicately curved blade fell away, perfect.

Two children were playing in the shade of the west wall. He could see no others so he stepped out of the shadows.

The man looked up, midway through a strike. The hand holding the hammer stone paused. He dropped it and reached casually for a spear lying nearby. Without picking it up he smiled. "Kaixo," he said. "Welcome."

Shelsan could imagine what he'd been thinking: if Shelsan were alone, there was no danger. If he were accompanied and intended harm, his spear would be of little use. Negotiation was the best option.

"I thank you," Shelsan replied. "Kaixo." He crossed his arms on his chest the way he'd seen Basatzaun do.

The other stood and crossed his arms, still smiling.

With few words and much gesturing they came to understand each other. Yes, the man implied, he had come from the sunrise-side, come to gather frozen tears (though they did not call them that), to make tools, and to carry them back to his home near a great lake. He did not know Basatzaun, but he had heard the name. He was a relative of an affiliated clan. Soon, before the wet-time rains, they would return to the sunrise-side. And yes, the hunting had grown difficult these last years.

One of the women proffered a wooden bowl. Shelsan took the soup gratefully and offered in return one of the birds hanging from his belt.

After they ate the man led Shelsan to the water and showed him how to cross from one island to the next. At the foot of the mountain toward the sunset-side, he said, was the best stone. It was just by the water. He couldn't miss it.

A narrow land bridge led to the first island. From there he had to cross a narrow gap to the second. He plunged in and gasped with the cold shock of it, but pushed on. The water rose to his knees, his waist, halfway up his chest. Then the bottom rose swiftly and soon he was on the second island. A short jump took him to the mountain itself. He made his way along the shore to the sunset-side. The sun poured down full on him, and his clothing dried. Soon enough he found the outcropping, a black nodule of volcanic stone larger than a handful of houses together.

Though the ground was littered with used cores and worked flakes, it seemed the stone could never be used up.

He tapped off a fine block, almost too heavy to carry back to the Place, carefully wrapped it in leather and bound it into his pack, then found a comfortable place to curl up in the sun. He slept through the afternoon, content with his prize, the meal he had eaten, the warmth. By the time he had made his way back to the other side the sun was low against the horizon.

He was walking briskly toward the camp in hopes the women had cooked up his bird when something, not a sound, but the absence of sound, warned him. No tapping, no quiet conversation, no laughter of the children. He bent low and made his way around the angles of the gully until he reached the camp. It was still and lifeless; the small fire was out, the scraps of wood scattered.

First he noticed the smell.

Then he saw the bodies.

Tsurinye

After Shelsan had gone, Tsurinye made Little Boren drink a kind of tea. When he slept, she disappeared into the forest.

She returned several hours later and set a full sack on the ground beside him. He was still sleeping. She went to Basatzaun and gestured, holding her fingertips together, making zigzag motions. In answer he took a rolled leather package from his kit, unrolled it, displaying a number of bone needles and thin stone blades. She examined them so closely her loose hair fell forward and concealed her face.

After some time spent picking up one after another, she chose a long blade and four needles so thin they were nearly invisible. When she tested the tips against her finger, crimson drops welled up. With a quick dip of her head she carried them back to Little Boren.

Basatzaun watched her walk away with a bemused expression. The girl's strange powers gave her an authority rare for one so young.

She held Little Boren's head in her lap and with the blade carefully shaved his head, brushing his long black hair into a pile at her side.

When she finished she took the hair to a fire and tossed it in, chanting words no one could understand.

Then she sat once more at his head and arranged a set of flat shells in a row, ready to her right hand. With slow, deliberate movements she ground into each shell a different mineral color or plant dye. Humming quietly to herself she dipped the needles into the colors and pressed the tips into the boy's skin, leaving behind small dots of color. She began with circles of red near his left eye, pausing only to wipe away drops of blood with a piece of flax cloth.

Tsurinye worked long hours, day after day, for six days, like one possessed. When Little Boren started to wake she fed him broth and more of her narcotic tea, and he slept as one dead.

The women brought food, and she ate it absently, contemplating her work. As soon as she finished eating she set to work again. Her concentration was so intense the others watched in awe. "It's the god," they said. "The god of the place, of the hunt, of the sky – some god – who has taken her like this. What does it mean?"

There were no answers, only questions.

The dots became lines. Interlocking curves and rays of crimson, black, green, and white grew like vines on the left side of Little Boren's face and scalp, transforming him from beardless boy to supernatural being, part human and part animal, part woman, part man. The patterns were not symmetrical but swirled and intertwined around his cheek, under his chin, and over the top of his head and ears until he had acquired an otherworldly and terrifying beauty.

Only then did Tsurinye lie down beside the boy and sleep herself as one dead. The next day she asked what it was she had done. Basatzaun told her to look at Little Boren. She saw only the right side of his face at first and threw a puzzled glance at Basatzaun. But when Little Boren turned and she could see the left side, she bit her lip. "He's very beautiful," she said. "I did that? I don't remember."

After that Little Boren recovered slowly but steadily. He slept much of the time, but when he awoke, always at his side the quiet girl was waiting. When he went to sleep, her hand rested on his forehead. She filled his universe, her dark hair against blue summer sky or the River of Stars. She said little, and the words she did murmur from time to time he did not understand. Perhaps they were to heal him, or to encourage him, because they were soft, and often repeated.

And so the days passed, and the nights, and the moon dwindled and died and grew fat again. Her words began to have meaning. "You are my chosen one," she said one day. "You came from the sky."

"No," he tried to protest. "I came from the Place, with Babi Shelsan."

"Shh." She put her finger to her lips and held them closed. "From the sky. It was what I saw, three summers now, a dark boy from the sky, and when you came I recognized you."

"I came from the Place. From First Egg."

She shook her head, smiling. "I know you," she repeated. "You are the antelope, the leaping one. From the sky. Be quiet now." There was no contradicting her.

Most people had drifted away from the camp, and the buildings stood empty. Only Basatzaun and a few of others remained, but they, too, were preparing to leave.

Though at times his leg pained him and he favored it, Little Boren could move around the remains of the camp. He went into the building and saw nothing but a broad, empty space. The bench on which he had sat with Shelsan was there, and the groove in the floor from the central pool was there, but these features seemed small and ordinary.

He came out into the sunlight blinking.

Tsurinye lay down beside him at night after that. Once she touched him, and said, "Now you are a man." She pulled him to her, and for the first time he made love.

After that neither one would leave the other alone. When he went into the forest to find food, or when Basatzaun took him to hunt, Tsurinye was with him. When she waded upstream to find freshwater shellfish or snails or frogs, he went with her.

It was growing colder. Basatzaun asked Little Boren if he wanted to come with them toward the sunrise, to their cold-time lands, but Little Boren said some day he would have to return to the Place. Mala needed him. Babi, if he came back, would need him also. And so Basatzaun and the remaining people left, and Little Boren and Tsurinye were left alone together.

So perhaps it was inevitable that one day in the dry-time he would see that her belly had grown, and his thoughts would return to Mala and the Place.

"It's time," he said, and she lowered her head so her hair fell forward again, and so they packed their things and walked away together.

Possession

"Who?" Widow Klayn asked, her voice husky. "Who will die?"

Mala did not answer at first. She was still staring into the dark eyes swimming in the enormous bony face of the aurochs bull. From time to time his withers rippled and clouds of flies rose up and quickly landed again. The huge tail brushed back and forth without ceasing, swatting at his flanks. The flies buzzed and swirled.

The bull stamped his forefeet, and puffs of dust rose up around them. He blew out through his nose.

"Who?" the widow repeated, but seemed uncertain, as if she no longer knew what she had heard.

All Mala's indifferent calm vanished. She put up her hands to fend something off, something unseen.

"What is it?" Widow Klayn's eyes were wide with horror.

There was nothing to see. The bull stood his ground, staring upward. Mala shivered and fell sideways as though struck. Her head, hanging over the edge, thrashed from side to side, and an eerie keening sound came from her. Her heels drummed on the roof, leaving a series of cracked depressions in the plaster. The widow tentatively reached to touch her, but Mala's movements were so violent and unpredictable that she squatted back on her heels and stared in horror.

The roof shook. A dark woman with a fat face pushed her head out of the entrance. "What's this?" she demanded, climbing out with a deep wheezing sigh. She glowered at Mala and kicked her tentatively. "This is my home, and you're making vermin fall on my hearth."

"Something's taken her," the widow cried.

"Why do I care? She's been sitting here tens of days and I've said nothing. Mostly she doesn't make noise, so I don't mind, but now she's kicking my roof." The woman walked curiously to the edge and looked down. Widow Klayn followed.

The bull had gone.

"Well?" the woman asked. "What's this all about?"

"There was a bull; it spoke to her. It said someone would die. At least I think that's what it was."

"So? Someone's always dying. No reason to kick down my roof. Take her next door. They won't mind, they're out at the grain." She disappeared down the ladder.

Foam bubbled at the corners of Mala's mouth, and the frantic drumming of her heels increased. Widow Klayn took a deep breath and dragged her by the shoulders to the next roof. She sat by the moaning woman and asked the spirits of the air and land and water, the marsh bird, the Bull Himself, to ease this torment, but nothing seemed to relieve the pressure.

Only when the day was dying did the fit subside. Mala sat up and looked around. For the first time since the boy had died her eyes were dry.

"What was it?" Widow Klayn asked.

"Dark," Mala said. "And cold. So cold." Her voice could not have been colder when she said, "Someone will die. I'll see to it."

The Snare

The man's head was crushed. Fragments of bone and brain trickled out in a thin wash of fresh blood, so it had not been long since he was killed. Shelsan listened but heard only birds calling and wind over stone.

The women lay huddled against the gully wall. He saw the many small puncture wounds, but whoever had killed them had retrieved their arrows.

The two children were gone. The food had vanished with them.

Whatever their clan, Shelsan thought, they were a family and deserved to stay together, so he placed the bodies in a line. The ground was too hard to dig, and he had nothing with which to dig anyway, so he offered them to the vulture gods, saying: "These were hunters who did not keep the heads of their Grands, who had no Egg but the world. They should return to the air and earth on their own. It is the old way. Take them, please."

A slight breeze blew down the gully. He stayed upwind to wait in shadow, his back to the sunrise gully wall. The birds appeared early the next day, first one, then more, circling up from the lake. Gradually they descended until the boldest landed and waddled toward the bodies. The others followed and soon they were at work. With wet, tearing sounds and low gargling in their throats they tore at the skin, plucked out the eyes. Within an hour the bodies were scraps of flesh and bone. By mid-day nothing remained but clean bone and scraps of cartilage.

The birds lifted clumsily into the air, circled, and coasted away on the hot air rising above the stony ground.

He was alone beside the lake at the foot of the Mountain of Frozen Tears. Shelsan spoke to the spirits again, telling them they had done well. Then he set off toward the Place, carrying his burden of frozen tears.

He must have grown careless, for he had not yet walked half a day when a dozen of the mud people came down out of the trees in silence and seized him. They bound his arms behind his back and led him, stumbling, into the forest.

9 Now

The Media Get the Message

The news storm around Alice blew wars, recessions, and international brinksmanship right out of the global headlines.

"It won't last," Satchi said. "Tempest in a teapot."

Jones would not be sidetracked by skepticism. "You worry too much. Enjoy the moment. Alice hit a nerve, a global one."

"I don't get it," the excavator confessed. "Sure, she's unusual and deserves attention; she's exotic and scary. But she's not pretty, and she dates from the Neolithic. The public doesn't care about the Neolithic – no palaces, grave goods, treasure; no gallant warriors or gold masks. She's probably a skull wrapped in plaster, painted and decorated. Not that important, surely. We're digging a site rich in cultural history. We can learn more from phytoliths, human remains, architecture – hell, almost anything – than from one plastered skull. Damn it, Bryson, we've already seen the connections with the culture at Çatal. We might find evidence of trade between the two centers, commonality of subsistence, what they ate, how they lived, what they made. The bone evidence is already telling us about domestication and hunting, what animals were symbolically important. Archaeology isn't about flashy finds, it's about careful digging and painstaking analysis. Alice is just one more artifact, no more important than any other in terms of what it can tell us about these people. Why the fuss?"

But fuss there was. The phone in the office rang late into the night. Reporters cycled through by the hour, mingling with and opportunistically grilling other visitors. Emails of congratulation, criticism, or complaint were overwhelming the volunteers and the administrative staff. Requests for interviews poured in, and not just with Jones, with anyone – the academic specialists, the representative, students, even the kitchen workers and the guard at the gate.

Satchi and Jones watched Özgür welcome a vanload of tourists, apparently in some kind of trance. He wandered aimlessly with a beamish smile on his face and greeting everyone effusively. His occasional truculence seemed to have softened.

"The world wants magic," Jones said thoughtfully, tearing his eyes away from the representative. "There's a hunger for something different, something new, even alien. There are rumors Alice is a gift, planted here to teach mankind something essential."

"Huh? Aliens? Like the monolith in 2001? You're joking."

"Well, you have to admit she doesn't really look very human, does she?" Jones smiled. "Bright mirror eyes, head too big, funny nose, swirls and grooves in the face, small pits all over – for hair? Or something more alien, extraterrestrial, even?"

"Give me a break!" Satchi muttered.

Alice was on display. Mehmet was now posted inside the Secure Room to make sure visitors stayed behind a rope barrier. He performed these duties with enormous seriousness.

Jones decreed only a dozen people at a time could view her for no more than five minutes. A line had formed on the veranda. "Otherwise we'll never accommodate everyone."

Though Aynalı Tepe was far from Konya and the good hotels, the stream of visitors was continuing unabated into the sixth day. Parking inside the gate was full, and most had to leave their vehicles along the road outside the fence. Taxi and van operators were grateful to Jones Bey.

Lena Marie and Gayle strode through the main gate, followed by a dozen women and a couple of men. The group stopped just outside the Human Remains Lab and huddled around Lena Marie.

Jones murmured, "Dr. Troye is helping enormously. The goddess people are planning more visits, going on talk shows, blogging. She seems convinced Alice is a major discovery. Of course, eventually it'll die down and we'll drop below the radar, but later, when the documentaries come out, people will remember, don't worry." He sighed and stretched. "I'd better get going. A company that would like to help with funding will be here in a few minutes." He paused. "Remember, Satchi, the world needs its aliens, something to believe in."

Go Ask Alice

Lena Marie raised her voice. "Before we go in to go see Alice, are there any questions?" She looked each of her followers in the eye as if challenging – or daring – them to ask one.

An elderly woman in a straw hat took the bait. "Dr. Troye, why is it you believe Alice is the Goddess, and not just a piece of art?"

As a question it was such a soft and gentle lob that anyone listening might suspect Gayle had put her up to it.

Lena Marie's answer was firm. "All the iconography points to it," she said. "Her history goes far back into the Pleistocene, the Paleolithic, and Her image is buried deep in the human unconscious. One glance tells you Alice is the Terrible One. Vengeance, fear, and death are Her weapons. Her painted teeth are human. Symbolically this tells us, as it told the people who made Her, that, like the Furies in later Greek mythology, She is Avenger and Devourer. She incorporates outsiders into the group by swallowing them, bringing them into Her body. She says the coming patriarchy will not win easily! The warriors of the Bronze Age had to butcher their way to power. As Marija Gimbutas suggested, the Goddess was peaceful and benign, certainly, but I will state unequivocally that when affronted by male intrusion She bared Her teeth, and though She suffered temporary setbacks, She's been waiting in the earth all this time. Now She's returned."

The men murmured. To Satchi it sounded apprehensive.

"Well," Lena Marie said at the door to the Secure Room. "I suggest everyone prepare a question for Her. Ask silently and I'm sure She will answer. Though She can be terrible, Alice is woman-wisdom brought to light. She knows the ancient secrets, the ways of compassion and peace, of birthing and nurturing. She feeds and protects. Thus She is also the Balancer, the Even-Handed One, the Healer of individuals and the tribe."

Satchi shook his head, amazed at the sheer variety of what people wanted to believe. While he loved dirt and what it contained, he had no illusions others shared his obsessions. All these, though, the people standing in line, those gathered around Lena Marie, they had different agendas, but what bound them together was Alice.

Lena Marie concluded, "If you'll follow me, we'll go into Her presence." She knocked.

Mehmet opened the door and allowed the previous group to file out. Lena Marie led her group into the Secure Room ahead of the line.

What the Dead Bones Said

Satchi stuck his head into the Human Remains Lab to ask Lodewyk how he could work with all the noise and confusion.

The Dutchman grinned. "So far I manage to keep busy. Visitors aren't interested in my work, only Alice. Anyway, skeletons are a lot more interesting than visitors." He gestured at the bones. "This, for instance, is an infant burial from Trench One. Touching, these dead babies."

"Know what he or she died of?"

"No sign of trauma, but crowding people close together breeds communicable diseases, especially with domesticated animals nearby. So 'it' probably died of some infection. Infant mortality at this time was quite high. And it was still too young to tell whether it's a boy or a girl. Pity." He bent back to his work.

Satchi, with little to do for the moment, strolled around the lab, peering into plastic baskets full of bone fragments.

A few minutes later Lodewyk's graduate student peered through the glass of the door, mopping her red face with a bandana.

Lodewyk didn't answer her knock so she pushed the door open. Satchi saw her grin in relief at the blast of air-conditioning. "I've finished excavating the burial in Structure 1-3," she said.

"Sorry?" Lodewyk made a quick notation in his logbook and looked up.

"Structure 1-3, the house near the surface in layer one? Later than Alice, right next door? I've excavated the skeleton. Adult male, complete. Shall I bring him down?"

"Leave him. I'll come up tomorrow to see it *in situ*. Anything unusual?"

She shrugged. "Looks like he once had a pretty bad infection in his leg."

"Ah." Lodewyk looked at Satchi. "You see? Like I said, always disease."

"How do you tell?" Satchi asked.

Lodewyk replied, "Stop me if you know all this, because I tend to get a little . . . enthusiastic, but we can learn all kinds of things from bones besides sex, age, facial structure, and so on. For instance, we can determine quite a bit about an individual's lifestyle: if she was sedentary, the cross-section of the femur would be almost round; a more active person, a forager, say, would have an oblong femur, thicker front to back. It's a measure of the bone's bending strength. And then, diseases like arthritis are very visible on bones, and can tell you, for instance, if they were kneeling a lot, to grind grain, for instance. Then there's hyperostosis, an overgrowth of the bone on the top of the cranium, which can be caused by anemia, among other things. And of course teeth, don't get me started about teeth. Caries reflect diet. Poor nutrition or disease can appear in hypoplasias – grooves in the enamel. And of course with bone DNA we can discover things about relationship or hereditary diseases."

Satchi smiled. He realized Lodewyk was lecturing for the benefit of his student. "And the hole in the bone she mentioned?"

"Ah, yes. Bad infection leaves clues in the bone and gives insight into an individual's personal biography." He turned to the girl. "Is that what killed him, do you think?"

"No," she said promptly. "It had healed. I'd say it happened when he was an adolescent. This guy was an adult, somewhere between twenty and forty." She grinned sheepishly. "I haven't seen as many skeletons as Lodewyk, but I'm sure he survived the infection. He must have walked with a limp the rest of his life."

Precautions

It was a small hotel on a side street and commanded no grand view or inspiring vistas. Places like this, found in any city in the world, offered simple, fairly clean rooms and discreet, even indifferent, service. Its primary attractions were its acceptance of cash and its lack of curiosity about names.

Rolf Butcher gazed out his window at a small park, with its few listless trees and dry earth. Two benches, both unoccupied this time of day, were all the park offered in the way of amenities.

One of the cell phones he had purchased for cash two weeks ago at a stall in Harem on the Asian side of Istanbul purred softly and he let the curtain drop.

"Yes."

"I received your message." The voice was soft and cultivated, with a strong accent. Its faint warble showed he had taken the precaution of having it electronically altered.

"Yes."

"I would like to meet her."

"All right. What's your offer?"

The man said a number. Rolf restrained the impulse to whistle. "American?"

"That is correct."

Rolf doubled the figure. "Two separate events. Half now, half when you two meet. Introductions are expensive. No records."

After a moment's hesitation, the other agreed.

"It will take time to arrange," Rolf said. "By the way, what changed your mind?"

"Pardon?"

"About phones. You said you only trusted the mails."

"Ah. Things change."

"I see. A month to six weeks, then."

"I am a patient man," the collector assured him. The line went dead.

Rolf shrugged and tossed his own voice-altering device on the bed.

He then made a call of his own. "There's only one key," he said. "Find a way." He switched the phone off and gazed out the window for a few moments. The day was waning. The streetlights came on.

Rolf loved this country. He loved the wide sweep of its sky, the vast plains and attractive mountains. He loved the seemingly endless string of resorts along the Emerald Coast where the wealthy came to swim, soak up sun, and spend money. He loved the fact that Turkey was rich in history and archaeological sites. Anatolia was itself swimming in antiquities, many of them unregistered. To an expert like Rolf they meant profit, even the ones without provenance. Even the fakes. Or, perhaps, *especially* the fakes.

Alice, of course, was no fake. He was certain of that. He'd examined her carefully, seen enough of the soil, the fine cracks in her plaster, the idiosyncratic but Anatolian style. Alice really had been brought up from the depth of space and time.

He removed the SIM card from the phone, melted it in the ashtray with a Bic lighter, flushed the remains down the toilet, and went to the park. After strolling around its perimeter for a few minutes he discreetly dropped the cell phone into a trashcan and walked toward the commercial district, humming the theme of "La Vergine degli angeli" from Verdi's *La Forza del Destino*.

The global media storm had presented him with both a problem and a blessing: on the one hand it brought Alice great recognition and elevated her worth; on the other hand it made her too famous to handle easily should he be so fortunate as to get his hands on her.

So he was taking extra precautions.

Calamity

Sometimes Satchi loitered in Human Remains, telling himself the burials interested him. He'd begun to imagine a life for these people, how they had lived and died, how the one with a bad leg had been infected and managed to survive with a limp in a place and time when people had begun to depend on agriculture and the backbreaking labor it entailed.

Of course it had nothing to do with the fact that he could covertly watch Dr. Orbay through the glass partition between the labs. She was in three-quarter view, tapping on her laptop or examining fragments of obsidian under a binocular microscope. True, there was something about the way she pushed that strand of stray hair behind her ear as she bent over the microscope that drew his eye, but his interests in the Human Remains Lab were certainly purely scientific.

The site closed to visitors at five o'clock. As soon as the last ones were gone Afet would go into the Secure Room to study Alice's eyes, taking her tidy notes in a small, spiral-bound notebook. Satchi, bent over Lodewyk's shoulder as the Dutchman explained the arcana of porotic hyperostosis as evidence of iron deficiency anemia, would follow her with his eyes when she returned to Lithics and sat once more at her workbench.

Her concentration was fierce. An hour could easily pass while she motionlessly examined a small fragment of obsidian. Then suddenly she would stand up to stretch, clasping her hands together over her head. Her long black hair would cascade down the line of her spine when she twisted sideways twice.

When Satchi caught himself staring like that, he would mutter something vague at Lodewyk and walk resolutely up the mound. He had assigned Ben to help Francy finish the excavation of Structure 2-

1A, increasingly known as The Rabbit Hole, and that was surely more important than mooning over the lovely Turkish lithics specialist.

The excavation was crowded. One crew was expanding north toward the storage room. Ben and Francy meanwhile had cleared the plastered floor and the edges of the elevated platforms. Satchi watched them begin work on the obsidian cache near the hearth.

Francy pried up a flake of plaster. "Like a home safe. Treasure in the floor . . . What have we here?"

Ben leaned over. "Where?"

"There, see the three layers of plaster? It's burnt. There was a fire."

"This was the hearth area. There's always a fire."

"No, it's too big. After the fire they replastered, see?"

"I see. So?"

She glared at him. "How do I know? It's a bit of history. Probably the roof caught fire or something. It wasn't enough to destroy the house, so they weren't intentionally terminating it. They put out the fire and replastered. We can say that much, at least: there was a fire."

She called Lodewyk's student to start excavating the two infant burials.

"While she's working why don't you leave the obsidian cache and clear the east wall," Satchi suggested. "I've a hunch we're going to find something. This structure was special." With the tip of his trowel he scraped along the top of the wall, which had been knocked down to about 150 centimeters above floor level, clear now since the burial of the man with the hole in his leg had been removed. "You can see dozens of layers of plaster," he observed. "Mellaart would undoubtedly have called this a 'shrine,' especially after you found those two aurochs skulls on the floor near one of the support posts."

Francy and Ben chipped away at the dirt. When they found small fragments of colored plaster they passed them up to the other excavators, students, local men, and international volunteers. When they had reached a couple of centimeters from the wall Satchi began to fret, finally squatting in the Rabbit Hole to examine the dirt himself. Sometimes he used a magnifying glass to study the texture.

"What are you looking for?" Francy asked.

Satchi only grunted. "I'll take it from here."

"Something wrong with the way I'm working?" she asked, wiping the back of her hand over her forehead, leaving a streak of dust.

"No, why? Oh, no, sorry." Satchi backed away and waved her forward. He discretely watched as she went back to work. After a few moments he said, "Here, take my lucky trowel."

"What about me?" Ben muttered.

"If there's enough room by Lodewyk's student, you could continue excavating the cache."

"All right." Ben was clearly pleased to be given charge of his own excavation.

Francy scraped, pried, and brushed away the soil. It was late when she uncovered the first glimpse of plaster.

"Paint," Satchi breathed.

"Red," Francy added. "Looks like we do have wall art."

"And I've got a real treasure here," Ben announced, gesturing at his small excavation. Lying in it was an enormous obsidian core.

"DANTE gives two side chambers 2-1B to the west, and 2-1C to the north," Satchi said. "Nothing special about that. But there's Alice and now wall art. So there's something special about this place, all right."

It was going to be slow work to clean it and the hour was late, so he told them to close down for the night.

Later, when he passed the Lithics Lab, Afet looked up and smiled. Her teeth were perfect white.

Satchi Bennett could not imagine anything more catastrophic than the complex cocktail of emotions that struck him in that moment. He fled to the men's dormitory and skipped dinner. Only later did he venture out to attend Dr. Troye's evening lecture.

The Leisure of the Theory Class

The Seminar Room was crowded. Lena Marie's followers had already captured the prime seats in front, and Satchi had to content himself with a seat near the door in the last row of white plastic chairs.

He looked around, half-hoping to see the stone specialist, relieved when he didn't.

"I'm certainly gratified to see so many people here," Lena Marie began. "Gayle, lights, please."

The screen lit up with an image of Alice facing the camera. The flash had caught the mirrors, swamping detail around them. Lena Marie paused dramatically, letting the image sink in.

"This is Alice," she said slowly. "Most of you have already met Her, have spoken to Her. She is returned to the world, and not a moment too soon! We see the signs of our own ruin all around us. I won't dwell on the ecological degradation of Mother Earth, massive displacements of people, ongoing genocides, religious conflicts, or the growing gulf between rich and poor. You know all about these things.

"But our crisis is more than political, it is spiritual. In the millennia since Alice was created in the image of the Mother Spirit, we've lost our way and given in to unbridled greed and patriarchal excess."

Satchi began to fidget. His interest was the science. Dr. Troye was supposed to be an expert on mythology and folklore but she appeared to be giving a New Age political harangue.

He was chewing on a knuckle, only half-listening, when a presence loomed behind him. He turned to see the representative, who gave him a brief smile. His good humor was almost contagious.

Almost, but not quite, because Afet herself tiptoed in on his heels and found a place behind Satchi's chair. He gave her an awkward smile, twisted halfway around, but she was listening intently to the lecture and did not seem to notice. A pair of faint lines appeared between her strong, black eyebrows. He wasn't sure if it was disapproval or concentration.

". . . patterns of female representation," Lena Marie was saying. The images flashed on the screen beside her. "We see this in the figurines, for instance, the famous one from Çatal, of a fat woman, seated on a kind of chair, her hands on the backs of leopards, or another here, cupping her breasts. Yet another shows the fat woman from the front in the stereotypical pose, but her back is a skeleton. What are we to make of this? She is life-in-death and death-in-life, of course. She is both immortal, fecund and nurturing, and a reminder of our mortality.

"Which brings us back to Alice."

The face returned to the screen. She turned and tapped it. "The nose, for example, is vaguely animal. What is it? Snout? Muzzle? Beak? It is not uncommon to find masks or other depictions of half-human, half-animal creatures. Humans evolving before our eyes out of the animal world, as indeed we did."

Satchi was finding it hard to concentrate on what she was saying. Something about half-humans? A faint delicate, floral aroma surrounded him. It certainly wasn't the representative, who smelled mostly of Turkish tobacco.

He forced his attention back to the lecture.

". . . snake, bird, leopard, even cow."

So she was continuing with the animal theme. What kind of animal would Afet be? Something slender and graceful, a doe or a water bird, perhaps.

"These animals were sacred. They died that humans might live, and they always came back to life again. They meant abundance. But as we began to domesticate them, especially the caprids and ovids, the goats and sheep, they lost their supernatural status. They became like us. Ordinary."

Afet stirred and moved further into the room. Satchi breathed out slowly. He could no longer smell her perfume.

Suddenly he was angry. He'd been married. That was an aggravation he certainly didn't need again. In fact, the last thing he needed was a woman in his life. They were a distraction. Fortunately his wife had left him and he hadn't regretted it. She must have found someone else by now.

The image on screen changed to the back of Alice's head. "Here we see the pockmarks suggesting there was a wig, hat, or some other kind of decoration for the head. Although She is strange looking, we must remember this was a living being in its day, an otherworldly Presence in the human, domesticated domain. To Her makers She was alive. But we should not expect Her to be realistic. She was a manifestation of the spiritual realm, but human too, and She had something on Her head. Further research may reveal what that was."

Satchi glanced sideways again. Afet was brushing her hair back over her ear. She put the tip of her fingernail between her lips. There was an extraordinarily intense quality to her listening.

"As a quasi-human, quasi-spirit, She had the power to reconcile dualities: life and death, man and woman, night and day, peace and war. She still does."

This produced a smattering of applause, mostly from the front row.

They were plunged then into a series of images from other cultures, other times. Lena Marie showed them plastered skulls with painted eyes from 'Ain Ghazal, figurines from the Ukraine and Greece, masks from tribal cultures today, crude folk toys from Mexico, Paleolithic "Venus" figurines. Sometimes Satchi could actually see the resemblances Lena Marie insisted were there. Mostly he could not.

Finally he stood and edged his way toward the entrance. Afet, against the back wall, was listening to the lecture with a rapt expression.

Satchi snorted quietly. Best to stay away from women.

He went back to the dormitory. When the others with whom he shared the room returned he pretended to be asleep. He watched the quality of the light outside change with the hours. Finally he fell into a troubled sleep. There were birds everywhere.

Speed Dial

Right after breakfast Özgür grabbed a glass of tea, lit a cigarette, and pulled out his cell phone.

He'd taken to pacing up and down the veranda. The visitors sometimes complained about the smoke that trailed behind him, but he paid no attention. Aynalı Tepe was beginning to rival other famous sites in Turkey, Hittite Hattusas, for instance, or even Ephesus. Jones was talking of building a museum. This was Özgür's realm, and he could smoke if he wanted to. Others might not acknowledge it publicly, but here he was king.

As soon as the archaeologists had brought up the remarkable find he had called his cousin Nevra. It was the day the television people were first here. The head, he told his cousin, was much more important than any obsidian mirror, and he wanted credit. "I found Aynalı," he insisted, and Nevra answered, "Of course, Özgür, of course." Nevra often had that patronizing tone, but what did it matter? He would get the credit. In the middle of that call Bennett had come out and glared at him, like he was making too much noise. Perhaps it was because he was so excited. He had a right to be excited then, and he had a right now. After all, this time the mirrors weren't just for putting on makeup or whatever the people back then had done. This time they were part of something else.

Jones had dismissed his first mirror. Özgür had studied a couple in the Ankara Museum and thought Jones might be right, the mirrors couldn't be that important. They were quite dark and murky. Mirrors shouldn't be black. But then that woman had shown the image of the Goddess, as she called her, and the mirrors were very bright.

He pressed the button to speed-dial his cousin. There was something special about those mirrors.

Not the Territory

The flow of visitors took up again in the morning. Lena Marie and Gayle had settled in for a lengthy stay. Stachi devoted himself to the ongoing excavation.

That afternoon they were ready to clear the wall. During the previous days' excavation they had removed several buckets of small plaster fragments, probably from the destroyed upper section. The conservator would see if she could piece them together to recreate the painting, but from their size and condition Satchi didn't hold out much hope.

On the remaining lower wall, however, the plaster was in good shape, and the dirt came away easily.

The spot of red paint proved to be part of a small rectangle inset with white squares. Little by little they cleared enough to reveal a double row of such rectangles.

"Have you seen anything like this?" Satchi asked.

"The map from Çatalhöyük," Francy answered immediately.

Ben said, "Don't be silly."

"Why is it silly?" Francy demanded. "Red squares with insets."

"Well, for one thing, this isn't Çatal."

"If it looks like the map to me, it looks like the map. Get a life."

Ben couldn't suppress his grin. It always happened like this when he argued with her. "You're talking about the so-called map of the town, the one Mellaart thought contained a volcano and that is probably a leopard skin?"

"Yeah, that one."

"OK." He cocked his head and squinted at the pattern on the wall. "But it could be a board game," he suggested. "What do you think, Satchi?"

"Wall art isn't my field, but it does look a bit like the one at Çatal."

"Calico?" Francy suggested. "Tablecloth from an Italian restaurant? Anyway, the pattern is cut off at the top."

"OK," Satchi traced it in the air. "We have two rows of seven, hand print at the end. White squares inside the red. Some black wavy lines along the bottom near floor level. The top row is cut off, so, yes, there could have been more rows." He shrugged. "We'll never know unless we found enough plaster in the fill to account for the rest of the wall and Hellä can reconstruct it."

Francy shook her head. "The pieces are really small. I think they hauled it away. Some day maybe we'll find it in a dump somewhere."

"But it is a painting, isn't it? We've found art."

"And some amazing obsidian, and bull's heads," Ben added. He gestured at Lodewyk and his student bent over the two small open graves. "Not to mention two infant burials."

Lodewyk glanced up and indicated the tiny bones with the tip of his trowel. "This one was really young, probably just a few days, if not stillborn. It was wrapped in woven grass. The other's a toddler, legs tied back to make the body smaller. They placed a mat and a shell on it." He stood. "OK, let's get them down to the lab."

Francy's grin grew a little wild. "I bet this was a haunted house. Everything, the wall paintings, the obsidian, those burials, the fire, it all means something." She took off her cap and her wild red hair exploded. "Boo!" she shouted at Ben.

What's Bred in the Bone

Satchi stepped into Human Remains. In the next room Afet stood over the huge obsidian core, the fingertips of one hand resting on it as if she were absorbing knowledge directly into her body. Satchi thought in truth she probably was.

He tore his eyes away. "What do you know about this guy?" he asked the specialist about the male skeleton reassembled on a table.

"There's a saying," Lodewyk told him. "'What's bred in the bone will come out in the flesh.' I think here it's the other way around: the flesh did this to the bone, so now we can read that he suffered from periostial reaction and inflammation. That hole in the tibia was caused by draining pus."

The hole was the size of a quarter and perfectly round. "Looks like a bullet hole," Satchi said.

Lodewyk laughed. "Not a gun, of course, but something broke the skin of his lower leg. The wound got infected. Maybe he just fell, but it's more likely he was shot by an arrow."

It happened that Afet looked straight into Satchi's eyes the moment Lodewyk spoke the word "arrow."

10 Then

Full Circle

Little Boren's wound healed, and though he walked with a slight limp, he was strong again, and a man, so a few days after Basatzaun and the others left, he said, "We'll just walk toward the warm and the sunset and find the Place." He was more hopeful than certain, for there were gaps in his memory, but it didn't seem important that he couldn't remember details of his journey here. He was with Tsurinye, who smiled and took his hand and gestured for him to lead, saving her words.

They left the green hills and cool woods and descended along the river until they could turn toward the warm. Along the way they gathered wild grasses and nuts. He built snares the way he had seen Babi do, and sometimes caught rabbits or birds, and they feasted; other times they ate grubs or snails or she knew where to find tubers. Living came easily. There were signs of food everywhere: plants ripening in their time, the presence of water, the trampled ground or scat that told them where the animals were going, and why. Each day they would spend a pleasant hour or two seeing to their needs. The rest of the time they walked without haste or concern. He was careful of her and her growing belly, but if he made too much fuss she frowned and pushed him away.

After they had walked along the edge of the swamp, now dried to hard dust, there came a day when he sniffed at the air. "It will rain soon."

She only smiled, and he knew that he was stating something obvious to her. Yet she made no reproach. He was from the sky, and if he wanted to tell her something she already knew, so be it.

Little Boren didn't know what to make of this, so he put it aside with a smile of his own.

By then they had reached Dak's Cave, where Babi had told him the story of Water Bird, and of the Giant people who had driven her into exile, and how she built the Nest. "We stop here," he said.

He made a fire, and they ate.

Afterward they sat with their backs against the cliff and watched the clouds piling up over the distant mountains. He scratched in the sand in front of him and found scraps of frozen tears arranged in a semicircle, like a crescent moon, and remembered placing them there. How long ago had it been? He thought of time, the moons growing and dying, his change from child to man. He touched his face with a fingertip, the face that had made him jump when he'd seen it reflected in the river it had grown so dark and hairy. It was the face of a demon or a god, yet it was his face, too. He had changed, and could not go back to being a boy.

"Babi told me stories in this place," he said, rearranging the fragments. "That was on our way to the Mountain of Frozen Tears, which I have never seen. Babi must have gone there and returned home by now; I will be glad to see him again. But I am thinking about life, Tsurinye, about changing. What we call time is a strange thing. It has always been coming, and going, and coming back again, like the moon. But there is something else about it, something I don't understand. Water Bird made the Nest, and the world keeps changing and not going back. Do you know the Grands are buried in the floor, many of them, one after another. They don't come back, Tsurinye. The Grands are there, but they don't change. Their bones are always the same, and I think the Place must be higher every time we take down a house and put up a new one. If the Place gets taller, then it doesn't go and come and go again, like the moon. I don't understand this."

After thinking it over he kicked sand over his semicircle of stones and sighed.

"I've seen the Giant people, Tsurinye, the ones that drove Water Bird away from the unchanging place, and they are just people like us, even though they are fierce, and shot me through the leg."

His language was now a mix of hers and his, and she understood him. So he told her the story of Water Bird, and the Nest, and of First Egg, the Place where they were going. As he finished his tale the wind blew colder, and clouds covered the sky, and the world went dark. Thunder crashed around them and lit them up in terrific wild flashes of red light. The sky opened.

The rain put out the fire and washed sheet after sheet of dirt and sand over it, and the place where he had buried his semicircle of stones, and they moved back into the cave where it was dry, and there they slept.

Harvest

It was the first rain, and the harvest was not quite over.

Shelsan huddled near the wall of a round, leaky hut dug an arm's length into the ground. The crash of the storm against the thatch was deafening. Water seeped through the walls, and the trickles carried small rivulets of dirt to pool near his feet.

He shared the round building with seven others, including the two children from the Mountain of Frozen Tears. They were all slumped in silent exhaustion. Each night their arms and hands were intricately bound so they could only bring their hands to their mouths. Their ankles were tied together, fixed with braided flax cord to a central wooden support post.

He stared out through gaps in the wattle at the circle of rude hovels around an open space. He could count them on the fingers of two hands: nine, including this one. Behind them the animal pens were crammed with beasts. A rude palisade surrounded the whole miserable place.

They'd been forced to work, dragged forth every morning and returned every evening to be tied up like animals to sleep in their own waste. During the day they cut sheaves, piled them up, bound them, and carried them to the village past the burial ground, for these people laid their dead in fields and not in the house as was proper.

These people grew their grain all around the village and not half a day's walk away as they did at the Place, where the stands of wheat were supplements to what they gathered. They had cleared away useful plants to make way for the grain on which they depended. He'd seen no stores of wild plants at all. With so much growing nearby like this, he thought, they should have enough, more than enough.

Yet they always wanted more. The village was overrun with little ones and animals crying, bleating, and mewling for food. For nearly a moon now he had passed his days bent near the ground swinging a curved stick embedded with flint, cutting the stalks close to the ground. Few seeds fell from the stalks; instead of collecting seed in baskets as Mala did when she went to her stands, these people carried the stalks to the central place through an opening in the wooden palisade and beat them, sending seeds and chaff flying. It was heavy labor, but they acted as if it were a celebration, as if this was the way it should be, and despised Shelsan for not knowing how to cut. They hit him until he learned. "We need more food for the children," they said in their rough variation of Basatzaun's language. Though he could barely understand them, the meaning was clear enough. "To feed the animals. More. Work faster."

The next morning the rain stopped, and they were dragged back to the fields under heavy, low clouds, but the remaining grain was flattened into the mud and already beginning to rot. The men stood around gesturing, ignoring the slaves. Finally they were dragged back to the hut and tied as usual. Then the men entered the biggest house and discussed all day. Shelsan could hear their angry voices.

One of the women brought bowls of food. Otherwise the slaves were left alone.

Shelsan watched. Late in the morning the men came out frowning. "There will not be enough," the one in the tall crow-feather headdress shouted at the women and children. "So we must be strong. We will make sacrifice against thin bellies come wet-time, we will ask the gods for help. We will offer them something good." He paused, his hands outstretched, dropped them and smiled. "But for now the harvest is over. Tonight we celebrate."

To Shelsan the cheering that followed lacked enthusiasm, but he was a stranger here, a slave, and perhaps could not know the true depth of the people's joy.

By then the clouds had passed away and the earth breathed out a wet, uneasy mist into a thin, pale sky. This valley seemed to trap the mist hovering over the empty fields, the thick, dark mud, and the rotting wooden palisade. He wondered if this fence was intended to keep slaves in or strangers out? Then he remembered Basatzaun telling him that sometimes his people raided places like this.

Late in the afternoon the celebrations began with drumming and strange, skirling singing. A line of masked dancers snaked around a fire. Toward dusk the men tied a sheep and two goats between two posts near the fire and took turns chopping at their necks with stone axes, and their animal screams blended with increasingly frenzied human cries of dancers imitating the slaughter.

Two men came into the hut. One squeezed the muscles of Shelsan's leg and calf while the other forced his mouth open and examined his tongue and teeth. They spoke rapidly and laughed. After they were gone Shelsan spit on their footprints in the dirt floor. The other slaves tried to move away from him, as if they knew that something had made him dangerous.

As dark was falling a man brought him something to drink. He turned his head away. The man pulled his hair, tipping his head back, and forced liquid into his mouth. He recognized it from the hunters' ceremonial building. It burned. He swallowed some, and spit the rest in the man's face. The man drew back his hand to strike him, then laughed and went away.

He fought to keep strange images from his mind and focused on the fire, which grew in size and power as darkness fell and the smoke from roasting meat rose into the night. The feasting began. Some stopped dancing to eat, and others took their places, grew wilder and more daring, leaping over the fire and kicking up sparks that flew and swirled this way and that.

Heat from the fire washed into the hut in waves. The thatch had dried, and the rivulets of mud that had trickled down the walls only yesterday were solid ovals on the floor by his feet. Soon all the slaves were soaked with sweat.

Shelsan watched the dancers for a long while, despite the heat. The dancers wound between the two killing posts, leaping higher, spinning faster. They ran in lines and leapt the fire, and the swarms of sparks filled the air like fireflies.

When they began fixing new ropes to the posts, though, to prepare for the final sacrifice, he knew who it would be.

Pinnak and Temkash

Pinnak and Temkash were pushing their way through dense underbrush toward the river when they heard the bull. They were far downstream of the Place, approaching the mouth where the river spread out into a broad, shallow lake.

For the past dozen days fires had been sending up lines of smoke that darkened several parts of the circle of sky. Then last night it had rained hard, and the smoke was gone this morning. Now the day had been hot and already the underbrush was dry again, the leaves wilted and gray.

"There should be more rain." Pinnak was lifting aside a strand of willow when the sound came and he stopped dead.

"Bull," Temkash whispered. "Big one, from his sound."

Pinnak moved forward. The willows ended. What should have been a lake was a vast desolate expanse of cracked mud. The river had dried to a weak trickle.

The bull faced them, standing in mud up to his fetlocks. His head was massive, his horns broad; one tip was cracked.

Pinnak backed away. The bull snorted and lifted one forefoot with a sucking sound. Underneath the mud was thick and wet. "It's the god," Pinnak said. "The biggest of them all." He put out his hands in supplication.

"Don't move," Temkash breathed.

"I'm not."

The bull lifted the other forefoot and pawed at the air. Again he blew air from his nostrils. Somewhere overhead an eagle screamed. Pinnak backed into the willows.

The bull stepped forward daintily, raising his hooves and pushing them back down into the mud. He stopped a few body-lengths from the two men. His brown eyes were large, liquid, and malevolent; this was a warning.

After a long beat during which neither man breathed, the bull turned and walked with great dignity toward the trickle of water from the river, stepped up its course onto gravel, and slowly receded into the distance.

"What did he want?" Pinnak asked. His voice shook.

Temkash frowned. "There is a change coming," he said. "Beware. You heard the eagle."

"The rains? He means the rains?" Fear shook Pinnak's voice. The Place suffered terribly when there wasn't enough water. "But it rained last night."

"Not for long," Temkash replied. "Not enough. Look at the sky. It will be some time before there is rain again."

Pinnak shivered. "Can't you do something?"

The Pretender waved his hand. "I'm a healer." He spoke as if that said it all.

Pinnak shook himself and regarded the wasteland, his hands on his plump hips. Pinnak had never suffered from a drought. "We should grow more food ourselves. We don't have enough for the cold-time, and look at this!"

"You did not bring me all this way to discuss food, nor rain, nor visitations of bull gods," Temkash said. "You knew it was dry. It is the same as last year."

"No, it's more dry than last year. The rain is already later. We must do something. That's what the bull was saying to me. We must change our ways."

From the way he waited, arms folded across his chest, Temkash was neither agreeing nor disagreeing.

"Your half-sister," Pinnak began tentatively.

"Your cousin," Temkash replied.

"She's planning something."

"What do you know of this?"

Pinnak started across the plain. After a moment Temkash followed. They stopped far from the line of dying willows. "The Widow Klayn says Mala is not right in her head. Not since Shelsan and the boy left. Not since the little one . . ."

Temkash controlled himself. The little one had been a problem ever since he'd fought the Sun Demon. "She speaks against me," he said. "Though my half-sister. She's angry because of the boy. But Sun Demon took him. There was nothing to be done. Nothing."

"But Shelsan has become his father, and he is of the Locust Clan."

"What of this? You were speaking of Mala, and Widow Klayn."

"Mala is not right in the head. I am Pinnak, her cousin, but *she* lives in the house of First Grand. When he comes back, Shelsan will be Head and will become a Grand. That is not right. He is old and follows the old ways, but the Place is changing, Temkash. You know this as well as I. There are many people and many Eggs in the Place, perhaps too many. They squabble over clay to make brick. They squabble over who is crossing their roof, who harvests their grain, who has fed or stolen their goat. Life is difficult in the Place these times. Do you not feel it?"

Temkash walked a few paces toward the sunrise, then back toward the sunset, deep in thought. "What you say is true, Pinnak. What do you propose?"

"Someone must guide the people, tell them what to do," Pinnak said gravely. "One must be above the others, as the gods are above men. It's the only way."

Temkash almost smiled. "And who would it be, this man who will tell the People what to do?"

Long Road

The frenzied beat of the harvest festival drums had become a loud, unending din of two hands or more of people pounding on posts, animal skulls, and stones. Sharp screams shot like arrows from one side to the other. Once or twice a child wandered too close to the fire and had to be dragged out, crying in pain.

The dancers replaced their small masks with grotesque, oversized animal heads that mixed antlers and feathers, staring eyes and gaping teeth. The masks trailed trains of straw and flax that swirled and waved in the air. When dragged through the fire they caught burst into flame and sizzled up to the mask, and the dancer would scream in pain or fear. This amused the others, who bent double and slapped their legs.

When the two men who had examined him earlier pushed aside the ragged hanging over the door, Shelsan's eyes narrowed. His nerves were tight as the string of a fire bow. They undid his feet and roughly hauled him upright. He let his weight sag, as though through fear or exhaustion, and they had to drag him.

One of the children screamed, and the men turned to see flames licking through the wattle. The roof thatch caught with a loud whoosh and the small room filled with smoke. Shelsan kicked hard, connecting with someone. There was a grunt and the hands holding him fell away.

He backed toward the flames. The heat was intense but he pushed his bound elbows toward them. The flax rope caught, sputtered, caught again. He gritted his teeth against the pain. The smell of his own charred flesh made him gag, but he remained until the smoking fiber fell away. It seemed everyone was screaming, and the room swirled with shapes flickering in and out of sight in the flame-lit smoke.

Wall posts and wattle collapsed in a shower of sparks. Three quarters of the building was ablaze, and the fire was spreading fast. Shelsan moved away from the heat and tripped over the boy. He picked him up and the rope holding his feet suddenly gave way, burned through. Holding the screaming boy close to his body, Shelsan sprinted three paces toward the wall of flames and leapt up and through.

He landed in chaos. Clouds of choking smoke spackled with sparks rippled across the village, obscuring the fire itself. The gods, those from below the earth, the fire gods and the earth gods, possessed men and women alike. Most had thrown away their masks and stumbled blindly into one another, shouting incoherently. Children cowered away from the flames or lay trampled in the dust.

Those same gods were with him. The boy had fallen into silence against his shoulder. He drifted here and there with the rushing mob, but no one noticed. When he had made his way outside the circle of huts and past the animal pens, he eased carefully through a rotten section of the palisade to freedom. From the glow of the burning village he could see he and the boy were in the field where the mud people buried the dead.

Homecoming

Mala crouched in her home, surrounded by her losses. She counted them, over and over, the Grands buried to the cold, to the sunrise and to the sunset, the little ones under the hearth. First Grand, First Egg; Second Grand, First Egg; Distaff Second Grand, First Egg; Third Grand or Distaff Third Grand, Second Egg, or was it First? There were so many! Often she lost count and had to start again.

The rain had come and gone. She had forgotten to close the entrance and water had poured in. Now it was drying, and the room, which once had seemed so spacious it could accommodate four hands of people for Temkash's ceremony . . . Temkash! Though he was family, he did not speak truth. She had known this as soon as the Bull spoke to her, had said someone would die. For Mala, too many had died already; her heart had shriveled. She put her hand over her breastbone and felt it beating there, steady as the solstice drum, powered by her anger, which was a hard, black frozen tear, like that mirror they had found after the ceremony. That mirror was her heart, black and hard and shiny. It reflected darkly whatever it saw, stuck into the wall plaster in the niche next to Grand's skull. Shelsan had wrapped the skull in fresh plaster before he left, but it was blind. The mirror, though, stared into the room and saw everything that happened there. It was staring at her now.

She knew, sudden as the sharp forked strike of lighting in the night, that Temkash had dropped that thing deliberately for her to find, that it was not her heart at all, it was his eye left to watch her. He knew everything she did and thought. She could not hide, not even here, in the dark with only those few stars above the entrance for light. Their light caught the mirror where it was, creating a faint glow. She stood in sudden rage and ripped it from the wall, knocking it sideways.

It flew, hit the horns of the great bull fixed into the roof post, and fractured. Two pieces fell to the floor. She kicked them away.

The fight went out of her and she slumped. For a long time she crouched on the floor between the two sleeping platforms and stared up into the entrance. Stars wheeled away, and were replaced by others.

A shape appeared there, barely visible. It leaned down toward her. "Mami? Babi?"

"Who are you?" Her voice shook. "What are you?"

"Don't you know me?" the shape said, stirring above the opening. "Mami?"

"Little Boren?" Little Boren had gone with Shelsan on his Walk of the World, and they had not returned. He was dead.

"Yes," he said. "Little Boren."

Mala stood. "Come," she said, though it wasn't possible. The Bull had told her someone would die, and she was sure it was Little Boren. Or Shelsan. Or both.

"I'm not alone."

"Come," she repeated. "Wait, not alone?"

She went poked in the hearth with a stick. "Not alone," she muttered. "Not alone. It can't be Little Boren. Not alone, then with Shelsan. He left with Shelsan, he should be back with him."

She turned over ash with the stick. There must be a coal in there, a small lump of charcoal she could coax back into life. She had cooked a meal, had she not? She couldn't remember, but it must be so. She breathed into the hearth, and ash swirled around her like a flight of midges. A faint hint of warmth reached her cheek. She blew again and saw a faint orange gleam. She broke off clumps of dried dung and crumbled the fragments near that small source of warmth, and at last something flickered into life. She fed it more clumps and squatted back with a sigh. Soon there were flames, and smoke curling out from under the lip of the opening in front. When the fire was going, she lit a few oil lamps and put them around the room, smoothed back her hair and called out, "Come."

Little Boren climbed backward down the ladder, and she saw from the side of his face who it was, but when he turned she gave a gasp. "I thought I knew your voice, but this is Vulture Demon come into my home." She made gestures against the evil.

"No, I'm truly Little Boren, Mami." He stood at the bottom of the ladder looking at her. "You know me. You are my Mami."

"You have the form of Little Boren, but not the face. That is the face of Vulture Demon."

The loops and tangents smudged by his faint beard were strange and frightening. His hair was long and knotted, too, and he was too big, filling the space under the roof entrance. "Yet I am he." He turned the right side of his face to her again.

Mala's grief, which had given way to fear, now gave way to joy, and she fell to sobbing with the sheer relief of it. "Ah," she said, coming to him. She laid her cheek on his left shoulder, then her other cheek on his right. He did the same. "You are Little Boren, but you are not." She kept her eyes closed and touched the terrifying side of his face with trembling fingertips, tracing the line of his nose, the arch of his eyes, his chin.

"Yes, Mami. I am changed. Open your eyes. Look at me."

She opened her eyes and stared hard. "Who has done this?"

"My mate."

"Mate?" She stepped back. "Not Shelsan?"

"No, Mami, not Shelsan. He is here, is he not?

Mala frowned. "Here? No, not here. He was with you."

Little Boren looked grave, but after a moment he brightened. "He's delayed, that's all."

Mala said, "And this mate of yours, she's not from the Place, surely. A stranger?"

"Not to me, Mami, and soon she will not be a stranger to you. Her name is Tsurinye, which means White in her language."

Mala looked at the entrance. "Call her."

Little Boren did, and Tsurinye climbed down awkwardly. He gave her his hand to descend the final step and she stood shyly before Mala.

Mala sniffed, then touched the girl's face and hair. "She's going to have a child. Yours?"

"Yes, Mami."

Mala sniffed again, smiled, and embraced the girl, pressing cheek to shoulder. After a quick look at Little Boren the girl did the same.

Mala offered them cold wheat cakes and they ate in silence.

"Tell me of Shelsan," Mala said at last. Her joy had turned cold in her breast again.

"He went to get Frozen Tears for Temkash nearly two moons ago at least. I don't remember well because I was sick."

"Sick?"

"Arrow wound. Tsurinye cured me. She is a great healer, Mami."

Mala smiled sadly, thinking that she had need of a healer, that she had not been right since her men had left. But this girl was a stranger, and not of the People. What would Pinnak and the others say? Her mind began to wander, and she lapsed into silence.

Later, she said, as if to herself, "It has not been good here."

Counting the Dead

Shelsan carried the boy through the night. At dawn he fell exhausted in a grove of pines and slept, despite the throbbing of his burns. They had come far from the village. He hoped far enough.

Later he looked at the child lying on his side, his knees drawn up and his hands pressed together before his face, and knew at once he was dead.

He left the body for the vultures and walked swiftly on, knowing the vultures might well bring the people who grew their food. His hands and forearms ached from the burns, but they would heal quickly and he ignored the pain.

His captors had brought him three day's walk toward sunrise. If he went the other way he should come back to the Mountain of Frozen Tears, where he could find another core to replace what they had taken.

His first task was to find some stone suitable for making into cutting edges. He wandered along a creek bank until he found a boulder. It was not ideal, but would do for now. With a rounded hammer stone he chipped until he had a cutting edge he could grip by the back.

He used this to cut a heap of tough grass, and spent much of the afternoon weaving the stalks together to make a carrying basket. When he was satisfied, he filled it with such nuts and tubers as he could gather and felt would travel. The next day he cut and peeled rounds of bark and tied it into a cylinder closed at the bottom. Braided grasses worked as a sling, and he could now carry his tools over his shoulder. More of the plant material made sandals; they would not last long, but he could always make more as needed on the way. It took time, but allowed him to rest. Whenever an opportunity presented itself he cut branches and made a staff, an ax handle, a spear. He worked on these as well whenever he paused.

On the second day he found the skull and antlers of an unfamiliar kind of deer. He broke off one of the antler tines and had a fine tool for pressure flaking. This too went into his kit. It would be useful when he had some frozen tears to work into real blades and arrowheads.

That afternoon he trapped three rabbits. After he had eaten them he prepared the skins. It would take a lot of skins to make a cloak against the growing cold, but he had time.

When he reached the mountain and saw the scattered bones of the dead boy's family, he felt the sudden weight of all the dead heavy inside him, and his steps dragged. He crossed the islands and collected a magnificent core of frozen tears, better than the one the villagers had taken. It was more than enough to pay the Pretender, and so he began the long journey back to the Place. As he walked he started to see more clearly the little one and the infant girl he had buried near the hearth.

The people of the village also haunted him. They had attacked without reason, had injured Little Boren. They had been about to sacrifice him to their strange gods, and they kept other People to work for them. They were without honor, or poetry, or grace. They depended on the food they grew, and the food could not grow without them. They threw their dead into the ground outside the village. They did not care for their dead, and would always be afraid.

They were the real slaves, he realized, bound to the soil, the crop, the round of work.

Day after day he walked under clear, dry skies. As he walked, and hunted, and worked his stone, the dead became more than memories, the slaves in the hut, the boy, and his family he had put out for the vultures, all the others. They were faint, cold shadows that flitted always at the edge of seeing, companions on his homeward journey.

Perhaps he was getting old and forgetful. There had been so many dead to remember. The ones he had buried, and those who came before, those someone else had buried under floors below his floor, floors of earlier houses, back to the First Grands. Mala had told him their stories, their lives and deaths, and where they were under First Egg. It was for him to remember, and to teach those stories to Little Boren.

He knew then that the Place had been growing over time. The land was nearly flat in all directions, yet the Place had grown above it. The Nest was old and held all the Grands that had come and gone. They were still there, down in the earth.

Of course there were others who were forgotten, whose lives had ended far from the place. The woman lost in the marsh, for instance, or those who never came back from hunting, like Big Boren. They may have carried no magic, and have been of little value, but they, too, were dead, and were of the People, and had known how to live. They were not like the people who grew all their food.

Shelsan stopped one night at Dak's Cave where he had told Little Boren the story of Water Bird, and before he slept he counted all the dead on his fingers. There were many. He had been captured for a reason. It was a warning.

He would return to the Place and would tell them they should keep to the old ways. Those who grew their own food grew sour and violent and reckless. The People must never give in to that temptation.

The dead were talking at him, though. They were telling him it might already be too late.

11 Now

Evil Eye

"It's evil," Gayle said.

Lena Marie tucked in her chin. "Don't be silly."

Gayle's rings flashed in the shaft of early sunlight crawling toward them when she waved her hand, taking in the Secure Room. "I've been thinking it for some time, Lena Marie. I don't think this is the Goddess, I think it's a devil. It's an evil force."

Lena Marie's good-natured laughter tinkled an arpeggio up and down the scale. "Come, Gayle, why would you say such a thing? She's magnificent."

They were by the window. The sun had just painted Alice a brilliant orange. Lena Marie added, "Look at Her. You can't call Her evil!"

Gayle glanced and looked away. "Yeah, she's spectacular all right." The head seemed to glow from within, her red and black lines writhing as if alive. "But I *can* call it evil. She's done something awful. I feel it."

"You feel it? Now you're being superstitious," Lena Marie said firmly. "The Goddess may be frightening, but She is not evil."

"Yes, she can be frightening when it serves her purpose." Gayle shook her head, somehow managing to demote the goddess to lower case. She rubbed the nape of her neck. Despite the air-conditioning and the early hour, it was damp with sweat. She looked at her palm with disgust and wiped it dry on her jeans. "Lena Marie, think about it. She's disfigured, incised with horrific lines, red like blood running from those ghastly eyes; she has a beak and painted teeth. She was made to scare people, to do something horrific."

"Don't be so culture-bound," Lena Marie snorted. "She's scary to us, that's all. You're reacting like a typical male Western rationalist in the presence of a force both ancient and spiritual."

As Lena Marie uttered this last word the sun caught Alice's sunken eyes. The two women raised their hands against the glare.

"There's an Arab proverb," Gayle muttered. "'The evil eye empties houses and fills tombs.' She's a tomb filler, this one."

"I can't have you talking like this." Lena Marie gazed lovingly down at Alice. "She's beautiful. Do not talk like that in the Presence."

"Lena Marie, you're deluded. She's ugly and sinister. Evil."

"How dare you talk to me like that?" Lena Marie avoided Gayle's eyes. "I won't stand for it. Even at Her most terrible, the Goddess is never evil."

Gayle wanted to cry out in frustration. Instead, she bit her lip and tasted blood.

Dead Reckoning

Lodewyk spoke too soon when he had told Satchi no one was interested in skeletons. Ever since Jones had trumpeted the mystery of the three burials, "probably related," in the Rabbit Hole where they had found Alice, the Human Remains Lab had been besieged by near-constant interruptions. After several days of this aggravation Lodewyk taped newspaper over the lab windows and locked the door from the inside.

Satchi used his own key. "What's this?" he asked, holding the door open.

"I can't get anything done," Lodewyk complained, looking up from his workbench. "Close, please."

"I thought no one was interested in skeletons."

"Ha, ha, ha."

As he turned to close the door, Satchi glimpsed Afet staring thoughtfully out her window at the mound. There was nothing to see but a line of visitors climbing to the summit and a lot of dead weeds. "Anything new?"

The two small skeletons – the tiny infant and the larger toddler – lay on their backs on the workbench under the windows. Their spines, ribs, arms, and legs were organized in approximately normal articulation. Small, hand-written tags identified them as Units 2333 and 2452.

Unit 2104, the adult with the hole in his tibia, was still on the table in the center of the room. Lodewyk was entering numbers on a form.

He measured the top of the femur with a pair of calipers. "I won't put this in writing," he muttered, staring at the scale on his instrument. "Not yet, anyway. And I'll deny it if you tell anybody, but I think Jones may be right, these three are related."

"Related how?"

Lodewyk stabbed the air with the points of the calipers. "*Stront!* Without DNA how can I know for certain? Perhaps they were siblings, the adult and two children. The two small ones were buried near the hearth in the same house, and probably around the same time. From the soil it seems the youngest was probably wrapped in some kind of grass basket or shroud. The adult was buried later, in the successor house to the east. You see?" He smiled brightly. "It would be really interesting. Or," he added thoughtfully, "the later burial was their father."

"You deduce all this how?"

"Well, according to Ben Vierra one burial was under six layers of plaster, the other under eight, so there were two layers between burials. That would give us a relative time between them. If they plastered once a year, then there were up to three years at the most between the burials."

"That may be too conservative," Satchi said. "They probably plastered more often."

"There you go!" Lodewyk exulted. "Call it a year."

"But there was the fire," Satchi added. "Events like that change the pattern."

"Yes, and they plastered only three more times, once for the fire and twice after that. Then they destroyed the house, and the adult, the man with the hole in his leg, was buried next door. I suspect he might be the one who buried the two small ones. What do you think? The ages would be about right, especially if neighboring houses reflect kinship."

Satchi grinned. "So why won't you put that in writing?"

"Bah." Lodewyk began to measure the ribs.

Satchi stared thoughtfully at the hole in the leg. "How old did she say this guy was when he died?"

Lodewyk looked up from his measurements. "Him? Between twenty and forty."

"And he was buried in the later house . . ."

"Yes. Does that mean something?"

Satchi shook his head. "I don't know. If they're related, I find it poignant, like a glimpse of family history. We're trying to read individual lives from such fragmentary evidence. We know at Çatal there isn't much evidence of violence, if any – no arrowheads in the skeletons, no defensive walls. This place was the same. Does that mean they were peaceful, living together in harmony?"

Lodewyk laughed almost heartily. "Under the benign rule of the Goddess? Right, indeed, humans living in perfect harmony, that's a lovely image, but has that ever happened in the long, sad history of our species?"

Satchi watched Afet cross her lab to tap on her laptop. She frowned at the screen for a few minutes and went back to the workbench. She held a small piece of obsidian up to the light and a smile played around her lips. She was so obviously savoring the color, or the transparency, or some other quality. Satchi spontaneously smiled in response.

"What?" Lodewyk said, looking at him sharply. "You find the question amusing?"

"Oh, no, I was wondering what killed him in the end? How did Unit 2104 die?"

Lodewyk shrugged. "Disease, probably. People living this close together . . ."

"Yes, so you've said many times."

"Or some kind of toxin."

"Poison?"

"I didn't say that. There's no sign of another injury, only the deformations of the leg bones where he had the infection. No evidence of cumulative toxins that would leave a trace. Bone analysis might show us more, but for now he looks pretty healthy."

"So you don't know?"

"No, but there were plenty of environmental toxins around, heavy metals, poisonous food, tainted meat, mushrooms, septicemia – the list goes on. Or maybe he inhaled carbon monoxide from the hearth. Or ingested some kind of naturally occurring fluoride compound. We can run some tests. My guess, though, is he died of a sudden illness. The world has never been particularly safe."

"You brought up poison," Satchi insisted. "Can you look for traces?"

"Sure. Anything's possible. You would want me to be looking for murder here?" Lodewyk was only half serious.

"Murder's a big word for an archaeologist."

"But not for a forensic pathologist, or even an old bone man like me."

"Sure, why not?" Satchi said with a grin. "After Alice, Jones would love a good murder mystery."

Air Play

Rolf waited on the flight deck, absently checking his harness and listening to the captain shout at his crewman. The captain finished and turned to give a thumbs-up. The motor kicked in and the boat moved away from the dock. Once in open water it headed east and picked up speed.

The crewman helped Rolf get the canopy of the parasail inflated, and within seconds he lifted off the deck and into the sky.

He had paid for a tow to Manavgat and back. An hour of this would give him a bird's-eye view of the coast and some alone time to think. With wind rushing past him, the astoundingly clear water below, the distant boat buzzing ahead, and the fertile coast to his left, he floated gently away from the resort and was soon paralleling the Emerald Coast under clear skies. Every road, inlet, beach, and building was etched in exquisite detail.

Much had changed since he had first entered the antiquities business almost a quarter century ago. Art from Central and South America, from Asia, Africa, the Mediterranean, everywhere, had been liberated in enormous quantities and sold to dealers and collectors. Collecting and dealing in artifacts, art objects, and cultural materials was an ancient and honorable activity. In the old days one could count on a museum somewhere to bid. Attention to legality or provenance was not high in anyone's priorities. Curators were as interested as collectors, and museum collections depended on people like Rolf, people whose scruples were flexible, to fill them.

All that had changed. There were laws almost everywhere against trafficking in antiquities. There was the 1972 UNESCO Convention on World Heritage requiring the return of stolen antiquities . Although most museums wanted to hang on to them, the countries of origin, in many cases, wanted them back, and museums everywhere—Boston, the Getty, even the Met—were forced to surrender important parts of their collections. It was all a matter of national prestige.

Archaeologists were whining these days that looting destroyed knowledge, all that nonsense about "context"! As if it mattered where an artifact was today. Some people who like old things take care of them better than archaeologists do.

And then there were the forgeries! The Getty Museum was caught up in terrible controversy just because it turned out some kouros statue they had bought for a fortune was probably a fake.

Ego, Rolf thought, watching the beaches roll past. From time to time he dipped and banked, swooping in for a closer look at sunbathers or yachtsmen. Ahead he saw a small deserted beach in a cove that looked promising. He banked left and dropped down. Rocky headlands blocked both ends. The sandy strip was narrow and the shelf dropped off, so it wouldn't be very attractive to swimmers. He saw no obvious trail from the road, which passed a kilometer or two inland.

He committed its location to memory so he could take another look on the way back, and returned to his musing.

National prestige, scholarship, heritage, he thought, were really just ego. Those people below, the very rich, the well-to-do, and the economizers, were small packets of national ego. They came from England, Germany, Sweden, from every continent and every culture, which they believed they represented when they sat on a beach in Southern Turkey.

Many of them, more than enough, wanted to participate in the great world art market. It was Rolf's business to accommodate them.

But now Interpol, the FBI, and other agencies were interfering in the trade of historic (and prehistoric) artifacts. They had started to call it "looting," as if Rolf himself looted. He was no tomb raider. He'd seen the looter's hole on top of Aynalı Tepe and deplored it. Digging through the past without a permit might be unethical, but mostly it was simply undignified and inefficient. He preferred to let others do the dirty work. If archaeologists dug things up, well, they got their data. After that, there was no reason Rolf shouldn't get their objects.

He rose swiftly at the end of his tether until he was nearly over the boat and his parasail lost lift. He loved that moment when the sail stalled and he plunged down, picking up speed. For him it was perfectly safe. The boat was still moving, the line tautened, the parasail filled, and he rose as swiftly as he had descended.

He was a resourceful man, flexible, adaptable, and unafraid of risk. He could bank and turn. If markets changed, methods changed. Profit endured. With the museum market drying up he had turned naturally enough to private collectors, believing they would never be as profitable as museums with their hefty endowments and wealthy patrons, and that his business was either going to shrink or he was going to have to work harder.

To his surprise it appeared the ranks of new global billionaires had grown exponentially. While the Arabs and Japanese had tapered off in their buying habits, there were now so many new-rich in Asia, India, and the Americas that the market had grown only more lucrative.

True, national pride had impeded traffic. Museums were more cautious, fearing lawsuits. Greece wanted the Elgin Marbles back. Italy wanted a collection of Sicilian Roman silver returned. Lawyers were everywhere, making trouble.

But individual ego rushed in to fill the gap. There was ample profit in personal ego too.

If an artifact came to his attention, and if one of his clients expressed an adequate interest, Rolf would make the effort. And an artifact had come to his attention.

Sun glinting off the curve of the river at Manavgat caught his eye. The boat began a long graceful curve back toward the west.

He decided, going past that small beach, that it was ideal. It might as well be named Smuggler's Cove.

Mother Love

"Whatcha doing?" Francy asked.

Ben tipped sideways to peer at her from behind the flat screen. It was Saturday morning and the shades of the computer lab were down. "Working," he said.

"Yeah? What a surprise. In semidarkness, too. And, whatcha doing?"

He waved at the screen. "Jones asked me to make an interactive model of the Rabbit Hole."

She looked at it. "Cool." She pulled up a chair and sat next to him. "I said there'd be niches. I bet there was a skull in that one."

Ben laughed. "I know. There was lip on the top of the wall there. I thought it was probably the bottom of a niche, so I put one in. Dr. Jones wants this 'visualization' for the Alice exhibit. So there she is, on her post in the middle of the room."

"Where's the light coming from?"

Ben shrugged. "Ambient. I can put some lamps around if you like." He dragged a few icons into the room and put them on the floor. The lighting changed, and now Alice looked like a cliché from a horror movie, a tortured face lit dramatically from below.

Francy's lip twitched. "You think it really looked like that? All spooky, like you used to do with the flashlight at camp?"

"Speak for yourself," Ben said. "I didn't go to camp."

"Come on. You never tried to scare people with that old trick?"

"Well . . ."

"Anyway, she really does look like Alice Cooper in outrageous makeup, especially with all those sticks and feathers stuck in her head."

"Dr. Troye keeps talking about wigs or hair or something. I just added some stuff. I got the files from the illustrator. Nifty, huh?"

With a grin he rotated the room so they were looking down over the back of Alice's head toward the south wall. A glow came from the entrance in the ceiling. The ladder slanted down toward the hearth where an animated fire crackled. Smoke drifted toward the entrance.

"It's so cool you can do all that, I mean with the smoke and fire and everything."

Gayle poked her head in the door. "What can he do that's cool?"

"Come on in," Francy said.

"Sorry, I was just going by and heard you say it's so cool." Gayle's smile was apologetic.

"Look what he's done!" Francy rested her hand on Ben's shoulder for a moment. He glanced up at her and she trailed her fingers down the slope of his shoulder before removing it.

Gayne bent toward the screen. "You're right, the detail is amazing. Those bags and baskets of food, that bearskin on the floor, the bull's horns set in the . . . is that a support post? And the clothes hanging on the wall, it's fantastic! Even the fire looks real." After a moment she added, "Do you really think Alice was just sitting on top of a pole like that?"

"What do you mean?" Ben leaned back to stretch. "The debris of the pole was under her, set in the floor."

Gayle shook her head. "No, I mean maybe she was like those plastered reed sculptures at 'Ain Ghazal in Jordan. They were maybe a millennium earlier, sure, and they didn't have human bones, of course. But their bodies were just sketched in, so they were probably dressed. Maybe these people did the same things, put clothes on the pole or something, to make her look like a real person. The clothing could have disappeared, leaving just the pole."

"It's possible, I suppose." Ben was skeptical. "There was no evidence of textiles or anything, no impressions in the dirt that we could see that something woven might have left."

Gayle shrugged. "Maybe they removed it before they destroyed the house."

172

"Yeah, maybe. She'd have been about the height of a short person. And it's true that when the house was destroyed they left more of it standing than was normal."

"And they didn't rebuild it," Francy reminded him.

"No, you're right. They filled it in and abandoned it. For the rest of the occupation the Rabbit Hole was a garbage dump. Kinda weird, all right. What were they thinking?"

They contemplated in silence the back of the head, the fire in the hearth, the dazzle of sunlight above the entrance.

Francy suddenly tapped the screen with a blunt, rather dirty fingernail. "See how she's looking toward the south? Toward the hearth?"

"Yes," Gayle said. "I see what you mean. It's wonderful. I can't wait to tell Lena Marie, though she may not like it."

"What?" Ben asked. "What do you mean?"

Francy gave him her well-duh look. "She's facing the burials."

"So?"

"So she's not a goddess; she's human."

Ben shook his head. "I still don't get it."

"They're her kids. She's a grieving mother, watching over their graves."

"Or the opposite," Gayle said. "She's the one who killed them."

No Crocodiles

Daily routine returned to Aynalı Tepe. Most of the journalists left, the wall painting was undergoing stabilization and conservation, the large obsidian core was in Afet's lab, and the hard drives in the Computer Lab were filling up with digital photographs and hours of video. The specialists were overwhelmed with data recording and analysis.

Lodewyk removed the newspaper taped over his windows. He had shipped small bone samples of the three skeletons to a laboratory in France for analysis but did not expect results for some time. He was able to continue working in peace. "It won't last," he told Satchi. "It never does around here. Jones sees to that. Don't think there are no crocodiles just because the water is calm."

He was right. Two days later the portable X-ray equipment arrived.

Satchi led the technician to the Secure Room, and within a few minutes Alice's interior took shape on a laptop screen. Ben could hardly contain himself. "She does have a skull!" he exulted.

Confirmation prompted Jones to call a videoconference with *ArchaeologyNowOnline*. "Alice was once a living person," he announced. He was standing under the awning beside the Rabbit Hole. "The question we ask, of course, is what purpose could all that decoration possibly have served? Other plastered skulls from the region are painted simply, with sketchy shell or bitumen eyes, and sometimes a nose. Most archaeologists believe they belonged to ancestors and were decorated as a form of reverence or to identify with a lineage. But Alice is different. She has grooves, paint, pits for hair or some kind of head covering, and, strangest of all, those famous obsidian eyes. We've never seen anything like this level of elaboration. Someone went to a lot of trouble – the amount of work that went into her making is astonishing. Of course we'd like to know why. Though," he added with a laugh, "we probably never will."

"Excuse me," Lena Marie called out. She was double protected from the sun by the awning and a broad-brimmed straw hat. Her nose had started to peel.

Jones gestured her forward and introduced her to the camera. "Dr. Troye is convinced Alice is a depiction of the Mother Goddess. Her interests in the Goddess are well known. Lena Marie?"

"Thank you, Bryson. I would be the first to admit the difficulty of knowing with absolute certainty what artifacts from the remote past may have meant to the people who used them, but there is considerable scholarship that supports my belief that Alice is a unique representation of the Mother Goddess. And I have a pretty good idea what She was doing."

Jones lifted one of his thick, blond eyebrows. "Do you?" He kept his tone neutral.

"Yes," she answered firmly. "I'm prepared to stake my reputation on it."

Jones was self-assured and diplomatic. "And what was she doing?"

"Watching over Her children."

Jones hesitated only a moment before saying, "What gives you that idea?"

Francy squeezed Ben's upper arm. "The bitch," she whispered. "That was my idea."

"I know. Gayle must have told her."

"She was standing in the center of the room, facing south toward the hearth where the two babies were buried. Do you not find that suggestive?" She must have realized she was being too aggressive and softened her tone. "What other explanation could there be for Her very careful position in the room. Alice is a head, set on a post at head height. The two graves were near the hearth in front of Her." She shook her own head and the brim of her hat flapped like waves. "No, She was a guardian. Those two children were extremely important to the community. It's as if we could see a nascent hierarchy beginning to emerge. This house was very near the center of the settlement, which suggests it was one of the oldest, perhaps even the original. After the children's deaths it was never rebuilt. She was put there as a memorial."

Jones smiled. "Like a tombstone?"

"More than that. She was there as a living guardian. The house is a place sacred to the dead. Alice was there to warn away intruders, anyone who might want to desecrate the tomb of those two children."

Jones laughed pleasantly. "Like archaeologists?" he asked.

"Yes, like archaeologists."

Line of Sight

Afet spent several hours before the Secure Room opened to visitors staring into Alice's face. She leaned forward to look into the reflecting eyes. She shone lights on them, measured their diameters, analyzed their reflectivity. She had the X rays pinned to the wall of her lab, and spent much of the rest of the day looking at them.

One morning as usual she stood, stretched, walked around Alice, returned to the table, and stared some more. She entered numbers in her laptop and ran calculations.

Mehmet arrived to open up to the day's visitors, now reduced to a handful. Afet smiled at him and hurried away, carrying her laptop. Back in her own lab she stared at the screen until breakfast, where she addressed Satchi directly for almost the first time. "I can't figure it out."

He was piling white cheese on a slice of bread. "Can't figure out what?" He took a bite and looked at her.

Her expression was puzzled. It was also, he realized, adorable.

"Her eyes," she said. "The polished obsidian."

He stopped chewing. "What about it"

"They're . . . focused."

"Focused?"

"Is that not the right word? Hollowed out."

"You mean concave?"

"Yes, that's it, concave. They focus on something. You can see it if you shine a light into them just right."

"Are you saying what I think you're saying?"

"This is the Neolithic, 9,000 years ago. It probably wasn't intentional, but these mirrors suggest a sophisticated understanding of optics. They were focused. That's not supposed to be possible in the Stone Age, even if it is the New one."

The Problem of Authenticity

After their conversation Jones thought Lena Marie was right, the archaeologists were intruding, but his concern was with the impact of all the visitors on Alice. She was attracting attention, and that was putting her at risk.

He saw Satchi the following afternoon. "Could you bring Afet and Özgür to the office for a brief meeting."

"What is it?" Satchi asked when they were all there and seated around the desk.

Jones paced. "Alice is attracting a lot of attention," he said slowly.

"Yes?"

"I think we should preserve her."

"Come one, Bryson, of course we should preserve her. What do you mean?"

Afet was watching Jones curiously. She glanced over at Özgür, who was examining his fingernails.

"I'd like to make a replica," Jones said.

Satchi sat up. "What? That's not ethical.

"A replica," Jones repeated. "As an experiment."

Satchi shook his head. "That would cost . . ."

Jones interrupted. "I know it won't be cheap, not if we want a good one, and we would need the best. But we can pay from the experimental archaeology budget. When we have it, we'll put it on view and secure Alice. We might even have Hellä do the conservation work on the authentic Alice here – cleaning, preservatives, everything."

Satchi shook his head. "First of all, that should be done in a proper museum lab. Second, people come here to see the real Alice, not a fake. Third, we need to get on with the dig, not waste more time with this tourist attraction."

"The tourist attraction helps pay the bills," Jones said. "The funding entity likes the international attention Alice is bringing. It makes it more generous. And it's not going to be a fake, Satchi. The original will be safe and sound and getting the best of professional attention."

"Who's going to make such a replica?" Satchi demanded. "We don't have anyone here with the skills, and we couldn't spare them if we did."

"Don't worry, I know someone."

Özgür stirred. "Excuse me, Jones Bey, but you do not propose to remove Alice for someone to make a copy?"

"Not a copy, a replica," Jones insisted. "An experimental reconstruction to help discover how she was made."

The representative shook his head. "No. The object cannot leave the premises."

"Just for a few days?"

"No, Jones Bey, I am sorry, but Alice must stay in the Secure Room. She is my responsibility."

Jones sat down at his desk and tented his fingers, deep in thought. After a moment he sighed. "All right, Özgür. We have X rays, high-resolution digital photos, and all the data. A skilled artist can work from that." He looked around. "Are we all agreed?"

Reluctantly Satchi nodded. Jones had made a convincing case, but he was still uneasy. "You're going to announce that what people see is a replica, that the original is locked up, right?"

"Don't worry," Jones reassured him. "I'll handle it all."

"All right."

Afet nodded.

"Well, then," Jones said brightly. "It's agreed."

The Dealer

Jones introduced Satchi, Afet, and Özgür to a spare Georgian from Batumi on the Black sea. "He is an old friend," Jones said. "We can rely on him."

The dealer nodded at the three with an elaborate sigh, his narrow frame rising and falling in sections – shoulders, elbows, hands, accompanied by eyebrows and mouth turning down and up in counterpoint.

He ran his hand over his carefully groomed white hair. The sense of exasperation he projected did nothing to diminish his urbane, polished exterior. "Dr. Jones, I have agreed to see you, but what you ask . . ."

Jones interrupted, "I know it's unusual, but you've done this sort of thing before. It's an exercise in experimental archaeology, for presentation purposes only. And of course we'll pay."

"I know," the dealer answered thoughtfully. "This is not my worry, but this is a rush, you say?"

"It would be good to have it sooner rather than later."

"Then it would be best if we could work from the original."

"I know, but I'm afraid that is not possible."

"I see. You wouldn't want it to leave the site."

Jones tilted his head in what might have been assent. "Mr. Tasköprülüzâde is the representative and he decides. Besides, discretion is important. The replica will go on display as soon as we receive it."

"And the original?"

"Will be sequestered; we need to stabilize it. We'll announce that we've made this replica for research purposes and are displaying it because the original is too valuable, too fragile. What you do must be good, as good as you can make from our data."

"Of course. Regretfully, it will cost."

Jones assumed an aggrieved, thoughtful air and stared at the shaft of sunlight racing up the bookcases on the east wall. The light winked out. It was now officially evening.

"Not too expensive," the dealer conceded. "Just because of the rush, and the conservation materials."

Jones sighed with elaborate resignation and smiled. "All right."

"It will look as if it has been cleaned. We'll make it and paint it with an acrylic-silane mixture to consolidate. It's the only way to explain why it will look new."

Jones sighed. "All right. How quickly can you do it?"

The dealer's eyebrows arched into two perfect half circles. "Three weeks," he said.

"All right," Jones agreed. "The media want to see her, but displaying her much longer risks serious damage. All that breathing, and of course exposure to theft."

The dealer made a decision and nodded. "Very well, I will do it for you, Dr. Jones."

"Half now," Jones said expansively. "Half when you deliver."

The dealer managed to look insulted. "My reputation is my life. I always deliver."

"I know, I know," Jones said soothingly. "Not always legally, but you do deliver."

"I don't know what you're talking about." The dealer looked like a well-groomed poodle, but his eyes were pained.

"I apologize," Jones said. His humility was patently false.

"All right. I can manage the skull, and we will need some good obsidian. I know someone who can make the eyes, but we need a good core from the original place. Göllü Da I suppose."

"Correct," Afet agreed. "The data is all there. I suppose as long as the skull remains plastered no one could detect a difference, but in a good museum laboratory you might not fool anyone . . ."

"We're not trying to fool people," Jones said. "Just preserve the real Alice."

The dealer nodded. "All right. Now, you said you had the data."

Jones withdrew the disk from the pocket of his safari jacket. "It's all there – photographs, measurements, X rays, spectroscopic analysis – everything," he said.

"Three weeks from today," the dealer said, sliding the disk into the computer concealed in the desk. His monitor sprang to life and threw a blue glow onto his forehead. He looked up. "Any time after noon."

Network

Rolf was satisfied. When he explained to the captain of the parasailing boat he would have another charter for him in a few weeks, the captain understood perfectly and doubled the usual rate.

"Half when we meet next. The rest when the job is finished," Rolf agreed. "And I'll need a yacht for a week, with a skipper who knows how to keep quiet."

The captain nodded. He had a cousin in Bodrum on the Aegean coast. "He's your man," the captain said. "Very quiet, my cousin Mustafa. Very efficient."

"I'll need to assure myself it's suitable," Rolf said.

"Of course, of course, *efendim*. I will call him."

Mustafa agreed to meet Rolf the next day. He could give him a complete tour of the *Island Princess*. "Tourists love the name," he said.

"Twenty-one meters, twin 760 horsepower engines . . ."

"Fast?"

"Cruise at twenty knots, top speed twenty-four. Do you need something faster? I have a cousin . . ."

"Everyone here has cousins. No, that's fine."

Rolf kept nothing in external storage, neither real nor virtual. Everything was in his head. He had memorized lists of names, locations, specialties. He could rattle off chemical compositions, the effects of acid on bone or clay, the aging effects of dirt or the reflective qualities of various stabilizing plastics and epoxies. He knew plane and bus schedules and bank account numbers.

He didn't like leaving a paper trail.

In Antalya he turned in his rental car and caught the afternoon flight to Istanbul. The next day he flew into Bodrum.

The *Island Queen* was sufficiently innocuous, neither too ostentatious nor too shabby, and fast enough. Mustafa could operate it himself.

Rolf made a down payment. "I'll expect you to be on call," he said. "This may happen at the last possible moment. You may have to bump other clients."

Mustafa counted the wad of New Turkish Lira in his hand with one hand, riffling through the new bills. "*Problem yok.* No problem, *efendim.*" He held up the money. "This assures you my complete attention."

Rolf caught the evening flight to Ankara and from there took a bus to Amasya in the east, where he spent a week in discussion with a man named Sevket whose skill, discretion, and cupidity were absolutely reliable.

He returned to Konya by a series of buses, paying cash. Upon arrival he made a phone card call. Everything was in place. He went to a hotel and slept the untroubled sleep of the absolutely innocent.

# 12 Then

Shelsan's Return

Shelsan did not ask himself why he did not go straight to the Place, walk across the roofs to Mala's house, call down to her. After all, he carried a message: he'd seen what happened to the mud people who grew all their food. Yet at Dak's Cave he came to understand he was reluctant to deliver it. He knew what the People, especially Pinnak, would say, and so he delayed his return.

His burns were almost healed. Since he could work easily again, he spent a day making a new grass cloak. Dry-time may have gone on too long, but it was almost over.

Despite the cold, he felt no urgency. Little Boren would have recovered or not, and would return home, or not. Mala would be waiting, or she would not. Widow Klayn, too, would be there, or not. The gods would help him, or they would not. Too much had happened the past few moons, and night always followed day as death followed life.

He thought it would be best to return with food, so he moved past Sand Hook, away from the Place and deeper into the swamp. There had been no rain since the storm many days ago in the mud people's village, and there was less water than normal for this time of year. The river barely flowed a hand's breadth deep. The lake was a vast reach of drying mud. He found a hidden spot near a sluggish stream that fanned out onto a broad, wet meadow. Here he crouched on his haunches in a reed thicket.

His back was turned against a cold breeze from the northwest. He rubbed his cheek, feeling the rasp of his beard but hearing only the soft sibilance of water.

The herd was there, as he had known it would be. Something had told him this, and so he knew. Perhaps it was the dead, still talking to him.

The low stream ran cold against its bank: there had been rain somewhere in the mountains to the south, and so the rains, too, were returning.

Shelsan listened for light sniffing sounds, the shifting of their body weight, the squelch of hooves. A slight thinning of the darkness told him a chip of moon would soon throw faint silver fire on wet hides.

He looked toward the sunrise-side, toward the Place, but it was too dark in spite of the stars. Though the moon would not help – it would be too old, almost gone – Shelsan knew it was coming, just as the rain was coming, because everything that had come before returned.

But the moon hesitated to show itself: clouds threw gray veils across the stars. A thin drizzle hissed on his cloak, which felt heavy on his shoulders.

For a time he dreamed he was back in the place, before the boy died. Little Boren offered him something, a mirror of frozen tears.

He flared his nostrils and breathed in silently. It was wrong: there was no smell of burning, of soup or cooked meat, of a woman's musk in a warm house. In the back of his nose he found only the cold rain, the manure of the aurochs, the swamp beyond, and a faint bitterness underneath it all. Even his own sweat had disappeared, vanquished by the cold.

He pulled his cloak closer at his throat and leaned forward, staring into the darkness downstream, and jerked back at a brief, sharp sting of silver on the water's surface, for in that moment the moon cleared the low mountains and flashed through a gap in the clouds before the cloud mouth closed on it again.

Something cried in the darkness to his right, not from the swamp but from the wide swampy plain where the herd stirred restlessly. A cat was hungry. Shelsan closed his eyes and reached with his ears, but the cry did not repeat. This was strange. Usually the cat spoke twice.

Night

The drumming in Pinnak's house lasted all night. Mala climbed onto the roof, but there was nothing to see but the cheerful red glow of his hearth fire visible inside the lean-to that protected his entrance. She thought of stamping on his roof to get the sound to stop, but the night was cold. She shrugged and went down again.

She could not sleep, and soon was back on the roof. The sheep in the angle between their houses, Pinnak's sheep, were no longer there. This was the first time she realized this, that the sheep didn't stamp and bleat, that there was no smell of dung. Pinnak had removed them to his pens just outside the Place, and she hadn't noticed.

Well, she'd been busy. All those weeks she had lost mourning for those she believed were dead, she had to make them up. Every day until yesterday she'd gone out to gather. Many plants were ripe in this season just before the cold-time, when the rains fell and then turned to snow. If they didn't gather what they needed, she and Tsurinye, they would have empty bellies before wet-time.

How could she have left it so long? She hadn't visited her crops to the warm-side, either.

Finally, a handful of days before, they had gone. The lentils and peas had already begun to rot, and there were only half as many as last year. They spent long days searching for wild seeds, the last dry-time tubers and nuts. All the places Mala knew, the named places, gave up less than the year before. Her own crop was asking something of her. If only she had been there when it rained. If only.

She stood on the roof, waiting for something to happen. While she waited the clouds moved in, and a cold rain pattered on the roof and drowned out the drumming from Pinnak's house.

In Dreams

He was dreaming again. How many times had he fallen asleep?

He had come here as if he could walk into the night away from the torment that gnawed at him, that kept him moving around the house he shared with Mala and Little Boren. Often lately it had driven him out into the cold-time. True, he should be finding food. Food was scarce since the gods spoke through the earth and the houses fell. They lost many. Three moons had come and gone since then. Each cold, dark night he had marked the moons as they came and went on the plaster by the hearth. It seemed important to know how many had come and gone.

The women had gathered, and the bins were full until the gods shouted and the ground shook, and then they were no longer full. The edge of the great building that was the Place had fallen away. The Nest had turned on its nestlings, had killed three of his aunts and all their children, taken away half his extended family. He hadn't slept well since then, and was constantly in motion.

Only the Widow Klayn could help him rest. He saw her, curled on her sleeping platform under the goat wool blanket she had woven herself, the one with the red pattern of broken lines, her full breasts fallen to the side, spilled into his hand. He could put his lips on them and sleep.

Shelsan shook himself, and the vision vanished. Cold water trickled down the back of his neck. He shifted position to ease the ache in his legs.

Why did he think the gods had just spoken through the earth? Those gods, were they speaking to him now, through this vision? What were they trying to tell him?

It had happened once that he remembered, but long ago: the ground had heaved under them. Things hanging from the rafters swayed, Grand's skull fell from its niche. But that was all. No walls had fallen; no one had died. Two of those aunts lived still. That was when Big Boren was still alive, before Shelsan had moved in with Mala and Little Boren. It was long ago, when he was young.

And not once had he slept beside the Widow Klayn.

The Leopard

Something moved in the deep dark. The beasts were unhappy, he heard it in the way they slept, the uneasy snorts and shuffling hooves.

So the cat was close now. He opened his eyes, keeping them away from a faint jagged line of silver on the water. Vague shapes rose out of the darkness and reached for him: trees along the far edge of the meadow, the nearest aurochs, its back to him, the ghost-glow of its wet hide, the water. It was young, not even a yearling. The pattern of its movement didn't change. The cat did not concern him, but it should, it should.

Like the cat and the aurochs, Shelsan knew the stream lived. It would grow angry, swollen and hungry, and would seize whoever came close. It had taken old Singer the last cold time. The bank crumbled under her. And that was near home, where there were others around, fetching water up from the stream, pushing over it in their fragile reed boats, netting small fish and crustaceans. She cried out once and was gone. The others beat the water with sticks, but she did not return. They searched for days before giving up. There were many before her, would be many after. But the water took her, pulled her in, carried her away. They never again saw her thick arms with the flesh hanging from the bones, her high cheekbones with shiny spots on their points, her ill-temper and bad breath. Now there was another Singer, and the old one sang through the new one less and less.

The cat was close. The bitter aftertaste of her smell caught in his throat, drowning the mud and animal scents. He knew she would strike soon, though he could not yet feel her presence (it was a she; this time of year he could smell that too).

His skin prickled. Did she was come for him? He shifted and readied his spear.

Suddenly she was there beside him, crouched within a hand's breadth, so close he could touch her wet side, feel the heaving bellows of her ribs. Her ears were back. There was little light, and she was dark, but he could see that, and could see also the frost form when she breathed out. She took three long shuddering breaths and leapt in one fluid movement across the stream onto the back of the calf that had wandered too close. Shelsan stood and threw his spear. Already the herd was running, their hooves sucking at the mud, their snorts quickly fading.

The cat snarled at him. Her yellow eyes caught the faint moonlight. He had thrown the spear truly; it caught her just under the chin. The snarl turned to a cough, and she threw herself sideways, pawing at the thing sticking in her, and was lost in the darkness. Clouds covered the moon, and the drizzle turned to rain.

He started up, as if to cross the stream, thought better of it. The herd was gone, and if she were only wounded he would never see her coming, though he could smell her blood.

Shelsan settled back and waited. He sniffed at the air. Yes, it would snow soon. The moon was just a sliver amid thick clouds, and the stars had the shape of cold-time. Rain fell for a time and then it didn't fall. Slowly, as always, detail swam toward him out of the darkness, and color swam back into the world.

The calf was dead, only slightly mauled, and the cat was gone. The shaft of his spear lay broken on the ground; she had taken his good flint point.

Despite the rain Shelsan could see the trail, so he followed. She wasn't far, and smaller in the daylight than she seemed in the dark. He slit her belly open and peeled off her skin. He could not take any leopard bone into the Place, so he had to leave the head. He draped the skin over his shoulders and packed his flint point.

Then he lashed the calf's body to two poles and dragged it home.

The sun, though it was covered by cloud, was overhead when he finally reached the Place and could smell wood smoke again. He called out. After a time three Sorrow Clan cousins climbed down to meet him. "You're back," one said, and it was as if he had never gone.

They hauled up the calf, Shelsan pushing from below. It had spilled its guts and his hands and face were covered with slime. Once the body was over the lip of the roof he wiped his hands on his cloak and climbed after it.

Smoke rising from chimney holes all across the broad uneven landscape of flat roofs flattened into a long gray blade that fanned out over the swamp into gray mist.

A few flakes of snow twirled around him. The cousins squatted around the calf and discussed its division.

Widow

"Come," Widow Klayn said in answer to Shelsan's call.

She was seated cross-legged, her back against a square pillar. Smoke from her hearth hung in thick layers among the ceiling beams. When he was there, she said simply, "It's you."

"Yes." He squatted in front of her and placed the package at her feet. "Aurochs, a calf."

"I see that." She unwrapped the meat and looked at it thoughtfully.

"I'll come back later." He stood.

"No, stay." She pushed away some baskets on the plaster floor beside her and patted the cleared space. "You were gone. Now you're back." She leaned toward him to touch his arm, and he sensed her breasts, as in the dream.

He sat with a sigh and closed his eyes. Accumulated fatigue washed through him.

Darkness swirled with vague shapes. Small sounds, some known, others strange, arose and faded. He awoke with a sharp grunt.

She had unwrapped the meat. The calf's head stared at her and she turned it around. He could tell by the set of her shoulders that she knew he was awake again, but she only took the small joint of the calf's leg and placed it carefully on the leather wrapping. After looking at it for a long moment, she picked up a flint knife, cut the meat away from the bone, and started slicing it into long strips. Then she pounded on the bone with a round stone, cracked it open, and scooped the marrow into a baked clay pot.

Only when she was done with this task did she look at him.

"Thank you," she said with a sad smile. She started to hang the strips from a beam over the hearth.

"Here," Shelsan said, taking them from her. "Let me."

She leaned against him for a moment. Then she pushed him away. "Go to Mala. She has not been well. Some demon took her. Then Little Boren came back and she was better. But she's changed. You should go."

He sighed. "I know."

A sudden gust of wind sucked some of the smoke away through the entry, clearing the room for a few moments and sending down a blast of chill air.

Painting the Dead

Three days had passed and Shelsan said, "I will paint the dead. They have been speaking to me; I have been counting them. It is time I gave Little Boren their stories."

Though Mala spoke little in those days, the house was livelier now that Shelsan was back, and Little Boren was there with his woman, Tsurinye. In the wet-time she would give birth, and then they would be five.

"Do what you must," Mala answered, as if it no longer mattered.

He spread a mat on the sunrise platform, and sat on it cross-legged, and prepared the shells for the paints, the red, the white, the black, the three colors of paint, and ground the paints, for this was to be an important lesson, a re-creation of former lives, of former deaths.

Little Boren and Tsurinye sat on the platform across from him and watched.

The wall was white. The day before it had been covered with paintings of black wings, but they reminded them of the boy gone under, so he had spread a thick coating of white clay from the riverbank with his hands, and now it was white.

Now, today, this day, he took brushes made from sticks and some bristles from the pig he had killed just before he and Little Boren had left on the Walk of the World. He selected one and dipped into the shell of red. He painted a series of squares across the wall in rows and sat back, looking at them. After a few moments he blew on the first one he had painted, touched it with his finger. It was dry.

"I start with First Egg," he said. "This."

"No, Babi," Little Boren said. "That is four sticks enclosing a space."

Shelsan looked at him. "I am doing this," he said. "I ask you, is not a house like four sticks that enclose a space? You will listen and you will watch, for this concerns you. First Grand Father was buried under the cold-side wall, toward sunrise, here." With another brush he put a patch of white inside the red. "Later they took his skull from the ground. That is his head there!" He pointed with the tip of the brush at the skull he had plastered those moons ago before they had buried the nameless boy.

He crossed the white with a red line. "First Grand is bones, but no skull, and for that reason I put this line through his place. This means his skull is above, in the human world."

He stood suddenly and stamped his foot on the sleeping platform. "And I know if we dig down here, in this place, we will find Second Grand's bones, under the floors below the floors below this one. He is there. How do I know?"

"Someone told you," Little Boren said.

Tsurinye looked down and smiled.

"That is correct." Shelsan said, sitting once more. "Now here is First Grand Mother." And he painted her grave.

He moved to the next square. "These are the Second Grands." He added generations to the house. "And then, when that house was terminated and built again, there were more Grands to bury, and sometimes children toward the warm-side too." He used a new column for the reconstructed house.

Little Boren stopped him once. "But how do you remember all this, Babi?"

Shelsan's face was stern. "Because someone told me, as you said, and as I am telling you."

"But did they paint the wall, as you are painting the wall? Did they, Babi?"

"Too many questions," Shelsan said, but he softened his voice. "No, they did not paint the wall, Little Boren. They only told me, and I remembered."

"Then why are you painting this, Babi?"

"Because I feel it is better. There are many dead now. This way we can see them and remember."

"Why did they tell you, Babi? Why didn't they tell Mami? She is the Daughter of all the Grands. You are from the Locust Clan and not from Sorrow, as we are, as Mala and I are."

"True. But I was often with Mala's Grand when I was a boy, and no son of his lived, so he had no man to tell the story of the Grands, and so he told me. And I have stayed with Mala since your father left. And that is enough."

He drew in the children and the Grands, generation after generation and Egg after Egg, until he had filled all the squares on the wall. At the last he asked, "And who is this?" He pointed at the two small marks on the warm-side.

"Little Sister and Little Brother," Little Boren said.

Shelsan smiled. "From now you will be called Boren, for you are no longer little. It is for you to remember what I have done this day. Look hard at this, and remember the dead." He put the imprint of his hand on the wall to show it was finished.

He looked at what he had done. Had he forgotten anyone? He counted the houses, the burials in each one, and it seemed they all were there, remembered. All the dead, until now.

Clans

The sun had disappeared, and the moon. The nights were long and cold and dark. The air was often thick with snow, and the vast marsh frozen hard. The People stayed inside, making tools and telling stories. The cold-time, which had come so late, stayed beyond its season.

There were times when Shelsan went out to hunt, and came back empty-handed. Once or twice he was lucky, and they had meat for another week, another month.

The days passed, the snow fell silently and piled high on the roofs, and Tsurinye grew large in the belly.

At the darkest time the Clans met. Locust and Sorrow and Wind were bound together through the Mothers and the Grands, but it was the men who gathered in Pinnak's house, while his women consulted in another.

Pinnak's room was filled with red light and smoke. A skin of hot mint tea went around, and the men grew somber or jolly as befit their natures.

"We cannot go on like this," one man said, the oldest of the Sorrow, Mala's Clan. "We are many, and food is growing short. We have bellies to fill and nothing to fill them with."

"You should have tended your grain patch," Pinnak said. "You would have food for cold-time. My storage bins are full."

"Are they?" the other asked skeptically. "You may show us these bursting storage bins if you like." He glanced toward the back, the cold-side, where two small round doors led to the bins. But it was dark, and impossible to tell if they were full or not. "You have been industrious, have you, Pinnak? Or is it your women who have done this for you?"

Pinnak rose to his feet, his face red.

Shelsan broke in. "Pinnak is right," he said, and the other settled down again. "And he is also wrong. I have seen what happens to the people who grow all their food and tend only to their flocks. They have forgotten how to hunt, how to find their food where it waits for them, where the gods, the animal spirits, and the plant spirits have put it."

Pinnak started to speak, but Shelsan cut him off. "What happens to those people is hunger. Not just in the cold-time, but all the year. They can never have enough."

Pinnak broke in then. "That is a lie. They have enough if they grow enough. If they work."

Someone said, "You mean if the women work," and everyone laughed.

Shelsan stabbed at the air with his fingers. "The more they work, the worse it is, because they increase in numbers, and there are always more mouths than there are stands of grain. If we do the same, we, too, will increase, and the hunger will grow. It is easy to see what will happen."

Pinnak snorted. "Easy! It is easy to see if we grow food, we will have food. If there are more children, there are more People to plant and tend and harvest. That is how there will always be enough food."

Shelsan shook his head, but said nothing further, and the discussion turned to other things. Later, back in the Egg, he said to Mala, Boren, and Tsurinye, "There will be trouble."

Pinnak

There were days when some of the People moved onto the roof and cooked outside. A few went hunting, though game was scarce. Snow covered the ground and even the river had frozen.

The month before the birthing moon Shelsan and Boren spent much of the day with the flock in their pen at the sunrise-side. As soon as enough early green showed through the melting snow they would turn it out, but the wet-time was late. Forage was getting low, and the People with flocks talked of nothing but their worry.

On the way back over the roofs they came across Pinnak standing beside their stack of dried dung fuel near the entrance to First Egg. He gave them a crafty look. "I was just on my way home." He smiled slyly. "It's good to see you tending your flock, Shelsan. You can see there is no need for hunting if you have a flock."

"Don't count on it too much, Pinnak. We have brought the plants and animals to us, but we should not depend on them alone. You can see that new growth is late this year, yet we have ewes to feed, and some grow sick. They depend on us too much. It is not right."

"Right? What do you mean of right? We are the People, and we do as we wish. To survive, to grow, we must have flocks and fields. That is what is right."

Boren listened silently, looking from one to the other.

"What is right," Shelsan replied, "is to go to the food, follow it as it moves through the seasons. Balance, Pinnak."

Pinnak continued without listening. "We will increase. You said it yourself."

"I said it myself?" Shelsan was taken aback.

"Certainly. You said yourself we would grow in numbers."

"That was a warning, not a wish."

Pinnak laughed. "Why? Why should we not grow numerous, and fill the land. It is empty now."

"Empty?" Shelsan said. "The land is not empty, Pinnak. It is filled with plants and animals and spirits. The land is a living thing, Pinnak."

The fat man shook his head, spreading his hands wide. "No, Shelsan. We will grow prosperous, and spread wide. This land is ours."

"Ours? How can it be ours?"

"We use the land to grow food, to tend our flocks, and that makes it ours, as the house we build and live in is ours. As our noses and eyes are ours."

"You forget something, Pinnak."

"What is that?"

"Where did we come from?"

"Waterbird Mother . . ."

"No, before Waterbird Mother. Where did we come from? Don't you wonder? We came here from somewhere else. Why? Why did we leave?"

"Waterbird Mother was driven away by the Giants."

"No, they were not Giants, Pinnak. I've seen them. Waterbird Mother was driven away by people who tended their food, people who had forgotten how to follow it and tried to make it follow them. They had grown too numerous, and hungry and desperate, and drove the People away, so the Grands came here long ago."

Pinnak sucked on his lip as if he tasted something bad, shrugged, and walked away.

Fire in the Air

The trouble Shelsan foretold came on a cold, moonless night. The season had been most unusual, colder and wetter than normal. First the rains were late; then they turned to snow or froze into balls of ice and kept the People inside much of the time.

Shelsan stirred fitfully. He was running from something when Mala shook him. "Shelsan!"

"What is it?" he murmured. His feet were moving. "What?"

First it was the sound, a crackling near the hearth. It was disturbing. He wanted to sleep but the air was full of smoke. He sat up. "Boren! Tsurinye!"

They looked around wildly. Tsurinye huddled against Boren, clutching his arm, her eyes wide. The darkness was thick, but the smoke was thicker, the only light was a faint red glow from the hearth. As the crackling grew louder, red appeared above them, where the dried dung was stored. Sparks began to spit down onto the hearth and floor. Suddenly with a terrible gulping sound the ceiling erupted into flame.

Shelsan grabbed Mala and dragged her toward the ladder, but the heat drove them back.

The entrance was growing larger as the flame ate away, crawling toward the cold-side. A family of mice fell from the ceiling and ran in circles on the floor, shrieking in tiny voices. A sheet of sparks showered down, then another, and a stretch of ceiling opened to the sky. Plaster from the floor above cracked and tumbled down in sheets, leaving only the beams to burn. Flame jerked toward the cold-side, billowing smoke. Over the hearth now the beams were all that remained, wrapped in fire. A wind was blowing up there, and the tongues danced. Smoke blew back into the house, bringing cold air that changed direction and sucked away, and the heat returned.

Soon the ladder itself would burn. "Quickly," he shouted. "We must get out!"

Tsurinye coughed.

"Go!" Shelsan cried, grabbing her and pushing her ahead of him through the swirling smoke. They ran over blazing thatch. She scrambled up the ladder and stood on the ledge of the warm-side wall, reaching down to help Mala. Boren came up, and at last Shelsan. The roof was burning away from them toward the cold-side. The dung pile collapsed into the house and scattered fire everywhere. Baskets and clothing erupted into flame. The ladder collapsed in a shower of red stars.

Theirs was the only house with fire in the air. Neighbors had come onto their roofs to watch. The old man to the cold-side was wrapped in his moth-eaten bearskin. He stood across from them, coughing and shivering.

Pinnak heaved his bulk from his house and stood on the edge of his roof staring at the fire as it crept across Mala's roof, across the roof of First Egg. "Looks like your fuel caught fire," he said.

The beams collapsed, one after the other, in showers of sparks and flame.

Rain began to fall in large, cold drops.

13 Now

Locking Up

Alice was on display in the center of the table. Dim light from the bulb over the locked laundry door outside filtered through the barred window and bathed her in a pearly glow. The ordinary low-wattage bulb was for safety, in case anyone took a walk around the Dig House after bedtime. Everything was quiet.

Earlier that day, after everyone else had gone, Özgür had been standing by the courtyard door. It was still light then, and a shaft of sun had caught Alice's eyes just right. The effect had been shocking. Özgür was not particularly superstitious, but his hands had trembled when he turned the face away from the door. He felt as if the dead had come to take him.

He took a last look around the Secure Room, but the head was just a dark smudge, inert and harmless.

The exhausting day was finally over. After the tense uncovering of the obsidian eyes there had been a storm of questions from specialists. There were media people constantly under foot, that breathy American woman babbled at him about the Mother Goddess, and there was that German, or French guy, whatever he was, blustering around as if he were single-handedly funding the project.

Özgür even had to endure the disconcerting stare of that admittedly attractive stone expert from Istanbul. She seemed to be thinking every time he was near the object he was going to break it. The nerve of her thinking he didn't know what he was doing! All day he'd been in motion, fretting that too many people were in the room, that the object would get breathed on, touched, even taken.

The courtyard was deserted. A number of the staff were on the roof. He could hear the distant sound track from *Indiana Jones and the Raiders of the Lost Ark*. It seemed they watched it projected against the wall up there at least once a month.

The seminar room below the movie was still occupied by reporters writing stories on Alice or editing video. Turkey had certainly changed since Özgür was young. It was catching up with the rest of the world.

Jones and some of the others had driven back into Konya to celebrate, but Özgür had to stay nearby. The object was his responsibility. No, the object was his, period.

He was contemplating the tranquil scene with satisfaction when Lodewyk Barhydt came down the stairs from the roof. "Good evening," the Dutchman said cheerfully. "How can anyone watch Indiana Jones when we have the real thing here?"

The representative was feeling too good not to be friendly. "Hello," he said. He turned to pull the door to the Secure Room closed when Lodewyk said, "Let me take just one more look."

"I must close up."

"Just a quick look?"

Özgür stepped back so the Dutchman could look through the small frosted glass window in the door.

"She's astounding, isn't she?" Lodewyk asked. "Are you sure she's safe?"

Özgür was insulted. "Of course. The door is double-locked and cannot be opened without the key. This is the only one." He lifted the brass key that hung on a ribbon around his neck, then pulled the door firmly closed and carefully locked it. He tucked the key back into his shirt, tugged at the knob a couple of times, and said good night.

He left Lodewyk standing by the door and walked to his car by the guard's house.

It was a pleasant evening, and so pregnant with hope and possibility that he remained behind the wheel of his car with his eyes closed for a few minutes, relishing the silence, the triumph.

With a deep breath he put the car in gear and drove to the village of Çalikükköy. The poplar trees were dark, vaguely threatening shapes against the star-filled sky.

New Friends

There were six men in the café-bar. Two were strangers. Four locals were, as always, huddled over two *tawula* boards. Concentration on the dice and counters of their endless tournament was broken only by an occasional gesture for a refill of tea or thick Turkish coffee. Cigarettes smoldered in a trio of ashtrays.

The strangers looked up when Özgür opened the door, smiled, and nodded. He nodded back and crossed to the bar. "*Efes, lütfen,*" he said, but the proprietor had already placed an open beer on the counter. Özgür took it to an empty table.

One of the strangers lifted his glass and gestured at a bottle of rakı and a bowl of ice cubes, inviting him over. Özgür tipped his beer at them in greeting and looked away. The last thing he wanted now was more conversation. He sipped contentedly. The project was going as he had hoped. Alice had been a happy find and was attracting international attention. His earlier conversation with Nevra had also gone well: the Ministry would grant him credit. True, the American had brought it up, and DANTE had first detected it. But Özgür had kept control. It had been a good idea to deny permission at first, then offer the permits. That way they understood who was the real boss.

One of the strangers approached. "Come drink with us," he said genially. "We're strangers here."

Özgür examined him. He was well dressed and spoke easily, with a faint accent that suggested he might not be Turkish. The other was dressed the same. What, he wondered, were they doing in an out-of-the-way village like Çalıkükköy?

Only one thing could draw strangers to this place: Aynalı Tepe. Perhaps they were from the media and wanted to ask him about the artifact. He was, after all, Özgür Tasköprülüzâde, discoverer of Alice. This could be his good luck. "Thank you," he said, standing up. "No camel route is long if you're in good company."

Only later would he remember another proverb: "The cock that crows too early gets his head cut off."

Afet

"They're too small," Afet said, tucking a neat cube of stewed lamb into her mouth and chewing thoughtfully.

Satchi said, "Too small for what?"

She put down her fork and circled her thumb and forefinger. "That's not big enough to make a useful mirror," she replied. "The size of an eye. I've never seen anything like them."

"I don't think anyone has," Satchi replied. Her English was very faintly seasoned with Turkish vowels. Unlike Özgür's accent, he found it charming. "But there are many things we'll never understand. You know, at Pinarbaşi there was a little semicircle of obsidian chips near a fire. Charcoal dated to our period, though of course the fire could have been a hundred years later, or earlier. Someone arranged them while sitting by a fire, perhaps. Ritual or play? What do we make of it? We'll never know."

They were dining on the roof terrace where it had all started three years before. The night was similar, balmy and soft as an embrace. The only noticeable difference in the surroundings was the office building that had been under construction across the street was now finished. Even this late the lights were on in many of the offices. They were like eyes, Satchi thought.

How had he ended up here, dining alone with her? Everyone else seemed to have something important to do. Jones was with one of his corporate contacts. Ben and Francy were searching for a club.

So here he was, seated opposite a woman he had just met, with nothing to do but watch her eat and say something meaningless from time to time. She didn't demand anything, yet he wanted to please her. She was calm, and serious, and comfortable to be with. Above all, she made no secret that she appreciated him. "We have something in common," she had said at the beginning of the meal. "We're both interested in dirt. Of course, in my case it's volcanic and in larger pieces and clean, but dirt just the same, wouldn't you say?" When she asked this she looked directly into his eyes and the world around him had gone dim.

She resumed eating, one small bite after another, and after a few moments he too took up his fork. When their plates were gone they both sat back at the same time and caught each other's eyes. "Why?" he asked.

Her fine dark brows knitted together.

"I mean, why do you like dirt, stone? It's not . . . ordinary."

"For a girl, you mean?"

"For anyone. But yes, for a girl."

"Because when I was young I liked pretty things, like most girls. Shiny things. My father was a physical anthropologist with an office full of the usual masks, baskets, and so on, and stone tools. One of them was a blade, very ordinary, black, and new, a piece of really inferior stone, clumsily worked by one of his students. But despite its poor quality, that blade fascinated me. It was the deepest black, yet the way it caught the light sometimes it ran silver along the edge. And that edge was sharp. I'd hold a sheet of paper by one side and slice it like it was smoke or mist. The paper would curl, as if the blade was the prow of a boat cutting through water. I always thought it was magic that something so ancient and natural, something that had been forged in the earth by such completely violent and destructive inhuman forces, could be so easily worked into something useful and beautiful." She gave a little laugh and shrugged. "That's why."

Their table was near the railing where he had first met Özgür. From behind him the moon brightened her eyes, which sparkled with silvery highlights, not at all like obsidian mirrors, but closer, human and intimate. They glowed with life. It might be the moonlight that caused it, but no, he thought, it was that small, shy laugh that imparted such life to them. Not the moon at all.

Thinking of Özgür reminded him that they had left him in charge of the site, and for a moment the smallest ripple of disquiet disturbed the surface of his perfect happiness.

He leaned forward and asked if she wanted dessert.

Survey Marker

Lena Marie and Gayle stood next to the survey marker at the highest place on the mound. The plain, frosted by the moon, stretched in all directions. They could see the faint silhouettes of mountains, but most of the world was made of stars.

"If only the awning weren't here," Lena Marie breathed, dipping her head toward the dark shadow of it. "Then the view would be perfect. Can't you feel it, Gayle, the lives of those people, standing on their rooftops 9,000 years ago and looking around them like this, the way we are now? We are completely connected to them. What did they see?"

"Swamp, mostly," Gayle said.

"Yes," Lena Marie agreed emphatically. "Yes! Swamp, the dark, damp, fecund, mysterious basin teeming with life. The trees like hair, the moonlight reflected off sheets of water in all directions. The harvest was fast approaching then, as now. It would be Goddess time. The richness of the earth, nursing Her people; the moon, waxing toward fruition, our cycles, Her cycles." She swept her hand, taking it all in, the vast expanses of space and time, the turning stars.

"Except now it's dry and turned into farmland," Gayle reminded her, ever the pragmatist. "Back then they would have depended more on nature."

"Yes, but She was here," Lena Marie went on, dismissing the comment. "The Goddess suffused this place with love; and with terror, sharp pain, sorrow . . . and with sweet comfort, too. You saw it in Her face down there, in Her mirrored eyes. You did, didn't you? You did see it. You looked into those eyes, and you saw yourself. They are the perfect metaphor from 9,000 years ago. Soon enough She would become Athena, Hekate, Kali. And with Her, so we would be empowered, too."

Gayle said nothing of the disquiet she always felt, looking at Alice.

The night was windless and held the two women standing side by side in its warm embrace.

Good Company

The evening grew ever more convivial. Özgür accepted a rakı on top of his beer. Soon he threw his jacket across a chair and watched it slide to the floor. This was enormously entertaining. He unbuttoned the top of his shirt. These strangers were no longer strange, but fellow Turks, countrymen, though they came from Sophia. For some reason this too was hilarious, Turks in Bulgaria! They all laughed merrily.

"Oh, no, no, no. I shouldn't," he said, holding out his glass to be refilled. This too produced gales of laughter.

The *tawula* players had frozen in place. Özgür had to stare hard to confirm that the smoke from their cigarettes was still in motion. "They hardly move," he whispered.

"What do you do, Özgür?" one of the men asked, staring up at the flickering blue fluorescent bulb over the bar. At first Özgür thought he hadn't really spoken.

But when the question finally got through, he almost stood up to declaim, "I am an archaeologist."

"Sit down, Özgür, and tell us more."

They told him to sit down. That meant he *had* stood up.

"I'm in charge," he said, still standing. "See?" He pulled out the key on its red ribbon. This was quite easy now that he had unbuttoned his shirt. He held the key. The fluorescent restaurant light made it gleam strange shades of brass and blue. Very carefully he tucked it away again. "I'm in charge, you see, because I have the key. And the man who has the key is in charge. Wouldn't you agree?" He knew he was insisting. Why was he insisting? He buttoned his shirt over the key with thick, clumsy fingers.

Some time later the three of them were walking along a road drenched in silvery moonlight. Often they bumped into one another. When they did, they clutched their sides in laughter. Off-key Turkish folk songs rose into the night air. Somewhere a dog barked. Özgür said, "The dog that barks does not bite." The others clapped him on the back and told him he was a funny fellow indeed.

Later still the moon was at the top of its arc, and Özgür was seated beside the road, which was made of dirt. Dirt was his friend. Satchi had told him dirt was a magical substance, like a fairy powder. He bent his face low over the road and sniffed the dirt. It was dusty and hot. "I'm thirsty," he announced.

From somewhere a bottle of water appeared. He drank it down greedily.

"Thank you," he said, using the most elaborately formal structure, as befitted his new friends. He took a deep bow, and toppled forward, turning in the air. Laughter shredded from his mouth and rose swiftly into the air above him, shrinking into silence. He fell for the longest time into the darkest possible abyss.

Glimmers

Their silence was companionable, as befitted two women in tune with the stately rhythms of the earth. They stood for a long time over the survey marker, meditating on planting, nurturing, and on the coming harvest. Great processions of stars followed one another down the western sky and under the earth, burial for Altair, and Vega, and soon Deneb. "You see the faint orange patch just up and to the left of Deneb?" Lena Marie asked.

"No. The moon's too bright."

"Come, Gayle. Just look."

"I don't have perfect vision," Gayle complained. "Not like you."

Lena Marie turned in surprise. "No contact lenses?"

"They give me headaches."

"Oh. Well, if you could see it, you would see the North American Nebula. There are lots of nebulas near Deneb. And you know what they are? Nurseries for stars, our universe giving birth."

Gayle shaded her eyes with her left hand and squinted but she still couldn't see. "It would be very far away, I suppose."

"Yes. Very far."

The Dig House was below the shoulder of the mound to their right. The moon cast a phosphorescent pall over the weeds, the tops of the poplars along the road, the vast, empty plain. In the still air it was witch light, fairy light, elf light. For the moment they could have believed they were the only two people left alive in the world.

The moon was near the jagged mountains on the horizon when they started back. Looking down at the Dig House, which lay in a pool of shadows, it seemed to be holding its breath, as if waiting for something to happen.

"That's silly," Lena Marie breathed. "It's not a person."

"Pardon?" Gayle asked. "Did you say something?"

"No." Lena Marie waved her hand negligently.

"Because I thought you said it's not a person."

"It was nothing, the Dig House, nothing," Lena Marie said. "Random thought."

"You said it was silly," Gayle insisted. "You said . . . What's that?"

There was an eldritch fire in the courtyard, a flicker of light that came and went, came and went.

"I don't know." Lena Marie shaded her eyes, as if doing that would help her see in the dark. "It looked like a light."

"It's gone now," Gayle said.

They watched, but the flicker did not recur. Lena Marie rubbed her eyes wearily. "I must be getting old," she said. "I could have sworn we saw something."

"Moonlight playing tricks," Gayle suggested.

When they were halfway down the hill they heard a car start up down the road near the poplar trees. "Someone's out late," Gayle remarked as the car drove away.

Lena Marie shrugged. "Kids," she said. She expected such behavior from the young. "Lovers, probably. With the Goddess's blessing, I must say."

"I wonder," Gayle said.

"Come, now, Gayle. This is a magic place, full moon, the Presence all around us. What a day, and what a night this has been!"

Call

Rolf flipped the portable phone open before the end of the first ring. "Yes?"

A man whispered, "We've taken delivery." The line went dead.

Aftermath

Something wet touched his face. Özgür's eyes flew open and he pushed himself back in horror. He could see nothing but two large, faintly glowing eyes. His head was splitting.

A tongue touched his forehead again, followed by a whiff of hot breath and the gentle tinkle of a bell. "Go away!" he shouted. The beast backed away.

He realized the moon was gone behind the western mountains. That's why it was so difficult to see, that and the pounding in his head. He touched the animal's side and felt wool. His touch was rewarded with a gentle bleat, restless shifting, and more soft clangs of the bell.

Sheep. It was a sheep. He almost collapsed with relief.

Where was he? His memory was shrouded in cobwebs. He had drunk an Efes at the bar. There were those two men, Turks from Bulgaria. Nice men; they had offered him drinks.

No matter how hard he tried to remember what happened afterward, no images appeared. He pressed the heels of his hands against his eyelids, and his eyes exploded into sharp pyrotechnic arcs of white phosphorus and red afterimages. With his eyes open he could just make out the edge of the road, the horizon dark against a pale splash of stars.

He saw no human light in any direction, but at least there was a road. With considerable difficulty he got his bearings. The road ran east and west. One direction was as good as another. Surely there would be a town or a farmhouse. He started walking.

The sky ahead of him grew pearl gray, then lavender, and the stars dissolved. Venus was bright as the point of a knife above the horizon; then she, too, faded and he found himself squinting at the topmost edge of the sun. It must be 5:30 in the morning.

He walked like one of the dead. The pounding in his skull acquired a rhythm, which after some time he realized was that of his footfalls on the dirt. He stopped, but the pounding continued. It improved slightly when he paced his steps to fall between the thumps in his head.

Fields rose up on all sides, wheat nearly ready for harvest. The fields repeatedly grew sharp in detail and faded away, a new rhythm, out of sync with the others. A flock of sheep dotted the far side of a fenced meadow, sleeping. One or two stirred and began grazing. He stopped to watch. Stupid sheep, life was easy, wasn't it? Just sleep, wake, eat. Then get killed and eaten.

He thought he might be hungry, but the idea of food sent a spear of nausea through him. No, he was thirsty.

Thirst. There was something about thirst. Yes, he had been thirsty and someone had thrust a bottle into his hand. He had drunk it down. This was a random image, out of time, out of context. Had it happened yesterday or long ago? He didn't know.

He saw his feet, walking, and that was when it hit him so hard he staggered: they had been walking along a road. This road?

He felt frantically for the key around his neck and sank to the ground when he discovered it still hanging on the ribbon inside his shirt, nestled among the dark hair of his chest.

When he recovered he examined the key. It was the key to the Secure Room. Alice was safe. He held the key in his fist and mouthed a brief prayer of thanks to Allah.

But they wanted something; they had drugged him, those fellow Turks. He had fallen for it like a common tourist. They had given him the water.

He sniffed the key.

It smelled of wax. He could see traces of it in the grooves. Someone had taken an impression.

He began to comprehend the true depth of his troubles

Dawn

Satchi and Afet parked outside the Dig House just as the sun was clearing the horizon. They were still laughing when they got out of the car and walked, arm in arm, into the courtyard.

The early risers, specialists mostly, were sitting around the veranda sipping cups of instant coffee. People wandered out of the dorms, rubbing their eyes. "Hell of a day yesterday," someone said. "Hell of a day. Hard to go back to work."

Satchi went into the kitchen for coffee. He and Afet sat next to each other on white plastic chairs holding their cups and watched the day come to life. The air was still, the sky a faultless blue. Fragrance rose from the flowers planted around the court.

At 6:30 the kitchen staff arrived from town in two cars. The workday started at seven for the dig crew.

Satchi made a low hum.

Afet responded with a grunt of agreement.

They sipped their coffee. Behind them they could hear the sound of the women chopping vegetables, clip-clip-clip, accompanied by low conversation.

Lodewyk came by and gave Satchi and Afet a strange look. He walked on a few paces toward his lab and turned.

"You two just get back?" he asked politely.

"Mm," Satchi said.

Afet smiled at the Dutchman.

"You drove to Konya?"

Satchi nodded.

"You must have gotten up early," he persisted.

Satchi shook his head. "Didn't go to bed."

"Really? You don't look tired."

"Not," Satchi said.

"And Jones, the others?"

"Coming later with people from the Ministry. Nevra, probably."

The Goddess women appeared, faces freshly washed and still damp. "Glorious morning," Lena Marie called out, raising her arms toward the cardinal directions one after the other. "Blessings."

"Blessings," Gayle murmured.

"Come then, let's go see Her."

"Can't," Satchi said. "Rep's not here yet."

Lodewyk and Lena Marie spoke at the same time. "No?"

"His car's still gone. He closed up last night, probably went to celebrate or something. He's been acting as if he just got married to Alice."

"He does have a look about him," Lodewyk agreed.

"OK," Lena Marie said brightly. "We'll just go have a look through the window, then, shall we?"

"Shouldn't we have coffee first?" Gayle asked.

"Oh, come on. Just a peek." The two women walked toward the Secure Room.

"She takes Alice very seriously," Lodewyk remarked.

Satchi shrugged. It was a glorious day.

Lena Marie screamed. She started banging on the Secure Room door. "She's gone!"

Satchi got up slowly and walked without haste. "Come now," he said. "It can't be."

Lena Marie turned toward him, hunched like a bird of prey. "Then where is She?" she hissed.

Satchi peered through the window. Bright morning sunlight flooded the table in barred shafts.

It was empty. He grunted. "Özgür shouldn't have handled it, but he must have put it somewhere else."

He knew even as he said it, though, that Alice was truly gone.

Iskembe

Özgür hunched over a bowl of the traditional Turkish hangover remedy: *iskembe*, tripe soup. The throbbing in his head had retreated, leaving behind a cloudy void and a dark hollow in his stomach. He didn't want to go back to Aynalı Tepe; he wanted to go to the other side of Turkey, somewhere around Lake Van, in the mountains. He wanted to start a new life under a different name.

How could this happen? Those Bulgarians knew exactly who he was and what he did. Why did they choose him? And why had he told them he was important? He'd been bragging. It was the rakı, that's what it was. They had cheated him. It was their fault, not his.

He had to get away.

This was stupid. He couldn't flee to the east. They would find him wherever he went in Turkey. Cousin Nevra would hunt him down.

He had lost the most important find in Turkish archaeological history! Could he emigrate somewhere? Where? What would he do? All his careful plans had collapsed. He pushed the bowl away and leaned back with his eyes closed, fingering the ribbon around his neck. He tried not to think.

Slowly his head cleared. He opened his eyes and looked down at his hand. The key lay in his palm.

There had been a theft. Alice was gone. He had no doubt about this at all; there was no need to check. Özgür was a realist.

But he still had the key! There was nothing to tie him to the theft. Nothing, that is, except the two men, and the *tawula* players, and the barkeeper. But what did they know? The *tawula* players probably didn't even notice him. The proprietor had sold him an Efes, but that's not a crime. He had gone out with the two strangers after a few glasses of rakı, true, but what did that mean? Would they even connect Özgür's visit to the bar to the theft of the artifact?

He had an alibi too. He had been at the bar. There were witnesses. He was in town, not at the site. He couldn't have been the thief!

All he had to do was go back to the dig, make a big show of taking out his key, and discover the theft. No one could possibly suspect him. He had the key!

An enormous weight left him just like that. *Iskembe* was a miracle cure.

14 Then

Year, Turning

It seemed that wet-time, the time of flood and sun, of melt and green, would never come, that they were trapped in an unending cold-time.

Shelsan fashioned a new ladder from scraps of wood and sinew and fixed it against the warm-side so they could climb out onto the flat mud brick of the wall. Through long nights they huddled under a shelter of branches on the sunrise-side sleeping platform. The fire had spared his painting of the dead, the stories of all those burials through the generations and house reconstructions and they slept next to it, in close communion with the ancestors, huddled together.

During the day Mala crouched before the hearth and fed small, damp bits of dried dung to the fire. Smoke billowed from the fitful blaze, but without a roof over their heads it escaped easily into the gray, leaden skies. Some days the rain turned to fat flakes of snow that hissed on the dome of the hearth, ran in rivulets down the sides, and pooled over the graves of the boy and his infant sister.

Mala began to cough and took to the sleeping platform. Her forehead grew hot. Shelsan wrapped her upper body in the skin of the leopard he had killed to give her strength and power, but she shivered and moaned.

Tsurinye took over the cooking, holding her swollen belly with one hand. Later she sat by Mala and sang, but her songs passed uselessly into the sky with the hearth smoke.

Late in the afternoon she stopped and sat, head down, hair falling over her ears, and stared at Mala's face. Suddenly she said, "Boren! Come."

He approached and she waved toward the sunset platform. "Sit there."

He did so, puzzled. Light bounced from the white floor and walls. Light reflected from the painted wall tinted the lines on Boren's face a faint red. Tsurinye stared at his face for a long time, then asked for her tools.

As she had on Boren when he was Little Boren, she now worked on Mala's face. After dark she worked by lamplight, sketching the lines and loops, the red tears and black welts on her forehead and down her cheek. By the time morning leaked into the Egg she was tapping a point of frozen tears into the woman's chin, adding red, adding black.

Boren said, "The pattern is the same as mine." Tsurinye did not answer. Boren added, "But it is the other side of her face you are doing."

Toward the middle of the day she fell backward and could not be roused until another night had come and gone.

Passing

The next day Mala's eyes were unnaturally bright and she was weak, but she had stopped coughing, and took some food. Shelsan cleared his throat and squeezed Tsurinye's shoulder. Then he climbed outside.

The remaining bit of roof over cold-side of the house still protected the storage chambers. Their hoard of lentils and grain, though small, remained dry. He sat there and carefully sharpened a set of hand axes. When he was finished he said, "Come, Boren. Though it's not yet the season, we must cut new beams. Call the cousins. We cannot wait longer for the year to turn to wet-time, and the world to make us warm again."

Meager snow had fallen in the night and the roofs of the Place were dusted white. Mist filled the air, flakes twisted and fluttered in a fitful breeze. Flares of sunlight stabbed through and disappeared. When Shelsan and Boren stepped onto the mud brick of their wall and moved toward the opening between First Egg and Pinnak's house, their footprints melted into the white. When they stepped across the opening between their roofs and looked down into the pit between them, they saw that all the waste both houses had thrown there was also covered. Pinnak's sheep, like everyone's in cold-time, were penned just outside of the Place. Dogs barked in the distance.

All around them the People, tired of the dark and cold, and of the gloom inside, shivered around fires under rough roof shelters. Their voices were muffled and calm. Some, despite the cold, were playing games of chance, throwing bones and moving stone counters on grids scratched into the roof plaster.

Shelsan started across Pinnak's roof, Boren limping at his side. At once there was a shout from inside, and Pinnak's fusty bearskin hat popped from the entrance. He rose into the light and they could smell the flax oil on his recently trimmed beard. "Hey, what?" he growled, climbing to his feet and blocking their way. "It is not right, you crossing my roof."

"Not right?" Shelsan spoke mildly, though his voice was taut as a bowstring.

"Ssah," Pinnak hissed. "This is my house. You disturb my family."

"We have never denied you the right to cross our roof," Shelsan said, his voice tightly controlled.

Pinnak looked away. "Well, yes, but you see, you have no roof," he said. "Things have changed since you went away."

"Things have changed since I returned."

Pinnak's eyes flashed. "What's that to mean?"

"What I say." Shelsan gestured behind him at the yawning pit of First Egg. "You are correct, we have no roof."

Pinnak pulled at his beard, frowning. "It wasn't my doing," he muttered.

"What? I could not hear."

"I said," Pinnak shouted, "it wasn't my doing."

"Ah?" A smile twitched at the corners of Shelsan's mouth. "It wasn't? Was there Sky Fire that night? Did the Sky Bull roar and awaken me? It is possible, Pinnak, that sky spirits threw down the fire and set our roof ablaze. But we awoke not to the roar of the Heaven Bull, but to smoke in our house and fire in our roof. Only the rain came, the tears of the gods weeping for us, perhaps. It saved us, didn't it, that rain? And it seemed that made you unhappy."

Pinnak reached for his spear rack. "Do you accuse me?"

"Don't try my patience, Pinnak. I say that our house is open to the cold-time sky and yours is not. I say that snow falls on our hearth, and on the graves of our children. I say that had it not been for the rain, we would be hungry now, if we lived at all. I say that it is strange the fire should come like that, in the time of rain. These things only I say."

Pinnak held a spear, his head thrust forward. "Best you say nothing more."

Shelsan did smile then, though the smile was cold and without mirth. "I must rebuild my roof, Pinnak, and the light is short. Let us pass."

The fat man shrugged but made no move to step out of their way.

The old man on the cold-side roof shouted, "Let them pass, Pinnak."

The cousins, those who lived on the warm-side and others on the sunset-side, shouted agreement. Four of them joined Shelsan and Boren. "Let us pass, Pinnak."

Pinnak shrugged and stepped aside. "Things have changed, Shelsan," he muttered, so the others could not hear. "Don't forget that. It is not your house you speak of, it is Mala's. Hers is the line of First Egg."

Shelsan frowned. "So that is it? That is what has changed since I went away? Yes, Mala told me. You would become heir of First Egg?"

"I said nothing," Pinnak mumbled.

Shelsan shrugged. "Thank you, cousins," he said to the four who had joined them.

They wound their way to the warm-side house, and so crossed onto the roof beyond Pinnak's. Hard pellets of snow swirled around them, and soon enough, when they turned back to look, Pinnak was hidden behind a curtain of white.

Building the Sky

Shelsan, Boren, and the others passed nights at Dak's Cave huddled by a small fire and days cutting beams, which they then dragged back to the Place over ice and drifted snow. Twice they had to wait for blizzards to pass. Even with the cousins to help, it was slow work. Although his leg obviously pained him, Boren never complained. By the time they had the beams in place the days were visibly longer. The darkest time was over.

Mala sat in silence on the pallet, her bright eyes darting here and there, watching Shelsan and Boren framing the new roof and laying down cross-beams from first to last light. They thatched with bundles of lake-reed. Finally, one cold, clear day, they plastered with silt mud from near the river.

Pinnak watched it all in silence, his mouth twisted into a grim smile, his eyes glittering. Boren often stared back, but Shelsan touched his arm. "Don't look at him, Boren. He wants this house. He won't have it as long as Mala lives."

"Why?"

"This is First Egg. He thinks it will make him bigger."

"He's big enough already," Boren said.

One evening as twilight was gathering around them and the sunset horizon was a green line, Boren said quietly, as if he had been thinking for some time and decided to speak, "Things are changing, aren't they, Babi? The clans no longer mesh. Locust won't speak with Leopard. The People are tense and angry, and it's not just this long cold-time. It didn't feel like that with Basatzaun. It didn't feel that way before we went on the Walk of the World. Only since I came here with Tsurinye."

"You're no longer a boy, Boren. You see now as a man."

"No, Babi, it is more than just seeing. Since the sacrifice of the bull, since I drank from Basatzaun's cup, things have changed. Perhaps it is Tsurinye, because she made my face like this, that people see me differently, too. No one has spoken of it, but they show what they feel, and now when they see Mala, the way her face matches mine, they draw back. They are afraid of Tsurinye, Babi. It would not have been that way before. In days past there have been strangers in the Place, and they were welcome, the way we were welcomed by Basatzaun, who is now related to me. You told me this yourself." He looked toward Pinnak's house and added, "Also, there is something between Pinnak and Temkash."

Shelsan showed his teeth. "Ah, Boren, I am also angry also with Temkash."

"You have not given him the frozen tears he wanted."

"No, and I will not. My anger remains. But Temkash has joined with Pinnak and so I have buried the frozen tears beside the boy."

"I helped you do that, Babi."

"Then you know why."

"I remember Little Brother died, Babi, and say you are right to keep the frozen tears for our family. But this is something more I feel, something in the People, something hidden that flows like wet-time water under ice. It is a danger in the Place."

The last light left the sky. Shelsan sighed. "I know, Boren. I, too, feel it."

Light

The floor, blackened from the fire, disappeared under a new coat of white lime plaster. "Now," Shelsan said, "we can live again, between sky above and earth below, between the Spirits and the Grands."

Mala smiled weakly, but she smiled, and as the days went by she moved about the house again, though always in silence.

Tsurinye's term grew close. Then, one fitful night when it seemed wet-time must surely come at last, she cried out in the night, and began to breathe hard, her face twisted in pain.

Mala walked a circle around the pregnant woman, sweeping the air with her hands. "Go, spirit, come, spirit," she said, looking at the beams and supports of the ceiling. She turned to the opening in the roof. "Go through the sky opening and leave this woman, spirit of earth, spirit of death. Come through the sky opening and guard this woman, spirit of sky, spirit of light."

Shelsan and Boren stood back against the warm-side wall beside the hearth. They kept their feet on the place of Frozen Tears, and were careful to keep them off the places where the two younglings had been put into the floor.

Mala whisked the air with a cedar branch, filling First Egg with its smell.

Tsurinye was breathing fast and hard when Mala pushed the men outside. "The time is close. You must leave now," she said. "Go fetch the Widow Klayn."

At the top of the ladder she looked hard at Shelsan, then disappeared down into the darkness.

After they had brought the Widow Klayn back, Shelsan and Boren sat on the edge of the sunrise wall and waited. The sounds from inside were clamorous and strange, but at last there was a small cry and silence.

Widow Klayn emerged. "Tsurinye has birthed a small one, a girl," she said. "Her name is Arghinye, which, she says, means Light."

Wet-Time

Snow faded at last from the fields, and faint green dusted the wet ground. The mood of the Place seemed to lighten, if only a little, and someone said the People should celebrate the return of the good spirits to the new land. Even Pinnak looked less sour, and though he didn't smile he lifted his hand in greeting when Shelsan or the others came up into the sky.

Shelsan said he waved because he had built a new rack for his spears, six of them with long, delicate leaf-shaped blades, and he wanted everyone to notice them. "He doesn't care that his blades are weak," Shelsan said. "Those spears are not for killing."

"What could they be for but killing?" Mala asked, a rare break in her silence.

They sat around a small, new hearth on the roof. A thatch awning shaded them from the sun. It was still chilly, but dry and clear. Thin pillars of smoke rose from fires all across the plain of roofs. The Place had come alive again at last. From cold-side came the sound of singing. Distant animal sounds – bleats of the lambs and kids, dog barks, the stamping of feet – floated on the aromatic breeze. Arghinye sucked loudly and Boren secretly watched as if he feared some harm, as if evil spirits walked among them.

"His spears are only to show others he has things of value." Shelsan was carving a wooden toy for the baby. "He thinks they give him size, importance."

Boren tore his eyes away from his woman and child. "Babi," he said, always respectful. "They do make him important. He has convinced them that this year the Great Feast should come on the Unborn Moon. Others listen when he changes the ways."

"This is true, Boren. Always it was the Water Bird Festival at the time of the Grown Moon, two days before the Wasting begins."

"Yet the People have agreed now to what he has told them."

"And how does this happen?" Shelsan asked, examining the wooden figure of a woman holding a baby to her breast. He scraped a bit of wood away and handed the object to Tsurinye.

Boren said, "The clans look to him. The men ask him what to do. He determines pairings for Sorrow and Locust. This never was before – even I, young as I am, know it. I chose Tsurinye and she chose me. We did not ask you, we did not ask Basatzaun. Now Pinnak tells the People who they can take into their Houses, where to send the flocks, where to build. Have you not seen this?"

"I have seen it, Boren, but Pinnak is only one among many."

"I fear it is more than that."

Final Combat

It was not long after this that Shelsan and Boren met the great bull, which they called Mala's Bull.

The land was wet, wetter than last year. The river now ran fast from the warm-side, from the mountains where Dak's Cave was, and the lake water rose, flooding the willow brakes. Birds gathered in great numbers, and the People could eat again. There were eggs, fish, snails, and frogs. More hunting parties went out, and low boats made of reeds dotted the water. Families went upstream to build dams, and their weirs grew full. Those with livestock took their flocks to higher ground. The Place was almost empty. Of those remaining most slept up-side on the roof.

Mala remained in her silence and despair, certain someone was going to die. Boren, Tsurinye, the baby, Shelsan even: one of them was marked. Once, in the deepest night, she had whispered how the Bull had told her; Shelsan told her to go back to sleep, it was a dream.

"No, Shelsan, it will come to pass."

"People are always dying, Mala. It is the way of the world. Your Bull has given you no secret."

"You're wrong, Shelsan. Wrong to say this, wrong to defy the gods. It is the Bull, the one with the broken horn tip, the one who killed Widow Klayn's man. Now he is my Bull. He spoke to me." She drew a sharp breath in through her teeth, her eyes flashing. "He spoke to me," she repeated.

Shelsan said nothing. What was there to say? She would believe it was her Bull, and how could he say no? He had not been there.

Next morning as sunlight seeped into the sky he said, "Come, Boren. Call the cousins. Today we will hunt, for tomorrow is the Feast and we must bring wild meat in praise of the spirits."

On the next roof Pinnak squatted on his heels, gently tapping on a core of frozen tears. "That will be a lovely blade," Shelsan said to him. "Come with us now, we will hunt. Bring your new blade. You can see if it will last more than one use."

"You are funny, Shelsan, but you know I do not hunt. I have my herds, my stands of grain, and my sheep and goats have multiplied this year. These are the things of power now, Shelsan. Hunting is of days gone." He sighted along the graceful point, tapped away a tiny imperfection, looked again. Sunlight was caught in the translucent stone, a shooting star down the dark triangle.

"No, Pinnak, you should come. It is said the aurochs herd that came so close to the Place in the last hot season has drifted toward the hills to the sunset-side. Boren and I are going." Shelsan smiled. "What do you say, Pinnak? Time for a hunt."

Pinnak grunted. He lifted a shaft, still green and uncured, and fitted the tanged blade to its end. Shelsan started to point out the wood would probably warp as it dried, but stopped. The image of the great bull came to him and seemed to tell him to keep his council. He gave Pinnak a wave.

At the sunset-side they met a party of a dozen cousins, all men in their prime, and set out. They walked along the edge of a marsh spreading in irregular sheets across the land. The water reflected hard light as the sun climbed the sky. Tamarisk trees were in leaf, and the rushes were growing tall.

Boren's leg slowed them, and he apologized.

"It is not important, Boren. Mala's Bull said someone would die, and you almost died. Yet we cut the beams and dragged them back. You grow strong. Do not worry, you can hunt." He sent the cousins ahead. "Perhaps he meant someone *might* die, and not *will* die."

Boren insisted. "If you'd had someone whole to help you, you could have built the roof sooner. Mala might not have gotten sick. If you had someone whole you would be with the others hunting, not back here with me."

"Be quiet, Boren. Mala is well, and we are hunting now, you and I." From far away they heard shouting. The cousins would bring back meat. It was not important that Shelsan and Boren do the same. It was enough they were together, hunting.

They could smell fresh dung of the aurochs long before they saw them. Shelsan led the way to the upwind side, and they crept close.

Mala's Bull stood on a slight mound, his head low, the broad arc of his horns scraping the dirt. The slight breeze brought the sound of his labored breath. Each inhalation rasped deep in his throat, followed by a low gurgling.

He faced a younger bull. This would be his final challenge. His opponent stood fast, legs spread, head up. He glared at the old one, pawed the ground, lowered his head and charged.

Mala's Bull stood his ground, his great horns ready. The challenger, who expected more, skidded, hooked his horn into the old one's side.

Mala's Bull bellowed and twisted his head, nicking the young one on the shoulder. The challenger trotted a few meters away and turned.

The old bull was finished. His labored breathing was broken by long periods of silence as he gathered the energy for another breath. A line of blood slowly connected his nostrils with the ground.

His harem of five cows stood in a circle around them, watching his agony. Their calves stuck close, their attention on the magnificent, broken figure at the center of this drama. They ignored the younger bull.

Mala's Bull lifted his head and snorted a long loop of bloody saliva, but his eyes flashed with his old pride and arrogance. Shelsan and Boren could clearly see the polished tip of one horn and the dull, shattered tip of the other. The beast's eyes met theirs and held them.

Then, with a deep, resigned groan, he toppled to the ground and lay motionless.

Bucranium

The cows shuffled a few paces toward the body and backed away.

The challenger waited. Finally he turned and with a disdainful toss of his head walked away. The cows led their calves after him, leaving the huge body to Shelsan and Boren.

He had been old, older than they had imagined, and his meat was tough. After some discussion they decided to leave the body and bring back only the head. It was a long, sweaty job cutting it free, but at last they managed to detach it, strip off most of the flesh, and remove the brain. Shelsan looped some bark cord around the horns and slung it on his back.

When they placed the skull at her feet, Mala's eyes widened in recognition, but she said nothing. She had dreamed often enough of what would happen, or of what was happening in the other realms beyond sky or under the earth. And now she sensed them gathering, the birdmen, the man-beasts, the others that could not be named. They were coming, as the Bull had told her. Someone would die.

She and Tsurinye polished the skull, and Shelsan installed it on the sunrise-side pillar at the foot of the sleeping platform above the other skull, the other horns.

The next night would be the first night of the Unborn Moon, the night of the Feast.

Unborn Moon

The People gathered. Those who had been away hunting or scattering seed for their stands of grain returned by mid-afternoon. The Feast would begin outside the Place, on the side away from the river, on the flat place the men had prepared.

Pinnak darted everywhere, one moment urging the men to scrape and clear a larger space in the scrub. Later he had a gang filling dirt into the wet hollows. When sufficient space was cleared and packed and dry, he had Temkash perform a successful ceremony to hold off the rain, for the sky remained empty of clouds.

As the underworld swallowed the sun, Pinnak was directing the construction of a pile of brushwood high as a man. Soon sparks danced in the air. From other fires came the smell of roasting lamb and kid. The women brought down huge wooden platters of tubers and bowls of lentil stew.

Small groups huddled close to their family fires. Women used tongs to draw from them hot clay balls. These they dropped into great wooden bowls, making the water in them hiss and steam. From time to time they added things. There was an air of suspense, as if they were waiting for the moon to rise. It was a still evening that carried only the soft murmur of conversation. Children moved soberly through the crowd, with none of their usual raucous play. It seemed more like death rites than celebration. Darkness closed on the gathering ground like a thick skin curtain.

A mounting sense of anticipation rippled through the crowd. The children, who had been practicing their dances for the last hands of days, began to fidget as the meal came to an end, eager to put on their costumes, get in line and begin. Some of the youngest slept, though they would certainly wake when the music began.

Finally Pinnak announced in a loud voice, "It's the Unborn Moon. Water Bird will come."

Someone began to tap a soft, slow, steady beat on an aurochs skull with a stick. Across the camp other drums joined, at first reinforcing the beat, then varying it.

Out of the shadows the first line of dancers appeared, reddened by the glow of the great fire. The People gathered in a circle. Shadows leaped across their faces.

Water Bird appeared, enormous, great wings spread, long stilt legs scissoring. A screech came from some instruments nearby, and the bird lifted her head, turned it right, turned it left. The child dancers scattered under her feet in fear. Water Bird was terrible, circling the fire, bending down to stare into the faces of the People. Even Pinnak, puffed up with importance, shrank back from her look.

The drumming grew louder, more insistent. Men emerged out of the shadows in a long line, then a second line, and a third, circling the fire inside the line of spectators, the women and children, who had now shed their costumes. Twangs and shrieks from flutes and bow-strings joined the music. It began to syncopate, stagger its rhythm. Water Bird stalked away.

Pinnak was soon puffed up again, seated beside the Pretender, who looked off into the darkness and took no part. From time to time Pinnak tapped him on the arm and said something, but Temkash only frowned and looked away.

Cups went around and the People drank. The drink was hot and comforting, and they began singing long, repetitive refrains that spoke of their migration from the cold sunrise-side, of Water Bird settling in the Place, the Nest, and how the People were Her children.

Boren leaned back with a contented sigh. "Even if it isn't the real Water Bird Festival," he said, "it is familiar."

"Not to me," Tsurinye said with a small laugh. "The music is strange, transformations stranger. No one tells us what festival to have; we know. Here Pinnak tells People what to do, and they do it. And of course we don't have a Water Bird."

They drank more, and lights began dancing before Shelsan's eyes. He had trouble seeing the woman with the small baby at her breast. Did he know her? Of course, she was the one Boren brought back from the Mountain of Frozen Tears. Her name was Tsurinye. "You have a Bull," he said thickly.

"Yes, but none has ever been like Mala's, whose horns are the greatest I've seen."

"He waited for us," Boren said. His words, too, started running together, as if they had been frozen and were now melting. "He knew we were coming, and he waited. We were supposed to bring him back. You saw that, didn't you, Babi? You saw that he was waiting."

"Yes."

Boren shook his finger. "Yes," he mumbled. "We saw he was waiting."

He sat beside Mala. The firelight flickered, the decorated halves of their faces separated by the plain. Shelsan saw the two faces run together for a moment. He rubbed his eyes and looked again and the faces were one, distorted with lines, dots, loops, tears of blood, each side the image of the other. He couldn't tell which was Mala, which was Boren. An icicle of fear dropped through him and he turned to Tsurinye, but she was feeding the baby. He looked away.

The music picked up, and the People's feet were pounding the ground, making it shake. Heads rose and fell in unison. Boren jumped up and joined them, his arms around two others. Their heads were tossing wildly and their eyes were flashing. They paused to drink more of the tea, only to plunge right back into the dance. Smoke from the fires now drifted among the People and obscured the stars.

Night Spirit

Mala drew the leopard cloak around her shoulders and fell into a reverie. Spider webs floated among the dancers, lifting and falling, sinuous draperies of woven air through which the dancing progressed. The sound was very far away.

She was a child again, watching the reflection of wild flames against the wall, holding her mother's skirt as she pounded grain in a wooden urn. The soft padded thumping it made. The grain began whole, seeds spilling into the dark wood, disappearing over the brim of it, and then her mother lifted the big wooden pestle and thrust it down. It made that thump. Soon the grain was powder in the urn, and the women tipped it into a woven basket, the special grain basket, not the kind they had buried the stillborn baby in. She had woven it herself from special flowering wild grass. It had smelled so sweet. Her mother's cheerful hearth, the orange flame dancing lightly over the flat disk of dried dung, its thick, pungent smoke.

She took a step, then another, pulling the leopard tighter around her shoulders. Not that it was cold. She needed the protection. The bull had spoken and she was worried. Best to move away from the movement, it was making her dizzy. She turned toward the darkness, away from the great fire, and walked unsteadily. There was water there, and dry land, and plants bursting into green. She stood in the center of a dark place and looked away. Were those stars over her head? Yes, they were.

Her bull loomed in the dark there, eyes soft in regard. She knew what he had told her now, that someone would die. All things happened at once, her life, the lives of others. She was the last of her line. No daughter to the lineage. The bull breathed out, a hollow sound. Yet the bull was also dead, his cranium set into the sunrise post of First Egg. He had gone over ahead of her, leading the way. Yes.

She took a deep breath, taking in the smells of the night, of the season of growing things, the dark, flat smells of the Unborn Moon.

It was her last breath.

Something slipped over her head and settled around her neck. Shelsan had made her a necklace, she thought, even as it tightened around her throat. How kind of him. He wasn't her man, not really. Big Boren had been, but he was gone, and Shelsan had taken care of her. She was grateful to him. She wanted to turn, to tell him how she felt, but she couldn't turn.

There was no need to turn. Her Bull stood before her in full sunlight, his massive shoulders as powerful as ever. He looked into her eyes. Their eyes met in that moment across whatever divided them. There was no river, no mountain between them. She went to meet him; he came to meet her. They were one.

A pressure built up in her eyes, and the dark began to swim with spirits, so many, they were beyond counting.

One of them rushed toward her like the very darkness itself and carried her away.

15 Now

Questions

Word of the catastrophe spread quickly through the project community. Everyone understood Alice's loss would mean the certain end of the Aynalı Tepe Project: permits would be withdrawn, foreign archaeologists expelled from the country if not thrown in jail, Jones's reputation would be in ruins, Satchi would probably have to get a real job, and the students would have no future. Aynalı Tepe would be toxic to everyone involved. Thus it was important that the loss be kept confidential and Alice recovered if at all possible.

Satchi ordered a search and summoned Mehmet. The guard's shock at the loss was so palpable Satchi felt guilty just asking him if he'd seen or heard anything suspicious. No, Mehmet insisted. He and his wife had gone to bed at eleven. Everything was quiet. Everyone who was leaving had already left, even Mr. Tasköprülüzâde, who sat in his car for a few minutes before driving off. Mehmet locked the gate and no one had come through after that until early this morning when Doctor Bennett and Dr. Orbay returned from Konya.

He wrung his hands, his eyes imploring. What could he do to help? He was ready to do anything. He loved his job; he loved Professor Jones, and Doctor Bennett, all the people working here.

"Don't worry, Mehmet. We'll find her. We have to," Satchi added under his breath.

Jones arrived in a spray of gravel and leaped from the car. "What the hell happened?"

"She's gone," Satchi said.

"I know that. How?" This could well have been the first time anyone had seen Jones genuinely upset. He understood the consequences.

Satchi shrugged. "The Secure Room door is still locked. Özgür has the only key. We can't go inside until he gets here."

"So. Where is he?"

"I don't know."

"You checked the windows, I suppose?"

Satchi shrugged. "Of course; and the roof. If there were a crawl space I'd have checked it, but there is no way into the Secure Room without the key. No one here took her."

"Özgür?" It was the obvious question.

Again Satchi shrugged.

"No," Jones muttered. "Not likely. He has even more to lose than we do, unless someone offered him an awful lot of money, and even then I don't think he'd take it. Damn!"

The desolate feeling grew more palpable as the hunt progressed. Deep down, everyone knew Alice was lost. No matter how many times they shaded their eyes and squinted through the windows of the Secure Room, the table remained stubbornly empty.

When Lodewyk's student came down from the mound to announce she'd finished excavating burial in of Structure 1-5, the others stared as if she were mad. "What is it?" she asked, bewildered.

"Alice is gone," Lodewyk said.

"I didn't know. I've been up there since dawn. I wanted to finish today. I don't understand."

"No one understands," Satchi assured her. "Not yet, anyway."

Alice on the Road

Alice was snug in her box, and her box, wrapped in blankets, was snug in the trunk of a new Honda sedan.

For many hours the car glided in full daylight at a sedate, legal pace over toll highways and winding back roads. Its windows were darkened. It passed in silence through small towns. Once it stopped for gas. While a young boy filled the tank, the driver leaned against the front fender near the passenger door and sipped a glass of tea.

By the time the car was out of sight again, the boy had forgotten about it.

The landscape changed from plain to fairy towers of volcanic tufa to steep mountains. By late afternoon the Honda was cruising north through low rolling hills, a clear horizon in every direction.

Near dusk it passed a sign indicating Amasya was 17 kilometers ahead, slowed and stopped. A narrow dirt road disappeared into fields of wheat to the right.

After a moment's hesitation the car turned and drove without haste until it disappeared into the sea of waving grain.

First Steps

Two young policemen, a patrolman and an officer, arrived shortly after Jones. The officer was perplexed. "Why does someone take a skull?" he asked in passable English.

"No one has *taken* the skull," Jones said. "We don't for the moment know where it is, that's all." He turned to Satchi. "I'm not sure I understand why these policemen are here."

The excavator shrugged.

"Excuse, please," Mehmet interrupted. "I called. It is a matter for police, no?"

The guard seemed so worried and unhappy, Jones could only nod. "Of course, Mehmet." Turning back to the policemen he said, "I'm sure you understand this is a highly confidential matter."

"Yes," the officer said slowly. "I understand it is confidential. I just don't understand why does someone take a skull."

"It's archaeologically significant," Jones replied. "It's like others from the region, but in many ways it is unique."

The officer shook his head. "I do not understand." He turned to Mehmet and asked a long string of questions in rapid Turkish.

Mehmet translated, "He apologizes that he is not an archaeologist and doesn't understand the significance. He says an old skull is worth nothing except to the family. He wants to know for what reason someone would want it."

"Tell him," Jones said glumly, "that *this* skull is really old, and valuable to a lot of people, for many reasons."

After a further lengthy exchange Mehmet said, "What different reasons might there be? The policeman thinks it might be helpful to his investigation if he knew what kinds of people would be interested in such a thing and why they would want to take it."

"I see. Well, I, for one, am interested because I want to know how people and societies developed, what significance objects have for ritual or social meaning. Knowing this helps us understand why we organize ourselves the way we do. But I'm an archaeologist, and I wouldn't steal something from my own project, especially when doing so would have serious consequences for me and my team."

He saw Lena Marie Troye standing near the door to the Secure Room, apparently in shock. "That woman over there is interested because she believes the skull has religious significance, as indeed it may. I sincerely doubt she would take it, either. Some may find it beautiful and desire to own it, others might be willing to sell it to them. There are people who believe the skull belongs to ancestors of people who live here today, and so represents the patrimony of Turkey." Jones' shoulders slumped. "The fact is, we just don't understand how it could be missing. Özgür has the only key and he's . . ." He looked up.

Mehmet spoke again with the policeman. "He asks where is Mr. Özgür. I have told him Mr. Tasköprülüzâde left late last night and has not yet returned."

Satchi interrupted. "Lodewyk said he spoke to Özgür as he was locking up and watched him drive away. The door was definitely locked, and Alice was definitely inside. Özgür wouldn't take it, I'm sure. So unless he lost the key, or gave it to someone, he's not a suspect. On the other hand, the matter may be solved when he gets here. After all, he was the last person to see Alice."

"Well, there you are," Jones said, and at that moment the representative drove up.

"I am here," Özgür called from his car window. "You will begin to study Alice now, isn't it so?" He noticed the policemen for the first time, though he was parked next to their car. "Something is wrong?"

"Alice is missing," Jones said. "You don't happen to know where she is, do you?"

There followed a long and very complicated series of expressions on Özgür's face. Many were indecipherable, though shock was clearly one. "This is impossible," he stammered at last. "I forbid it. I am in charge. Who has done this thing? Why . . ."

Jones interrupted. "Where have you been, Özgür?"

"No, no, Mr. Dr. Jones, I am at home, not feeling well this morning."

The police officer asked, in English, if he lived in Çalikükköy.

"I have rented a place there for the summer, yes. Usually I live in Konya."

Jones nodded at Mehmet. While the guard and the others plunged into a four-way discussion with Özgür and the two policemen, Jones took Satchi by the arm and led him the length of the veranda. "These guys aren't going to find anything any time soon," he said under his breath. "We're going to have to do our own investigation."

"They're the police," Satchi replied. "It's their job."

"Well, good for them if they beat us to it, but we can't count on them. They'll be too slow and time is short. We have to contain this before it gets out, so we have to find Alice. That's Plan A, find Alice."

"What's Plan B?"

"I'm working on it."

"I see," Satchi said. "Well, we're in Turkey. My command of the language is limited, and unless you're prepared to surprise me, yours is even more so. We have a handicap."

Jones smiled for the first time since he'd arrived. "What about your girlfriend?"

Satchi started. "Girlfriend?"

"Dr. Orbay. She's Turkish and fluent in English. She's . . . well, she's a woman and might be able to learn things we, as strangers, couldn't."

"This is a Muslim country."

"Exactly. Furthermore, she's beautiful."

"You're shameless."

Something ferocious appeared in Jones's smile. He didn't disagree.

In the World

"What," Lena Marie said to Gayle, "if Alice got loose?" They were up on the mound. It was curiously deserted with everyone searching for Alice at the Dig House. A few students were walking the periphery of the fence, heads down. They looked very small from up here.

"Excuse me?"

"What if She got loose, Gayle? What if She's gone a-wandering on Her own? Don't you see what it would mean, Alice loose in the world again?"

"I'm really not following this, Lena Marie. Are you trying to say Alice *escaped*? That a dead person's skull wrapped in plaster managed to get out of a locked room *by itself*? You can't be serious."

"Gayle, now really, what do you take me for? Of course I don't think Alice escaped without help. She influenced someone to liberate her, that's all. She's the Goddess. You'd agree with that, wouldn't you?"

Gayle sniffed.

They looked into the Rabbit Hole. A beetle was struggling to climb up the painted wall but kept falling back onto the clean plaster of the floor, which, except for the excavations of the burials and the darker circle where Alice's post had been set into it, was pristine, as if newly made.

"She did something back then, Gayle. Something powerful. She healed, or She influenced the spirits in some way to help Her people. No, don't say anything. I know your theory. She did something evil. I don't believe it."

"But what if she did, and now, as you say, she's out in the world?"

"Fiddlesticks," Lena Marie snorted. "The Goddess is benign. If She freed Herself from the clutches of archaeologists, it's because She has a mission. We should honor that."

Sunlight poured through the translucent awning like honey and filled the excavation. "I hope you're right," Gayle said. "Because if you're wrong, it's going to get really ugly."

Feed Your Head

A hanging lamp threw a harsh circle of light over the two men contemplating the grotesque face on the table. The top of the head seemed to glow. "It is a frightening object, is it not, this thing your men have delivered," one said. He was squat, almost as wide as he was tall, but the thumb and index finger that pinched his lower lip were surprisingly long and elegant.

"Frightening?" Rolf replied. "That would depend on how you looked at it, Sevket. Personally, I find profit, not fear, in that endearing face."

Sevket's curling wave of dark brown hair gave off an odor of lilacs when he bent forward from his thick waist to look into Alice's eyes. His forehead grazed the shade of the lamp and set it in motion, giving the head an eerie semblance of life. "One can see oneself in them," he said, straightening carefully and stopping the shade.

"Yes," Rolf agreed. "Obsidian, fine polish, very good work."

"Who put them there?"

"Pardon?"

"What is this object?" He wiped both palms over his pompadour, causing it to lie flat and spring up again. "Where is it from?"

Rolf looked around. In the shadows were shelves crammed with objects, four shuttered windows, three overstuffed chairs, and a stand of professional photographic lights, tripods, and other equipment. "It's Neolithic," he said slowly.

The man gave him a sharp look. "You will pay for my expertise. Please do not insult me."

"Aynalı Tepe."

"That is what I suspected, Mr. Butcher. This would be the famous Alice, then."

"I don't have much time," Rolf interrupted. "When I was here before you said you were the best."

"I am. There is no need for concern," Sevket said simply. He turned toward the door to the back. "Ahmet! Come!"

A man in his late twenties appeared in the doorway. "Yes, *efendim?*" His hands and overalls were dusted with white powder.

"Ahmet is my associate," Sevket told Rolf. "He's very . . . gifted. Take a look at this, Ahmet."

"Yes, *efendim.*" The youth walked slowly around the table. "I've never seen anything quite like it. The eyes, very interesting, don't you agree, *efendim*, that the eyes are most interesting?" His accent in English was strong, but he was fluent.

"Yes, Ahmet, the eyes are particularly interesting. Can you do it?"

Ahmet looked offended. "You ask this of me?"

His boss smiled. "It is only to reassure our client, Ahmet."

"Ah, well, then." Ahmet relaxed. "We will need a skull. It is skull inside, is it not?"

"Yes," Rolf said.

"You have X rays?"

"No."

"Then we will make some, we'll need as close a match as possible. We can get a skull, can't we, *efendim?*"

The man waved a hand negligently. "I know people."

Ahmet continued, "Female?"

"Probably."

Ahmet nodded. "The art is in the patina of the plaster, the color, any scratches or pits, discolorations . . . We'll have to consolidate, clean it up. It will be easier to copy if it's smooth, without the impressions of soil. The client will like it better, too."

"Yes, Ahmet," Sevket interrupted. "What else?"

The young man looked at Rolf. "You know the source of the obsidian?"

"Almost certainly from Göllü Dağ,"

"All right, then we will need obsidian from Göllü Dağ." He picked up a magnifying glass and studied one of the eyes. "A good core," he added. "I know someone who can grind, very discreet." He shook his head and laid the glass on the table.

"If you work the obsidian, won't they know – obsidian hydration, that sort of thing?" Rolf asked.

Ahmet nodded. "To test, they'd have to take out the eyes; they won't do that."

Sevket said, "The mirror will not be a problem."

"Ah, good," Rolf said. "The plaster?"

Sevket shook his head, sending lilac through the room. "Plaster is Ahmet's specialty. He will analyze and reproduce. You need not to worry about the plaster. Now, if you will excuse us, Ahmet and I, we will take measurements and photographs. You may come back early next week. Tuesday morning would be fine."

Rolf made a half-bow and went toward the door.

The man called after him, "Only one thing for you to worry about, Mr. Butcher."

"I'm not worried," Rolf lied.

"Very well. But this head of yours, it's very old, and it doesn't look friendly."

"What do you mean?"

Sevket shrugged. "Evil, Mr. Butcher. It is said these things don't like to be removed from their homes. It is said they may take revenge."

"Don't be silly," Rolf answered. He stepped out into the night, the shrill of insects and a gaudy splash of stars. With a sigh he climbed into the car. Back on the highway he turned toward the lights of Amasya.

Plan B

Lunch at the Dig House was a desultory affair. Work had stopped. Lodewyk stayed in his lab, and when Satchi asked him to lunch he said he wasn't hungry. Most of those who *were* eating picked at their food, discussing Alice in hushed tones. Lena Marie offered to call a psychic of her acquaintance, but no one took her seriously until later in the afternoon when the futility of the hunt was obvious to everyone.

Satchi had expected an explosion from Özgür, but after his initial posturing and his interview with the two policemen, he seemed to grow detached and even smiled from time to time. "Don't worry, everything will be fine," he said.

"Where does he get that idea?" Ben asked Francy.

She put her hand on his arm. "Oh, Ben." It wasn't much of an answer. He understood then what wishful thinking was.

The day wore on. Satchi and Jones huddled in the Secure Room. From time to time Özgür stuck his head in, but did not interrupt them.

Afet Orbay was seated at a table in the Seminar Room, interviewing the local members of the team – the site workers, custodians, and house staff – one by one.

In the middle of the afternoon Jones stopped by to ask if she had learned anything useful. She shrugged. "No one saw anything. You know most of them had left long before the artifact disappeared."

Jones waved. "Keep trying. We have to get to the bottom of this. I'll send Satchi to help."

They interviewed the camp manager, students, and conservators and a parade of specialists. Although most of the Turkish specialists spoke English, it seemed to go faster if she handled those in their first language. Among them were the palaeoethnobotanist, an architectural expert, and specialists in stamp seals, figurines, and beads.

Satchi took over for the Europeans and Americans on the team, including a Swedish photographer and a visiting isotope chemist from Denmark who had arrived only that morning.

They finished toward four o'clock and closed up the Seminar Room. In the courtyard he and Afet found Jones frowning at the afternoon sun, as if blaming it for kidnapping Alice.

Satchi said, "You're thinking of Plan B?"

"Yes, it's time," Jones said. "Everyone's been questioned?"

Satchi handed Jones the sheets from their interviews. Except for the glimmering lights Lena Marie and Gayle had reported, no one had seen or heard a thing.

"I'll need your help," Jones said, looking them over. "This is going to be more difficult than I thought."

"And what exactly is Plan B?" Satchi asked.

"The replica."

"We can't do that," Satchi said instantly. "It's not ethical."

"Think it over. I'm not sure we have a choice. Afet, would you get Özgür for us, please."

She nodded and went in search of the representative.

"It might not be a good idea bringing Özgür into this," Satchi said.

Jones gave his wolfish grin. "We need his support. Plan B is a desperate measure, Satchi, but I see no other."

"All right," Satchi reluctantly agreed. "I suppose he'll cooperate. It's true the loss of Alice would ruin him, too."

Ripple

Satchi took the wheel of the project van. Jones graciously offered Afet the front seat.

"Is he expecting us?" Satchi asked.

"Yes, and he's not happy."

Twelve hours after they had discovered Alice was missing they stopped in front of the dealer's house. They could see the second floor above the wall along the road. There was no sidewalk. The wrought iron gate set into the wall creaked open.

Schedule Change

Jones was right, the Georgian was not happy. "Dr. Jones, we have known each other for, how many are the years? I don't see how . . ."

Jones interrupted, "I know it's unusual, but this is an emergency situation."

"Mm-hm . . . ." The dealer peered out through a narrow gap in the shutters. A vertical bar from the setting sun divided his face. He turned and sat at an ornate teak desk. The only object on its leather surface was a very sleek, recent model computer monitor; there was no visible sign of keyboard or any other component. "I fear the object is too well known. It's been all over the media, the television, and Internet. It will be on T-shirts before we can order them printed ourselves. I think this makes a special problem."

"You owe me," Jones said.

The dealer spread his hands. "I know, Bryson Bey, but . . ."

Jones insisted. "We now need it in four days, max. I can't hold off any longer than that."

The dealer's eyebrows arched into two perfect half circles. "We've come far, but that does not leave us much time."

"No," Jones agreed. "We need it a little sooner than planned, that's all."

The dealer made a decision. "Very well, I'll do my best. Come back on Monday."

16 Then

Under the Tamarisk

Shelsan saw Mala sleeping near a tamarisk not far from Sand Hook. The sun, still out of sight, was approaching the horizon, and the mountain called Water Bird Landing showed purple. Light twinkled on the open marsh and cast low shrubs into black relief. The world was about to catch fire.

Shelsan, splashing across a creek toward her, shook away a persistent sound. What could that low buzzing have to do with him? Shadows pooled under the bushes, but all around was ripening with green. Soon enough the sun would bring it all into brilliance.

It was strange she had wandered so far away. True, she had been possessed by some malign spirit since he and Boren had left, and then she'd been sick, too. But she'd been so much better lately, less worried about what the Bull had told her, and last night she was nearly happy.

He and Boren, and the mother of Boren's little girl, too, had been searching since the dazzling Mirror Star wandered up ahead of the sun, and they noticed she had not returned to the Feast.

He called from the creek bank to wake her, "Mala!"

Boren, some distance away, shouted. "You found her?"

"Yes."

It was stranger still she did not move, did not sit up and rub her eyes and smile.

Moments later Shelsan and Boren stood over her amid cloud of flies dancing like a soul fragmented, spiraling up, spiraling down. All the sounds of dawn were submerged in their insistent hum.

Tsurinye arrived, little Arghinye slung at her hip. "What?"

"Sent over," Boren said. "She's gone." The story was clearly told in the staring red eyes, the way her swollen black tongue filled the opening of her mouth, the dark bruises on her neck.

Shelsan muttered, *"Pinnak!"* His voice was tight as the skin on a wooden drum.

"We can't know that." Boren squatted on his heels and touched her face. The flies rose angrily. Already they were setting their eggs.

Shelsan turned on him. "You think it was spirits did this thing? This isn't Tsurinye healing, Boren. Someone choked her life and sent her over. Who do you think?"

Boren took his hand away and the flies landed, turned her face a shimmering, iridescent black. "Yes. Took the leopard cloak, too."

Shelsan stood for a long time. The sun lit him red, then yellow. Fire on the line of earth separated above from below, a moment of delicate balance, especially this day. Tonight would see the first chip of the Growing Moon. It should have been a time of hope.

"We must move her," Tsurinye said in a hollow voice. Her silhouette loomed against the rising sun so her eyes were empty darkness, her face in shadow. Beyond her a dark speck floated in a slow oval against the sky.

Boren, troubled by her expression, stood. "Tsurinye?"

She took a step, another, spun once in a circle as if scanning the horizon. She tilted her head. "Yes," she said, but it was not an answer. She walked to the tamarisk, entered among reddish-brown branches feathery with small, pink flowers. She turned, and the branches closed over her. The baby made a startled sound.

Boren and Shelsan watched closely. The flowers trembled, though there was no breeze. Tsurinye made a low moaning, rising and falling. The flies were humming. Light clarified.

Then she waddled into the open in a crouch. Her head was back, her eyes closed against the early light. Arghinye stared from her pouch, wide-eyed and silent.

Boren started forward, but Shelsan stopped him. "Wait."

Tsurinye stood, opened her eyes and said, "I've seen what to do."

They carried Mala, accompanied by the flies, far away toward the sunset-side, to the place where Shelsan and Boren had watched her Bull die. By the time they had placed her body on the raised ground the sun was overhead.

The herd was gone, the field empty except for the headless skeleton of the Bull. The distant purling of water of a wet-time creek and the calls of bird and insect were the only sounds.

They waited.

The spot in the sky had followed them, joined by others. They swooped in a tightening oval and swung low with a beating of black wings.

The vultures had come for Mala, last Grand and Mother of her line.

A Turn

Days passed, and the Grown Moon had come. Shelsan and the others returned to the Place. When asked about Mala, they said only that she was gone.

Pinnak called a meeting of the Sorrow Clan. When it was over and the others had dispersed, he stepped across the roofs and called down the entry. "It is decided," he said. "Mala is gone. With no daughter the lineage ends. Through Boren the line would continue, but though he was of the Sorrow Clan, his is not the right to First Egg. You must leave."

There was no reply. He shrugged his fat shoulders and descended the ladder. Sunlight poured down the hole and reflected off the white walls, filling the place with a luminous presence.

But the hearth was cold. The house was empty, all belongings gone, all the clothing and traps, the weapons, even the skull of First Grand. Pinnak moved around the place, testing the surfaces of the raised platforms. He inspected the color of the walls, the cleanliness of the floor.

He puzzled for a time over the strange painting of red squares inset with white. Some odd ceremony Shelsan had performed, perhaps for Boren's initiation. The only symbol he knew was the handprint at the end. Pinnak shrugged. He would leave it, though the rest was a mystery.

No matter, the house was ready for him. Too bad about First Grand; it would have added status, but no matter. He thought only briefly of what might have become of Shelsan and the others. This was First Egg, his right to take as first son of Mala's mother's brother. It was only good that Shelsan and Boren had seen that. He went back up into the sky and called his women to come back down with him, and bring the children.

He would be First Grand, founder of a new lineage. His desires, and his alone, would guide the People.

Last Rights

The rains of the wet-time had grown gentle and warm and gradually ceased. Abundance was everywhere.

Shelsan's little group picked its way across the floodplain, splashing through the wet to dry land. They camped at Dak's Cave, trapping birds and gathering wild food. It was his preference, and Tsurinye's way. Boren, despite his leg, grew strong at hunting, quieter and more patient than any of the People Shelsan had known. "Because of what happened," the young man said. "First Basatzaun and his initiation; then, when Tsurinye cured me, when I went somewhere else, I came back as I am."

Shelsan could only dip his head in affirmation. Boren did not lie.

At the beginning of warm-time they left Dak's Cave and wandered through the mountains farther to the warm-side, going places where no one they knew had gone. When they came to a sand beach by endless water, Tsurinye said, "Salt, like the lake near where we met."

"So you were right, Babi. You did smell salt then."

Shelsan nodded.

"And look," the young man said, holding out a shell. "It's the same as the one we put on Little Brother when we put him down near the hearth."

"It was his favorite toy."

"I'll keep it for Arghinye, then."

There were people along the coast, hunters like themselves, and they spent time with them. Later they drifted back inland.

In the hottest days of the warm-time they returned to the Field of Mala's Bull.

Mala was bone still bound with ligament. The birds had carried away the rest. Ants and beetles had emptied her skull. She had gone to the sky. "We will send down the bone," Shelsan said. "She deserves to share the sky with the young, with Little Brother and Little Sister and the others who died before their time, but her bones join with the Grands in the Under."

They opened the soil at the edge of the raised place and arranged her so she faced the sky.

Shelsan sat on the edge of the pit, hands dangling between his knees, staring into her empty eye sockets. Finally, with a sigh, he started to scoop dirt onto the bones.

Tsurinye stopped him. "We need that," she said, tapping the skull.

Shelsan frowned. "She is the last of First Egg," he said. "We do her no honor by keeping it."

"Not honor," Tsurinye said. "Her will. She spoke to me in the tamarisk. Did you not hear? She whispered in leaf, spoke through flower. She told what she wants."

Boren stared. "Why would she tell you?"

"Because I listen."

Boren spread his hands. "What, then, does she want?"

Tsurinye shifted the baby to the other hip. "Pinnak took her life, as Shelsan guessed. This she told me. Pinnak has taken First Egg. This too she said. She wants it back."

Shelsan looked at the sky, then down at the gray bone of her forehead. "And if we carry this back, she will help us recover First Egg?"

Tsurinye shook her head. "No, you will never again live in First Egg. No one will. It will be for her, for Mala, her place."

She spoke with such certainty that Shelsan said nothing more. He pulled his stone knife from his belt and bent to work separating Mala's skull from her spine.

The Offer

"You can have my house," Pinnak said with a gracious wave of his hand when Shelsan and the others returned.

The roof of First Egg was littered with bundles of wood, clumps of fodder tied to frames, heaps of half-made or half-rotted mats, baked clay pots, many of them broken, terra cotta toys for the children, and the children themselves. Steam twisted up from mounds of fresh dung near the entrance. White smoke rose from a hearth at the cold-side where the women were preparing peas and lentils.

In high warm-time many of the People were away, but for those like Pinnak who remained life had moved up-side. The People only descended for grain from storage in the cool dark.

"We cannot live there," Shelsan said pleasantly. "It stinks of Pinnak and his kind."

Pinnak's smile was lopsided. "Rebuild it, then. End the old. You can even take from my stretch of mud by the river for new brick."

"Your mud is shit that runs."

Pinnak shrugged.

"But we will use it to rebuild," Shelsan agreed. After a moment he added thoughtfully, "Perhaps you should do the same, Pinnak. Perhaps you should rebuild."

"Why should I do that, Shelsan? I like the walls as you have painted them, though I wonder what ritual led you. First Egg is my right. It is good you left it, took your things."

"Yes, it is good, for First Egg is now cursed. Mala is unhappy, Pinnak. She knows what you did."

A cloud passed over the fat man's face. He took off his leather cap and rubbed his hand over his balding head. "She cannot know," he muttered, replacing his cap. "It is not true, what you say."

Shelsan showed his teeth. Even Pinnak could not mistake it for a smile.

Moving In

They slept on the distaff cousins' roof.

Shelsan and two of the cousins passed their days by the river cutting mud from the bank. Once Temkash, who lived near, came by and said, "That's Pinnak's mud." To this Shelsan made no reply. Eventually the Pretender went away.

They squared the mud into long, flat bricks a double hand-width wide and nearly the length of a man. Shelsan set out row after row to dry in the sun beside the Edge wall.

Meanwhile Boren, with the help of other cousins, began to dismantle Pinnak's house. They took down the hearth and cleared the floor. Then they set to work on the roof, sweeping up the litter Pinnak had left and carrying it to the pit of an abandoned house three buildings toward the sunset-side. When the roof was bare, they scraped the plaster and pounded it to dust with wooden hammers.

When they pulled up them up, the roof-reeds crumbled to black, soggy ruin in their hands. Insects swirled up. Vermin in the thatch scurried away or fell shrieking into the house below. Pinnak's women were sloppy housekeepers. Boren said First Egg would suffer with such a man. Shelsan said it did not matter. First Egg was cursed until Mala had it back.

They stored such roof beams as were still usable in the pen between houses.

When it was time, they pounded against the mud-brick of the walls, shattering it, and Tsurinye and some female cousins from Shelsan's Locust Clan sifted the dirt. Slowly, as the walls came down, clean brown powder filled the floor, covering the platforms.

Finally it was finished, and among the other houses crowded together in the center of the Place was a smooth, level platform.

They put the dried mud bricks on planks and carried them by twos back up the ladder and across all the roofs, and one by one they laid new walls on top of the old ones and mortared them with mud.

The walls grew in this way until at last they could set the roof. A few days later they plastered it, and the house was finished.

Out of the corner of his eye Pinnak watched them move in with their sacks of grain and lentils, the head of First Grand and Shelsan's worn spears. If Shelsan or Boren glanced at him, he looked away.

The next evening Shelsan, Boren, Tsurinye, and the cousins were relaxing on the roof with bowls of hot mint tea. Shelsan worked intently with a shaft straightener, a stone tablet with a hole bored in it. Already he had a stack of smooth arrow shafts beside him.

Suddenly he looked up to see Pinnak staring at him from across the gap between the houses. "Did you hear Mala last night, Pinnak?" he asked in a friendly way.

"What are you talking about?"

"Mala. Didn't you hear her?"

"How could I hear her? She went over the night of the Feast, the Unborn Moon."

Shelsan said, "Oh, no. No one ever said she went over. She left, that's all. But last night she was there, outside in the night, crying, down in the pit where you kept your sheep, remember? I'm surprised you didn't hear."

"I don't believe you."

"Really?"

"She made no sound. I would have heard."

"Perhaps you were busy with your women?"

Pinnak spit to avert evil.

Shelsan added thoughtfully, "No, I don't believe she's gone, Pinnak. I think perhaps she went wandering, that's all, like old Sekkab's Third Grand."

"Don't be stupid," Pinnak said. "I'm certain she went over. I am living in First Egg now, as is my right now she is gone."

Shelsan persisted. "How can you be certain, Pinnak? How can you be certain she's dead?"

"I . . . never mind. She's gone over. I know," he muttered.

It was Shelsan's turn to spit. "Well, Pinnak, gone over or not, she's back, and she's looking for something. Or somebody."

Pinnak shifted uncomfortably.

"She has her eye on you, Pinnak. Yes, I think you can depend on it."

The fat man froze. After a few moments he shook himself. "No," he said emphatically and hurried to the shelter on the cold-side where a group of Sorrow Clan elders were waiting. He sat among them on a mat under the lean-to, apparently at ease. From time to time he said something and they all laughed. But each time he glanced over at Shelsan and the others to see if they were watching.

Shelsan busied himself with his arrow shafts, but he was smiling.

"Good," Tsurinye said. Arghinye nuzzled softly at her breast. "Mala lives."

Invocation

Though it was the warm-time, they avoided Pinnak by sleeping inside. One evening, shortly before they would have to go to the grain stand to harvest, they were sitting around the hearth inside. The roof entrance was open, and a light breeze fluttered the hangings.

Tsurinye was holding Mala's skull. Suddenly she said, "You put plaster on First Grand. You covered his eyes and nose and mouth and painted it red."

Shelsan glanced at First Grand in a niche on the sunrise wall. "Yes. It seems very long ago."

"This is your custom, this living with the Grands. To me it is strange. We do not keep skulls."

"You don't live in one place as we do," Boren said. "The Grand is the House, its spirit."

"But even though it is strange, I have seen we must do this for Mala. She is the mother of Boren. That makes her the Grand of this family." Tsurinye held the skull up to face the two men.

Shelsan looked at her. "Would Mala truly want to have her skull covered and painted, like a Grand?"

Tsurinye tilted her head, her brow furrowed. "Why do you ask this?"

He turned away with a shrug. "Mala speaks to you. She must do this because you are the mother of Boren's child, and Boren is her son. So I thought perhaps she asked for this. The Grands often demanded it."

Tsurinye shook her head and her long hair flew in intricate spirals and fell still. "Not to make her a Grand, no, but I know it must be done."

He spread his hands. "If you say it must be done, then it will be." He crawled through the hole to the sunrise-side storage room.

Tsurinye looked deeply into the empty eyes of Mala's skull. The bone was dry, warm, smooth, and curiously light. The inside was clean. "It is difficult," she said softly. "She is there, yet not there." After a moment she shook herself. "We must summon her, Boren. We must call her back."

"I don't understand." He held the sleeping baby on his lap.

Tsurinye gave him a sharp look. "You will."

Shelsan crawled back with what he needed. "This is the finest lime for plaster, the same I used to renew First Grand."

Tsurinye, whose name meant White, and who spoke the language of the Place with an alien emphasis and oddly sharpened vowels, began to speak. "I ask the spirits, I ask the spirits," she said. "I ask the spirits to send us Mala, to bring her back, to let her return. This I ask them."

As she spoke she shaped the air around Mala's skull with her hands, as if smoothing plaster on it herself. Shelsan saw between her palms the way the air took on flesh, grew large. He saw the eyes when Tsurinye drew them with her thumbs. He saw Mala's dark, coiled hair spray from her skull as feather, as fur, as wheat stalk.

"We call her back as Water Bird," Tsurinye murmured. "We call her back as Mala, Mala as she was. We call her back as Mala's Bull, also, who spoke to her at the edge of the Place, at the edge of the Nest. We call her back as Boren.

"She will be all of them, she is all of them, as she was all. Your story, Shelsan, your capture and escape, the dead boy in the village, the family near the Mountain of Frozen Tears, Water Bird Mother, Mala's Bull, Boren's wound, his initiation into the tribe of my people, all are here. Can you see them? We will put them into this thing, this head, these bones, and we will put in yet more. We will put in the evil that is Pinnak, your neighbor, Mala's cousin. All will go into this thing that we make, this thing that is Mala, and will always be. Her Bull, and the hard weather that held us through the winter, my long walk to the Place with Boren, our hunt, our journey to the Big Salt Lake. All will be part of her. We will put in the fire that was in the air, the roof that fell burning onto us. It does not matter that Pinnak set the fire. It does not matter that he killed Mala. He lives now with Mala's Bull, set into the house post, the tree that holds the roof of the Nest. He lives under the eye of the Bull, under the horns of the Bull. He will end there.

"Mala will return. We will bring her back; this thing that we make will bring her."

Getting Ahead

Tsurinye, Boren's woman, sorted through the baskets they had left with the distaff cousins when they moved out of First Egg. There were pots and cups, wooden spoons and small containers of spice, sacks of dried fruit and hackberries. "These," she said, taking out the two pieces of Temkash's mirror.

Shelsan and Boren looked. "It was a mirror, but it's broken," Shelsan said.

"Yes. Can you work them?" She placed her thumbs over Mala's eye sockets.

"To fit in there? Why?"

"Her eyes were bright," Tsurinye said, looking at Boren. "With these she can see."

"See what?" he wanted to know.

"What she needs to see. Boren will keep the plaster moist."

Shelsan got his stone and antler hammers, his pressure flakers. He held one of the frozen-tear mirrors, and tapped gently. A small piece detached. He put his thumbs into Mala's sockets, closing his eyes. He felt the depths, the sharp orbital ridge and the curve of bone at the back. He tapped again.

Slowly the mirrors took shape until they filled the sockets. One stuck out too far and he tapped again, releasing more frozen tears from its back. He took some fine grit and ground the eyes smooth, over and over, checking the way they caught the light.

When they fit perfectly, Shelsan caught a glimpse of his own eye brightly reflected and involuntarily let out a moan.

"Now," Tsurinye said. "The plaster. Cover everything except the eyes. Can we do that?"

"Everything?"

"Yes, even her jaw."

Shelsan set aside his stone-working tools without a word and pulled the baskets of burned lime to his side. He mixed some with water in a shallow clay bowl and kneaded it.

Tsurinye scooped some out and rubbed it between her fingertips. "Yes," she said, passing the skull to Shelsan. "Now we are ready. Flat on the under side."

Shelsan's smile was dry, but he dipped into the bowl and covered the bottom of the skull, filling the hollow of her jaw and all the pits and openings, smoothing the white paste over the uneven bone with his thumb. He pressed plaster into the nasal opening. Soon the skull was covered, leaving only the mirror eyes.

"More over the forehead," Tsurinye said.

Shelsan added plaster, smoothing the round dome.

"A little narrower. She needs to look more like a bird."

"A bird? You said she was to be the Bull."

"That too. Now the nose, like a beak."

They worked through the night, shaping, discarding, reshaping. Tsurinye was never satisfied. Shelsan started falling asleep and jerking himself awake. Once little Arghinye cried out, and Tsurinye took time to nurse her. As soon as the child finished, though, she came right back. "Shelsan, wake."

Boren slept fitfully. When a lamp went out she asked him to refill it. Toward the darkest time of the night she declared the work useless and ordered Shelsan to remove all the plaster.

He mixed more and they started over. "This time," she said, "fill the inside first."

"It will never dry if we do that. The plaster shrinks and changes shape."

"Sand," she said. "Fill with sand. It must be dry and she needs weight."

Light seeped into the house. When the plaster was finally to Tsurinye's liking, she took a bone point and began to inscribe the same patterns of loops and swirls of Boren and Mala's tattoos.

"Tomorrow, when it is dry, we will paint," she said.

"And then?" Boren asked.

"And then we wait." Tsurinye took the sleeping baby, stretched out on the fern-padded platform and went to sleep.

17 Now

Plan B Executed

Plan B worked flawlessly. The days of waiting had passed in a state of palpable anxiety, yet against all odds Alice's disappearance remained confidential. The Turkish policemen had not returned, the phones were silent, and the Aynalı Tepe Project returned to work with a façade of normal routine.

Jones brought the new Alice back from Konya in a cardboard box late Monday evening. He and Özgür installed it in the Secure Room and announced that she had been recovered. The next morning when visits resumed, the team's mood had lightened.

Only Ben, who danced a quick dance with Francy in front of the Secure Room, asked Satchi where Alice had been.

Satchi grinned sheepishly. "That must remain confidential." The words almost stuck in his throat, but he managed to add, "Everything's fine now."

Of course it wasn't fine, since the real Alice was still missing.

Afet swore she couldn't tell this was the fake. "There may be subtle differences in paint color or small imperfections in the soil stains, and maybe I could find them under a microscope, or do pixel-by-pixel comparisons of the spectroscopic data, but no visitor will guess, especially if now we say it's been cleaned and consolidated."

"It's not a fake," Jones insisted. "It's a replica."

"At the moment it's a fake," Satchi said. "We can't forget that. No one knows it's a replica, so it's a fake."

Lena Marie was especially grateful to see Alice. "You frightened me," she told the head. "Don't do that again."

Gayle rolled her eyes. "What?" Lena Marie asked.

"Nothing. I'm glad it's back, even if it does seem fishy she suddenly turned up like that."

Package

Sevket walked around the two heads several times. "No," he said. "I can't tell."

Ahmet grinned happily. "That was the idea."

"Which one is the real one?"

Ahmet looked stunned. "Which? Uh, this . . . No, that . . ." When he saw the look on Sevket's face he burst out laughing. "I'm just playing. The one on the right."

Sevket almost managed to smile. "All right. Pack them up. Butcher will be here in a few minutes."

Both boxes were closed and sealed. Ahmet was about to mark them when Sevket called him into the back room for something. It wasn't important, and he was grumbling when he returned. Sevket was so fussy sometimes. He started to mark the side of a box with a felt marker pen, but hesitated.

The bell rang. The client had arrived.

He told Sevket the original was on the right, didn't he? Yes, he was certain he had said that. He always put originals on the right, copies on the left; it was a habit. But when he packed them, did he really put the original in the right-hand box? It depended on which way he was facing. He was now facing the front door, but when Sevket had inspected them, the heads were facing the door, so the original, from here, would be on the left.

He no longer felt certain. He started again to mark a box, then changed his mind and reached for the other. After another moment's hesitation he marked it.

What difference did it make? His copy was as good as the original.

Homecoming

Tuesday night Jones was on the phone. Through his office window he saw a large moon flood the mound in silvery light. "Yes, Dimitri," he was saying. "Lodewyk got the DNA results back from the labs.

Apparently they could get mitochondrial specimens with good genetic information. . . Yes, Dimitri, they recovered over 800 base pairs from crystal aggregates inside the bone, I understand, and amplified them by polymerase chain reaction. The three skeletons are almost certainly related." The moon shifted infinitesimally. Shadows gathered under the awning over the Rabbit Hole. "I agree one hundred percent, Dimitri, it *is* unusual, but not impossible. The Jericho heads used lime plaster too. Alice has more elaborate decoration . . ."

Someone knocked. "Come in," he called. "No, I wasn't talking to you, Dimitri."

Mehmet put his head in. "Excuse, please, Jones Bey."

Jones cupped his hand over the receiver. "Yes?"

The guard very carefully placed an open cardboard box on the desk.

Jones took one look at its contents and said into the receiver, "I'll call you back tomorrow, Dimitri. Something's just come up." He hung up. "Where's did you find this?"

"Back of the guard house, Jones Bey. Just now I am taking out trash and see. So I opened."

"This has been there since last week?"

Mehmet shook his head. "No, Jones Bey. It was not there before, I think."

"You think? When *was* the last time you took out the garbage?"

Mehmet looked sheepish. "Five days, or six?"

"So it could have been there since Alice disappeared?"

"Yes, Jones Bey. I am sorry. Will I lose my job?"

"No, no." Jones got up and closed the blinds. "It's all right, Mehmet. Nothing says when you have to take out your garbage. You've done well. Very well. Don't worry. Leave it here, and remember, not a word to anyone about this. Not even your family."

Double Vision

Jones found Satchi and Afet on the roof watching the moon. "Come," he said from the top of the stairs, crooking his finger.

They followed him to the office where Özgür was waiting.

"Our lucky day," Jones said.

They looked into the box. "Alice," Satchi murmured.

"Yes, Alice. Behind the guard house."

"But we looked there!" Satchi protested.

Jones shrugged. "Not well enough, it seems. The thieves must have panicked and left it. Probably they intended to come back and Mehmet found her first."

"I don't think so," Satchi said.

"What do you mean?"

Satchi gestured at the head. "It's too clean. No dirt marks."

Afet put on a pair of white cotton gloves and delicately removed Alice from the box. She set her on the desk and turned the desk lamp down onto the strange bird-woman face. She hummed to herself, walking slowly around the desk, viewing the head from all angles.

"What do you think?" Jones asked.

Afet squatted down and squinted. "It's very good," she said.

"What do you mean, it's very good? Of course it's very good. All we have to do is put the real Alice back and hide our replica until . . ." He stopped when he saw her expression. "This is Alice, isn't it?"

"Perhaps," Afet said gravely. "But as Satchi said, she's been cleaned."

"That means they brought her back," Satchi said. "She wasn't here the whole time."

"But this is Alice?" Jones insisted.

Afet squinted at the ceiling.

Jones stared in disbelief. "You mean you don't know?"

Satchi, Afet, Jones, and Özgür stood in a dejected group. The obsidian eyes reflected twin images of Jones's desk lamp onto the west wall, leaving the rest of the room in shadow.

"It must be Alice," Özgür mumbled. "It must be." If possible, he seemed even more nervous than he had when Alice disappeared, as if two Alices were worse than none.

Afet said, "If it isn't Alice, it's a good copy, Dr. Jones, as good as yours, very good work. There can't be many people in Turkey who could do work like this."

"Why would they have to be in Turkey?" Satchi asked. "It could have been taken over the border to Syria, or even into Iran. Plenty of skilled forgers – I mean artisans – there."

"I refuse to believe this is not real!" Jones exclaimed

Afet stood. "But Dr. Jones, such is possible, no? We have a copy. If we can have one, so can whoever took the original. They are clever, the people who took her – we still don't know how they managed it." She avoided looking at Özgür, but they all knew he was the only one with a key. They also knew he was away when Alice disappeared. Either he gave the key to someone or there was another explanation they couldn't imagine.

Jones tugged at his lower lip. "You're saying there may be *three* Alices."

"That," Satchi said, "would be two too many."

"If there can be three, there could even be more," Afet offered.

"Great!" Satchi rolled his eyes.

"Well!" Jones brightened. "We don't know there's a third. Copies are not cheap, I can tell you. This is mere speculation."

"Like so much of archaeology," Satchi muttered.

"All right, it's true this introduces a measure of ambiguity, but in reality it changes nothing. We will assume this is the original, at least for now. The thieves cleaned her up, did a decent job of consolidation for us, then, because Alice is so well known, they got cold feet and returned her."

"What if this isn't the original . . . ," Satchi began. "If anyone finds out . . . ."

"They won't," Jones said firmly. "We've been lucky so far, but if word does get out, we'll just say we used the replica to protect the original, which we have here. Afet, I'd like you and the conservator to examine it. Let's make sure this one is."

"What if it isn't?" she asked. "Hellä will know."

"Damn. You're right, we can't let her know the one on display is a replica. OK, we keep this among the four of us. Do your best, Afet. At least you can examine the eyes." He closed the box. "Tomorrow," Jones said. "Look at it tomorrow."

At Sea

The charter boat cruised at a leisurely pace over slow swells away from the small beach Rolf had facetiously named Smugglers' Cove.

It had turned out the beach's real Turkish name meant the same thing, a fitting irony, since Rolf had brought the artifact down undetected and was about to smuggle it out of the country. He had paid his Bulgarian associates and sent them to Antalya for a well-deserved vacation. He was headed toward his rendez-vous with the *Island Princess*. Everything was going according to plan.

The beaches, sunbathers and tourists, the restaurants, bars and nightclubs of the Emerald Coast had dwindled to a dark line. Ahead were international waters, where subtle tensions between countries would make intercepting the transfer of the strange plastered head from Aynalı Tepe extremely improbable.

True, he was breaking his own rules by handling the transfer personally, but he told himself this was especially delicate . . . and especially lucrative. His mysterious Asian buyer was willing to pay extremely well. There was no one else he could trust with a project of this magnitude.

The captain swept his hand around the bridge and said to his guest, "As you asked, *efendim*, I have not brought my incompetent imbecile of a first mate with me. As you wished, I am piloting this boat completely by myself alone. You can count on me, *efendim*, and you must not be concerned also for my cousin, Mustafa. Mustafa will be there. We have spoken today already. And, he has GPS," he added proudly.

"So he told me," Rolf answered.

"You are paying him. He will be there." This logic seemed so self-evident that as far as the captain was concerned the bargain was already concluded.

"Yes." Rolf glanced at his Rolex. "And I believe I am also paying you to take me out to meet him."

The captain pressed his lips together and advanced the throttle. Moments later the black, motionless smudge of the *Island Princess* appeared on the horizon exactly where it was supposed to be.

Reasonable Doubt

"I can't say for sure," Afet confessed. "The obsidian is the right color. If this is a copy, it's even better than yours."

"Replica," Jones said reflexively.

"That's it, then," Satchi stretched. "Alice is back and we have a museum quality co- . . . replica."

"We should think it through," Jones insisted. "Just in case."

"OK," Afet said. "Either this is Alice, or it's a remarkably good copy."

"It doesn't make sense," Jones mused. "Why would they make a copy and give it to us?"

"To keep the original and make us think we had it. We'd never know until it was too late; by then the original would be long gone and we would be in no position to admit it."

"Maybe they returned the original and kept the copy," Jones suggested.

"Why would they do that?" Satchi wondered. "Someone wanted Alice, that's for sure. Stealing it took planning and skill. Someone was willing to take those risks, and pay for them. Alice is far too well known to be on the open market, so it has to be a private collector. The thief replaces the original with a copy, and no one ever knows. Brief consternation at the site, then it blows over."

Jones shook his head. "Far better to give the collector the copy, don't you think? Let him think he got the original. It all blows over, we get the real Alice and drop the matter. The thief gets his money, and no one's the wiser."

"Wishful thinking," Satchi said. "Collectors always want the real thing. They believe in authenticity, that there's some kind of aura around an original artifact that isn't there with a copy. History somehow clings to it. We believe the authentic Alice is important because it holds data, all the information in her bones, her stone mirror eyes, her plaster. Of course, we'd have to disassemble her in order to know if this is the real one, but we believe authenticity is important. Just like the collector."

"But think about it," Jones said. "It would really be in the thief's interest to return the original to us. How would a collector know? He doesn't have the data, nothing to compare it to, and he can't ask anyone."

"Or she," Afet said.

"Most collectors are men."

"But when the Aynalı Tepe Project publishes?"

"Then the collector feels even more smug because he thinks he has the original and we have the fake."

"Replica," Afet said.

"No," Jones corrected. "Ours is a replica, theirs is a fake. If the collector gets a fake thinking it's real, and we have the original plus a museum-quality replica, everyone's happy."

"Unless this one's the fake," Afet said. "There's reasonable doubt."

Özgür dropped into the desk chair and put his head in his hands. "I get headache." His English grammar was deteriorating rapidly.

"All right," Jones said briskly, rubbing his hands together. "Let us summarize. We are in possession of two Alices, one of which is *probably* the original. If neither one is original, how could we tell?"

Afet shrugged. "Compare with the original X rays?"

"That would mean asking Lodewyk, unless one of you is particularly competent with skeletal remains. No? Well then, do we want to bring him in?" Jones asked.

Satchi arched his eyebrows. "Now, that's a question, isn't it?"

"If this is a fake, and the other is the replica, then someone has the original and our research would be compromised. It's dishonest," Satchi said, reddening.

"Yes, Satchi, but we believe this is the original Alice, made here some time around 6900 BCE. It was put on a post in a house for reasons unknown. The house was dismantled and she was buried there. This we know. It'll have to be enough."

Satchi grumbled, but in the end he agreed. Unless a third Alice appeared, perhaps on the antiquities market, there was nothing they could do.

But . . .

The next morning toward eleven Bryson Jones received a phone call from a certain Capitaine Poliveau at Interpol. "We have a report from the Turkish police," he said in precise English lightly seasoned with Belgian French. "A missing plaster skull, non?"

"Oh, that," Jones said dismissively. "Yes, not a plaster skull, a skull covered with plaster, and yes, it did go missing, and the police were here, but . . ."

The policeman interrupted. "We have looked into the matter."

"There's no need . . ."

"You must understand, M'sieur, the antiquities market is how do you say, awash? Yes, awash, in rumors – and in forgeries, too, I fear. So, we are busy these days, you understand, very busy. Especially with material from Iraq, or supposed to be from Iraq, or assumed to have been looted there. Much of it is inauthentic, you understand. Much. However, we have been looking into your lost plaster skull, M'sieur, and I'm afraid I have little to report."

"Yes, that's . . ."

"Yes, please, I would like to ask one or two questions. You see, we, my office that is, have received some vague intelligence of a collector in the market for prehistoric work. This is a new collector, we are told, and not one on our list. You understand this is from an informant who heard it from someone he knew, who may, in turn have overheard it in a nightclub somewhere. Nothing at all reliable, not at all."

"Yes, there are . . ."

"Still, this collector is in China. Shanghai, specifically."

"Shanghai?"

"No, I assure you, nothing definite. Just that such a person exists and is looking for Anatolian prehistory. No one speaks specifically of a plaster skull, yet I wonder, considering your, ahem, considerable reputation, if you have heard anything, in light of the fact that the funding of Aynalı Tepe Project comes largely from a company called Shanghai Holding Trust?"

"No," Jones said sharply. "I haven't heard anything like that."

"Nothing at all?"

"Certainly not. Our funder is a reputable man, a wealthy supporter of archaeological projects. I understand he also funds a dig in the Andes. I'm quite certain he wouldn't be interested in doing anything illegal."

"Ah, well, then, that's disappointing, I suppose, but I'm sure you'll let us know if you should come across anything along those lines. Now, secondly, Dr. Jones, I have in front of me a report, a brief report, you understand, just a paragraph, a rumor, almost, or a whisper, just a *soupçon*, if you take my meaning, that someone is making a copy of such an object. We think perhaps we know who is doing this. So my question is, should this collector be from Shanghai – that is, should in fact this person actually exist – then perhaps these two facts are connected, if you follow my reasoning, M'sieur. Might you have heard anything?"

"Well," Jones began smoothly, "we do sometimes make replicas of unusual archaeological finds. In fact, it's not at all unusual, and is, as I'm sure you know, Capitaine Poliveau, a form of experimental archaeology. We sometimes do this to see if we can deduce something about methods of manufacture."

"Yes, of course."

Jones took a deep breath. "The Aynalı Tepe Project has, in fact, made one such. Perhaps that could be the source of your, um, rumor?"

"Ah, perhaps."

"Furthermore," Jones pressed on, falling, as he sometimes did at moments of high tension, into a faintly British cadence, "there's been a bit of a mix-up, I'm afraid. It's entirely my fault, of course, but, you see, I simply haven't had time yet to inform the Turkish police, but we have recovered the artifact. Unharmed, thank goodness."

There was a long silence. Finally the captain sighed. "I see."

"Really," Jones continued. "It only just happened. It was misplaced, that's all. These things do happen, despite all precautions. Terrible to cause such a fuss about it, but under the circumstances we felt it was best to err on the side of caution."

"Quite."

"So I'm sure this has nothing to do with a hypothetical collector from Shanghai."

"I'm relieved to hear it, Dr. Jones," Capitaine Poliveau said dryly. Before hanging up he asked, "You haven't happened across any information about certain artifacts from Iraq, have you? No? Well, don't hesitate to call if you do."

The Island Princess

Mustafa was smoothing his magnificent moustache and exuding good cheer. His hand was only figuratively out for his second payment.

Rolf set the cardboard box on the deck. "Where's your passenger?"

Mustafa shrugged. "He did not come, *efendim*."

"Not come?"

"No, *efendim*. I waited."

"You called the number I gave you?"

Mustafa looked grieved. "Of course, *efendim*, but the number no longer functions."

"No longer . . ."

"We can go back to Bodrum if you wish. Perhaps he was detained."

"Back to Bodrum? No. Let me think."

"Would you like a drink, *efendim*? I have champagne."

"Mineral water, please."

While Mustafa rummaged in the stores, Rolf looked at the empty sea.

He had a stolen artifact, a chartered yacht, over 200,000 euros in expenses, and no client.

The situation did not look promising, but Rolf Butcher was a resourceful man. There were a number of places he could go, places with complicated political contexts, places where a stolen prehistoric artifact could still find a home.

Mustafa handed him a glass. "Where to, *efendim*?"

Rolf waved his hand vaguely. "East. Stay in international waters."

Goddesses

They replaced the original Alice (if, Satchi reminded himself, that's really what it was) in the cardboard box, which they labeled "ATP Experimental Archaeology Replica Specimen #43854" and locked it in a cupboard in the Secure Room.

The replica remained on view. Evenings Lena Marie Troye, Professor of Folklore, stayed with her until the small hours of the morning, "communing," she said, "with Her ancient wisdom." From time to time she pounded on her laptop. Gayle told her she would break the keyboard, but Lena Marie replied only that she was writing a Major Work that would rock the Goddess community.

Alice, she insisted, was the original, the archetype for all to follow.

"Don't you see, Gayle, inside the living Goddess was a once-living person. Plastered skulls were common, but Alice is different. She's no revered ancestor, to be daubed and painted as an act of household piety. She was the physical culmination of a long Goddess tradition going back to the Venuses of the Upper Paleolithic. She *is* the very moment when the divine became flesh and the flesh became divine, thousands of years before Jesus Christ."

Alice's Revenge

Rolf found a cell phone signal off the coast of Syria and made a call. Two hours later it was returned. "Yes."

One of the Bulgarians said, "Interpol has issued an advisory," and disconnected.

So his mysterious client from Asia had panicked because of a silly Interpol advisory? Despite all his precautions he was going to lose a fortune because some peasant billionaire from China got cold feet!

He made another call.

"No, my friend," the man on the other end replied. His voice was very distant and the connection kept dropping. "No one will take on such a project, I'm afraid. With all this trouble about Iraqi antiquities, potential customers have gone to ground. I'm truly sorry, but this is not a good time."

"Not a good time? What do you mean, not a good time?"

But the connection was lost for good.

Rolf clung to the belief that he could still salvage the deal, but everywhere he met the same response. Though he stayed in international waters as much as possible, he had to risk going closer to shore for his cell phone. He wasn't going to discuss this on a clear radio channel.

Finally Mustafa informed him they would have to refuel.

"All right, go back to Bodrum," Rolf said at last. "I'll see what I can do there." He was going to have to smuggle Alice back *into* Turkey!

A mile out of Bodrum a sleek vessel marked *Sahel Güvenlik*, the Turkish Coast Guard, hailed them. Two young officers politely requested permission to board. They had a warrant for a search.

Rolf carried his box to the railing. After a moment's anguished hesitation he tipped it over and let Alice slide out. The splash she made seemed very small. "Sevket, you bastard," he murmured, as she fell. "You were right, she is cursed." He watched the head make three slow spirals before vanishing into the deep blue waters of the Mediterranean.

When the policemen approached, Rolf was standing at the railing holding the empty box.

"We'll take that," the officer said. He took the box from Rolf and handed it to his subordinate.

"You have nothing on me," Rolf muttered. "It's an empty box."

The officer shrugged. "It was not empty when it left Amasya. This we know. We've been speaking with some friends of yours. Interpol, you see." He looked over the side and shrugged again. "Perhaps they will send divers."

Rolf said nothing.

The officer continued, "We also investigate the theft of an object from a place called Aynalı Tepe some days ago. We find there was a copy made of this object. I myself don't understand why someone would take such a thing, a human skull covered with plaster, but such is the nature of police work. Interpol suggests we speak with a man named Sevket. So we speak with this man, now is in our custody, and this man has spoken of you at some length, Mr. Butcher. So, you see, regrettably, I must place you under arrest."

Season's End

Season Three was over. Many of the students and specialists had already left. Satchi Bennett, Afet Orbay, Bryson Jones, Lodewyk Barhydt, Ben, Francy, and a handful of others were seated at a large table on the roof of the hotel where it had all started.

Jones was congratulating Ben on DANTE and teasing him about his dissertation, when someone approached the table. "Özgür!" Jones cried. "Join us." He moved over to make room.

"I wanted to say," the representative said formally, "how grateful I am, Jones Bey, for what you have done here. Also, I want to apologize for any problems I may have created for you and your people."

"Problems, Özgür?"

"You laugh at me, Jones Bey, but sometimes I was perhaps not as helpful as I could have been."

"Nonsense. You were terrific."

Özgür spread his hands. "Please. There was the matter of the head." He leaned forward, tapped Jones on the knee confidentially, and continued in a low voice, "I wanted to confess . . ."

"Stop right there. I won't hear another word. I don't want your confession. None of us do. We have had a very successful season and are here to celebrate. We, you, and I and this fine team, will have many more seasons to come. It's true we put a lot of effort into Alice, and found a terrific object, and our sponsor seems happy about it, because he's written a big check for next season, and I'm sure it's because of Alice."

"But we still don't know which one is the real Alice," Satchi said.

"Perhaps not," Jones agreed. "And without destroying them one by one and testing them, doing hydration on the inside of the obsidian eyes, for example, or matching the skull with DNA, we'll never know. Perhaps it's better we live with the Alices we have, and not worry too much about authenticity at this point."

Satchi shrugged. "It's true that's not the point of archaeology as far as I'm concerned. I want to understand the past, study it, and bring it to light. Alice was just one artifact, and perhaps not the most important for our work, after all."

"Right," Jones agreed. "We're interested in the full complex of factors, from climate to resources, from symbols to folkways, all help tell the story of what happened. For example, . . . No, you tell him, Afet."

She nodded gracefully. "Well, Özgür, I've been looking at the sequence of obsidian and comparing it to Çatalhöyük. There was a change in the way they worked it at both places, with a shift to more labor-intensive, less useful, and more decorative points. This certainly happened at Aynalı Tepe near the end of the occupation. I wondered if there was a connection between abandonment and this shift." She shrugged. "It's an intriguing question."

Jones grinned happily. "Alice was a good find, Özgür, wonderful, really. True, she caused us some bother, but in the long run, as Satchi said, she was far from the only important find we'll have. Many interesting questions remain." He thought for a moment. "Of course, Alice *was* most important for Dr. Troye. Speaking of whom, did you hear she's presenting her paper, 'Spirit Made Flesh: The Mother Goddess of Aynalı Tepe,' at a New Neolithic Conference at Gravidian College? No? Well, I'm sure she'll launch Alice off into the world on her own. So you see, Alice no longer needs us."

Özgür shifted awkwardly, then leaned back and relaxed. "Very well, Jones Bey," he said, louder now. "I am happy to tell you I will be the representative once again next year."

Ben patted Özgür on the back. "Congratulations. They must like you in Ankara."

"Yes, thank you," the representative said modestly. "I think perhaps they do."

Later Satchi and Afet wandered to the railing to look at the moon. Though it was full, it struggled to compete with the lights of Konya.

Afet took Satchi's arm. "The people of Ayalı Tepe must have looked at just such a moon. I wonder what they thought."

18 Then

Harvest and Plant

It was the height of the warm-time. The marshes dried and grew hard, and the game wandered away into the mountains, toward Angry Bear or Water Bird Landing. The heat grew fierce on them and the People scattered, many to harvest the grain at their stands, others to gather materials for weaving, or wood for weapons and tools. Some were rebuilding, and the riverbank was thick with drying bricks. When the heat was at its most intense the Place was nearly empty. Only the elders, the sick, mothers with very young children, and a handful of others remained.

They were sitting on the roof of Pinnak's old house. Shelsan, facing First Egg, said slowly, "There is no one in First Egg but Pinnak now."

Tsurinye, holding the baby's two pudgy hands in her own, said, "His women are warm-side at their stand of grain. They have taken their children and their cutting tools to harvest, but he will stay in First Egg. So he has said. I heard this from several of the cousins of the Sorrow Clan. I believe it is because he is too fat and lazy to help."

"He thinks himself too important," Boren added bitterly.

"What does Mala say, then, eh, Tsurinye?" Shelsan asked. "You've prepared her; she's ready. I just don't know what for."

Boren looked sharply at him. He had seldom seen Shelsan be so direct.

"It is just past the Unborn Moon. We wait through the Gaining for the Grown," she replied. The baby let her fingers slip from her mother's hands and abruptly sat down. Her expression was so comical Tsurinye laughed. After a moment caught between crying and laughing, the baby opened her mouth wide and crinkled up the corners of her eyes. Though she made no sound, her delight was enough to lift all their spirits.

"Why do we wait for the Grown Moon?" Boren asked. "We could . . ."

As he spoke Pinnak came onto his roof and stretched his fat arms to the sky. He pointedly ignored them. He was the master of First Egg, heritor of the lineage, chief of the Sorrow Clan. It was his world.

He touched one of his spear tips, jerked his hand away. "Aiee," he cried, licking a drop of blood from the end of his finger. Abruptly he set off across his neighbors' roofs without a backward glance.

Tsurinye's eyes followed him. "That is how it must be," she said.

The Moon began its Gaining. People came and went. The roofs grew a dense forest of hanging cloth, new mounds of drying dung, racks of spears and arrows, some early harvest grain bundles, debris from working tools of obsidian and flint, stacks of crudely dried clay pots, bundles of reeds and beams for roofing. Lines of smoke from cooking fires were few, and children's laughter was rare. There was both peace and melancholy at the Place. The days were hot, the nights warm.

All around the marsh had turned brown.

And still the moon was Gaining until one afternoon Tsurinye said, "The Grown Moon will arrive tomorrow. Boren, you must ask a cousin for help. Have her tell Pinnak one of his children is sick, probably that puny one from Second Woman. You can say a runner came from their stand toward the sunset, and ran back. She should tell Pinnak Second Woman is bringing the boy back, they will be here when the Moon starts to fall from the sunrise- to the sunset-side. The boy will need a healing exactly then. Sun Demon wants the child. Pinnak is almost as child-proud as he is fat."

"How do you know all this?" Boren asked.

"Don't be thick, Boren. I healed you. I see what must be done, and I've been here long enough to know, too, what Mala wants. You told me what happened to Little Brother. I know the ways of healing. What we will do now is just the other side of the Healing Mirror."

Boren stared in wonder. Though she spoke the People's language slowly, and with many stops, she was wiser than anyone he knew. Even Shelsan was silent. Only Mala could have matched her for knowledge of their ways. "Then what?" he asked.

"When you see him go to fetch Temkash, call me."

He nodded.

"And I will need a tree, a trunk as tall as you, Boren. And after Pinnak leaves I will need Mala's leopard cloak, the one she wore the night she died. You will find it down in First Egg where Pinnak has been keeping it."

Setting the Stage

They watched from their roof as the cousin called at the entry, was invited down, and disappeared into First Egg. Some time later she reappeared and nodded at Boren. Pinnak emerged a few moments later and set off across the roofs toward the Edge without a backward glance, moving as swiftly as his bulk allowed.

As soon as he had vanished behind the tangle on the rooftops, the cousin came over to their roof. "Thank you," Boren told her.

Tsurinye handed baby Arghinye, sleeping soundly in her arms, to the cousin.

"It won't be long," Tsurinye said.

The cousin dipped her head, and carried the baby to her own house three roofs away and vanished down her entry.

Shelsan, Boren, and Tsurinye leaped silently onto the roof of First Egg. Boren handed a lamp to his woman before he climbed into Pinnak's house with a bundle of digging tools.

Shelsan carried the newly cut post down the ladder. Tsurinye followed with the lamp and Mala's skull.

The Grown Moon was approaching the zenith of a cloudless sky. Its brightness dimmed the stars.

Tsurinye set the lamp down and marked a place in the center of the room. "Here!"

Shelsan and Boren dug through the plaster and set the post, packing soil around the base.

"You know what to do," Tsurinye whispered to Boren. He nodded and crawled into the back storage room. A moment later he returned with the jaguar cloak.

She handed Mala's skull to Boren, and she and Shelsan returned to the roof. She walked around the opening, looking thoughtful. Finally she went to their roof and fetched a small, vaguely human figure made of bundled reeds, which she set at the house corner facing the entrance.

"He won't see it," Shelsan muttered. "The entry blocks it from the direction he'll come."

Without a word she lifted the entrance flap and stared into the dimly lit interior. With a swift gesture she ripped the flap away, kicked over the crude lean-to and dropped it all over the side of the house into the sheep pen. "Now he'll see it," she said.

She squatted on the brick wall to the warm-side looking into the entrance for a time. "Tilt her head back," she called down to Boren. "The jaguar cloak is good, but she must be looking at the entrance."

When Boren returned up-side she placed the lamp in front of the reed figure and arranged a cord of fiber from its back across to their roof, where they concealed themselves behind the stack of dried dung.

"How long?" Boren asked.

"When the Grown Moon is directly over our heads," Tsurinye said.

When the Grown Moon poured silver light straight down they heard a sheep bleating three roofs away.

Moments later Pinnak appeared, closely followed by the Pretender, already dressed in his bear and vulture-feather helmet.

Pinnak Descends

Pinnak leaped onto the roof of First Egg. "Come on," he called to Temkash. "There's a light. They must be back."

Tsurinye touched fire to the string and watched it burn away from them. The flaming tip dropped into the triangular space between the two houses. The spark climbed up the outside wall of First Egg and approached the reed figure as Pinnak and Temkash approached it.

"What is that?" Pinnak asked.

Temkash had stopped. "Don't go near it!" he said.

"It's a man, but who?" Pinnak leaned forward. "Someone is trying to . . ." The reed figure caught fire. "Spirits!" he shouted, leaping back.

The figure exploded in a shower of sparks. Pinnak backed away into the arms of Temkash, who pushed him away.

"No," the Pretender shouted. He pulled off his bear headdress. "No. This is bad magic."

"What do you mean, magic?" Pinnak tried to sound strong, but his voice squeaked and his fat body trembled.

Temkash only shook his head and walked away, clambering onto the cold-side roof. He turned once before he disappeared and stared, wide-eyed, at Pinnak. "No." And he was gone.

Pinnak stood in petrified silence. Finally, with a great effort, he made his way to the opening, approaching it cautiously from the side opposite the glimmering remains of the burnt man. The coals glowed red in the dark.

"What happened to my shelter?" he murmured. His head jerked this way and that. "What is this? Water Bird Mother, what is this?" The whites of his eyes glowed like pale stones in the moonlight.

He muttered a prayer, backing toward the entrance, repeating the same incoherent words over and over. He felt with one fat foot for the first rung of the ladder and stepped down. Step by step he lowered, until his head disappeared below the roof. The prayer was muted, almost inaudible.

Tsurinye stood. Boren and Shelsan followed. They watched tensely.

Suddenly a piercing wail rose from First Egg's dark entry, accompanied by a frantic scrambling. The cry went on and on, inarticulate, otherworldly. It was the sound of mindless fear, naked and raw. When it stopped, they could hear Pinnak fall in the sudden silence.

The old man on the cold-side stood up. "What was that?" he called.

"Don't know, old man," Shelsan answered. "Perhaps something has happened to Pinnak."

"Oh," the old man said, falling into a fit of coughing. "Is that all?" He lay down again, grumbling about the noise neighbors made in the middle of the night.

"We'll see what it was," Shelsan called to him, but the old man only coughed and turned away. His wife, who had sat up, lay down again.

One by one Shelsan, Boren, and Tsurinye descended into First Egg.

Mala stood in the middle of the room, her leopard cloak spread around her like vulture wings. Her tattooed face stared up. Her eyes reflected two small but very bright moons.

Even Shelsan, who knew of her making, felt a stab of fear.

Pinnak's body lay beside the hearth, his head at an unnatural angle. His eyes were wide open, staring toward the demon-woman in the center of the room as if she were the dead come to get him.

Perhaps it was the moonlight, but Shelsan thought that despite her fearfully scarred and tattooed face, her Water Bird beak and mirror eyes, Mala was smiling.

Endings

The Sorrow Clan held a feast for Pinnak's going over. People said it was the grandest farewell anyone had seen since Water Bird Mother first made the Nest. Someone brought an aurochs back from Angry Bear, and there was five-moon lamb from Pinnak's flock. His grain, harvested from the foothills toward Dak's Cave, had been threshed and made into flat bread. Wasting Moon, adrift in the night sky, was partly obscured by smoke from the cooking fires.

Late in the night some of the elders sat in council just outside the Place, near the open ground where so recently they had celebrated the Feast of the Unborn Moon. Shelsan sat among them. Boren watched from the outer circle, still too young to participate, but old enough to observe.

"We must decide what to do with the body," Tzam, Pretender of the Spider Clan, said.

Some wanted to carry Pinnak away from the Place.

"He was cursed," Tzam continued. "You can see it on his face. He must be removed from the Place or he will bring evil."

Others, though, wanted to bury him in First Egg, since he was the son of Mala's mother's brother and so the last of the lineage. "First Egg was his," a man of Sorrow Clan said. "His women and children should live there."

Shelsan stood. "I speak as Mala's man. We heard him fall, Boren and Boren's Woman and I, and we went down into First Egg. As you all know, I lived there and know it well. We three brought Pinnak up to the roof, and laid him out under the Grown Moon. No one has dared go down into First Egg since we brought Pinnak up. As you say, Tzam, the house is cursed. What happened is on his face, in his eyes. A terror. So, even though he was my slant cousin through Mala, I agree with Tzam. We must remove him from the Place for the good of all the People."

Many in the circle murmured agreement.

"More," Shelsan continued, holding up one finger. "First Egg must end."

The silence that followed was stunned. It was inconceivable to end First Egg, which was the original Nest, the place Water Bird Mother had built for the People, where the People hatched.

The old man from the cold-side stood and spoke to this. "It will mean the Place has an empty place, a dead place, at its very center. It will put death at my side." He fell to coughing and had to stop.

Another stood. "To end First Egg could mean the Place itself will begin to die from the center."

There was an outcry that went on until the night was nearly gone. The Place was theirs, they said, home, hearth and haven. They had always lived in the Place. It could not end.

Temkash crouched against the wall near the Edge, and said nothing. When the discussion was at its most heated he stood in and climbed the ladder to the roof and disappeared toward his own dwelling.

But what could they do? Shelsan was obviously right, First Egg had to end. They could only hope for the best.

Finally they agreed that Pinnak would be carried from the Place by his closest kin and given to the sky at the Great Marsh. They set off at first light, but his bulk made the journey arduous, and halfway there they put him down near where the river dispersed into the open, which was now a plain of cracked mud.

Even before they had turned their backs to return to the Place the insects and animals were burrowing into Pinnak's open, staring eyes.

Shelsan's Shelter

So it came to pass that Shelsan and Boren killed First Egg.

They left Mala, her skull, her head, where it stood in the center of the room, taking only the leopard cloak for Shelsan to wear. It had served Mala well, but he had killed the cat, so it was for him to carry its power.

They prepared and cleaned the dirt, as if planning to rebuild. Beginning with the tops of the walls they dismantled the mud bricks, smashed them to powder, and dusted them over the plaster floor, the hearth, the sleeping platforms. They filled the grain pits and sprinkled dirt into the back storage rooms; they filled the side chamber where Little Boren had once slept when not yet a man.

As the warm-time cooled they piled clean dirt around Mala; her post sank in the sea of dust until only her head with its hair of spiky feathers and dried grass remained above the level of the fill. The tops of the walls came down to meet the new floor, and at last she was completely covered. With her sank Shelsan's memory painting of all the dead.

"Mala will watch the place where the roof entrance had once been," Shelsan sang.

Boren sang, "She will guard the Grands, buried floor by floor beneath her. She will watch over the two little ones near the hearth."

And Tsurinye sang, "She has become the Grands, she has become the sky."

"The earth has found its balance," sang Shelsan, and they all echoed the words.

"I left the frozen tears from my trip to the Mountain," Shelsan said. He sat with the others on the edge of their wall, feet hanging into the pit that had once been their home. "The frozen tears belonged to her. Not to Pinnak, and not to Temkash. To her, to Mala."

So First Egg vanished. A level place surrounded by the walls of neighboring houses covered it over.

People said it was a dangerous place, a cursed place, an evil place, a dark opening in the center of their world, and at first they avoided it, speaking of it only in hushed tones.

But memory faded, and there were fewer and fewer places set aside for the emptying of baskets of night soil, household waste, hearth sweepings, bone and stone fragments, chaff and forage straw. The Place was crowded, and more families wanted to build.

So although at first they avoided First Egg, within a year or two even Shelsan and Boren and the cousins began to throw their waste into the pit. The following year goats and sheep shivered in the cold-time where First Egg had been. In the wet-time it was a muddy place of straw and human waste and trodden forage.

Light

The Moons Gained and Wasted, and the cold-times and warm-times came and went. The old man from the cold-side was older now than anyone had ever been, so they said. He seldom spoke, but waved his hand slowly when he recognized someone. His woman, hunched at his side, grew more silent and withdrawn, and one day was no longer there. He coughed a few more moons, and then they had to put him under the floor of his house.

There had not been enough rain this year, and almost no snow. Many of the People had left the Place, and some did not come back, leaving empty houses, dark, desolate places already crumbling. Fewer fires burned on the roof terraces.

The People seldom spoke of these changes. When they did, they shrugged and said People had left before, and had come back, and strangers had come, too, and stayed. Since Water Bird Mother made the Nest there had always been People in the Place. It would always be.

Shelsan, Boren, Tsurinye, Widow Klayn, the cousins, and the cousins' children gathered on the roof at the end of the wet-time. Arghinye had grown chubby and always under foot, always asking questions, always laughing. She did not notice the empty houses, nor the scarcity of water. Instead she tugged at Shelsan's cloak. "Why do we call it Angry Bear?" she demanded, pointing at the mountain to the sunset-side.

Tsurinye was peeling tubers. She stood with a sigh, holding her swollen belly, and let the debris fall into the open space beside their house, brushing it from her apron.

Shelsan combed his fingers through his graying beard. "Angry Bear is a spirit," he said gravely. "If we respect the spirit, if we call him by his name, if we thank him, he will give his blessing. Many aurochs live there now, around the feet of Angry Bear. We go there, your father and I, and we bring back meat, don't we?"

"Yes."

"Well, all the mountains are spirits. You know that, little one. And the streams, the Great Marsh, Sand Hook, Dak's Cave, where we went last dry-time, they are all spirits."

"I know," the girl insisted. "But why? Why is the Bear angry?"

"Why does the Wasting Moon follow the Grown?" Shelsan asked with a smile. "You ask too many questions." He touched her black hair indulgently, and soon enough she was holding up some leaves she had gathered outside the Place. "Can we eat these? What're they called? Should we cook them?"

Late in the dry-time Arghinye's brother was born, and Shelsan moved in with Widow Klayn. This brought him into the Wasting Moon Clan. Soon after that he became the father of a boy and a girl, twins, and surprisingly both of them lived.

No one noticed when Temkash died. He did not come onto his roof for many days, but his neighbors thought nothing of it. He often stayed inside, talking to himself. Only when the smell became strong did they venture onto his roof and call down to him. When they saw he was gone, they took away from his crowded house what they thought useful, the dried plants, the bits of stone and wood. They left him lying on his floor, and his face dried and became black, and his ribs broke through, and the mice nibbled at him. His house slumped, the brick walls softened and ran, the plaster on his roof blew away, and when the wet-time came the rains filled his Egg. Later in the wet-time the river flooded and cut under the outer wall of his house. The river swirled around the bricks and they dissolved and the river carried away what was left of Temkash himself, and in time, he became a story men told their children.

"If you don't behave," they would say, "Temkash will come to get you."

To the Sunset

Cold-times and warm-times came and went. One clear, chilly afternoon near the end of the wet-time, Boren started down the ladder into the house when suddenly his bad leg folded under him. He made only a small cry of surprise.

Tsurinye sang over his body in her own language, and the girl joined her. The boy, still too young, only stared solemnly through the night while the cousins came and went, bringing things to offer the family.

When Tsurinye stopped singing at first light, Shelsan said, "He goes with Mala now, and all the Grands, to sky and earth, mountain and water. Soon I will follow."

The next day he cut into the platform near the cold-side, sunrise-side. They wrapped Boren in a cloak of plaited grass and laid him on his back in the shallow pit. Shelsan repaired the platform over the grave, and they ate in silence while the plaster dried. Then Shelsan stood, put his hand on Tsurinye's shoulder, touched the two children, and returned home to Widow Klayn.

Shortly after Boren's death three men came to the Place, people from the cold-side, and from the sunrise-side. Tsurinye spoke with them. "The land has grown dry," she told Shelsan. "They say the mud people have grown more numerous, and the land cannot feed them all. They say Basatzaun was injured in a fight with them and now he is sick." After a long silence she said, "I most go to them, to my people, to Basatzaun."

"I know," Shelsan said. "Tell them we, too, are numerous. And animals are scarce, too, except for our flocks. We barely have enough food for the Place. Each year it grows more difficult. Each year there is less water in the wet-time, and the dry-time lasts longer."

"I will take the children," Tsurinye said. "But I will return."

"No, Tsurinye," Shelsan said. "There is nothing more for you here." He turned to the widow and the sturdy twin boys he had made with her, seated together in a shaft of sunlight from the entry. "There is nothing more for us, either."

So it happened that the day came when the wet-time ended, and on that day Tsurinye said, "We will go now. You are right, Shelsan. It is not good to stay so much in one place. People become what they were not, and should not be."

Shelsan watched her walk away toward the warm-side, following the path he and Little Boren had taken so long ago. Arghinye, he could see, was already asking questions of her mother, and the boy, trotting at her side, seemed to be asking his sister his own questions. He stroked the gray hair of his beard until they were out of sight.

With a sigh he took the Widow Klayn's hand and turned to the three hunters. "Where will you go from here?" he asked. His command of their language was limited, but they understood him. One pointed toward the sunset side. Shelsan followed his finger toward Angry Bear Mountain and nodded. "Then we will go with you," he said.

Epilog • NOW

Wonderland

Then there were three.

One fell slowly through many meters of saltwater and gently touched down on the sea floor, where a current carried her away. She was a small thing, and although divers arrived to look for her, they searched without success. During the following days, the plaster loosened. Her expression softened and let go, the lines and swirls, the tears and cuts, the bird-beak and upper lip melted and flowed together. The plaster dissolved and floated away, leaving a naked skull with two obsidian mirrors as eyes. New currents rolled it along a sandy bottom until it bumped against a stone outcropping and lay on its back, the reflecting eyes staring up at the surface. Undertow played with it, rocking it back and forth. The mandible with its remaining teeth detached from the skull and lay still. She rolled again on the sea floor. One of the eyes fell out. Still further along in her journey she came to a halt in a tangle of sea grass. The other eye fell.

Silt from a nearby river gradually settled over the rounded dome, covering it. The eye sockets filled with dirt, where sea grass grew, its fronds swaying to and fro. Silt piled up and covered the bone, leaving for a time only the brow ridge, until it too was finally hidden forever from human sight.

A second Alice found a home in a special display case in the Konya Museum. She is identified as the original plastered skull from Aynalı Tepe, perhaps the head of a Mother Goddess. Every year more visitors came, some to see, some to worship: tourists, art historians, nationalists, cosmopolitans, locals, and all found something frightening, or noble, or transcendental in this famous face. A forty-five minute video of Bryson Jones describing the excitement of the find played continuously in a special room.

A third, identified as an exact replica, remained on display in the Secure Room at Aynalı Tepe, amid selections of terra cotta figurines, flint daggers, obsidian projectile points, and fragments of wall paintings too small and insignificant for the museum in Konya. Eventually, because it was a replica and not the original, it was shipped to Connecticut to become the centerpiece of the new Gravidian College Museum of the Goddess, where some still believe it possesses supernatural powers to do good.

Glossary

absolute dating Determination of age with reference to specific measurements based on **radioactive decay**, *dendrochronology*, **varves**, or historical evidence.

adze Large handheld stone chipped to form a **blade** for chopping or digging.

aerial archaeology Remote sensing or photography conducted from airplanes, balloons, or satellites.

AMS (accelerator mass spectrometry) Radiocarbon dating that measures the concentration of 14C isotopes instead of counting their radioactive decay; it is most generally used to find the composition of a physical sample.

anthropology Study of humankind, including physical evolution, social systems, and material culture.

archaeomagnetism Use of magnetic properties of artifacts and soils that result from human activities, especially burning, for dating hearths and kilns and for remote sensing (magnetometer surveys and magnetic susceptibility surveys).

arrowhead Weapon point or tip made of stone, bone, metal, or other material usually fixed to an arrow. Larger ones may be spear points or knife blades.

artifact Object made or modified for human use.

assemblage Group of artifacts found together in a single context such as a grave or a household.

association Refers to artifacts or other items found together in the same layer or context.

asymmetrical Projectiles or tools with opposing sides of dissimilar contours, shape, or form.

awl Pointed tool for marking surfaces or making small holes.

ax Large chopping tool, sometimes with a groove for hafting to a handle.

bioarchaeology Study of organic archaeological material such as DNA, bone, and faunal or plant remains to learn more about past populations.

biosphere The part of the earth and its atmosphere in which living organisms exist or that is capable of supporting life; also, the living organisms and their environment composing the biosphere.

blade Narrow, sharp-edged **flake** of stone whose length is more than twice its width.

borer Tool that has been retouched to a point.

burin Chisel-like implement made from a flake or a blade.

burnish To make shiny or lustrous by rubbing or polishing.

calibration Correction of measurements to eliminate errors; for example, use of a calibration curve derived from tree rings to convert radiocarbon age estimates into calendar years.

Çatalhöyük Major Neolithic (c. 7,000 BCE) cluster of dwellings on the Konya plain southeast of the city of Konya; first excavated by James Mellaart in the early 1960s and currently under investigation by a large team led by Ian Hodder: www.catalhoyuk.com.

ceramic Of or pertaining to pottery.

characterization Definition by scientific analysis of the distinctive minerals, elements, or isotopes characteristic of specific sources of raw material such as quarries or **obsidian** nodes.

chopper River pebble or rock with varying degrees of working to obtain a sharp edge for chopping.

chronology Science that deals with the determination of dates and the sequence of events; the establishment of relative or absolute dating systems.

chronometric dating Absolute dating based on regular and measurable "clocks," such as the rate of decay of radioactive isotopes.

civilization Loose term normally referring to social groups living in complex settlements and using a writing system, such as Mesopotamia, Egypt, and Mesoamerica.

classical archaeology Study of Greek and Roman sites and material culture.

conservation Preservation and care of ancient sites and landscapes or laboratory techniques for stabilizing objects and structures.

context The time and space setting of an artifact, feature, or culture; the context of a find is its position on a site, its relationship through association with other artifacts, and its chronological position.

core Stone such as **obsidian** or flint from which **flakes** or **blades** have been struck and removed by percussion to make tools or projectiles.

cross-dating Relative dating technique that attributes similar ages to two strata, components, or sites on the basis of the recovery of similar artifacts from each; the use of an artifact whose age is known elsewhere, to date a new site.

Cultural Resource Management (CRM) Protection and conservation of archaeological and historic sites and landscapes; called "heritage management" outside North America.

debitage Flakes and chips from stone as a by-product of tool production; often the most abundant artifacts found in prehistoric archaeological sites.

dendrochronology Dating of past events or climatic changes through study of tree-ring growth.

denticulate Having a finely toothed (toothlike) or serrated edge.

diffusionism Belief that ideas and cultural and technological developments moved and spread over space and time from a single point of origin.

DNA Material in living organisms that carries genetic information.

domestication Process of genetically adapting animals and plants to better suit the needs of human beings; exploitation and selective breeding of plants and animals begun in Near East during the Neolithic.

ecology Interaction of living organisms; for archaeology, the relationship between humans and their natural environment.

electronic distance measurement (EDM) Surveying equipment that uses laser or infrared beams for high-precision measurement over long distances.

end-scraper Thick **flake** or blade retouched at one end used for scraping hides and other materials.

environmental archaeology Study of the interactions between human beings and the environment, from landscape and general climate to agriculture and specific foods.

Epi-Paleolithic European period and cultures immediately after the end of the Würm (Alpine) glaciation, about 10,000 BCE.

ethnoarchaeology Ethnographic study of contemporary peoples, with a focus on material culture and the formation processes that create archaeological deposits. *See also* **ethnography; middle range theory.**

ethnography Anthropological study of contemporary cultures.

evolution The change from generation to generation in how common inherited characteristics are within a population, the mechanisms that regulate these changes, and the long-term collective effects of such processes. Genetic variations are acted on by mechanisms such as natural selection: organisms that have combinations of traits that help them to survive and reproduce will generally have more offspring. In doing so, they pass more copies of these beneficial traits on to the next generation, leading to advantageous traits becoming more common in each generation, while disadvantageous traits become rarer.

experimental archaeology Simulation and/or replication of ancient activities, structures, and artifacts to study their performance, ideally with carefully designed scientific observation and controls.

field archaeology, fieldwork Refers to archaeological work on sites or in regions, including **field survey**, excavation, and preservation activities.

field survey Multidisciplinary study of the long-term settlement history of a region and its environmental setting through systematic examination of the ground surface visually or through remote sensing. *See* **landscape archaeology.**

fieldwalking Systematic recovery and recording of **artifacts** recovered from ploughed field surfaces.

flake Thin, flat asymmetrical piece of **flint** or other stone struck from a **core**.

flotation Use of liquids to recover seeds and other organic materials from excavated soil; dried soil is placed on a screen, water is gently bubbled up through the soil. Seeds, charcoal, and other light material float off, and tiny pieces of stone, bone fragments, and other relatively heavy materials are left behind.

gender Refers to issues of male and female identity and behavior in the past and the ways they may be represented archaeologically; for example, through burial practices or the layout of settlements and buildings.

Geographical Information System(s) GIS Range of computer graphics techniques to analyze maps, images, sites, and finds. GIS has become essential for interpreting fieldwork data.

geophysical surveying instruments Equipment designed to locate and record buried sites by measuring the electrical resistance, magnetism, or other physical properties of the soil using, among other instruments, resistivity meters, magnetometers, and ground penetrating radar (GPR).

glacials and interglacials Succession of Ice Ages alternating with temperate conditions deduced from evidence of changes in the natural and physical environment.

Göllü Dağ "Mountain with Lake"; source for the obsidian at **Çatalhöyük** and other Neolithic sites.

grave goods Selection of personal items placed in a burial as gifts to take into an afterlife or to indicate the sex, social status, or religion of the deceased.

haft Shaft or handle for a stone tool.

half-life Time taken for half the radioactive isotopes (for example, radiocarbon) in a sample to decay; measuring the amount of residual radioactivity helps estimate the age of a sample.

hand-ax Somewhat flat stone tool that has been completely worked and retouched on both faces; used for cutting or chopping.

heritage Those aspects of past landscapes, structures, and artifacts that continue to survive.

historical archaeology Study of the material remains of past societies that also left behind documentary evidence; this subfield of archaeology studies the emergence, transformation, and nature of the modern world.

hoard Collection of artifacts buried together at the same time. *See* **assemblage.**

Holocene (postglacial) Geological period beginning about 10,000 years ago and continuing into the present.

Höyük Turkish for "tumulus"—artificial hill, mound, or **tell**.

interpretive archaeology Assortment of theoretical approaches emphasizing individual experience over general processes; associated with **postprocessual archaeology.**

isotopes Atoms having the same atomic number but differing in atomic weight and mass number (that is, in the number of neutrons). For most elements, both stable and radioactive isotopes are known. Radioactive isotopes of many common elements, such as carbon and phosphorus, are used as tracers in medical, biological, and industrial research. The very slow and regular transmutations of certain radioactive substances, notably carbon-14, make them useful as "nuclear clocks" for dating archaeological and geological samples. Isotopes are fundamental to several radiometric dating techniques including **radiocarbon, potassium-argon**, and uranium series and are used to detect variations in diet from bones, among other things.

landscape archaeology Examination of sites in their wider environmental context by using archaeological, ecological, and historical information to interpret them regionally and over time.

lithics Of or pertaining to stone; lithic artifacts include ground and chipped stone tools and their manufacture debris (**debitage**).

magnetic dating, magnetic surveying, magnetometers *See* **archaeomagnetism**.

material culture Range of physical evidence observed by archaeologists and anthropologists, from artifacts to structures.

Mesolithic (Middle Stone Age) Period between the old and new stone ages (about 15,000–10,000 years ago), when people were still hunter-gatherers using a tool kit of multiple small stone blades. *See* **Epi-Paleolithic.**

midden Deposit of usually domestic waste material: food, trash, and garbage.

middle range theory Theoretical models of human behavior in specific contexts, based on fragmentary evidence of prehistoric sites and structures and modern ethnoarchaeology.

Neolithic (New Stone Age) Period during which humans took up a more settled way of life, living in communities, growing crops, and domesticating animals; also called the Sedentary Divide, the Neolithic Revolution, or Agricultural Revolution; in the Near East the Neolithic dates from approximately 10,000 BCE–4000 BCE and contains both pottery and prepottery phases.

New Archaeology Movement that emerged in the United States in the 1960s proposing a scientific approach to archaeological questions by designing models, suggesting hypotheses, and testing them. Also known as **processualism.**

obsidian Natural volcanic glass—clear, black, brown, or green in color—that in many parts of the world is one of the finest raw materials for making flaked tools.

obsidian hydration Dating technique in which relative age is estimated by the depth of water accumulation inside a worked surface as seen under a microscope.

open-area excavation Uncovering of large continuous areas; contrasts with the box trench system developed by Mortimer Wheeler.

palaeo-, paleo- Greek prefix (from *palios*, meaning "ancient") attached to many natural and biological scientific terms.

Palaeolithic (Old Stone Age) Earliest of three subdivisions of the Stone Age; lasted several million years, from the first appearance of stone tools to the Mesolithic (about 15,000–10,000 years ago); divided into Upper, Middle, and Lower phases.

palaeomagnetism Natural magnetic properties and periods of north-south magnetic reversal of geological rocks and sediments; distinguished from **archaeomagnetism**, which is generated by human activities, such as heating clay.

palynology Study of pollen grains found in samples of soil from archaeological sites, peat bogs, and lake beds and the reconstruction of environments and climatic phases from the species present.

platform Flat surface of a stone core used for striking, from which a **flake** or a **blade** is detached.

Pleistocene Longest geological period, marking the advance and the withdrawal of the ice sheets that began about two million years ago and ended at the beginning of the **Holocene** 10,000 years ago.

positivism Approach to science and human society developed in the nineteenth century, characterized by the replacement of speculation by testable propositions; **New Archaeology** has been criticized for being excessively positivist.

postprocessual archaeology Reaction to **processualism (New Archaeology)** that avoids **positivism** in favor of more recent anthropological approaches such as symbolism and the role of material culture in social relationships.

potassium-argon dating **Absolute dating** technique based on the decay of a radioactive **isotope** of potassium.

prehistory Period before written history; because, by definition, there are no written records from prehistoric times, the information we have about prehistory comes from the fields of palaeontology, astronomy, biology, geology, anthropology, and archaeology.

pressure-flaking Process of making an artifact by removing surplus material in the form of chips and flakes by a pressing force rather than percussion.

processualism *See* **New Archaeology**.

radioactive decay Energy in transit in the form of high-speed particles and electromagnetic waves released by unstable **isotopes** at a constant rate; used in radiometric dating methods, such as **radiocarbon** and **potassium-argon**.

radiocarbon dating Most important **radiometric** technique for determining absolute dates by measuring the radioactive decay of carbon in the remains of once-living plants and animals.

radiometric dating Methods for measuring the decay of radioactive isotopes.

relative dating Assignment of an age to an artifact or assemblage in relation to other artifacts and assemblages, based on a sequences of contexts established by the **stratification** of archaeological sites, through changes over time of a **typology**, or through some geophysical analytic method such as **obsidian hydration** or **archaeomagnetism**.

remote sensing Use of aerial or satellite images to discover and interpret surfaces of buried archaeological sites, and the use on the ground of geophysical instruments to locate buried sites.

rescue archaeology Archaeological **fieldwork** and/or excavation prompted by threats from development, such as roads and buildings. It is an important component of **Cultural Resource (Heritage) Management**.

resistivity surveying Geophysical technique that measures the extent to which buried soils and features resist an electric current.

retouch Working of a primary stone **flake**, usually by the removal of small fragments, to form a tool.

sickle Tool for gathering cereal crops; usually **hafts** with embedded microliths (very small blades made of flaked stone) for cutting.

stratification, stratigraphy Examination of successive layers of deposits to establish a relative cultural chronology.

tanged points Projectile points with a tang (tapered end that fits into the handle) at one end to help fix it to a **haft**.

taphonomy The study of how archaeological sites are created by human activity and the conditions and processes by which organisms become fossilized, how animals and plants become part of the fossil record; taphonomic analysis also attempts to reconstruct the chronology of a variety of postmortem processes that have produced an **assemblage**. Many of these processes leave signatures on the surface of bone that, if properly identified, are a powerful method of assessing everything form natural and cultural formation processes to complex cultural rituals. Also called concept of site formation processes.

tell Mound common in the Near East formed by the accumulation of occupation debris, such as mud-brick, over long periods of time.

tepe Turkish for "hill"; often used for a mound or **tell**.

thermoluminescence dating (TL) Method of determining **absolute dates** for fired clay or burnt stone; it involves exposing minerals (quartz, feldspars, calcite, and clays) to heat until they emit light. Defects within the mineral crystal structure attract free electrons. As the result of heating these crystals, the electrons escape the crystal defects and migrate to another defect known as a luminescence center. This movement of free electrons results in the emission of photons that can be measured as a light signal. The amount of light obtained is related to the amount of radiation that the minerals have been exposed to in the natural environment since deposition.

tree rings Layers of new wood formed annually around the circumference of tree trunks; used to study environmental conditions as well as in dating. *See* **dendrochronology**.

typology Classification of things according to their characteristics; the chronological arrangement of artifacts separated into types according to changes over time in decoration, construction methods, function, materials, or form.

varve Annual deposit of silt on river or lake beds used for **absolute dating** if related to a dated reference point.

wheat Several types of grasses, such as Emmer and Einkorn, that were among the first domesticated grains in the Fertile Crescent, the historical region in the Middle East incorporating the Levant, Mesopotamia, and Ancient Egypt.

Würm glaciation Würm (in the Alps) and Weichsel (in northern central Europe) glaciations are the most recent glaciations of the **Pleistocene** epoch, which ended around 10,000 BCE. The general glacial advance began about 70,000 BCE and reached its maximum extent about 18,000 BCE.

Bibliography

Atkin, Tony (Ed.). 2005. *Structure and Meaning in Human Settlements*. University of Pennsylvania Museum of Archaeology: Philadelphia.

Atwood, Roger. 2004. *Stealing History: Tomb Raiders, Smugglers, and the Looting of the Ancient World*. St. Martin's Press: New York.

Bahn, Paul G. 1997.*The Cambridge Illustrated History of Prehistoric Art* (Cambridge Illustrated Histories). Cambridge University Press: Cambridge.

———— 2001. *Journey Through the Ice Age*. University of California Press: Berkeley and Los Angeles.

Balter, Michael. 2006. *The Goddess and the Bull: Catalhoyuk: An Archaeological Journey to the Dawn of Civilization*. Left Coast Press, Inc: Walnut Creek, California.

Bradley, Richard, 2002. *The Past in Prehistoric Societies*. Routledge: London.

Cauvin, Jacques. 2000. *The Birth of the Gods and the Origins of Agriculture*. Cambridge University Press: Cambridge.

Diamond, Jared. 2005. *Collapse: How Societies Choose to Fail or Succeed*. Viking: New York.

———— 1999. *Guns, Germs, and Steel: The Fates of Human Societies*. W. W. Norton & Company: New York.

———— 1992. *The Third Chimpanzee: The Evolution and Future of the Human Animal*. Harper Perennial: New York.

Edmonds, Mark. 1999. *Ancestral Geographies of the Neolithic: Landscapes, Monuments and Memory*. Routledge: London.

Edwards, Kevin J. 2003. *Scotland After the Ice Age*. Edinburgh University Press: Edinburgh.

Fowler, Brenda. 2001. *Iceman: Uncovering the Life and Times of a Prehistoric Man Found in an Alpine Glacier*. University Of Chicago Press: Chicago.

Garfinkel, Yosef. 2003. *Dancing at the Dawn of Agriculture*. University of Texas Press: Austin.

Gimbutas, Marija. 1982. *Goddesses and Gods of Old Europe, 6500–3500 B.C.: Myths, and Cult Images*. University of California Press: Berkeley and Los Angeles.

———— 2001. *The Living Goddesses*. University of California Press: Berkeley and Los Angeles.

Goody, Jack. 1977. *The Domestication of the Savage Mind*. Cambridge University Press: Cambridge.

Greenspan, Stanley I. 2004. *The First Idea: How Symbols, Language, and Intelligence Evolved from Our Primate Ancestors to Modern Humans*. Da Capo Press: Cambridge, MA.

Hayden, Brian. 2003. *Shamans, Sorcerers, and Saints: A Prehistory of Religion*. Smithsonian Books: Washington, D.C.

Hillier, Bill. 1989. *The Social Logic of Space*. Cambridge University Press: Cambridge.

Hodder, Ian. 1990. *Domestication of Europe*. Blackwell Publishers: Malden, MA.

———— 2001. *Archaeological Theory Today*. Polity Press: Cambridge.

———— 2003. *Reading the Past: Current Approaches to Interpretation in Archaeology*. Cambridge University Press: Cambridge.

Hodder, Ian (Ed.). 1996. *On the Surface: Catalhoyuk 1993–95* (British Institute of Archaeology at Ankara, Biaa Monograph No 22: the Catalhoyuk Project Volume 1). McDonald Institute for Archaeological Research: Cambridge.

———— 2005. *Inhabiting Catalhoyuk: Reports from the 1995–99 Seasons*. McDonald Institute for Archaeological Research: Cambridge.

———— 2006. *The Leopard's Tale: Revealing the Mysteries of Catalhoyuk*. Thames & Hudson: London.

———— 2006. *Catalhoyuk Perspectives: Themes from the 1995–99 Seasons*. McDonald Institute for Archaeological Research: Cambridge.

———— 2006. *Changing Materialities at Catalhoyuk: Reports from the 1995–99 Seasons* (Catalhoyuk Research Project) McDonald Institute for Archaeological Research: Cambridge.

Joyce, Rosemary A. 2002. *The Languages of Archaeology: Dialogue, Narrative, and Writing*. Blackwell Publishers: Oxford.

Kristiansen, Kristian. 1999. *Europe before History*. Cambridge University Press: Cambridge.

Larsen, Clark Spencer. 2002. *Skeletons in Our Closet: Revealing Our Past through Bioarchaeology*. Princeton University Press: Princeton.

Mithen, Steven. 2004. *After the Ice: A Global Human History 20,000–5000 BC*. Harvard University Press: Cambridge, MA.

———— 2006. *The Singing Neanderthals: The Origins of Music, Language, Mind, and Body*. Harvard University Press: Cambridge, MA.

Pearson, James L. 2002. *Shamanism and the Ancient Mind: A Cognitive Approach to Archaeology.* AltaMira Press: Walnut Creek, CA.

Praetzellis, Adrian. 2000. *Death by Theory: A Tale of Mystery and Archaeological Theory.* AltaMira Press: Walnut Creek, CA.

———— 2003. *Dug to Death: A Tale of Archaeological Method and Mayhem.* AltaMira Press: Walnut Creek, CA.

Rogers, Everett M. 1995. *Diffusion of Innovations*, 4th ed. Free Press: New York.

Rosen, Arlene Miller. 1986. *Cities of Clay: The Geoarchaeology of Tells.* University of Chicago Press: Chicago.

Sahlins, Marshall. 1972. *Stone Age Economics.* Aldine de Gruyter: New York.

Shanks, Michael. 1992. *Re-Constructing Archaeology: Theory and Practice.* Routledge: London.

Smith, Bruce D. 1998. *Emergence of Agriculture.* Scientific American Library: New York.

Tenner, Edward. 1996. *Why Things Bite Back: Technology and the Revenge of Unintended Consequences.* Knopf: New York.

Thomas, Herbert. 1995. *The First Humans.* Thames & Hudson Ltd: London.

Thomas, Julian. 1999. *Understanding the Neolithic.* Routledge: London.

Vialou, Denis, 1998. *Our Prehistoric Past: Art and Civilization.* Thames & Hudson: London.

Wade, Nicholas. 2006. *Before the Dawn: Recovering the Lost History of Our Ancestors.* Penguin Press: New York.

Wallace, Jennifer. 2004. *Digging the Dirt: The Archaeological Imagination.* Duckworth Publishing: London.

Wheeler, Mortimer. 1954. *Archaeology from the Earth.* Pelican: Baltimore.

Zangger, Eberhard. 2003. *The Future of the Past: Archaeology in the 21st Century.* Phoenix: London.

About the Author

Rob Swigart is a visiting scholar at the Stanford Archaeology Center. He is author of nine novels, including *Little America*, *The Time Trip*, and the *Book of Revelations*, as well as several works of interactive and electronic fiction. This is his second teaching novel after *Xibalbá Gate* (AltaMira Press 2005), which describes Late Classic Maya life.